Killing Me Softly

D0109682

Nicci French is a journalist and lives in London. Her first two novels, *The Memory Game* and *The Safe House*, were both bestsellers and are both published in Penguin.

Killing Me Softly

Nicci French

MICHAEL JOSEPH
LONDON

MICHAEL JOSEPH LTD
Published by the Penguin Group
Penguin Books Ltd, 27 Wrights Lane, London w8 5tz, England
Penguin Putnam Inc., 375 Hudson Street, New York, New York 10014, USA
Penguin Books Australia Ltd, Ringwood, Victoria, Australia
Penguin Books Canada Ltd, 10 Alcorn Avenue, Toronto, Ontario, Canada m4v 3b2
Penguin Books (NZ) Ltd, Private Bag 102902, NSMC, Auckland, New Zealand

Penguin Books Ltd, Registered Offices: Harmondsworth, Middlesex, England

First published 1999
1 3 5 7 9 10 8 6 4 2

Copyright © Joined-UpWriting, 1999

Filmset in Plantin Light
Typeset by Rowland Phototypesetting Ltd, Bury St Edmunds, Suffolk
Printed in England by Clays Ltd, St Ives plc

A CIP catalogue record for this book is available from the British Library

Hardback ISBN 0-718-14342-6
Trade Paperback ISBN 0-718-14341-8

To Kersti and Philip

He knew he was going to die. And he knew dimly, somewhere far inside himself, that he ought not to want to die. He should do something to save himself but he couldn't think what. Perhaps if he could make sense of what had happened. If only the wind and the snow would slacken. They had battered him for so long that he could hardly distinguish the sound from the cold and the stinging on his face. Always there was the struggle, the last struggle, really, to breathe oxygen from this air of eight thousand metres above sea-level, where humans weren't meant to live. His oxygen cylinders were long since empty, the valves frozen up, the mask nothing but an encumbrance.

It might be minutes, more likely hours. But he would be dead before the morning came. That was all right, though. He was drowsy and calm. Under his layers of windproof nylon, Gore-Tex, wool, polypropylene, he could feel his heart beating at twice its normal rate, a prisoner hammering frantically at his chest. Yet his brain was sluggish, dreamy. Which was a mistake, because they all needed to stay awake, keep moving, until they were rescued. He knew he should sit up, stand up, clap his hands together furiously, wake his companions. He was too comfortable. It was good to lie down and rest at last. He had been tired for such a long time.

He no longer felt cold, which was a relief. He looked down to where one of his hands, which had slipped from its mitten, lay at a curious angle. It had been purple but now – he leaned forward curiously – it was a waxy white. Strange that he should be so thirsty. He had a bottle in his jacket, which was frozen and useless to him. He was surrounded by snow, which was equally useless. It was almost funny. Lucky he wasn't a doctor, like Françoise.

Where was she? When they had reached the end of the line, they should have been in the Camp Three col. She had gone ahead and they hadn't seen her again. The others had stayed together, blundered around, lost all sense of direction, any feeling about where on the mountain they were, and had nestled hopelessly into this excuse for a gully. And yet there was something he had to remember, an object lost in his mind, and not only did he not know where it was, he didn't know *what* it was.

He couldn't even see his feet. This morning, when they had set out, the mountains had shimmered in the thin air and they had inched their way up the tilted sea of ice towards the summit in fierce sunlight that had spilt over the rim of the mountains, and glinted off the blue-white, bullet-proof ice and pierced their aching heads. There had been only a few cumulus clouds drifting towards them and then suddenly this swirl of stony snow.

He felt a movement beside him. Someone else was conscious. He turned laboriously to the other side. Red jacket, so it must be Peter. His face was entirely obscured by a thick layer of grey ice. There was nothing he could do. They had been a sort of team but were all in their own separate worlds now.

He wondered who else was dying on the mountainside. It had all gone so wrong. Nothing to do, though. He had a syringe in a toothbrush holder inside his snowsuit, full of dexamethosone, but grasping a syringe was beyond his powers now. He couldn't even move his hands to unstrap his backpack. What would he do, anyway? Where could he go from here? Better to wait. They'd find them. They knew where they were. Why hadn't they come yet?

The world beyond, the life before, these mountains, all that had now sunk beneath the surface of his sluggish consciousness, until only traces were left. He knew that every minute he lay up here, in the oxygen-deprived death zone, millions of his brain cells were being erased. A tiny part of his mind was watching himself die and was terrified, full of pity and horror. He wished it was over. He just wanted to sleep.

He knew the stages of death. He had watched almost with curiosity as his body protested against its environment here on the final ridges below the summit of Chungawat: the headaches, the diarrhoea, the gasping shortness of breath, the swollen hands and ankles. He knew he could no longer think clearly. Perhaps hallucinations would come to him before he died. He knew that frostbite had invaded his hands and feet. He couldn't feel any of his body, except for his charred lungs. It was as if his mind was the last thing that was left, still burning dimly inside his finished carcass. He was waiting for his mind to flicker and die out.

Pity he had never got to the summit. The snow felt like a pillow against his cheek. Tomas was warm. At peace. What had gone wrong? It should all have been so simple. There was something he had to remember, something wrong. There had been a wrong note. A piece of the puzzle didn't fit. He closed his eyes. The darkness felt healing. Life had been so busy. All that effort. For what? Nothing. He just had to remember. Once he had remembered, nothing else mattered. If only the howl of the wind would stop. If only he could think. Yes, that was it. It was so stupid, so simple, but he understood. He smiled. He felt the cold spread through him, welcoming him into the darkness.

I sat very still in the hard-backed chair. My throat hurt. The strip-lighting flickered and made me feel dizzy. I put my hands on the desk between us, fingertips lightly together, and tried to breathe steadily. What a place for it all to end.

Phones were ringing around us and conversation hummed in the air, like static. There were people in the background, men and women in their uniforms passing busily by. Occasionally they would look towards us, but they didn't seem curious. Why should they be? They saw so many things in here, and I was just an ordinary woman, with a flush in her cheeks and a ladder running up her tights. Who could tell? My feet ached inside their ridiculous ankle boots. I didn't want to die.

Detective Inspector Byrne picked up a pen. I tried to smile at him with all of my last hope. He looked across at me patiently, eyebrows bunched, and I wanted to cry and ask him to save me, oh, please. It had been such a long time since I had cried properly. If I started now, then why should I ever stop?

'Where were we, do you remember?' he asked.

Oh, yes, I remembered. I remembered it all.

One

'Alice! Alice! You're late. Come on.'

I heard a soft resistant grunt and realized it was coming from me. Outside it was cold and dark. I wriggled deeper into the bunched-up duvet, closed my eyes in a squint against the dim glimmers of winter light.

'Up, Alice.'

Jake smelt of shaving foam. A tie hung loose from his collar. Another day. It's the little habits rather than the big decisions that make you into a real couple. You drift into routines, inhabit complementary domestic roles without deciding to. Jake and I were the world trivia experts on each other. I knew that he liked more milk in coffee than in tea, he knew that I liked just a drop of milk in tea and none at all in coffee. He could locate the hard knot that formed near my left shoulder-blade after hard days in the office. I didn't put fruit in salads because of him and he didn't put cheese in salads because of me. What more could you want from a relationship? We were shaking down into a couple.

I'd never lived with a man before – I mean, a man with whom I was in a relationship – and I found the experience of assuming household roles interesting. Jake was an engineer and was limitlessly capable with all the wires and pipes behind our walls and under our floors. I once said to him that the one thing he resented about our flat was that he hadn't actually built it himself on a greenfield site, and he didn't take it as an insult. My degree was in biochemistry, which meant that I changed the sheets on the bed and emptied the swing-bin in the kitchen. He fixed the

5

vacuum cleaner but I used it. I washed the bath, except if he had shaved in it. I drew the line there.

The odd thing was that Jake did all the ironing. He said that people didn't know how to iron shirts any more. I thought that was deeply stupid and I would have got offended except that it's hard to stay offended as you lie watching TV with a drink while somebody else does the ironing. He bought the paper and I read it over his shoulder and he got irritated. We both shopped, although I always took a list and ticked everything off, and he was haphazard and far more extravagant than me. He defrosted the fridge. I watered the plants. And he brought me a cup of tea in bed every morning.

'You're late,' he said. 'Here's your tea and I'm leaving in exactly three minutes.'

'I hate January,' I said.

'You said that about December.'

'January's like December. But without Christmas.'

But he'd left the room. I showered hurriedly and put on an oatmeal-coloured trouser suit, with a jacket that came to my knees. I brushed my hair and coiled it into a loose bun.

'You look smart,' said Jake, as I came into the kitchen. 'Is that new?'

'I've had it for ages,' I lied, pouring myself another cup of tea, tepid this time.

We walked to the underground together, sharing an umbrella and dodging puddles. He kissed me at the turnstile, putting the umbrella under his arm and holding my shoulders firmly.

'Goodbye, darling,' he said, and I thought at that moment, He wants to be married. He wants us to be a married couple. With my mind on that arresting idea, I forgot to say anything back. He didn't notice and stepped on to the escalator, joining the descending crowd of men in raincoats. He didn't look back. It was almost as if we were married already.

I didn't want to go to the meeting. I felt almost physically incapable of it. The previous evening, I'd been out late with Jake

6

for a meal. We hadn't got in until after midnight and hadn't got to bed until one and then hadn't actually got to sleep until maybe two thirty. It had been an anniversary – our first. It wasn't much of an anniversary but Jake and I are short of them. Occasionally we've tried, but we've always been unable to remember our first meeting. We were around each other in the same environment for such a long time, like bees hovering around the same hive. We can't remember when we became friends. We were in a fluctuating group of people, and after a bit of time we had reached a stage where if somebody had asked me to write a list of my three or four, or four or five closest friends, Jake would have been on it. But nobody ever asked me. We knew all about each other's parents, schooldays, love lives. Once we got horrendously drunk together when his girlfriend left him, sitting under a tree in Regent's Park and finishing off half a bottle of whisky between us, half weepy, half giggly, generally maudlin. I told him that she was the one who was losing out, and he hiccuped and stroked my cheek. We laughed at each other's jokes, danced with each other at parties, but not when the music was slow, cadged money and lifts and advice. We were mates.

We both remembered the first time we slept together. That was on 17 January last year. A Wednesday. A group of us were going to see a late-night movie, but various people couldn't go and by the time we were at the cinema it was just Jake and me, and at one point during the film we looked at each other and smiled rather sheepishly and I guessed that we were both realizing that we were on a sort of date, and maybe we were both wondering if this was such a good idea.

Afterwards he asked me back to his flat for a drink. It was about one in the morning. He had a packet of smoked salmon in the fridge and – this was the bit that made me laugh – bread he had baked himself. At least, it made me laugh in retrospect, because he has never baked a loaf or anything else since. We are a takeaway-and-convenience-food couple. However, I did very nearly laugh then, at the moment when I first kissed him, because

7

it seemed odd, almost incestuous, being such good ordinary friends already. I saw his face getting closer to mine, his familiar features blurring into strangeness, and I wanted to giggle or pull away, anything to break the sudden seriousness, the different kind of quietness between us. But it immediately felt right, like coming home. If there were times when I didn't want that sense of settledness (what about all my plans to work abroad, to have adventures, to be a different kind of person?), or worried that I was nearly thirty and was this, then, my life?, well, I shook them off.

I know that couples are meant to make a specific decision to live together. It's a stage in your life, like exchanging a ring or dying. We never did. I started staying over. Jake allocated me a drawer for knickers and tights. Then there was the odd dress. I started leaving conditioner and eyeliner pencils in the bathroom. After a few weeks of that I noticed one day that about half of the videos had my handwriting on the labels. It's just that if you don't write down programmes you've taped, even in very small writing, then you can never find them when you want to watch them.

One day Jake asked me if there was any point in my paying rent for my room, since I was never there. I hemmed and hawed, worried, and didn't come to any firm decision. My cousin, Julie, came down for the summer to work before starting college and I suggested that she could park in my place. I had to move more of my stuff out to give her room. Then at the end of August – it was a hot early Sunday evening and we were at a pub looking over the river at St Paul's – Julie talked and talked and talked about looking for somewhere permanent, and I suggested she stay there permanently. So Jake and I were together and the only anniversary we had was the first sexual encounter.

But after the celebration, there was the reckoning. If you don't want to go to a meeting and you are worried about doing yourself justice or having injustice done to you, make sure that your outfit is ironed and get there on time. These are not exactly in the managerial ten commandments, but on that dark morning when

I couldn't face anything but tea, they seemed like a survival strategy. I tried to collect my thoughts on the tube. I should have prepared myself better, made some notes or something. I remained standing in the hope that it would keep my new suit smooth. A couple of polite men offered me a seat and looked embarrassed when I refused. They probably thought it was ideological.

What were they all going to do, my fellow passengers? I bet myself silently that it wasn't as odd as what I was going to do. I was going to the office of a small division of a very large multinational drug company in order to have a meeting about a small plastic and copper object that looked like a New Age brooch but was in fact the unsatisfactory prototype of a new intrauterine device.

I had seen my boss, Mike, being successively baffled, furious, frustrated and confused by our lack of progress with the Drakloop IV, Drakon Pharmaceutical Company's IUD, which was going to revolutionize intrauterine contraceptives if it ever made it out of the laboratory. I had been recruited to the project six months ago, but had become gradually sucked into the bureaucratic quagmire of budget plans, marketing objectives, shortfalls, clinical trials, specifications, departmental meetings, regional meetings, meetings about meetings, and the whole impossible hierarchy of the decision-making process. I had almost forgotten that I was a scientist who had been working in a project on the fringes of female fertility. I had taken the job because the idea of creating a product and selling it had seemed like a holiday from the rest of my life.

This Thursday morning, Mike just seemed sullen, but I recognized the mood as dangerous. He was like a rusty old Second World War mine that had been washed up on a beach. It seemed harmless but the person who prodded it in the wrong place would get blown up. It wasn't going to be me, not today.

People filed into the conference room. I had already seated myself with my back to the door so that I could look out of the window. The office lay just south of the Thames in a maze of narrow streets named after spices and the distant lands where they had come from. At the rear of our offices, always on the verge of being acquired and redeveloped, was a recycling facility. A rubbish dump. In one corner there was a giant mountain of bottles. On sunny days it glittered magically but even on a horrid day like this there was a chance that I might get to see the digger come along and shovel the bottles into an even larger pile. That was more interesting than anything that was likely to happen inside Conference Room C. I looked around. There were three slightly ill-at-ease men who had come down from the Northbridge lab just for this meeting and evidently resented the time away. There was Philip Ingalls from upstairs, my so-called assistant Claudia, and Mike's assistant Fiona. There were several people missing. Mike's frown deepened, and he pulled on his earlobes furiously. I looked out of the window. Good. The digger was approaching the bottle mountain. That made me feel better.

'Is Giovanna coming?' Mike asked.

'No,' said one of the researchers, Neil, I think he was called. 'She asked me to stand in for her.'

Mike shrugged in ominous acceptance. I sat up straighter, fixed an alert expression on my face and picked up my pen optimistically. The meeting began with references to the previous meeting and various droning routine matters. I doodled on my pad, then tried a sketch of Neil's face, which looked rather like a bloodhound's, with sad eyes. Then I tuned out and looked at the digger, which was now well at its work. Unfortunately the windows cut out the sound of the breaking glass but it was satisfying all the same. With an effort I tuned back into the meeting when Mike asked about plans for February. Neil started saying something about anovulatory bleeding and I suddenly and absurdly got irritated by the thought of a male scientist talking to a male manager about technology for the female anatomy. I took a deep breath to speak, changed my mind, and turned my attention back to the recycling centre. The digger was retreating now, its job done. I wondered how you could get a job driving something like that.

'And as for you . . .' I became aware of my surroundings, as if I had suddenly been disturbed from sleep. Mike had directed his attention to me and everybody had turned to survey the imminent damage. 'You've got to take this in hand, Alice. There's a malaise in this department.'

Could I be bothered to argue? No.

'Yes, Mike,' I said sweetly. I winked at him, though, just to let him know I wasn't letting myself be bullied, and saw his face redden.

'And could someone get this fucking light fixed?' he shouted.

I looked up. There was an almost subliminal flicker from one of the fluorescent light tubes. Once you became aware of it, it was like having somebody scratch inside your brain. Scratch, scratch, scratch.

'I'll do it,' I said. 'I mean, I'll get someone to do it.'

I was drafting a report that Mike could send to Pittsburgh at the end of the month, which left plenty of time, so I was able to spend the rest of the day doing not very much. I spent an important half an hour going through two mail-order clothes catalogues I'd been sent. I turned the page back on a pair of neat ankle boots, a long velvet shirt, which was described as 'essential', and a short dove-grey satin skirt. It would put me £137 further into debt. After lunch with a press officer – a nice woman, whose small pale face was dominated by her narrow, rectangular, black-framed spectacles – I shut myself into my office and put on my headphones.

'Je suis dans la salle de bain,' said a voice, too brightly, into my ear.

'Je suis dans la salle de bain,' I repeated obediently.

'Je suis en haut!'

What did 'en haut' mean? I couldn't remember. 'Je suis en haut,' I said.

The phone rang, and I pulled off the headphones. I was away from the world of sunshine and fields of lavender and outdoor cafés and back in dockland in January. It was Julie, with a problem about the flat. I suggested we meet for a drink after work. She was already seeing a couple of people so I rang Jake on his mobile and suggested he come to the Vine as well. No. He was out of town. He had gone to look at progress on a tunnel that was being dug through a site that was both beautiful and sacred to several religions. My day was nearly done.

Julie and Sylvie were there, at a corner table with Clive, when I arrived. Behind them were some wall plants. There was a vine motif in the Vine.

'You look awful,' Sylvie said sympathetically. 'Hangover?'

'I'm not sure,' I said, cautiously. 'But I could do with a hangover cure anyway. I'll get you one as well.'

Clive had been talking about a woman he had met at a party last night.

'She's a very interesting woman,' Clive said. 'She's a physio-therapist. I told her about my bad elbow, you know . . .'

'Yes, we know.'

'And she took hold of it in this special grip, and it immediately felt better. Isn't that amazing?'

'What does she look like?'

'What do you mean?'

'What does she look like?' I insisted.

The drinks arrived. He took a sip. 'She was quite tall,' he said. 'Taller than you. She has brown hair, about shoulder-length. She's good-looking, tanned, she had these amazing blue eyes.'

'No wonder your elbow felt better. Did you ask her out?'

Clive looked indignant but a bit shifty as well. He loosened his tie. 'Of course I didn't.'

'You obviously wanted to.'

'You can't just ask a girl out like that.'

'Yes, you can,' Sylvie interrupted. 'She touched your elbow.'

'So? I don't believe this. She touched my elbow as a physio-therapist, and that means she's asking for it, does it?'

'Not as such,' said Sylvie primly. 'But ask her. Ring her up. She sounds desirable to me.'

'Obviously, she was . . . attractive, but there are two problems. One, as you know, I don't feel that I've got over Christine properly. And secondly, I can't do that sort of thing. I need an excuse.'

'Do you know her name?' I asked.

'She's called Gail. Gail Stevenson.'

I sipped my Bloody Mary reflectively.

'Call her up.'

A look of alarm passed comically over Clive's features. 'What would I say?'

'It doesn't matter what you say. If she liked you, and the fact that she took hold of your elbow at the party means that she may have done, then she'll go out with you almost whatever you say. If she didn't, then she won't go out with you whatever you say.' Clive looked confused. 'Just give her a ring,' I said. 'Say, "I'm the person who had the elbow that you manipulated at whateveritwas party the other night, would you like to go out?" She might be charmed.'

Clive looked aghast. 'Just like that?'

'Absolutely.'

'What should I ask her to?'

I laughed. 'What do you want me to do? Fix you up with a room as well?'

I got some more drinks. When I returned, Sylvie was both smoking and talking dramatically. I was tired and only half listening to her. Across the table, I wasn't sure because I only heard fragments, I think that Clive was telling Julie about the secret meanings hidden in the pattern on the Marlboro cigarette box. I wondered if he was drunk or mad. I lingered over the last of my drink, feeling fuzzy round the edges. This was part of the Crew, a group of people who, mostly, had met at college and stayed together, looking out for each other, spending time. They were more like my family than my family.

When I got back to the flat, Jake opened the door as I put my key in the lock. He was already changed into jeans and checked shirt.

'I thought you'd be late,' I said.

'The problem went away,' he said. 'I'm cooking you dinner.'

I looked on the table. There were packets. Spiced chicken. Taramasalata. Pitta bread. A miniature steamed pudding. A carton of cream. A bottle of wine. A video. I kissed him. 'A microwave, a TV set and you,' I said. 'Perfect.'

'And then I'm going to have sex with you for the entire night.'

'What, again? You tunneller, you.'

Two

The following morning, the underground was more than usually crowded. I felt hot inside all my layers of clothing, and I tried to distract myself by thinking about other things as I swayed against the bodies and the train clattered through the darkness. I thought about how my hair needed cutting. I could book it for lunch-time. I tried to remember if there was enough food in the house for tonight, or maybe we could get a takeaway. Or go dancing. I remembered I hadn't taken my pill this morning and must do it as soon as I got to work. The thought of the pill made me think of the IUD and yesterday's meeting, the memory of which had left me more unwilling than usual to get out of bed this morning.

A skinny young woman with a large, red-faced baby squeezed her way down the train. No one stood up for her, and she stood with her child on her angular hip, held in place by the bodies all round her. Only the baby's hot, cross face was exposed. Sure enough, it soon started yelling, hoarse, drawn-out wails that made its red cheeks purple, but the woman ignored it, as if she was beyond noticing. She had a glazed expression on her pallid face. Although her baby was dressed for an expedition to the South Pole, she wore just a thin dress and an unzipped anorak. I tested myself for maternal instinct. Negative. Then I looked round at all the men and women in suits. I leaned down to a man in a lovely cashmere coat, till I was near enough to see his spots, then said softly into his ear: 'Excuse me. Can you make room for this woman?' He looked puzzled, resistant. 'She needs a seat.'

He stood up and the mother shuffled over and wedged herself between two *Guardian*s. The baby continued to wail, and she continued to stare ahead of her. The man could feel virtuous now.

I was glad to get out at my station, though I wasn't looking forward to the day ahead. When I thought about work, a lethargy settled over me, as if all my limbs were heavy and the chambers of my brain musty. It was icy on the streets, and my breath curled into the air. I wrapped my scarf more firmly around my neck. I should have worn a hat. Maybe I could nip out in a coffee-break and buy some boots. All around me people were hurrying to their different offices, heads down. Jake and I should go away somewhere in February, somewhere hot and deserted. Anywhere that wasn't London. I imagined a white beach and a blue sky and me slim and tanned in a bikini. I'd been seeing too many advertisements. I always wore a one-piece. Oh, well. Jake had been on at me about saving money.

I stopped at the zebra crossing. A lorry roared by. A pigeon and I scuttled back in unison. I glimpsed the driver, high up in his cab and blind to all the people below him trudging to work. The next car squeaked to a halt and I stepped out into the road.

A man was crossing from the other side. I noticed he was wearing black jeans and a black leather jacket, and then I looked up at his face. I don't know if he stopped first or I did. We both stood in the road staring at each other. I think I heard a horn blare. I couldn't move. It felt like an age, but it was probably only a second. There was an empty, hungry feeling in my stomach and I couldn't breathe in properly. A horn was sounded once more. Someone shouted something. His eyes were a startling blue. I started walking across the road again, and so did he, and we passed each other, inches away, our eyes locked. If he had reached out and touched me, I think I would have turned and followed him, but he didn't and I reached the pavement alone.

I walked towards the building that contained the Drakon offices, then stopped and looked back. He was still there, watching me. He didn't smile or make any gesture. It was an effort to turn away again, with his gaze on me as if it were pulling me back towards him. When I reached the revolving doors of the Drakon building and pushed through them, I took a last glance back. He was gone, the man with blue eyes. So that was that.

I went at once to the cloakroom, shut myself into a cubicle and leaned against the door. I felt dizzy, my knees trembled and there was a heavy feeling at the back of my eyes, like unshed tears. Maybe I was getting a cold. Maybe my period was about to start. I thought of the man and the way he had stared at me, and I closed my eyes as if that would somehow shut him out. Someone else came into the cloakroom, turned on a tap. I stood very still and quiet, and could hear my heart thudding beneath my blouse. I laid my hand against my burning cheek, put it on my breast.

After a few minutes I could breathe properly again. I splashed cold water on my face, combed my hair, and remembered to remove a tiny pill from its foil calendar and swallow it. The ache in my guts was fading, and now I just felt fragile, jittery. Thank God nobody had seen anything. I bought coffee from the machine on the second floor and a bar of chocolate, for I was suddenly ravenous, and made my way to my office. I picked the wrapper and then the gold foil off the chocolate with shaky, incompetent fingers and ate it in large bites. The working day began. I read through my mail and tossed most of it into the bin, wrote a memo to Mike, then phoned Jake at work.

'How's your day going?' I asked.

'It's only just started.'

I felt as if hours had passed since leaving home. If I leaned back and closed my eyes, I could sleep for hours.

'Last night was nice,' he said, in a low voice. Maybe there were other people around at his end.

'Mmm. I felt a bit odd this morning, though, Jake.'

'Are you all right now?' He sounded concerned. I'm never ill.

'Yes. Fine. Completely fine. Are you all right?'

I'd run out of things to say but I was reluctant to put the phone down. Jake suddenly sounded preoccupied. I heard him say something I couldn't make out to someone else.

'Yes, love. Look, I'd better go. 'Bye.'

The morning passed. I went to another meeting, this time with the marketing department, managed to spill a jug of water over the table and say nothing at all. I read through the research document Giovanna had e-mailed to me. She was coming to see me at three thirty. I phoned up the hairdresser's and made an appointment for one o'clock. I drank lots of bitter, tepid coffee out of polystyrene cups. I watered the plants in my office. I learned to say 'je voudrais quatre petits pains' and 'Ça fait combien?'

Just before one I picked up my coat, left a message for my assistant that I would be out for an hour or so, then clattered down the stairs and into the street. It was just beginning to drizzle, and I hadn't got an umbrella. I looked up at the clouds, shrugged, and started to walk quickly along Cardamom Street where I could pick up a taxi to the hairdresser's. I stopped dead in my tracks and the world blurred. My stomach gave a lurch. I felt as if I was about to double up.

He was there, a few feet from me. As if he hadn't moved since this morning. Still in his black jacket and jeans; still not smiling. Just standing and looking at me. I felt then as if no one had ever looked at me properly before and was suddenly and acutely conscious of myself – of the pounding of my heart, the rise and fall of my breath; of the surface of my body, which was prickling with a kind of panic and excitement.

He was my sort of age, early thirties. I suppose he was beautiful, with his pale blue eyes and his tumbled brown hair and his high, flat cheekbones. But then all I knew was that he was so focused on me that I felt I couldn't move out of his gaze. I heard my breath come in a little ragged gasp, but I didn't move and I couldn't turn away.

I don't know who made the first step. Perhaps I stumbled towards him, or perhaps I just waited for him, and when we stood opposite each other, not touching, hands by our sides, he said, in a low voice, 'I've been waiting for you.'

I should have laughed out loud. This wasn't me, this couldn't be happening to me. I was just Alice Loudon, on her way to have her hair cut on a damp day in January. But I couldn't laugh or smile. I could only go on looking at him, into his wide-set blue eyes, at his mouth, which was slightly parted, the tender lips. He had white, even teeth, except that the front one was chipped. His chin was stubbly. There was a scratch on his neck. His hair was quite long, and unbrushed. Oh, yes, he was beautiful. I wanted to reach up and touch his mouth, ever so gently, with one thumb. I wanted to feel the scratch of his stubble in the hollow of my neck. I tried to say something, but all that came out of me was a strangled, prim 'Oh.'

'Please,' he said then, still not taking his eyes off my face. 'Will you come with me?'

He could have been a mugger, a rapist, a psychopath. I nodded dumbly at him and he stepped into the road, flagged down a taxi. He held open the door for me, but still didn't touch me. Inside he gave an address to the driver then turned towards me. I saw that under his leather jacket he wore only a dark green T-shirt. There was a leather thong around his neck with a small silver spiral hung on it. His hands were bare. I looked at his long fingers, with their neat, clean nails. A white scar kinked down one thumb. They looked practical hands, strong, dangerous.

'Tell me your name?'

'Alice,' I said. I didn't recognize my own voice.

'Alice,' he repeated. 'Alice.' The word sounded unfamiliar when he said it like that. He lifted his hands and, very gently, careful not to make any contact with my skin, loosened my scarf. He smelt of soap and sweat.

The taxi stopped and, looking out, I saw that we were in Soho. There was a paper shop, a delicatessen, restaurants. I could smell coffee and garlic. He got out and once more held the door open for me. I could feel the blood pulsing in my body. He pushed at a shabby door by the side of a clothes shop and I followed him up a narrow flight of steps. He took a bunch of keys from his pocket and unlocked two locks. Inside, it wasn't just a room but a small flat. I saw shelves, books, pictures, a rug. I hovered on the threshold. It was my last chance. The noise from the street outside filtered through the windows, the rise and fall of voices, the rumble of cars. He closed the door and bolted it from the inside.

I should have been scared, and I was, but not of him, this stranger. I was scared at myself. I didn't know myself any longer. I was dissolving with my desire, as if all the outlines of my body were becoming insubstantial. I started to take off my coat, hands clumsy on the velvet buttons, but he stopped me.

'Wait,' he said. 'Let me.'

First he removed my scarf and hung it carefully on the coat-stand. Next, my coat, taking his time. He knelt on the floor and slipped off my shoes. I put my hand on his shoulder to stop myself toppling. He stood again, and started to unbutton my cardigan, and I saw that his hands were trembling slightly. He undid my skirt and pulled it down over my hips; it rasped against my tights. He tugged off my tights, collecting them into a flimsy ball, which he put beside my shoes. Still, he had hardly made contact with my skin. He took off my camisole and slid down my knickers and I stood naked in that unfamiliar room, shivering slightly.

'Alice,' he said, in a kind of groan. Then, 'Oh, God, you're lovely, Alice.'

I took off his jacket. His arms were strong and brown, and there was another long, puckered scar running from the elbow to the wrist. I copied him and knelt at his feet to pull off his shoes and socks. On his right foot, he had only three toes, and I bent down and kissed the place where the other two had been. He sighed softly. I tugged his shirt free of his jeans and he raised his arms like a little boy while I pulled it over his head. He had a flat stomach with a line of hair running down it. I unzipped his jeans and eased them carefully down over his buttocks. His legs were knotty, quite tanned. I took off his underpants and dropped them on to the floor. Someone moaned, but I don't know if it was him or me. He lifted one hand and tucked a strand of hair behind my ear, then traced my lips with a forefinger, very slowly. I closed my eyes.

'No,' he said. 'Look at me.'

'Please,' I said. 'Please.'

He unhooked my earrings and let them fall. I heard them clink on the wooden boards.

'Kiss me, Alice,' he said.

Nothing like this had ever happened to me before. Sex had never been like this. There had been indifferent sex, embarrassing sex, nasty sex, good sex, great sex. This was more like obliterating sex. We crashed together, trying to get past the barrier of skin and flesh. We held each other as if we were drowning. We tasted each other as if we were starving. And all the time he looked at me. He looked at me as if I were the loveliest thing he had ever seen, and as I lay on the hard dusty floor I felt lovely, shameless, quite done for.

Afterwards, he lifted me to my feet and took me into the shower and washed me down. He soaped my breasts and between my legs. He washed my feet and thighs. He even washed my hair, expertly massaging shampoo into it, tilting my head back so soap wouldn't run into my eyes. Then he dried me, making sure I was dry under my arms, between my toes, and as he dried me he examined me. I felt like a work of art, and like a prostitute.

'I must go back to work,' I said at last. He dressed me, picking up my clothes from the floor, threading my earrings through my lobes, brushing my wet hair back from my face.

'When do you finish work?' he asked. I thought of Jake waiting at home.

'Six.'

'I'll be there,' he said. I should have told him then that I had a partner, a home, a whole other life. Instead I pulled his face towards mine and kissed his bruised lips. I could hardly bring myself to pull my body away from his.

In the taxi, alone, I pictured him, remembered his touch, his taste, his smell. I didn't know his name.

Three

I arrived back at my office out of breath. I grabbed some messages from Claudia's outstretched hand and went into my office. I flicked through them. Nothing that couldn't be put off. It was already twilight outside and I tried to catch my reflection in the window. I felt self-conscious about my clothes. They seemed strange on me because they had been taken off and put back on again by a stranger. I worried that it would seem as obvious to other people as it seemed to me. Had he fastened some button wrongly? Or maybe some bit of clothing had been put on over some other bit. It all seemed fine, but I wasn't sure enough. I rushed to the lavatory with some makeup. In the unforgiving bright light I checked in the mirror for puffy lips or visible bruises. I did some remedial work with lipstick and eye-liner. My hand was trembling. I had to bang it against a sink to steady it.

I rang Jake's mobile. He sounded as if he was in the middle of something. I said that I had a meeting and I might be late home. How late? I didn't know, it was completely unpredictable. Would I be back for supper? I told him to go ahead without me. I replaced the phone, telling myself that I was just trying to make things neat. I would probably be home before Jake was. Then I sat and thought about what I had done. I remembered his face. I sniffed at my wrist and smelt the soap. His soap. It made me shudder and when I closed my eyes I could feel the tiles under my feet and hear the shower pattering on the curtain. His hands.

There were one of two things that could happen, by which I meant that there were one of two things that *should* happen. I didn't know his name or address. I wasn't sure that I would be able to find his flat even if I wanted to. So if I came out at six and he wasn't there, it would be finished with in any case. If he was there, then I would have to tell him firmly and clearly the same thing. That was that. It was a mad thing to have done and the best thing to do was to pretend that it hadn't happened. It was the only sane course.

I had been dazed when I had returned to the office, but now I felt clearer-headed than I had for weeks, full of a new kinetic energy. Over the next hour I had a brief chat with Giovanna and then made a dozen phone calls with no small-talk. I got back to people, made arrangements, queried figures. Sylvie rang and wanted to chat but I told her I would see her tomorrow or the next day. Was I doing anything this evening? Yes. A meeting. I sent some messages, disposed of the papers on my desk. One day I wouldn't have a desk at all and I'd get twice as much done.

I looked across at the clock. It was five to six. As I was searching around for my bag, Mike came in. He was taking a conference call before breakfast on the next day and he needed to go over things.

'I'm in a bit of a hurry, Mike. I've got a meeting.'

'Who with?'

For a moment I thought of pretending I was meeting someone from the lab but some flicker of a survival instinct prompted me not to. 'It's something private.'

He raised an eyebrow. 'Job interview?'

'Dressed like this?'

'You *do* look a bit rumpled.' He didn't say any more. He probably assumed that it was something female, gynaecological. But he didn't go away either. 'It'll just take a second.' He sat down with his notes, which we had to go through point by point. I had to check one or two of them and phone somebody about another. I made a promise to myself that I wouldn't look at the clock a single time. What did it matter anyway? Finally there was a pause and I said that I really had to go. Mike nodded. I looked at my watch. Twenty-four minutes past six. Twenty-five past. I didn't hurry, even after Mike had gone. I went to the lift feeling relieved that events had sorted themselves out. It was best this way, all forgotten.

I lay at an angle across the bed with my head on Adam's stomach. His name was Adam. He had told me that in the cab on the way over. It was almost the only thing he had said. Sweat was running down my face. I could feel it everywhere: on my back, on my legs. My hair was wet. And I could feel the sweat on his skin. It was so hot in this flat. How could anywhere be so hot in January? The chalky taste in my mouth wouldn't go away. I raised myself up and looked at him. His eyes were half closed.

'Is there anything to drink?' I asked.

'I don't know,' he said sleepily. 'Why don't you go and look?'

I stood up and looked for something to put around me and then thought: why? There was almost nothing else to the flat. There was this room, which had a bed and lots of floor space, and there was the bathroom, where I had had my shower earlier, and there was a tiny kitchen. I opened the fridge: a couple of half-squeezed tubes, some jars, a carton of milk. Nothing to drink. I was feeling the chill now. There was a bottle of some kind of orange juice on a shelf. I hadn't drunk diluted orange squash since I was a child. I found a tumbler and mixed some, drank it in a couple of gulps, mixed some more and took it back into the bedroom, living room, whatever it was. Adam was sitting up, leaning against the bedhead. Briefly, I allowed myself to remember Jake's bonier, whiter shape, the jutting collar-bone and knobbly spine. Adam was looking at me as I came in. He must have been watching the doorway, waiting for me. He didn't smile, just gazed intently at my naked body, as if he were committing it to memory. I smiled at him, but he didn't smile back and a feeling of intense joy rose up in me.

I walked across and offered the glass to him. He took a small sip and handed the glass to me. I took a small sip and passed it back to him. We emptied the glass like that, together, and then he leaned across me and placed the glass on the rug. The duvet had been kicked off on to the floor. I pulled it up over us. I looked around the room. The photographs on the chest and the mantelpiece were all of landscapes. There were some books on the shelf and I examined them one by one: several cookery books, a large coffee-table book about Hogarth, the collected works of W. H. Auden and of Sylvia Plath. A Bible. *Wuthering Heights*, some D. H. Lawrence travel books. Two guides to British wild flowers. A book of walks in and around London. Dozens of guidebooks in a row and in piles. A few clothes were hanging on the metal runner or neatly folded on the wicker chair by the bed: jeans, a silk shirt, another leather jacket, T-shirts.

'I'm trying to work out who you are,' I said, 'by looking at your things.'

'None of it's mine. This place belongs to a friend.'

'Oh.'

I looked round at him. He still wasn't smiling. I found it unsettling. I started to speak and then he did give a slight smile, shook his head and touched my lips with one finger. Our bodies were close together anyway and he moved forward a couple of inches and kissed me.

'What are you thinking?' I said, running the fingers of one hand through his soft, long hair. 'Talk to me. Tell me something.'

He didn't answer immediately. He slid the duvet off my body and moved me on to my back. He took my hands in his and raised them above my head on the sheet as if they were pinioned. I felt exposed like a specimen on a slide. He gently touched my forehead and then ran his fingers down over my face, my neck, down my body and they came to rest in my belly-button. I shivered and wriggled. 'Sorry,' I said.

He leaned right forward over me and touched my belly-button with his tongue. 'I was thinking,' he said, 'that the hair under your arms, here, is just like your pubic hair. Here. But not like the lovely hair on your head. And I was thinking that I like your

26

taste. I mean, all your different tastes. I would like to lick every bit of you.' He was looking up and down and over my body as if it were a landscape. I giggled, and he looked into my eyes. 'What's that for?' he asked, with a look almost of alarm in his eyes.

I smiled at him. 'I think you're treating me like a sex object.'

'Don't,' he said. 'Don't make jokes.'

I felt myself blushing. Was I blushing all over my body? 'I'm sorry,' I said. 'I wasn't. I like it. I feel blurry.'

'What are *you* thinking?'

'*You* lie back,' I said, and he did. 'And close your eyes.' I ran my fingers over his body, which smelt of sex and sweat. 'What am I thinking? I think that I'm completely mad and I don't know what I'm doing here but it was . . .' I stopped. I didn't have words for sex with him. Just remembering it sent little ripples of pleasure through me. I felt a throb of desire again. My body felt soft and new and open to him. I curled my fingers on to the velvety skin of his inner thigh. What else was I thinking about? I had to force myself. 'I'm also thinking . . . I'm thinking that I have a boyfriend. More than a boyfriend. I live with somebody.'

I don't know what I expected. Anger, maybe, evasiveness. Adam didn't move. He didn't even open his eyes. 'But you're here,' was all he said.

'Yeah,' I said. 'God, I am.'

We lay together for a long time after that. One hour, two hours. Jake always said that I can't relax for long, can't stay still, can't stay silent. Now we barely spoke. We touched. Rested. Looked at each other. I lay and listened to the sounds of voices and cars in the street below. My body felt thin and peeled under his hands. Finally I said I had to go. I showered and then dressed while he watched me. It made me shiver.

'Give me your number,' he said.

I shook my head. 'Give me yours.'

I leaned over and kissed him gently. He put a hand on my hand and pulled my head down. I felt an ache in my chest so that I could hardly breathe, but I shook him off. 'Must go,' I whispered.

It was after midnight. When I let myself into the flat, it was dark. Jake had gone to bed. I tiptoed into the bathroom. I put my knickers and tights into the washbag. I had a shower for the second time in an hour. The fourth time that day. I washed my body again in my own soap. I washed my hair in my own shampoo. I crawled into the bed beside Jake. He turned and mumbled something.

'Me you too,' I said.

Four

Jake woke me up with my tea. He sat on the edge of the bed in his towelling robe and smoothed my hair back from my forehead while I surfaced from sleep. I stared at him, and memory flooded back, disastrous and overpowering. My lips felt sore and puffy; my body ached. Surely he could tell, just by looking at me. I pulled the sheet up to my chin and smiled at him.

'You look lovely this morning,' he said. 'Have you any idea what time it is?'

I shook my head.

He looked theatrically at his watch. 'Nearly eleven thirty. Lucky it's the weekend. What time did you get in last night?'

'Midnight. Maybe a bit later.'

'They're working you too hard,' he said. 'Drink up. Lunch at my parents', remember?'

I hadn't remembered. Only my body seemed to have a memory now: Adam's hands on my breasts, Adam's lips at my throat, Adam's eyes staring into mine. Jake smiled at me and rubbed my neck, and there I lay, sick with desire for another man. I picked up Jake's hand and kissed it. 'You're a nice man,' I said.

He pulled a face. 'Nice?' He leaned down and kissed me on the lips, and I felt as if I was betraying someone. Jake? Adam?

'Shall I run you a bath?'

'That'd be lovely.'

I poured a stream of lemon bath oil into the water, and washed myself in it all over again, as if I could wash away what had happened. I hadn't eaten anything yesterday, but the thought of food was horrible. I closed my eyes and lay in the hot, deep, fragrant water and let myself think of Adam. I must never, ever see him again, that was clear. I loved Jake. I liked my life. I had behaved appallingly and I would lose everything. I must see him again, at once. Nothing else mattered except for the touch of his hands, the ache of my flesh, the way he said my name. I would see him once, just once, to tell him it was over. I owed him that at least. What rubbish. I was lying to myself as well as to Jake. If I saw him, looked again into his beautiful face, I would fuck him. No, the only thing to do was just turn away from everything that had happened yesterday. Concentrate on Jake; work. But just one more time, a last time.

'Ten minutes, Alice. All right?'

The sound of Jake's voice brought me to my senses. Of course I was going to stay with him. We'd get married, maybe, and have children and one day this would be a memory, one of those ridiculous things one had done once before growing up. I sluiced myself down one last time, watching the bubbles stream off a body that suddenly seemed strange to me. Then I climbed out of the bath. Jake held out a towel. I was aware of his eyes on me as I dried.

'Perhaps we can be a bit late, after all,' he said. 'Come here.'

So I let Jake make love to me, and tell me that he loved me, and I lay under him damp and acquiescent. I groaned with pretended pleasure, and he didn't know, he couldn't tell. It would be my secret.

We had spinach flan for lunch, with garlic bread and green salad. Jake's mother is a good cook. I lifted a piece of curly lettuce on to my fork and put it in my mouth, chewed slowly. It was difficult to swallow. I took a gulp of water and tried again. I'd never be able to eat all of this.

'Are you all right, Alice?' Jake's mother was looking fretfully at me. She hates it when I don't finish meals that she's cooked. Usually I try to have a second helping. She likes me better than

Jake's previous girlfriends because I usually have a large appetite, and eat several slices of her chocolate cake.

I speared a chunk of flan and pushed it into my mouth and chewed determinedly. 'Fine,' I said, when I had swallowed it. 'I'm getting over something.'

'Will you be all right for this evening?' Jake asked. I looked baffled. 'You know, stupid, we're going for a curry with the Crew over in Stoke Newington. Then there's a party if we feel like it. Some dancing.'

'Great,' I said.

I nibbled some garlic bread. Jake's mother watched me.

After lunch, we all went for a slow walk in Richmond Park among the docile herds of deer, and then, when it was beginning to get dark, Jake and I drove home. He went to the shops for some milk and bread, and I took out an old Interflora card from my wallet, with Adam's number on the back. I went to the phone, picked it up and dialled the first three digits. I put it down again and stood over it, breathing heavily. I tore the card up into lots of bits and flushed it down the lavatory. Some of the scraps wouldn't go down. In a panic, I filled a bucket with water and swilled them away. It didn't matter anyway, because I could remember the number. Jake came back then, whistling up the stairs with his shopping. It will never get worse than this, I told myself. Every day it will get a little bit better. It's just a question of waiting.

When we arrived they were all there in the curry house. A bottle of wine and glasses of beer stood on the table, and everyone's faces in the candlelight looked merry and soft.

'Jake, Alice!' Clive shouted, from one end of the table. I sat squeezed against Jake, my thigh against his, at the other end, but Clive waved me over. 'I called her,' he said.

'Who?'

'Gail,' he said, slightly indignantly. 'She said yes. I'm going to meet her for a drink next week.'

'There you are,' I said, making myself do an imitation of a person having fun. 'I'll become a freelance agony aunt.'

'I thought of suggesting that she come tonight. But then I thought the Crew might be too much for her on a first meeting.'

I looked around the table. 'The Crew sometimes seems too much for *me*.'

'Oh, come on, you're the life and soul of the party.'

'Why does that sound so dreary, I wonder?'

I was sitting next to Sylvie. Across from me was Julie with a man I didn't know. On the other side of Sylvie was Jake's sister, Pauline, who was there with Tom, her fairly new husband. Pauline caught my eye and gave me a smile of greeting. She is probably my closest friend and I had been trying not to think of her for the past couple of days. I smiled back.

I started to pick at somebody else's onion bhaji and concentrate on what Sylvie was telling me, which was about a man she'd been seeing, most specifically what they'd been doing in bed, or on the bed, or on the floor. She lit another cigarette and drew deeply from it. 'What most men don't seem to understand is that when they arrange your legs over their shoulders so that they can go deeper in, it can really hurt. When Frank did it last night, I thought he was going to pull my coil out. But you're the coil expert,' she added, with an earnestly analytical air.

Sylvie was the only person I knew who satisfied my basic interest in what other people actually do when they have sex. I was generally resistant about replying with confessions of my own. Especially now. 'Maybe I should introduce you to our designers,' I said. 'You could road-test our new IUD for us.'

'Road-test?' said Sylvie, grinning wolfishly, her teeth white and her lips painted bright red. 'A night with Frank is like the Monte Carlo rally. I felt so sore today that I could hardly sit down at work. I'd complain to Frank about it but he'd take it as some backhanded compliment, which I don't mean at all. I'm sure you're much better than I am at getting what you want. Sexually, I mean.'

32

'I don't know about that,' I said, looking around to see if anybody was listening to what we were saying. Tables, indeed whole restaurants, had a way of falling silent when Sylvie was talking. I preferred her alone in situations where there was absolutely no risk of being overheard. I poured myself another glass of red wine and half emptied it in a gulp. At this rate, and on a practically empty stomach, I'd be drunk soon. Maybe then I would feel less bad. I stared at the menu. 'I'll have, um . . .' My voice trailed away. I thought I'd seen someone outside the restaurant window in a black leather jacket. But when I looked again no one was there. Of course not. 'Maybe just a vegetable dish,' I said.

I felt Jake's hand on my shoulder as he moved across to our end of the table. He wanted to be near me, but just at the moment I could hardly bear it. I had an absurd impulse to tell him everything. I tilted my head on to his shoulder, then drank some more wine and laughed when everyone else laughed and nodded occasionally when the intonation of a sentence seemed to demand a response. If I could see him just one more time, I would be able to bear it, I told myself. There was someone out there. Obviously it wasn't him, but someone in a dark jacket was outside in the cold. I looked at Jake. He was having an animated conversation with Sylvie about a film they had both seen last week. 'No, he just *pretended* to do it,' he was saying.

I stood up, my chair scraping loudly. 'Sorry, just got to go to the bathroom, I'll be back in a minute.'

I went to the end of the restaurant, near the stairs that led down to the toilets, then glanced back. No one was watching me: they were all turned to each other, drinking, talking. They looked such a happy group. I slipped through the front door and outside. The cold air hit me so that I gasped as I breathed it. I looked around. He was there, a few yards down the street, beside a telephone box. Waiting.

I ran to him. 'How dare you follow me,' I hissed. 'How dare you?' Then I kissed him. I buried my face against his, pushed my lips against his, and wrapped my arms around him and strained my body against him. He pushed his hands through my hair and yanked my head back until I was looking into his eyes, then said, 'You weren't going to ring me, were you?' He rammed me up against the wall and held me there while he kissed me again.

'No,' I said. 'No, I can't. Can't do this.' Oh, but I can, I can.

'You have to,' he said. He pulled me into the shadow of the telephone box and undid my coat and felt my breast under my shirt. I moaned and tilted my head back and he kissed my neck. His stubble rasped against my skin.

'I've got to go back,' I said, still straining against him. 'I'll come to your flat, I promise.'

He took his hand from my breast and moved it to my leg and then up my leg and against my knickers and I felt a finger inside me.

'When?' he asked, looking at me.

'Monday,' I gasped. 'I'll come at nine o'clock on Monday morning.'

He let me go and raised his hand. Deliberately, so I could see, he put his shiny finger into his mouth and licked it.

On Sunday, we painted the room that was going to be my study. I tied my hair back in a scarf and wore some of Jake's old jeans and still managed to drop pea-green paint on my hands and face. We had a late lunch and in the afternoon we watched an old movie on television, arm in arm on the sofa. I went to bed early, after an hour-long bath, saying I still had a bit of a stomach-ache. When Jake climbed in beside me later, I pretended to be asleep, though I lay awake for hours in the dark. I planned what I would wear. I thought about how I would hold him, learn his body, trace his ribs and his vertebrae, touch the full, soft lips with my finger. I was terrified.

The next morning I got out of bed first, had another bath, and told Jake I would be working quite late, that I might have to go to a meeting in Edgware with clients. At the tube station, I rang Drakon and left a message for Claudia, saying I was ill in bed, and please on no account to disturb me. I flagged down a taxi – it didn't occur to me to go by underground – and gave Adam's address. I tried not to think about what I was doing. I tried not to think about Jake, his cheerful bony face, his eagerness. I looked out of the window as the cab crawled slowly through the rush-hour traffic. I brushed my hair again, and fiddled with the velvet buttons on my coat, which Jake had bought me at Christmas. I tried to remember my old telephone number, and couldn't. If anyone looked inside the taxi, they would just see a woman in a severe black coat on her way to work. I could still change my mind.

I rang the doorbell and Adam was there before I had time to arrange my smile, my jokey greeting. We nearly fucked on the stairs, but made it into the flat. We didn't take off our clothes or lie down. He parted my coat and lifted my skirt above my waist and pushed into me, standing up, and it was over in a minute.

Then he took off my coat, straightened my shirt and kissed me on my eyes and mouth. Healing me.

'We have to talk,' I said. 'We have to think about . . .'

'I know. Wait.' He went into the tiny kitchen and I heard him grinding coffee. 'Here we are.' Adam put a pot of coffee and a couple of almond croissants on the small table. 'I bought these downstairs.'

I discovered I was ravenous. Adam watched me eat as if I were doing something remarkable. Once he leaned forward and took a flake of croissant off my lower lip. He poured me a second cup of coffee.

'We've got to talk,' I said again. He waited. 'I mean, I don't know who you are. I don't know your second name or anything about you at all.'

He shrugged. 'My name's Adam Tallis,' he said simply, as if that answered all my questions about him.

'What do you do?'

'Do?' he asked, as if it were all far away and long ago. 'Different things, in different places, to get money. But what I really do is climb, when I can.'

'What? Mountains?' I sounded about twelve, squeaky and amazed.

He laughed. 'Yeah, mountains. I do stuff on my own, and I guide.'

'Guide?' I was becoming an echo.

'Put up tents, short-rope rich tourists up famous peaks so they can pretend they've climbed them. That sort of thing.'

I remembered his scars, his strong arms. A climber. Well, I had never met any climbers before.

'Sounds . . .' I was going to say 'exciting', but then I stopped myself from saying something else stupid and instead added, '. . . like something I don't know anything about.' I smiled at him, feeling giddy with the utter newness of it all. Vertigo.

'That's all right,' he said.

'I'm Alice Loudon,' I said, feeling foolish. A few minutes ago we'd been making love and staring into each other's faces with a rapt attention. What could I say about myself that made any sense in this little room? 'I'm a scientist, in a way, though now I work for a company called Drakon. They're very well known. I'm managing a project there. I come from Worcestershire. I have a boyfriend and I share a flat with him. I shouldn't be here. This is wrong. That's about all.'

'No, it isn't,' said Adam. He took the cup of coffee out of my hands. 'No, it isn't all. You've got blonde hair and deep grey eyes and a turned-up nose, and when you smile your face crinkles up. I saw you and I couldn't look away. You're a witch, you cast a spell on me. You don't know what you're doing here. You spent the weekend deciding you must never see me again. But I spent the whole weekend knowing we have to be together. And what you want to do is to take off your clothes in front of me, right now.'

'But my whole life . . .' I started. I couldn't go on because I no

36

longer knew what my whole life was meant to be. Here we were, in a little room in Soho, and the past had been erased and the future too, and it was just me and him and I had no idea of what I should do.

I spent the whole day there. We made love, and we talked, although later I couldn't remember what about, just little things, odd memories. At eleven he put on jeans and a sweatshirt and trainers and went to the market. He came back and fed me melon, cold and juicy. At one, he made us omelettes and chopped up tomatoes and opened a bottle of champagne. It was real champagne, not just sparkling white wine. He held the glass while I drank. He drank himself and fed me from his mouth. He laid me down and told me about my body, listing its virtues as if cataloguing them. He listened to every word I said, really listened, as if he were storing it all up to remember later. Sex and talk and food blurred into each other. We ate food as if we were eating each other, and touched each other while we talked. We fucked in the shower and on the bed and on the floor. I wanted the day to go on for ever. I felt so happy I ached with it; so renewed I hardly recognized myself. Whenever he took his hands off me I felt cold, abandoned.

'I have to go,' I said at last. It was dark outside.

'I want to give you something,' he said, and untied the leather thong with its silver spiral from his neck.

'But I can't wear it.'

'Touch it sometimes. Put it in your bra, in your knickers.'

'You're crazy.'

'Crazy for you.'

I took the necklace, and promised I would ring him and this time he knew it was true. Then I headed for home. For Jake.

Five

The following days were a blur of lunch-times, early evenings, one whole night when Jake was away at a conference, a blur of sex and of food that could be easily bought and easily eaten: bread, fruit, cheese, tomatoes, wine. And I lied and lied and lied, as I had never done before in my life, to Jake and to friends and to people at work. I was forced to fabricate a series of alternative fictional worlds of appointments and meetings and visits behind which I could live my secret life with Adam. The effort of making sure that the lies were consistent, of remembering what I had said to which person, was enormous. Is it a defence that I was drunk with something I barely understood?

One time Adam had pulled on some clothes to buy something for us to eat. When he had clattered down the stairs, I wrapped the duvet around me, went to the window and watched him head across the road, dodging through the traffic, towards the Berwick Street market. After he had vanished from view, I looked at other people walking along the street, in a hurry to get somewhere, or dawdling, looking in windows. How could they get through their lives without the passion that I was feeling? How could they think it was important to get on at work or to plan their holiday or buy something when what mattered in life was this, the way I was feeling?

Everything in my life outside that Soho room seemed a matter of indifference. Work was a charade I was putting on for my colleagues. I was impersonating a busy, ambitious manager. I still cared about my friends, I just didn't want to see them. My home felt like an office or a launderette, somewhere I had to pass through occasionally in order to fulfil an obligation. And Jake. And Jake. That was the bad bit. I felt like somebody on a runaway train. Somewhere ahead, a mile or five thousand miles ahead, were the terminus, buffers and disaster, but for the moment all I could feel was delirious speed. Adam reappeared around the corner. He looked up at the window and saw me. He didn't smile or wave, but he quickened his pace. I was his magnet; he mine.

When we had finished eating I licked the tomato pulp off his fingers.

'You know what I love about you?'

'What?'

'*One* of the things. Everybody else I know has a sort of uniform they wear and things to go with it – keys, wallets, credit cards. You look as if you've just dropped naked from another planet and found odd bits of clothes and just put them on.'

'Do you want me to put them on?'

'No, but . . .'

'But what?'

'When you went outside just now, I watched you as you went. And I mainly thought that this was wonderful.'

'That's right,' said Adam.

'Yes, but I suppose I was also secretly thinking that one day we're going to have to go out there, into the world. I mean both of us, together, in some way. Meet people, do things, you know.' As I spoke the words, they sounded strange as if I were talking about Adam and Eve being expelled from the Garden of Eden. I became alarmed. 'It depends what you want, of course.'

Adam frowned. 'I want you,' he said.

'Yes,' I said, not knowing what 'yes' meant. We were silent for a long time and then I said, 'You know so little about me, and I know so little about you. We come from different worlds.' Adam shrugged. He didn't believe any of this mattered at all – not my circumstances, my job, my friends, my political beliefs, my moral landscape, my past – nothing. There was some essence-of-Alice that he had recognized. In my other life, I would have argued vehemently with him over his mystical sense of absolute love, for I have always thought that love is biological, Darwinian, pragmatic, circumstantial, effortful, fragile. Now, besotted and reckless, I could no longer remember what I believed and it was as if I had returned to my childish sense of love as something that rescued you from the real world. So now I just said, 'I can't believe it. I mean, I don't even know what to ask you.'

Adam stroked my hair and made me shiver. 'Why ask me anything?' he said.

'Don't you want to know about me? Don't you want to know the details of what my work involves?'

'Tell me the details of what your work involves.'

'You don't really want to know.'

'I do. If you think what you do is important, then I want to know.'

'I told you already that I work for a large pharmaceutical company. For the last year I've been seconded to a group who are developing a new model intrauterine device. There.'

'You haven't told me about you,' Adam said. 'Are you designing it?'

'No.'

'Are you doing the scientific research?'

'No.'

'Are you marketing it?'

'No.'

'Well, what the fuck *are* you doing?'

I laughed. 'It reminds me of a lesson I had at Sunday School when I was a child. I put up my hand and I said that I knew that the Father was God, and that the Son was Jesus, but what did the Holy Spirit do?'

'What did the teacher say?'

'He had a word with my mother. But in the development of the Drakloop III, I'm like the Holy Spirit. I interface, arrange, drift around, go to meetings. In short, I'm a manager.'

Adam smiled and then looked serious. 'Do you like that?'

I thought for a moment. 'I don't know, I don't think I've said this clearly, even to myself. The problem is that I used to like the routine part of being a scientist that other people find boring. I liked working on the protocols, setting up the equipment, making the observations, doing the figures, writing up the results.'

'So what happened?'

'I suppose I was too good at it. I got promoted. But I shouldn't be saying all of this. If I'm not careful you'll discover what a boring woman you've inveigled into your bed.' Adam didn't laugh or say anything, so I got embarrassed and clumsily tried to change the subject. 'I've never done much outdoors. Have you climbed big mountains?'

'Sometimes.'

'Really big ones? Like Everest?'

'Sometimes.'

'That's amazing.'

He shook his head. 'It's not amazing. Everest isn't . . .' he searched for the right word '. . . a *technically* interesting challenge.'

'Are you saying it's *easy*?'

'No, nothing above eight thousand metres is easy. But if you're not too unlucky with the weather then Everest is a walk-in. People are led up there who aren't real climbers. They're just rich enough to hire people who *are* real climbers.'

'But you've been to the top?'

Adam looked uncomfortable, as if it was difficult to explain to someone who couldn't possibly understand. 'I've been on the mountain several times. I guided a commercial expedition in 'ninety-four and I went to the summit.'

'What was it like?'

'I hated it. I was on the summit with ten people taking pictures. And the mountain . . . Everest should be something holy. When I went there it was like a tourist site that was turning into a rubbish dump – old oxygen cylinders, bits of tent, frozen turds all over the place, flapping ropes, dead bodies. Kilimanjaro's even worse.'

41

'Have you just been climbing now?'

'Not since last spring.'

'Was that Everest?'

'No. I was one of the guides for hire on a mountain called Chungawat.'

'I've never heard of it. Is it near Everest?'

'Pretty near.'

'Is it more dangerous than Everest?'

'Yes.'

'Did you get to the top?'

'No.'

Adam's mood had darkened. His eyes were narrow, uncommunicative. 'What is it, Adam?' He didn't reply. 'Is it . . . ?' I ran my fingers down his leg to his foot and to the mutilated toes.

'Yes,' he said.

I kissed them. 'Was it very terrible?'

'You mean the toes? Not really.'

'I mean the whole thing.'

'Yes, it was.'

'Will you tell me all about it some day?'

'Some day. Not now.'

I kissed his foot, his ankle and worked my way up. Some day, I promised myself.

'You look tired.'

'Pressure of work,' I lied.

There was one person I hadn't felt able to put off. I used to meet Pauline almost every week for lunch and usually we'd wander into a shop or two together, where she would watch indulgently as I tried on impractical garments: summer dresses in winter; velvet and wool in summer; clothes for a different life. Today I was walking along with her while she did some shopping. We bought a couple of sandwiches from a bar on the edge of Covent Garden then queued at a coffee shop and then at a cheese shop.

I immediately knew I'd said the wrong thing. We never said things like 'pressure of work' to each other. I suddenly felt like a double agent.

'How's Jake?' she asked.

'Very fine,' I said. 'The tunnel thing is almost . . . Jake is lovely. He's absolutely lovely.'

Pauline looked at me with a new concern. 'Is everything all right, Alice? Remember, this is my big brother you're talking about. If anybody describes Jake as absolutely lovely, there must be some kind of a problem.'

I laughed and she laughed and the moment passed. She bought her large bag of coffee beans and two takeaway polystyrene cups of coffee and we walked slowly towards Covent Garden and found a bench. This was a bit better. It was a sunny, clear, very cold day, and the coffee burned my lips pleasantly.

'How's married life?' I asked.

Pauline looked at me very seriously. She was a striking woman whose straight dark hair could suggest severity, if you didn't know better. 'I've stopped taking the Pill,' she said.

'Because of the scares?' I asked. 'It's not really . . .'

'No,' she laughed, 'I've just stopped. I haven't changed to anything.'

'Oh, my God,' I said, with a half-scream, and hugged her. 'Are you ready for this? Isn't it a bit too soon?'

'It's always too soon, I think,' Pauline said. 'Anyway, nothing's happened yet.'

'So you haven't started standing on your head after sex, or whatever it is you're meant to do.'

So we chattered about fertility and pregnancy and maternity leave and the more we talked the worse I felt. Up to this moment, I had thought of Adam as a dark, strictly private betrayal. I knew I was doing something awful to Jake but now, looking at Pauline, her cheeks flushed red in the cold but also with the excitement, maybe, of impending pregnancy, and her hands clutched round the coffee, and the mist from between her narrow lips, I had a

43

sudden mad sense that all of it was operating under a misapprehension. The world wasn't as she thought it was and it was my fault.

We both looked at our empty coffee cups, laughed and stood up. I gave her a close hug and pushed my face against hers.

'Thank you,' I said.

'What for?'

'Most people don't tell you about trying for a baby until they're into their second trimester.'

'Oh, Alice,' she said reprovingly. 'I couldn't not tell you *that*.'

'I've got to go,' I said suddenly. 'I've got a meeting.'

'Where?'

'Oh,' I said taken aback. 'In, er, Soho.'

'I'll walk along with you. It's on my way.'

'That would be lovely,' I said, in anguish.

On the way Pauline talked about Guy, who had broken off with her suddenly and brutally not much more than eighteen months earlier.

'Do you remember the way I was then?' she asked, with a little grimace and looking, for the moment, just like her brother. I nodded, thinking frantically about how I was to handle this. Should I pretend to go into an office? That wouldn't work. Should I say I had forgotten the address? 'Of course you do. You saved my life. I don't think I'll ever be able to repay you for all you did for me then.' She held up her bag of coffee. 'I probably drank about that much coffee in your old flat while crying into your whisky. God, I thought I would never be able to cross the road again on my own, let alone function and be happy.'

I squeezed her hand. They say that the best friends are those who can simply listen and if that's true then I was the best of all friends during that terrible walk. This was it, I said to myself, the terrible punishment for all my deceptions. As we turned into Old Compton Street, I saw a familiar figure walking in front of us. Adam. My brain dulled and I thought I might even be going to

44

faint. I turned, saw an open shop door. I couldn't speak but I seized Pauline's hand and pulled her inside.

'What?' she asked in alarm.

'I need some . . .' I looked into the glass case on the counter. 'Some . . .'

The word wouldn't come.

'Parmesan,' said Pauline.

'Parmesan,' I agreed. 'And other things.'

Pauline looked around. 'But there's such a long queue. It's Friday.'

'I've go to.'

Pauline looked indecisive, shifting from one foot to another. She looked at her watch. 'I'm sorry,' she said. 'I'd better get back.'

'Yes,' I said, in relief.

'What?'

'That's fine,' I said. 'Just go. I'll phone you.'

We kissed and she left. I counted to ten, then looked out into the street. She had gone. I looked down at my hands. They were steady, but my mind reeled.

That night, I dreamed that someone was cutting off my legs with a kitchen knife, and I was letting them. I knew I mustn't scream, or complain, because I had deserved it. I woke in the early hours, sweating and confused, and for a moment I couldn't tell who it was I was lying next to. I put out my hand and felt warm flesh. Jake's eyes flickered open. 'Hello, Alice,' he said, and returned to sleep, so peaceful.

I couldn't go on like this. I had always thought of myself as an honest person.

Six

I was late for work because I had to wait for the art shop round the corner from the office to open. I stood for a while looking at the river, hypnotized by the surprising strength of its currents, spinning this way and that. Then I spent far too long choosing a postcard from the revolving racks. Nothing seemed right. Not the reproductions of old masters, nor the black-and-white photographs of urban streets and picturesque poor children, nor those expensive cards with collages of sequins and shells and feathers stuck decoratively in the middle. In the end I bought two: one a muted Japanese landscape of silver trees against a dark sky, and the other a Matisse-style cut-out, all joyful simple blues. I bought a fountain pen as well, although I had a whole drawer full of pens in my desk.

What should I say? I shut the door to my office, took out the two cards and laid them in front of me. I must have sat like that for several minutes, just staring at them. Every so often I would allow his face to drift across my consciousness. So beautiful. The way he looked into my eyes. Nobody had ever looked at me like that before. I hadn't seen him all weekend, not since that Friday, and now . . .

Now I turned over the Japanese card and unscrewed my fountain pen. I didn't know how to start. Not 'dearest Adam' or 'darling Adam' or 'sweetest love'; not that any longer. Not 'dear Adam' – too cold. Not just 'Adam'. Nothing then: just write.

'I cannot see you any more,' I wrote, careful not to smudge the black ink. I stopped. What else was there to say? 'Please do not try to make me change my mind. It's been –' Been what?

46

Fun? Tormenting? Stunning? Wrong? The most wonderful thing that has ever happened to me? It has turned my whole life upside down?

I tore up the picture of the Japanese trees and put it into the bin. I picked up the splashy cut-out. 'I cannot see you again.'

Before I could add anything else, I slipped the card into an envelope and wrote Adam's name and address on it in neat capitals. Then I walked out of the office holding it, and took the lift down to reception, where Derek sat with his security passes and his copy of the *Sun*.

'You couldn't do something for me, could you, Derek? This letter needs to go urgently and I wondered if you could send a bike for it. I would ask Claudia but . . .' I let the sentence hang unfinished in the air. Derek took the envelope and looked at the address.

'Soho. Business, is it?'

'Yes.'

He put the envelope down beside him. 'All right, then. Just this once, though.'

'I really appreciate it. You'll see it goes immediately?'

I told Claudia that I had a lot of work to catch up on and could she not put through telephone calls unless they were from Mike or Giovanna or Jake. She looked at me curiously, but said nothing. It was half past ten. He would still be thinking that at lunch-time I would be with him, in his darkened room, letting the world go hang. By eleven, he would have received the note. He would run down the stairs and pick up the envelope and slide his finger under the flap and read that one sentence. I should have told him I was sorry, at least. Or that I loved him. I closed my eyes. I felt like a fish on dry land. I was gasping, and every breath hurt.

When Jake had given up cigarettes a few months ago, he had told me that the trick was not to think about not smoking: what you are denying yourself, he'd said, becomes doubly desirable and then it's like a kind of persecution. I touched my cheek with one finger and imagined it was Adam touching me. I mustn't let myself picture him. I mustn't talk to him on the telephone. I mustn't see him. Cold turkey.

At eleven o'clock I closed the blinds against the grey, drizzly day, just in case he came to the office and stood outside waiting for me. I didn't look down into the street. Claudia brought me a list of people who had called and left messages; Adam hadn't tried to phone. Perhaps he was out, and still didn't know. Perhaps he wouldn't get the note until he came back to his flat to meet me.

I didn't go out for lunch, but sat in my dimmed office staring at my computer screen. If anyone had come in, they would have assumed I was busy.

At three, Jake rang to say that on Friday he might have to go to Edinburgh for a couple of days, on business.

'Can I come with you?' I asked. But it was a stupid idea. He would be working all day; I couldn't just take off from Drakon at the moment.

'We'll go away together soon,' he promised. 'Let's plan it tonight. We can have an evening in, for a change. I'll buy us a takeaway. Chinese or Indian?'

'Indian,' I said. I wanted to throw up.

I went to our weekly conference, where Claudia interrupted us to say there was a man who wouldn't leave his name but urgently wanted to speak to me. I told her to say that I was unavailable. She went away, looking interested.

At five, I decided to go home early. I left the building by the back entrance, and got a cab home through the rush hour. I put my hands over my face and closed my eyes when we drove past the main entrance. I was first home, and I made it to my bedroom – our bedroom – and lay on the bed, where I curled up and waited for time to pass. The phone rang and I didn't answer it. I heard the letterbox flap, something hit the mat and I struggled up. I had to get that before Jake did. But it was just junk mail. Did I want all my carpets specially cleaned? I went back and lay on the bed and tried to breathe calmly. Jake would be home soon.

Jake. I thought about Jake. I pictured the way he frowned when he smiled. Or the way he poked his tongue out slightly when he was concentrating. Or the way he hooted when he laughed. Outside it was dark and the street lamps glowed orange. I could hear cars, voices, children chattering. At some point I fell asleep.

I pulled Jake down to me in the darkness. 'The curry can wait,' I said.

I told him I loved him, and he told me that he loved me too. I wanted to say it over and over, but I stopped myself. Outside it rained gently. Later, we ate the cool takeaway from the silver-foil containers or, rather, he ate and I picked, washing it down with large mouthfuls of cheap red wine. When the telephone rang I let Jake answer, although my heart pounded furiously in my chest.

'Whoever it was put the phone down,' he told me. 'Probably some secret admirer.'

We laughed together merrily. I imagined him sitting on the bed in his empty flat, and took another gulp of wine. Jake suggested going to Paris for a weekend. You could get good deals on Eurostar at this time of year.

'Another tunnel,' I said. I waited for the phone to ring again. This time I would have to pick it up. What should I do? I tried to think of a way of saying, 'Don't call me,' without Jake being suspicious about it. But it didn't ring. Maybe I had just been a coward and should have told him to his face. I couldn't have told him to his face. Every time I looked at his face I climbed into his arms.

I glanced across at Jake, who smiled at me and yawned. 'Bed-time,' he said.

I tried. Over the next few days, I really, really tried. I wouldn't take any of his calls at the office. He sent me a letter there, too, and I didn't open it but tore it into shreds and threw it into the tall metal refuse container by the coffee machine. A few hours

49

later, when everyone else was at lunch, I went to retrieve it but it had been emptied. Only one little piece of paper was still there, with his slashing handwriting across it: '. . . for a few . . .' it read. I stared at the pen strokes, touched the scrap of paper as if a bit of him was left on it, indelible him. I tried to construct whole sentences around the three neutral words.

I left work at odd times, and by the back entrance, sometimes in great protective crowds of people. I avoided central London, just in case. In fact, I avoided going out. I stayed at home with Jake, closing the curtains against the vile weather, and watched videos on TV and drank a bit too much, enough anyway to send me blundering to sleep each night. Jake was being very attentive. He told me that I had seemed more contented over the past few days, 'not always rushing on to the next thing'. I told him that I felt good, great.

On Thursday evening, three days after the note, the Crew came round: Clive, Julie, Pauline and Tom and a friend of Tom's called Duncan, Sylvie. Clive brought Gail with him, the woman who had grabbed his elbow at the party. She was still holding on to his elbow now, and looking a bit bemused, as well she might, since it was only their second date and it must have felt like being introduced to a whole extended family at once.

'You all talk so much,' she said to me, when I asked her if she was okay. I looked around. She was right: everyone in our living room seemed to be talking at once. All of a sudden I felt hot and claustrophobic. The room seemed too small, too full, too noisy. I put my hand up to my head. The phone was ringing.

'Can you get that?' called Jake, who was getting beer from the fridge. I picked up the receiver.

'Hello.'

Silence.

I waited for his voice but there was nothing. I put the phone down and went dully back into the room. I looked around. These were my best and oldest friends. I had known them for ten years and in ten years' time I would still know them. We would still meet up and tell each other the same old stories. I watched Pauline talking to Gail, she was explaining something. She put her hand on Gail's arm. Clive approached them, looking nervously self-conscious, and the two women smiled up at him; kind. Jake came across and handed me a can of beer. He put his arm around my shoulder and hugged me. Tomorrow morning he was off to Edinburgh.

After all, I thought, it was beginning to get better. I could live without him. Days were going past. Soon it would be a week. Then a month . . .

We played poker: Gail won and Clive lost. He clowned around for her benefit and she giggled at him. She was nice, I thought. Better than Clive's usual girlfriends. He would go off her because she wouldn't be cruel enough to keep his adoration.

The next day I left work at the usual time, and by the main entrance. I couldn't hide from him for the rest of my life. I pushed my way through the doors, feeling dizzy, and looked around. He wasn't there. I had been sure he would be. Maybe all those times I had sneaked out of the back he hadn't been there either. A terrible disappointment rose in me, which took me by surprise. After all, I had been going to avoid him if I saw him. Hadn't I?

I didn't want to go home, nor did I want to wander across to the Vine to meet everyone. I suddenly realized how tired I was. It took an effort to put one foot in front of the other. I had a dull thudding ache between my eyes. I drifted along the street, jostled by the rush-hour crowds. I peered into shop windows. It had been ages since I bought any new clothes. I made myself buy an electric-blue shirt that was in a sale, but it felt a bit like force-feeding myself. Then I dawdled along in the dwindling crowd, going nowhere in particular. A shoe shop. A stationer's. A toy shop, where a giant pink teddy sat in the middle of the display. A wool shop. A book shop, although there were other objects that gleamed in the window, too: a small axe, a coil of thin rope. Warm air gusted from its open door, and I went in.

It wasn't really a book shop, though it had books in it. It was a climbing shop. I must have known that all the time. Only a few other people were in there, all men. I gazed around, noting the nylon jackets, gauntlets made from mysterious modern fabrics, the sleeping bags stacked on a large shelf at the back. There were lanterns hanging from the ceiling, and small camping stoves. Tents. Vast, weighty boots, gleaming and hard. Backpacks with lots of side pockets. Sharp-looking knives. Mallets. A shelf full of adhesive bandages, iodine swabs, latex gloves. There were sachets of food, energy bars. It looked like equipment for people venturing into outer space.

'Can I help you?' A young man with bristly hair and a puggish nose stood by my side. He was probably a climber himself. I felt guilty, as if I were in the shop under false pretences.

'Um, no, not really.'

I sidled across to the bookshelves and let my eyes slide over the titles: *Everest without Oxygen, The Fierce Heights, Roped Together, The Third Pole, The A–Z of Mountaineering, First Aid for Climbers, Head in the Clouds, A Kind of Grace, On Top of the World, The Effects of Altitude, K2: a Tragedy, K2: the Terrible Summer, Climbing for their Lives, On the Edge, The Abyss . . .*

I pulled out a couple of books at random and looked at their index under the Ts. There he was, in *On Top of the World*, a coffee-table book about Himalayan climbs. Just the sight of his name in type made me shiver and feel queasy. It was as if I had been able to pretend he didn't exist outside that room in Soho, didn't have a life except for the life he spent with me, on me. The fact that he was a climber, something I knew nothing about, had made it easier for me to treat him as some kind of fantasy figure; a pure object of desire, only there when I was there. But he was in this book, in black and white. Tallis, Adam, on pages 12–14, 89–92, 168.

I turned to the section of colour photographs in the middle of the book and stared at the third one, in which a group of men and a few women in nylon or fleece jackets, snow and rubble at their backs, smiled into the camera. Except he wasn't smiling, he was gazing. He hadn't known me then; he had a whole other life. He probably loved someone else then, though we had never talked about other women. He looked younger, less bleak. His hair was shorter and had more of a curl to it. I turned the pages and there he was, on his own and looking away from the camera. He was wearing sunglasses, so it was difficult to make out his expression or what he was looking at. Behind him, in the distance, there was a small green tent, and beyond that a swoop of mountain. He had thick boots on and there was wind in his hair. I thought he looked distressed, and although that was long ago, in another world and before me, I had an intense desire to comfort him. The agony of my renewed desire took my breath away.

I snapped the book shut and put it back on the shelf. I took out another book and again looked in the index. There were no Tallises there.

'I'm sorry, we're closing now.' The young man was back again. 'Do you want to buy anything?'

'Sorry, I didn't realize. No, I don't think so.'

I made it to the door. But I couldn't do it. I turned back again, snatched up *On Top of the World* and took it over to the till. 'Am I in time to buy this?'

'Of course.'

I paid and put it in my bag. I wrapped it in my new blue shirt, so that it was quite hidden.

Seven

'That's it, pull the left string down a bit, careful not to collide with that other one. There, isn't that satisfying?'

In each hand, I held a spool of string that twitched and snagged in the gusts of wind. The kite – Jake's present to me from Edinburgh – swooped above us. It was a rather swanky red and yellow stunt kite, with a long ribbon that slapped when the wind changed.

'Careful now, Alice, it's going to crash. Pull.'

Jake had an absurd bobble hat on his head. His nose was red in the chill. He looked about sixteen, happy as a boy on an outing. I tugged on both strings randomly, and the kite veered and plummeted. The strings went slack and it accelerated into the ground.

'Don't move. I'll get it,' yelled Jake.

He went running off down the hill, picked up the kite, walked with it until the strings were taut again, then sailed it up into the low white sky once more, where it pulled at its reins. I thought of trying to explain to Jake that the good bits of kite-flying – that is, when it was briefly airborne – didn't, as far as I was concerned, compensate for the bits where it was lying on the grass with the line having to be untangled by clumsy numb fingers. I decided not to.

'If it snows,' said Jake, back beside me and panting, 'let's go tobogganing.'

'What's got into you? You're a bit energetic, aren't you?'

He stood behind me and slid his arms around me. I concentrated on steering the kite.

'We could use that big kitchen tray,' he said, 'or just some

54

large bin bags. Or maybe we should buy a toboggan. They don't cost much and it would last us years.'

'In the meantime,' I said, 'I'm starving. And I can't feel my fingers.'

'Here.' He took the kite from me. 'There are gloves in my pocket. Put them on. What time is it?'

I looked at my watch. 'Nearly three. It'll be getting dark.'

'Let's buy some crumpets. I love crumpets.'

'Do you?'

'There's lots you don't know about me.' He started reeling in the kite. 'Did you know, for instance, that when I was fifteen I had a crush on a girl called Alice? She was in the year above me at school. I was just a spotty little boy to her, of course. It was agony.' He laughed. 'I wouldn't be young again for anything. All that worry. I couldn't wait to grow up.'

He knelt on the ground, carefully folded the kite and put it away in its narrow nylon bag. I didn't say anything. He looked up and smiled. 'Of course, being grown-up has its problems too. But at least you don't feel so awkward and self-conscious all the time.'

I squatted down beside him. 'What are your problems now, then, Jake?'

'Now?' He frowned then looked surprised. 'Nothing, really.' He put his arms on my shoulders, nearly unbalancing me. I kissed the tip of his nose. 'When I was with Ari I felt I was always on trial, and was never quite coming up to scratch. I've never felt that with you. You say what you mean. You can be cross, but you're never manipulative. I know where I am.' Ari was his previous girlfriend, a tall, big-boned, beautiful woman with russet hair, who designed shoes that I had always thought looked like Cornish pasties, and who had left Jake for a man who worked for an oil company and was away for half the year.

'What about you?'

'What?'

'What are your grown-up problems?'

I stood up and pulled him to his feet. 'Let's think. A job that's driving me insane. A phobia about flies and ants and all creepy-crawly things. And bad circulation. Come on, I'm freezing.'

We really did have crumpets, horrid plasticky things with butter running through the holes making a mess. Then we went to see an early-evening film, and there was a sad bit at the end which allowed me to cry. For once, we didn't join everybody for drinks at the Vine or a curry, but went to a cheap Italian restaurant near the flat, just the two of us, and ate spaghetti with clams and drank abrasive red wine. Jake was in a nostalgic mood. He talked some more about Ari, and about the women before her, and then we did the whole how-we-first-met routine again – which is every happy couple's best story. Neither of us could remember when we had first set eyes on the other.

'They say the first few seconds of a relationship are the most important ones,' he said.

I remembered Adam, staring at me across a road, blue eyes holding me. 'Let's go home.' I stood up abruptly.

'Don't you want coffee?'

'We can make some at home.'

He took it as a sexual invitation, and in a way it was. I wanted to hide somewhere – and where better than in bed, in his arms, in the dark, eyes shut, no questions, no revelations? We knew each other's bodies so well it almost felt anonymous: naked flesh against naked flesh.

'What on earth is this?' he said afterwards, as we lay sweatily against each other. He was holding *On Top of the World*. I'd pushed it under my pillow last night, when he was away in Edinburgh.

'That?' I tried to sound casual. 'Someone at work lent it to me. They said it was brilliant.'

Jake was flicking through the pages. I held my breath. There. The photographs. He was looking at Adam in a photograph. 'I wouldn't have thought it was your kind of thing.'

'No, well, it's not really, I probably won't read it.'

'People must be mad to climb mountains like that,' said Jake. 'Do you remember all those people dying in the Himalayas last year?'

'Mmm.'

'Just to stand on the top of a mountain and go down again.'

I didn't reply.

The next morning, it had snowed, although not enough to go tobogganing. We turned up the heating, read Sunday newspapers and drank pots of coffee. I learned how to ask for a double room in French, and to say that 'janvier est le premier mois de l'année', or 'février est le deuxième mois', and then I ploughed through some technical journals that I'd let pile up, and Jake went on with the climbing book. He was about half-way through.

'You ought to read this, you know.'

'I'm going to go to the shops to get something for lunch. Pasta?'

'We had pasta last night. Let's have a real greasy fry-up. I'll cook and you wash up.'

'But you never cook,' I protested.

'I'm changing my ways.'

Clive and Gail came round after lunch. They had obviously spent the morning in bed. They had a post-coital glow about them, and occasionally they would smile at each other as if they knew something we didn't. They said they were going ten-pin bowling and would we like to come too, and maybe we should ask Pauline and Tom.

So I spent the afternoon skidding a heavy black ball towards the skittles, and missing them every time. Everyone giggled a lot: Clive and Gail because they knew that as soon as this was over they would go straight back to bed, Pauline because she was planning to have a baby and couldn't believe how her luck had changed, Tom and Jake because they were nice men, and it's easier to join in than not. I giggled because everyone expected me to. My chest hurt. My glands ached. The echoey, overlit bowling hall made my head spin. I giggled until my eyes watered.

'Alice,' said Jake, at the same time as I said, 'Jake.'

'Sorry, go on,' I said.

'No, you first.'

We were sitting on the sofa with mugs of tea, about six inches apart from each other. It was dark outside, and the curtains were closed. Everything was silent, the way it is when snow falls and muffles all sound. He was wearing an old speckled-grey jumper and faded jeans and no shoes. His hair was all rumpled up. He was looking at me very attentively. I liked him so much. I took a deep breath. 'I can't keep on with this, Jake.'

At first, the expression on his face didn't change. I made myself go on looking into his eyes, nice brown eyes.

'What?'

I took one of his hands and it rested limply in mine. 'I have to leave you.'

How could I say it? Every word was like hurling a brick. Jake looked as if I had slapped him really hard, bemused and in pain. I wanted to take it all back, return to where we had been a minute ago, sitting together on the sofa with our tea. I could no longer remember why I was doing this. He didn't say anything.

'I've met someone else. It's all so . . .' I stopped.

'What do you mean?' He was staring at me, as if through a thick fog. 'What do you mean, leave? Do you mean you want to stop being with me?'

'Yes.'

The effort of that word rendered me speechless. I gazed dumbly at him. I was still holding his hand, but it lay nervelessly in mine. I didn't know how to let it go.

'Who?' His voice cracked a bit. He cleared his throat. 'Sorry. Who have you met?'

'Just . . . no one you know. It just . . . God, I'm so sorry, Jake.'

He passed a hand over his face. 'But it doesn't make sense.

We've been so happy recently. This weekend, I mean . . .' I nodded at him. This was more awful than I could have imagined. 'I thought – I – how did you meet him? *When?*'

This time I couldn't meet his gaze. 'It doesn't matter, that's not the point.'

'Is the sex so good? No, sorry, sorry. I didn't mean to say that, Alice. I can't understand it. You're leaving everything? Just like that?' He looked around the room at all our things, the whole weight of the world we had built up together. 'Why?'

'I don't know.'

'It's that bad, is it?'

His whole body was slack on the sofa. I wanted him to shout at me, get angry or something, and instead he smiled across at me. 'Do you know what I was going to say?'

'No.'

'I was going to say I thought we should have a baby together.'

'Oh, Jake.'

'I was happy.' His voice had a muffled quality. 'And all the time, you were, you were . . .'

'No, Jake,' I pleaded. 'I was happy too. You made me happy.'

'How long has it been going on for?'

'A few weeks.'

I watched him considering, revisiting the recent past. His face puckered. He stared away from me, towards the curtained window, and said, very formally: 'Will it make any difference if I ask you to stay, Alice? Give us another chance? Please.'

He didn't look at me. We both stared ahead, hand in hand. There was a great boulder in my chest.

'Please, Alice,' he said again.

'No.'

He took his hand out of mine. We sat in silence, and I wondered what came next. Should I say anything about sorting out my things later? Tears were rolling down his cheeks, into his mouth, but he sat quite still and made no move to wipe them. I had never seen him cry before. I put up a hand to wipe his tears away but he turned away sharply, angry at last. 'God, Alice, what do you want? Do you want to comfort me or something? Do you want to see me howl? If you're going to go, just go.'

I left everything. I left all my clothes and my CDs and my makeup and my jewellery. My books and magazines. My photographs. My briefcase full of documents from work. My address book and diary. My alarm clock. My bunch of keys. My French tapes. I took my purse, my toothbrush, my supply of contraceptives and the thick black coat Jake had given me for Christmas and went out into the slush in the wrong shoes.

Eight

It's at a time like this when you're meant to need your friends. I didn't want to see anybody. I didn't want family. I had wild thoughts of sleeping in the street, under arches somewhere, but even self-punishment had its limits. Where could I find somewhere cheap to stay? I had never stayed in a hotel in London before. I remembered a street of hotels that I'd glimpsed out of the window of a taxi the other day. South of Baker Street. It would do. I took a tube and walked past the Planetarium, across the road and a block along. There it was, a long street of white stuccoed houses, all converted into hotels. I chose one at random, the Devonshire, and walked in.

Sitting at the desk was a very fat woman, who said something urgently to me that I couldn't understand because of her accent. But I could see plenty of keys on the board behind her. This was not the tourist season. I pointed at the keys. 'I want a room.'

She shook her head and carried on talking. I wasn't even sure if she was talking to me or shouting at somebody in the room behind. I wondered if she thought I was a prostitute, but no prostitute could have been as badly, or at least as dully, dressed as I was. Yet I had no luggage. A little corner of my mind was amused by the thought of what kind of person she took me for. I extracted a credit card from my purse and put it on the desk. She took it and scanned it. I signed a piece of paper without looking at it. She handed me a key.

'Can I get a drink?' I asked. 'Tea or something?'

'No drink,' she shouted.

I felt as if I had asked for a cup of meths. I considered whether

61

to go outside for something but couldn't face it. I took the key and went up two flights of stairs to my room. It wasn't so bad. There was a wash-basin and a window looking down on a stone yard and across at the back of another house on the other side. I pulled the curtain shut. I was in a hotel room in London on my own with nothing. I stripped down to my underwear and got into bed. I got out of the bed and locked the door, then dived under the covers again. I didn't cry. I didn't lie awake all night pondering my life. I went to sleep straight away. But I left the light on.

I woke up late, dull-headed, but not suicidal. I got up, took my bra and knickers off and washed myself in the basin. Then I put them back on. I brushed my teeth without toothpaste. For breakfast I had a contraceptive pill washed down with a plastic beaker of water. I dressed and went downstairs. There seemed to be nobody around. I looked in at a dining room with a shiny marble-style floor where all the tables had plastic chairs around them. I heard voices from somewhere and I could smell frying bacon. I walked across the room and pushed open a curtain. Around a kitchen table were seated the woman I had met last night, a man of her own age and shape, evidently her husband, and several small fat children. They looked up at me.

'I was leaving,' I said.

'You want breakfast?' said the man, smiling. 'We have eggs, meat, tomatoes, mushrooms, beans, cereal.'

I shook my head weakly.

'You paid already.'

I accepted some coffee and stood in the door of the kitchen watching as they got the children ready for school. Before I left, the man looked at me with a concerned expression. 'You all right?'

'All right.'

'You stay another night?'

I shook my head again and left. It was cold outside but at least it was dry. I stopped and thought, orienting myself. I could walk from here. On my way down Edgware Road, I bought some lemon-scented wipes and toothpaste, mascara and lipstick from a chemist and then some simple white knickers. In Oxford Street I found a functional clothes shop. I took a black shirt and a simple jacket into the changing room. I put my new knickers on as well, wiped my face and neck with the wipes until my skin stung, then applied some makeup. It was just enough of an improvement. At least I didn't look as if I was about to be sectioned. At just after ten, I rang Claudia. I had been intending to make up something about going through my papers but once I got her on the line, some odd impulse made me fall back on partial honesty. I told her that I was having a personal crisis that I was having to deal with and that I was in no condition to appear in the office. I could hardly get her off the line.

'I'll think of something to tell Mike,' she concluded.

'Just remember to tell me what it is before I see him.'

From Oxford Street it was only a few minutes' walk to Adam's flat. When I reached the street door I realized that I had almost no idea of what I was going to say to him. I stood there for several minutes but nothing occurred. The door was unlocked so I walked up the stairs and knocked on the flat door. It opened. I stepped forward, starting to speak, and then stopped. The person in the doorway was a woman. She was alarmingly attractive. She had dark hair that was probably long but was now fastened up unfussily. She was dressed in jeans and a checked shirt over a black T-shirt. She looked tired and preoccupied.

'Yes?' she said.

I felt a sick lurch in my stomach and a flush of hot embarrassment. I had the feeling that I had fucked up my entire life simply to make a fool of myself.

'Is Adam there?' I asked numbly.

'No,' she said briskly. 'He's moved on.'

She was American.

'Do you know where?'

'God, there's a question now. Come in.' I followed her inside because I didn't know what else to do. Just inside the door were a very large battered rucksack and an open suitcase. Clothes were tossed on the floor.

'Sorry,' she said, gesturing at the mess. 'I got in from Lima this morning. I feel like shit. I got some coffee in the pot.' She held out her hand. 'Deborah,' she said.

'Alice.'

I looked across at the bed. Deborah pulled out a familiar chair for me to sit on and poured coffee into a familiar mug for me and a familiar mug for herself. She offered me a cigarette. I refused it, and she lit it for herself.

'You're a friend of Adam's,' I ventured.

She blew out a thick cloud of smoke and shrugged. 'I've climbed with him a couple of times. We've been on the same teams. Yeah, I'm a friend.' She took another deep drag and grimaced. 'Jesus. I've got jet-lag big league. And this air. I haven't been below five thousand feet for a month and a half.

'And *you*'re a friend of Adam's?' she continued.

'Only for a bit,' I said. 'We just met recently. But yes, I am his friend.'

'Yeah,' she said, with what I took to be a knowing smile that embarrassed me greatly but I held her gaze until her smile softened into something more friendly and less mocking.

'Were you on Chunga-whatever-it's-called with him?' Or: have you had an affair with him? Are you his lover too?

'Chungawat. You mean last year? God, no. I don't do things like that.'

'Why not?'

She laughed. 'If God had meant us to go above eight thousand metres, he'd have made us differently.'

'I know that Adam was involved in that awful expedition last year.' I was trying to speak calmly, as if I had come knocking on her door just to have this coffee and friendly chat. Where is he? I was screaming inside my head. I must see him now – before it's too late, although perhaps it is already too late.

'*Involved?* Don't you know what happened?'

64

'I know that some people were killed.'

Deborah lit another cigarette. 'Five people. The expedition's medical officer who was, uh . . .' She looked across at me. 'A close friend of Adam's. Four clients.'

'How awful.'

'That's not what I meant.' She took a deep drag on her cigarette. 'You want to hear about it?' I nodded. Where *is* he? She leaned back, all the time in the world. 'When the storm broke, the leader, Greg McLaughlin, one of the top Himalayan guys in the world who thought he'd worked out a foolproof method for getting dorks up a mountain, was out of it. He was acutely hypoxic, whatever. Adam escorted him down and took over. The other professional guide, a French guy called Claude Bresson, a fantastic sport climber, he was fucked, hallucinating.' Deborah rapped her chest. 'He had a pulmonary oedema. Adam carried the bastard down to the camp. Then there were eleven clients out in the open. It was dark and over fifty below. Adam went back with oxygen, brought them down in groups. Kept going out. The man is a fucking bull. But one group got lost. He couldn't find them. They didn't stand a chance.'

'Why do people do that?'

Deborah rubbed her eyes. She looked terribly tired. She gestured with her cigarette. 'You mean why does *Adam* do it? I can tell you why *I* do it. When I was a med student, I had a boyfriend who was a climber. So I climbed with him. People want a doctor along. So I go every so often. Sometimes I hang around at base camp. Sometimes I go up.'

'With your boyfriend?'

'He died.'

'Oh, I'm sorry.'

'It was years ago.'

There was a silence. I tried to think of something to say. 'You're American.'

'Canadian. I'm from Winnipeg. You know Winnipeg?'

'Sorry.'

'They dig the graves for the winter in the autumn.' I must have looked puzzled. 'The ground freezes. They guess how many people they think will die during the winter and they dig that many holes. There are disadvantages to growing up in Winnipeg but it teaches you respect for cold.' She put her cigarette in her mouth and held up her hands. 'Look. What do you see?'

'I don't know.'

'Ten fingers. Complete and unmutilated.'

'Adam has toes missing,' I said. Deborah gave an accusing smile and I smiled ruefully back. 'He *might* have just told me about them.'

'Yeah, right. That's different. That was a decision. I'll tell you, Alice, those people were lucky to have him out there. Have you ever been on a mountain in a storm?'

'I've never been on a mountain.'

'You can't see, you can't hear, you don't know which way is up. You need equipment and experience but it's not enough. I don't know what it is. Some people stay calm and think rationally. That's Adam.'

'Yes,' I said, and then left a pause so that I wouldn't appear too eager. 'Do you know where I can reach him?'

She thought for a moment. 'He's an elusive man. He was going to meet someone in a café over in Notting Hill Gate, I think. What was it called? Wait.' She walked across the room and returned with a telephone directory. 'Here.' She wrote a name and address on a used envelope.

'When will he be there?'

She looked at her watch. 'Now, I guess.'

'I'd better go.'

She led me to the door. 'If he's not there, I've got some people you might try. Let me give you my number.' Then she grinned. 'But you've got it already, right?'

All the way along Bayswater Road in the taxi I wondered if he would be there. I constructed different scenarios in my head. He isn't there and I spend the next few days living in hotels and wandering the streets. He is there, but with a girl and I have to spy on them from a distance to work out what's going on then follow him until I can get him alone. I guided the taxi just past the café in All Saints Road and walked cautiously back. I saw him straight away, sitting in the window. And he wasn't with a girl. He was with a black man who had long dreadlocked hair tied back in a pony-tail. In the taxi I had also been considering ways of approaching Adam that wouldn't make me look like a stalker but nothing had occurred. Possible strategies were rendered irrelevant in any case because, at the moment I caught sight of Adam, Adam caught sight of me and did a double-take like in the movies. Standing there with all my current worldly possessions – old knickers, old shirt, bits of newly acquired makeup – in a Gap bag, I felt like some pathetic Victorian-style waif. I saw him say something to the man with him and then get up and walk out. There was a strange ten seconds or so in which the man turned and looked at me, obviously wondering, Who the fuck is *she*?

Then Adam was on me. I had been wondering what we were to say to each other, but he didn't say a word. He held my face between his large hands and kissed me deeply. I let the bag fall and put my arms round him, as tightly as I could, feeling the old sweater he was wearing, and his strong body underneath it. Finally we moved apart and he looked at me with a speculative expression.

'Deborah told me you'd be here.' Then I started to cry. I let him go and took a tissue from my pocket and blew my nose. Adam didn't hold me and say, 'There, there.' Instead he looked at me as if I were an exotic animal that fascinated him and he was curious to see what it would do next. I composed myself to say what I had to say. 'I want to tell you something, Adam. I'm sorry I sent you that card. I wish I'd never sent it.' Adam didn't speak. 'And,' I paused before leaping, 'I've left Jake. I spent last night in a hotel. I'm just telling you this. This is not to put pressure on you. Just tell me to and I'll go away and you'll never have to see me again.'

My heart was beating painfully fast. Adam's face was close to mine, so close that I could feel his breath. 'Do you want me to tell you to go away?'

'No, I don't.'

'Then you're all mine.'

I gulped. 'Yes.'

'Good,' said Adam, not as if he were surprised, or joyous, but as if the obvious had been acknowledged. Perhaps it had been. He looked round at the window and then back at me. 'That's Stanley,' he said. 'Turn and give him a wave.' I gave a nervous wave. Stanley gave me a thumbs-up back. 'We're going to be staying in a flat round the corner that belongs to a friend of his.' *We*'re. I felt a wave of sexual pleasure inside me at that. Adam nodded at Stanley. 'Stanley can see that we're talking but he can't lip-read. We'll go back in for a few minutes and then I'll take you to the flat and I'm going to fuck you. Painfully.'

'All right,' I said. 'You can do anything you want.'

He leaned down and kissed me again. He ran his hand round to my back and then beneath my shirt. I felt his fingers under my bra strap, a nail running down my spine. He took a fold of flesh and pinched it hard, agonizingly. I gave a sob. 'That hurt,' I said.

Adam brushed his lips against my ear. 'You hurt *me*,' he whispered.

Nine

I was woken by the phone. The light felt painful against my eyes. It was near the bed, wasn't it? I found it by touch alone.

'Hello?'

I could hear some noises, traffic maybe, but nobody spoke and the receiver was replaced. I put the phone down. A few seconds later it rang again. I answered. The same nobody. Was there a sound on the line? Some whispering, very quiet. I couldn't tell. I heard the dialling tone once more.

I looked down at Adam's sleepily opening eyes.

'It's the old story,' I said. 'If a woman answers, hang up.' I tapped out four digits on the phone.

'What are you doing?' Adam asked, yawning.

'Finding out who called.' I waited.

'So?' he asked.

'A call-box,' I said finally.

'Perhaps they couldn't get the money in in time,' he said.

'Perhaps,' I said. 'I've got nothing to wear.'

'Why do you need anything to wear?' Adam's face was a few inches away from mine. He tucked some strands of hair behind my ear, then trailed his finger down my neck. 'You look perfect like that. When I woke this morning, I thought it must be a dream. I lay here, just looking at you sleep.' He pulled the sheet off my breasts and covered them with his hands instead. He kissed my forehead, my eyelids, then my lips, gently at first, and then hard. I tasted blood metallic inside my mouth. I slid my hands down his knotty back, on to his buttocks and pulled him against me. We both sighed, and shifted our bodies slightly; my

69

heart pounded against his, or was it his heart pounding against mine? The room smelt of sex, and the sheets were still slightly damp.

'For work, Adam,' I said. 'I need clothes for work. I can't just spend the whole day in bed.'

'Why?' He kissed the side of my neck. 'Why can't you? We have to make up for all the time we lost.'

'I can't just not go to work again.'

'Why?'

'Well, I just can't. I'm not that kind of person. Don't you ever have to work?'

He frowned but didn't reply. Then he very deliberately sucked his index finger and slid it inside me. 'Don't go yet, Alice.'

'Ten minutes. Ah, Christ, Adam . . .'

Afterwards I still didn't have anything to wear. The clothes that I had worn yesterday were in a sweaty heap on the floor, and I had taken nothing else with me.

'Here, put these on,' said Adam, and chucked a pair of faded jeans on to the bed. 'We can roll up the legs. And this. That'll have to do for the morning. I'll meet you at twelve thirty and take you shopping.'

'But I might as well just get my stuff from the flat . . .'

'No. Leave that for now. Don't go back there. I'll buy you some clothes. You don't need much.'

I didn't bother with underwear. I pulled on the jeans, which were rather loose and long but didn't look so bad with a belt. Then the black silk shirt, which brushed softly against my jumpy skin and smelt of Adam. I took the leather thong out of my bag and put it round my neck.

'There.'

'Beautiful.'

He picked up a brush and pulled it through my tangled hair. He insisted on watching me pee, brush my teeth and apply mascara to my eyelashes. He didn't take his eyes off me.

'I've gone to pieces,' I said to him in the mirror, trying to smile.
'Think about me all morning.'
'What are you going to do?'
'Think about you.'

I did think about him all morning. My body throbbed with the memory of him. But I also thought about Jake and about the whole world that Jake and I had belonged to together. There was a bit of me that couldn't comprehend how it was that I was still here, in my familiar office, stringing together well-worn sentences about the IUD and female fertility when I had thrown a bomb into my old life and watched it explode. I tried to imagine everything that had happened since I had left. Probably Jake would have told Pauline, at least. And she would have told everyone else. They would all meet up for drinks and talk about it and wonder and be shocked, and try to comfort Jake. And I, who had for so long been an established part of the group, would have become the object of their gossipy, shocked exchanges. Everyone would have an opinion about me; their own emphatic version.

If I had left that world – and I supposed that I had – had I then joined Adam's world, full of men who climbed mountains and women who waited for them? As I sat at my desk and waited for the lunch hour, I reflected on how very little I knew about Adam, about his past or his present or his planned future. And the more I realized that he was a stranger to me, the more I longed for him.

He had already bought me several pairs of bras and knickers. We stood half hidden by a rail of dresses and smiled at each other and brushed each other's hand. It was our first real date outside the flat.
'These are ridiculously expensive,' I said.
'Try this on,' he said.
He picked out a straight black dress, then a pair of tight-fitting

71

trousers. I tried them on in the changing room, over the top of my new underwear, and stared at myself in the mirror. Expensive clothes made a difference. When I came out, clutching the garments, he thrust a chocolate-brown velvet dress at me, with a low neck, long sleeves and skirt cut on the bias, trailing the floor. It looked medieval and stunning and the price tag told me why. 'I can't.'

He frowned. 'I want you to.'

We came out of the shop with two bags full of clothes that had cost more than my monthly pay packet. I was wearing the black trousers with a cream satin shirt. I thought of Jake saving up to buy me my coat and how his face had looked so eager and proud when he had handed it to me.

'I feel like a kept woman.'

'Listen.' He stopped in the middle of the pavement and people flowed past us. 'I want to keep you for ever.'

He had this knack for making flippant remarks turn deadly serious. I blushed and laughed but he stared at me, scowled almost.

'Can I take you out for dinner?' I asked. 'I want you to tell me about your life.'

First, though, I had to collect some things from the flat. I had left my address book there, my diary, all my work things. Until I had got them, I would feel I was half there still. With a sick feeling in my stomach, I rang Jake at work, but he wasn't there; they said he was ill. I rang the flat and he answered on the first ring.

'Jake, it's Alice,' I said foolishly.

'I recognized your voice,' he replied drily.

'Are you unwell?'

'No.'

There was a silence.

'Listen, I'm sorry but I need to come round and collect a few things.'

'I'll be at work during the daytime tomorrow. Do it then.'

'I haven't got my keys any more.'

I could hear him breathing on the other end. 'You really burnt your bridges, didn't you, Alice?'

We arranged that I should call in at six thirty. There was another pause. Then we both said goodbye, politely, and I put the phone down.

It's amazing how you don't really need to work at work, what you can get away with when you don't care. I wish I'd discovered that before now. Nobody seemed to have noticed how late I had arrived that morning or how long I took for lunch. I went to another meeting in the afternoon, where once again I said very little and was congratulated afterwards by Mike for being so incisive. 'You appear very in control of things at the moment, Alice,' he said nervously. Giovanna had said almost the same thing in an e-mail earlier in the day. I shuffled paper round my desk, slid most of it into the bin, and told Claudia not to put calls through. At just after five thirty I went into the ladies' and brushed my hair, washed my face, put lipstick on my sore lips and buttoned my coat up firmly so that no trace of my new, glossy clothes could be seen. Then I took my old familiar route back to the flat.

I was early, and I walked around for a bit. I didn't want to take Jake by surprise, before he was prepared for me, and I certainly didn't want to meet him on the street. I tried to think what I should say to him. The act of breaking off from him had immediately turned him into a stranger, someone more precious and vulnerable than the ironic, modest Jake I had lived with. At a few minutes past six thirty, I went to the door and pressed the buzzer. I heard feet running down the stairs, saw a shape approaching through the frosted glass.

'Hello, Alice.'

It was Pauline.

'Pauline.' I didn't know what to say to her. My best friend; the one I would have turned to in any other circumstance. She stood

73

in the doorway. Her dark hair was tied up in a stern knot. She looked tired: there were faint smudges under her eyes. She wasn't smiling. I realized that I was seeing her as if we had been apart from each other for months, not just a couple of days.

'Can I come in?'

She stood aside and I walked past her, up the stairs. My rich clothes whispered against my skin, under Jake's coat. Everything looked the same in the flat, of course it did. My jackets and scarves still hung on the hooks in the hall. A photograph of Jake and me, arm in arm and grinning widely, still stood on the mantelpiece. My red moccasin slippers lay on the living-room floor, near the sofa where we'd sat on Sunday. The daffodils I had bought at the end of last week still stood in the vase, though a little droopy. There was a cup on the table half full of tea, and I was sure it was the same cup I'd been drinking from two days ago. I felt bewildered and sat down heavily on the sofa. Pauline stayed standing, looking down at me. She hadn't said a word.

'Pauline,' I croaked. 'I know that what I've done is awful, but I had to.'

'Do you want me to forgive you, then?' she asked. Her voice was withering.

'No.' That was a lie, of course I did. 'No, but you are my closest friend. I thought, well, I'm not cold or heartless. There's nothing I can say in my defence, except that I just fell in love. Surely you can understand that.'

I saw her wince. Of course she could understand that. Eighteen months ago she'd been left, too, because he had just fallen in love. She sat down at the other end of the sofa, as far away from me as possible.

'The thing is this, Alice,' she began, and I was struck by how we were even talking to each other differently now, more formally and pedantically. 'If I allowed myself to, of course I could under-stand. After all, you weren't married, you didn't have children. But I don't want to understand, you see. Not at the moment. He's my big brother and he's been badly hurt.' Her voice wavered and, for a few seconds, she sounded like the Pauline I knew. 'Honestly, Alice, if you could see him now, if you could see how *wrecked* he is, then you wouldn't . . .' But she stopped herself. 'Maybe some day we can be friends again, but I'd feel like I was betraying him or something if I listened to your side of the story and tried to imagine how you must be feeling.' She stood up. 'I don't want to be fair to you, you see. Actually, I want to hate you.'

I nodded and stood up too. I did see, of course I did. 'I'll get some clothes, then.'

She nodded and went into the kitchen. I could hear her filling the kettle.

In the bedroom, everything was as it always had been. I took my suitcase down from the top of the wardrobe and placed it open on the floor. By my side of the neatly-made double bed was the book I had been in the middle of reading about the history of clocks. By Jake's side, was the climbing book. I took them both and put them in the case. I opened the cupboard doors and started to slip clothes off hangers. My hands were shaking and I couldn't fold them properly. I didn't take many, anyway: I couldn't imagine wearing clothes I had worn before; I couldn't believe that they would still fit me.

I stared into the wardrobe, where my things hung among Jake's: my dresses next to his only good suit, my skirts and tops among his work shirts that were ironed and neatly buttoned on to their hangers. A couple of his shirts had frayed cuffs. Tears pricked my eyes and I blinked them away furiously. What was I going to need? I tried to picture my new life with Adam and found that I couldn't. I could only imagine bed with him. I packed a couple of jerseys, some jeans and T-shirts, two workaday suits, and all my underwear. I took my favourite sleeveless dress and two pairs of shoes and abandoned all the rest – there was so much of it, all those shopping sprees with Pauline, all those greedy, delighted purchases.

I shovelled all my creams, lotions and makeup into the case

but hesitated over my jewellery. Jake had given me quite a lot of it: several pairs of earrings, a lovely pendant, a wide copper bracelet. I didn't know if it would be more hurtful to take them or not. I pictured him, this evening, coming into the room and finding out what I had removed, and what I had left behind, and trying to read my feelings from such insubstantial clues. I took the earrings my grandmother had left me when she died, and the things I had had before Jake. Then I changed my mind, and took everything out of the little drawer and chucked it in the case.

There was a pile of washing in the corner, and I fished out a couple of things from it. I drew the line at leaving my dirty underwear lying around. I remembered my briefcase, under the chair by the window, and my address book and diary. I remembered my passport, birth certificate, driving licence, insurance policies and savings book, which were in a folder along with all of Jake's personal documents. I decided against taking the picture on the wall above the bed, although my father had given it to me years before I had started going out with Jake. I wasn't going to take any of the books or the music. And I wasn't going to argue over the car, for which I had put down the deposit six months previously, while Jake still paid the standing orders.

Pauline was sitting on the sofa in the living room, drinking a cup of tea. She watched as I picked up three letters from the table that were addressed to me and slipped them into my briefcase. I'd done. I had one suitcase full of clothes, and a plastic bag full of bits and pieces.

'Is that all? You're travelling light, aren't you?'

I shrugged hopelessly. 'I know I'll have to sort it properly soon. Not yet.'

'So it's not just a fling?'

I looked at her. Brown eyes like Jake's. 'No, it's not.'

'And Jake shouldn't go on hoping you'll come back to him. Waiting in every day in case you turn up?'

'No.'

I needed to get out of there so that I could howl. I went to the door, picking up a scarf from the hook as I did so. It was cold and dark outside.

'Pauline, can you tell Jake that I'll do this . . .' I made a wide, vague gesture round the room, at all our shared things '. . . however he wants.'

She looked at me but didn't reply.

'Goodbye, then,' I said.

We stared at each other. I saw that she, too, wanted me to go so she could cry.

'Yes,' she said.

'I must look dreadful.'

'No.' He wiped my eyes and my snotty nose with a corner of his shirt.

'I'm sorry. It's so painful.'

'The best things are born out of pain. Of course it is painful.'

At any other time, I would have hooted at that. I don't believe pain is necessary or ennobling. But I was too far gone. Another sob rose in my chest. 'And I'm so scared, Adam.' He didn't say anything. 'I've given up everything for you. Oh, God.'

'I know,' he said. 'I know you have.'

We walked to a simple restaurant round the corner. I had to lean against him, as if I would fall over if I was unsupported. We sat in a dark corner and drank a glass of champagne each, which went straight to my head. He put his hand on my thigh under the table and I stared at the menu, trying to focus. We ate salmon fillets with wild mushrooms and green salad, and had a bottle of cold greeny-white wine. I didn't know if I was elated or in despair. Everything seemed too much. Every look he gave me was like a touch, every sip of wine rushed round my blood. My hands shook when I tried to cut up the food. When he touched me under the table I felt as if my body would crumble into soft fragments.

'Has it ever been like this for you?' I asked, and he shook his head.

I asked him who there was before me and he stared at me for

a moment. 'It's hard to talk about.' I waited. If I had left my whole world for him, he was going to have to tell me at least about his previous girlfriend. 'She died,' he said then.

'Oh.' I was shocked and also dismayed. How could I compete with a dead woman?

'Up on the mountain,' he continued, staring into his glass.

'You mean, on that mountain?'

'Chungawat. Yes.'

He drank some more wine and signalled to the waiter. 'Can we have two whiskies, please?'

They arrived and we downed them. I took his hand across the table. 'Did you love her?'

'Not like this,' he said. I put his hand against my face. How was it possible to be so jealous of someone who had died before he ever set eyes on me?

'Have there been a lot of other women?'

'When I'm with you, I know there's been no one,' he replied, which meant, of course, that there had been lots.

'Why me?'

Adam looked lost in thought. 'How could it not be you?' he asked at last.

Ten

Unexpectedly I had a spare few minutes before a meeting, so I dared myself and rang Sylvie. She is a solicitor and I had generally found it difficult to be put through to her in the past. It was usually a matter of her calling back hours later, or the following morning.

This time she was on the line within seconds. 'Alice, is that you?'

'Yes,' I said limply.

'I need to see you.'

'I'd like that. But are you sure?'

'Are you doing anything today? After work?'

I thought. Suddenly things seemed complicated. 'I'm meeting . . . er, somebody in town.'

'Where? When?'

'It sounds stupid. It's at a book shop in Covent Garden. At half past six.'

'We could meet before.'

Sylvie was insistent. We could both leave early and meet at a quarter to six at a coffee shop she knew off St Martin's Lane. It was awkward. I had to rearrange a conference call that had been scheduled, but I arrived at twenty to six, breathless and nervous, and Sylvie was already there at a table in the corner, nursing a cup of coffee and a cigarette. When I approached she stood up and hugged me. 'I'm glad you called me,' she said.

We sat down together. I ordered a coffee. 'I'm glad you're glad,' I said. 'I feel I've let people down.'

Sylvie looked at me. 'Why?'

This was unexpected, and I didn't feel prepared for it. I had come in order to be given a hard time, to be made to feel guilty.

'There's Jake.'

Sylvie lit another cigarette and gave a half-smile. 'Yes, there is Jake.'

'Have you seen him?'

'Yes.'

'How is he?'

'Thin. Smoking again. Sometimes completely quiet, and sometimes talking so much about you that no one else can get a word in edgeways. Weepy. Is that what you want to hear? But he will recover. People do. He won't be wretched for the rest of his life. Not many people die of heartbreak.'

I took a sip of the coffee. It was still too hot. It made me cough. 'I hope so. I'm sorry, Sylvie, I feel as if I've just come back from abroad and I'm out of touch with what's going on.'

There was a silence that obviously embarrassed both of us.

'How's Clive?' I blurted desperately. 'And whatsername?'

'Gail,' said Sylvie. 'He's in love again. And she's good fun.'

Another silence. Sylvie fixed me with a pensive expression. 'What's he like?' she said.

I felt myself going red and oddly tongue-tied. I realized with an ache of something I didn't quite understand that it – Adam and me – had been a hidden activity and none of it had ever been put into words for the benefit of others. We'd never arrived at a party together. There was nobody who saw us as a couple. Now there was Sylvie, curious for herself, but also, I suspected, a delegation despatched from the Crew to forage for information she could bring back for them to pick at. I had an impulse to keep it secret for a while longer. I wanted to retreat back to a room once more, just the two of us. I didn't want to be possessed and gossiped and speculated about by other people. Even the thought of Adam and his body sent ripples through me. I suddenly dreaded the idea of routine, of being Adam and Alice who lived

80

somewhere and owned possessions in common and went to things together. And I wanted it as well.

'God,' I said. 'I don't know what to say. He's called Adam and . . . well, he's completely different from anybody I've ever met before.'

'I know,' said Sylvie. 'It's wonderful at the beginning, isn't it?'

I shook my head. 'It's not like that. Look, all my life everything has gone more or less to plan. I was quite clever at school, quite well liked, never bullied or anything like that. I got on all right with my parents, not brilliantly but . . . well, you know all that. And I had nice boyfriends, and sometimes I left them and sometimes they left me, and I went to college and got a job and met Jake and moved in and . . . What was I doing all those years?'

Sylvie's well-shaped eyebrows shot up. For a moment she looked angry. 'Living your life, just like the rest of us.'

'Or was I just skating along, not touching anything, really, not letting myself be touched? You don't need to answer that. I was thinking aloud.'

We sipped our cooling coffee.

'What does he do?' Sylvie asked.

'He doesn't really have a job in the way that we all do. He does odds and ends to raise money. But what he really does is, he's a mountaineer.'

Sylvie looked authentically and satisfyingly startled. 'Really? You mean, climbing mountains?'

'Yes.'

'I don't know what to say. Where did you meet? Not on a mountain.'

'We just met,' I said vaguely. 'Just bumped into each other.'

'When?'

'A few weeks ago.'

'And you've been in bed ever since.' I didn't reply. 'You're already moving in with him?'

'It looks like it.'

Sylvie puffed at her cigarette. 'So it's the real thing.'

'It's something. I've been knocked sideways by it.'

Sylvie leaned forward with a roguish expression. 'You should be careful. It's always like this at the beginning. He's all over you, obsessed with you. They want to fuck you all the time, come in your face, that sort of thing –'

'Sylvie!' I said in horror. 'For God's sake.'

'Well, they do,' she said pertly, relieved to be back on familiar territory, reckless Sylvie talking dirty. 'Or at least metaphorically. You should just be careful, that's all. I'm not saying you shouldn't do it. Enjoy. Do it all, go wild, as long as it isn't actually a physical risk.'

'What are you talking about?'

She looked prim all of a sudden. '*You know.*'

We ordered more coffee and Sylvie continued to grill me, until I looked at my watch and saw it was just a few minutes until half past. I reached for my purse. 'I've got to go,' I said quickly. After I'd paid, Sylvie followed me out on to the pavement. 'So which way are you going? I'll come along with you, Alice, if that's all right.'

'Why?'

'There's a book I need to buy,' she said brazenly. 'You're going to a book shop, right?'

'It's fine,' I said. 'You can meet him. I don't mind.'

'I just want a book,' she said.

It was only a couple of minutes' walk away, a shop that specialized in travel books and maps.

'Is he here?' asked Sylvie, as we walked inside.

'I can't see him,' I said. 'You'd better go ahead and find your book.'

Sylvie mumbled something doubtful and we both wandered around. I stopped in front of a display of globes. I could always go back to the flat if he didn't show. I felt a touch from behind and then arms around me, someone nuzzling my neck. I turned round. Adam. He put his arms round me in the way that felt as if they were wrapped around me twice. 'Alice,' he said.

He let me go and I saw there were two men with him looking amused. They were both tall, like Adam. One had very light brown, almost blond hair, smooth skin, prominent cheekbones. He wore a heavy canvas jacket that looked as if it should have been worn by a deep-sea fisherman. The other was darker, with very long wavy brown hair. He wore a long grey coat that reached almost down to his ankles. Adam gestured to the blond man. 'This is Daniel,' he said. 'And this is Klaus.'

I shook their very large hands in turn.

'Good to meet you, Alice,' said Daniel, with a little bow of the head. He sounded foreign, Scandinavian maybe. Adam hadn't introduced me but they knew my name. He must have told them about me. They looked at me appraisingly, Adam's latest girlfriend, and I stared right back, willing myself to hold their gaze and planning another shopping spree very soon.

I felt a presence at my shoulder. Sylvie. 'Adam, this is a friend of mine, Sylvie.'

Adam looked round slowly. He took her hand. 'Sylvie,' he said, almost as if he were weighing the name in his mind.

'Yes,' she said. 'I mean, hello.'

Suddenly, I saw Adam and his friends through her eyes: tall, strong men who looked as if they had come from another planet, dressed in odd clothes, beautiful and strange and threatening. She stared at Adam, mesmerized, but Adam turned his attention back to me. 'Daniel and Klaus might seem a bit out of it. They're still on Seattle time.' He took my hand and held it against his face. 'We're going round the corner. Want to come?' This last was addressed to Sylvie and he looked sharply back to her. I swear that Sylvie almost jumped.

'No,' she said, almost as if she had been offered a very tempting, but very dangerous, drug. 'No, no. I've, er, got to . . .'

'She's got to buy a book,' I said.

'Yes,' she said, falteringly. 'And other things. I've got to.'

'Some other time,' said Adam, and we left. I turned and gave Sylvie a wink, as if I were on a train that was pulling out of a station and leaving her behind. She looked aghast, or awe-struck, or something. As we walked Adam put his hand on my back to guide me. We made a few turnings, the last of which took us into a tiny alley. I looked questioningly at Adam but he pressed a bell by an anonymous-looking door and when the catch was released we walked up some stairs to a snug room with a bar and a fire and some scattered tables and chairs.

'Is this a club?'

'Yes, it's a club,' said Adam, as if it were too obvious to need mentioning. 'Sit in the next room. I'll get some beers. Klaus can tell you about his crappy book.'

I went through with Daniel and Klaus to a smaller room, also with a couple of tables and chairs. We sat at one. 'What book?' I said. Klaus smiled. 'Your . . .' He stopped himself. 'Adam is pissed with me. I've written a book about last year on the mountain.' He sounded American.

'Were you there?'

He held up his hands. There was no little finger on his left hand. The ring finger was half gone as well. On his right hand half the little finger was gone.

'I was lucky,' he said. 'More than lucky. Adam pulled me down. Saved my life.' He smiled again. 'I can say that when he's out of the room. When he comes in I can go back to telling him what an asshole he is.'

Adam came into the room clutching bottles, then went out again and returned with plates of sandwiches.

'Are you all old friends?' I asked.

'Friends, colleagues,' said Daniel.

'Daniel's been recruited for another Himalayan package tour next year. Wants me to go along.'

'Are you going to?'

'I think so.' I must have looked concerned, because Adam laughed. 'Is there a problem?'

'That's what you do,' I said. 'There's no problem. Just watch your step.'

His expression became serious and he leaned in close and kissed me softly. 'Good,' he said, as if I had passed a test.

I took a sip of beer, leaned back and watched them talking about things I could barely understand, about logistics and equipment and windows of opportunity. Or, rather, it wasn't that I couldn't understand them, but that I didn't want to follow what they said in its details. I felt a glowing pleasure in seeing Adam and Daniel and Klaus discussing something that mattered intensely to them. I liked the technical words that I couldn't understand, and sometimes I sneaked a glance at Adam's face. The urgency of his expression reminded me of something and then I remembered. It was the expression he had worn when I had first seen him. When I had first seen him seeing me.

Later, we lay in bed, our clothes scattered where we had thrown them, Sherpa purring at our feet – the cat came with the property, but I had named him. Adam asked me about Sylvie. 'What did she say?' he asked.

The phone rang.

'You get it this time,' I said.

Adam made a face and picked it up. 'Hello?'

There was a silence and he put it down again.

'Every night and every morning,' I said, with a grim smile. 'Somebody with a job. It's beginning to give me the creeps, Adam.'

'It's probably a technical fault,' Adam said. 'Or someone who wants to speak to the last tenant. What did she say?'

'She wanted to know about you,' I said. Adam gave a snort. I gave him a kiss, biting his lovely full lower lip slightly, then harder. 'And she said I should enjoy it. So long as I didn't actually get injured.'

The hand that had been caressing my back suddenly held me

85

down on the bed. I felt Adam's lips against my ear. 'I bought cream today,' he said. 'Cold cream. I don't want to injure you. I just want to hurt you.'

Eleven

'Don't move. Stay just as you are.' Adam stood at the end of the bed, staring down at me through the viewfinder of a camera, a Polaroid. I stared back, muzzily. I was lying on top of the sheets, naked. Only my feet were under the covers. The winter sun shone weakly through the thin closed curtain.

'Did I go to sleep again? How long have you been there?'

'Don't move, Alice.' A flash momentarily dazzled me, there was a whir and the plastic card emerged, as if the camera had poked its tongue out at me.

'At least you won't be taking it to Boots to be developed.'

'Put your arms above your head. That's right.' He came over and pushed my hair away from my face, then stood back once again. He was fully dressed, armed with his camera, a look of dispassionate concentration on his face. 'Open your legs a bit more.'

'I'm cold.'

'I'll make you warm soon. Wait.'

Once again, the camera flashed.

'Why are you doing this?'

'Why?' He put down the camera and sat beside me. The two images were tossed beside me on the bed. I watched myself take shape. The pictures looked cruel to me, my skin looking flushed, pallid, spotty. I thought of police photographers in films at the scene of the crime, then tried not to. He picked up my hand, which was still flung obediently above my head, and pressed it against his cheek. 'Because I want to.' He turned his mouth into my palm.

The phone rang and we looked at each other. 'Don't pick it up,' I said. 'It'll be him again.'

'Him?'

'Or her.'

We waited until the phone stopped ringing.

'What if it's Jake?' I said. 'Making those calls.'

'Jake?'

'Who else would it be? You hadn't been getting them before, you say, and they started as soon as I moved in.' I looked at him. 'Or maybe it's a friend.'

Adam shrugged. 'Maybe,' he said, and picked up the camera again, but I struggled into a sitting position.

'I must get up, Adam. Can you put the bar fire on for me?'

The flat, the top floor of a tall Victorian house, was Spartan. It had no central heating and little furniture. My clothes took up one corner of the large, dark cupboard, and Adam's possessions were neatly stacked in the corner of the bedroom, still packed. The carpets were worn, the curtains flimsy, and in the kitchen a bare bulb hung above the small stove. We rarely cooked, but ate in small, dimly lit restaurants each evening before coming back to the high bed and hot touch. I felt half blinded by passion. Everything was blurred and unreal except me and Adam. All my life until now I had been a free agent, in control of my life and sure of where I was going. None of my relationships had really diverted me from that. Now I felt rudderless, lost. I would give up anything for the feel of his hands on my body. Sometimes, in the dark early hours of morning when I woke first and was lying unheld in a stranger's bed and he was still in a secret world of dreams, or perhaps when leaving work, before I saw Adam and felt his continuing rapture, I felt scared. The loss of myself in another.

This morning I hurt. In the bathroom mirror, I saw that there was a livid scratch running down my neck and my lips were puffy. Adam came in and stood behind me. Our eyes met in the mirror. He licked a finger, then ran it down the scratch. I pulled on my clothes and turned towards him.

'Who was before me, Adam? No, don't just shrug. I'm serious.'

He paused for a moment, as if weighing up possibilities.

'Let's make a deal,' he said. It sounded horribly formal but, then, I suppose it had to be. Usually details of one's past love life leak out in late-night confessions, post-coital exchanges, little snippets of information offered as signs of intimacy or trust. We had done none of that. Adam held out my jacket for me. 'We'll have a late breakfast down the road, then I've got to go and pick up some stuff. And then,' he opened the door, 'we'll meet up back here and you can tell me who you've had, and I will tell you.'

'Everyone?'

'Everyone.'

'. . . and before him, there was Rob. Rob was a graphic designer, he thought he was an artist. He was quite a lot older than me, and he had a daughter of ten by his first wife. He was rather a quiet man, but . . .'

'What did you do?'

'What?'

'What did you do together?'

'You know, films, pubs, walks –'

'You know what I mean.'

I knew what he meant, of course I did. 'God, Adam. Different things, you know. It was years ago. I can't remember specifics.' A lie, of course.

'Were you in love with him?'

I thought wistfully of Rob's nice face, some good times. I'd adored him, for a time at least. 'No.'

'Go on.'

This was unsettling. Adam was seated opposite me, the table between us. His hands were steepled together; his eyes were boring into me. Talking about sex was difficult enough for me anyway, let alone under this interrogation.

'There was Laurence, but that didn't last long,' I mumbled. Laurence had been funny, hopeless.

'Yes?'

'And Joe, who I used to work with.'

'You were in the same office as him?'

'Sort of. And no, Adam, we didn't do it behind the photocopier.' I ploughed grimly on. I'd been expecting this to be an erotic mutual confession, ending in bed. It was turning out to be a cold, dry tale of the men who had been both irrelevant and important to me in a way I didn't want to explain to Adam, here at this table. 'Then before that, it was school and university, and, well, you know . . .' I tailed off. The thought of going through the rather short list of boyfriends and drunken one-night stands defeated me. I took a deep breath. 'Well, if this is what you want. Michael. Then Gareth. And then Simon, who I went out with for a year and a half, and a man called Christopher, once.' He looked at me. 'And a man whose name I never knew, at a party I didn't want to go to. There.'

'That's it?'

'Yes.'

'So who did you have sex with first? How old were you?'

'I was old compared to my friends. Michael, when I was seventeen.'

'What was it like?'

Somehow the question seemed unembarrassing. Perhaps because it seemed so long ago, and the girl I had been was such a stranger to the woman I was now. It had been captivating. Strange. Fascinating.

'Awful,' I said. 'Painful. Pleasureless.'

He leaned across the table but still didn't touch me.

'Have you always liked sex?'

'Uh, not always.'

'Have you ever pretended?'

'Every woman has.'

'With me?'

'Never. God, no.'

'Can we fuck now?' He was still sitting quite apart from me, straight-backed on the uncomfortable kitchen chair.

I managed a laugh. 'No way, Adam. It's your turn.'

He sighed and sat back and held up his fingers, counting off affairs as if he were an accountant. 'Before you, there was Lily, who I met last summer. Before her there was Françoise for a couple of years. Before her there was . . . er . . .'

'Is it difficult to remember?' I asked sarcastically, but with a tremor in my voice. I hoped he wouldn't notice.

'It's not hard,' he said. 'Lisa. And before Lisa there was a girl called Penny.' There was a pause. 'Good climber.'

'How long did Penny last?' I had expected a catalogue of conquests, not this efficient list of serious relationships. I felt an acid rush of panic in my stomach.

'Eighteen months, something like that.'

'Oh.' We sat in silence. 'Were you faithful?' I forced myself to ask. I really wanted to ask if they were all beautiful, all more beautiful than me.

He looked at me across the table. 'It wasn't like that. They weren't that sort of exclusive thing.'

'How many times were you unfaithful?'

'I used to see other people.'

'How many?'

He frowned.

'Come on, Adam. Once, twice, twenty times, forty or fifty times?'

'Something like that.'

'Something like *forty* or *fifty*?'

'Alice, come here.'

'No! No – this is – I feel awful. I mean, why am I different?' A thought struck me. 'You haven't . . .'

'No!' His voice was sharp. 'Christ, Alice, can't you see? Can't you feel? There's no one except you now.'

'How do I know?' I heard my voice wail. 'I feel I arrived a bit late at the party.' All those women crowding his life. I didn't stand a chance.

He stood up and walked round the table. He pulled me to my feet and cupped my face in his hands. 'You know, Alice, don't you?'

I shook my head.

'Alice, look at me.' He forced my head up and looked deep, deep into me. 'Alice, will you trust me? Will you do something for me?'

'It depends,' I said, sulkily, like a cross child.

'Wait,' he said.

'Where?'

'Here,' he said. 'I'll be back in a minute.'

It wasn't a minute, but it was only a few minutes. I had hardly finished a cup of coffee when the doorbell rang. He's got a key, I said to myself, and didn't respond, but he didn't come in and rang again. So I sighed and went down. I opened the door and Adam wasn't there. A toot made me jump. I looked round and saw that he was sitting in a car, something old and nondescript. I walked over and bent my face down to the driver's window.

'What do you think?'

'Is it ours?' I asked.

'For the afternoon. Get in.'

'Where are we going?'

'Trust me.'

'It had better be good. Shouldn't I lock the house?'

'I'll do that. I've got to get something.'

I seriously thought of not obeying but then walked round to the passenger side and got in. Meanwhile Adam ran in through the front door and returned a minute later.

'What were you getting?'

'My wallet,' he said. 'And this.' He tossed the Polaroid camera on to the back seat.

Oh, God, I thought, but didn't say anything.

★   ★   ★

I stayed awake long enough to see that we were leaving London on the M1 but then, as I always do when being driven anywhere, I fell asleep. When I was jolted awake for a moment, I saw that we were off the motorway in scrubby, wild countryside.

'Where are we?' I said.

'It's a mystery tour,' Adam said, with a smile.

I drifted off to a half-sleep and when I woke up properly noticed an old Saxon church by the road in an otherwise featureless landscape. 'Eadmund with an A,' I said sleepily.

'He lost his head,' said Adam, beside me.

'What?'

'He was an Anglo-Saxon king. The Vikings caught him and killed him and cut him up and scattered his body all over the place. His followers couldn't find him and there was a miracle. The head shouted, "Here I am," until they found it.'

'I wish that bunches of keys did that. I've often wished that my house keys would shout, "Here I am," so that I wouldn't have to search every single pocket of everything I own to find them.'

At a fork in the road there was an ornate war monument with an eagle on it to people in the RAF. We went right.

'We're here,' said Adam.

He pulled into the side of the road and switched off the engine.

'Where?' I said.

Adam reached into the back of the car for the camera. 'Come,' he said.

'I should have brought my boots.'

'We're only walking a couple of hundred yards.'

Adam took my hand and we walked away from the road, along a path. Then we turned off the path, into some trees and then up a slope, slippery with leaves still decaying from last autumn. Adam had been silent and thoughtful. I was almost startled when he began to speak.

'I climbed K2 a few years ago,' he said. I nodded and said something affirmative but he seemed lost in his own world. 'Lots of great, great climbers have never done it, lots of great climbers have died trying. When I was at the top I knew intellectually that it was almost certainly the greatest climbing thing I would ever do, but I felt nothing. I looked around but . . .' He made a contemptuous gesture. 'I was up there for about fifteen minutes, waiting for Kevin Doyle to join me. All the while I was calculating the time, checking my equipment, going through the supplies in my head, deciding on the route down. Even as I looked around, the mountain was just there as a problem.'

'So why do you do it?'

He scowled. 'No, you don't get my point. Look.' We were emerging from the trees on to some grass, almost moorland. 'This is the landscape I love.' He put his arms round me. 'I was once here before, and I thought it was one of the loveliest spots I had ever seen. We're in one of the most crowded islands on earth but here we are on a patch of grass that's off a path that's off a track that's off the road. Look at it with my eyes, Alice. Look down there, the church we passed nestling in the land as if it had grown there. And look round there at the fields, under-neath it but they seem close up: a table of green fields. Come and stand here, by this hawthorn bush.'

Adam positioned me quite carefully and then stood facing me, looking around, as if orienting himself precisely. I shook him off, bewildered and uncomfortable. What had all this to do with his dozens of infidelities?

'And then there's you, Alice, my only love,' he said, standing back and looking at me, as if I were a precious ornament he had put into a shop window. 'You know the story that we are all broken into two halves and we spend our lives looking for our other self. Every affair we have, however stupid or trivial, has a bit of that hope that this might be it, our other self.' His eyes turned dark suddenly, like the surface of a lake when a cloud has moved in front of the sun. I shivered in front of the hawthorn bush. 'That's why they can end so badly, because you feel you've been betrayed.' He looked round and then back at me. 'But with

94

you, I *know*.' I felt myself gasp, my eyes water. 'Stand still, I want to take a photograph of you.'

'Christ, Adam, don't be so odd. Just kiss me, hold me.'

He shook his head and raised the camera in front of his face. 'I wanted to photograph you here, in this place, at the moment that I asked you to marry me.'

There was a flash. I felt my knees give way. I sat down on the damp grass and he ran forward and took hold of me. 'Are you all right?'

Was I all right? A feeling of extraordinary joy rose up in me. I stood up and laughed and kissed him on the mouth, firmly: a pledge.

'Is that a yes?'

'Of course it is, you idiot. Yes. Yes yes yes.'

'Look,' he said. 'Here she is.'

And there, indeed, I was, open-mouthed, wide-eyed, taking shape, colours deepening, outline hardening.

'There we are,' he said, handing it to me. 'It's a moment, but it's also a promise. For ever.'

I took the picture and put it in my purse. 'For ever,' I said.

Adam seized my wrist with an urgency that startled me. 'You mean it, don't you, Alice? I've given myself before and I've been let down before. That's why I brought you here, so that we could make this vow to each other.' He looked at me fiercely, as if he were threatening me. 'This vow is more important than any marriage.' Then he softened. 'I couldn't bear to lose you. I could never bear to let you go.'

I took him in my arms. I held his head and I kissed his mouth, his eyes, the firm jaw and the hollow of his neck. I told him I was his, and he was mine. I felt his tears on my skin, hot and salty. My only love.

Twelve

I wrote to my mother. She was going to be very surprised. I had only told her that Jake and I had separated. I hadn't even mentioned Adam before. I wrote to Jake, trying to find the right words. I didn't want him to hear it from anyone else first. I met more of Adam's friends and colleagues – people he had climbed with, people he'd shared tents with and crapped with and with whom he had risked his life – and everywhere we went I could feel Adam's appraising eyes on me, making my skin prickle. I went to work and sat at my desk, loose with remembered and anticipated pleasure, and pushed paper around desks and sat in meetings. I meant to ring up Sylvie, and Clive, and even Pauline, but somehow I always put it off. Almost every day now we would receive silent phone calls. I got used to holding the receiver a bit away from my ear, hearing the raspy breathing and putting the phone back on its stand. One day wet leaves and earth were pushed through our letterbox, but we ignored that as well. If occasionally I felt anxious, the anxiety was drowned out by all the other turbulent emotions.

I learned that Adam cooked great curries. That television bored him. That he walked very fast. That he mended the few clothes he owned with meticulous care. That he loved single malt whisky and good red wine and wheat beer, and hated baked beans and bony fish and mashed potatoes. That his father was still alive. That he never read novels. That he was almost fluent in Spanish and French, the bastard. That he could tie knots with one hand. That he used to be scared of enclosed spaces, until he was cured by six days in a tent on a two-feet deep ledge on the side of

Annapurna. That he didn't need much sleep. That his frost-bitten foot still hurt him sometimes. That he liked cats and birds of prey. That his hands were always warm, however icy it was outside in the streets. That he hadn't cried since he was twelve and his mother died, until the day I said I would marry him. That he hated lids to be left off jars and drawers to be left open. That he took showers at least twice a day, and clipped his nails several times a week. That he always carried tissues in his pockets. That he could hold me down with one hand. That he rarely smiled, laughed. I would wake up and he would be beside me, staring at me.

I let him take photographs of me. I let him watch me in the bath, on the lavatory, putting on makeup. I let him tie me down. I felt at last as if I had been turned inside out and all my private internal landscape, everything that had belonged only to me, was known. I think I was very, very happy, but if this was happiness, then I had never been happy before.

On Thursday, four days after Adam had asked me to marry him and three days after we had gone to the register office to post our banns, sign forms and pay money, Clive rang me at work. I had neither seen him nor spoken to him since the ten-pin bowling, on the day I left Jake. He was polite and formal, but asked me if Adam and I would like to come to Gail's thirtieth birthday party. It was tomorrow, Friday, nine o'clock, with food and dancing.

I hesitated. 'Will Jake be there?'

'Yes, of course.'

'And Pauline?'

'Yes.'

'Do they know that you're asking me?'

'I wouldn't have rung you without talking to them first.'

I took a deep breath. 'You'd better give me the address.'

I didn't think Adam would want to go, but he surprised me. 'Of course, if it's important to you,' he said casually.

97

I wore the dress he had bought for me, chocolate-brown velvet with long sleeves, deep neck and slashed, swirly skirt. It was the first time I had got dressed up for weeks. It occurred to me that, since Adam, I had, bizarrely, paid little attention to what I wore or how I looked. I was thinner than I had been, and pale. My hair needed cutting and there were dark smudges under my eyes. Yet I felt, examining myself in the mirror before we left that evening, that I looked beautiful in a way that was new. Or maybe I was just ill, or mad.

Gail's flat was in a large, rickety house in Finsbury Park. When we arrived there, all the windows were lit up. Even from the pavement we could hear music and laughing voices, and see the shapes of people through the open curtains. I clutched Adam's arm. 'Is this a good idea? Maybe we shouldn't have come.'

'Let's go in there for a bit. You can see everyone you need to see, and we can go and have a late meal afterwards.'

Gail opened the door. 'Alice!' She kissed me exuberantly on both cheeks, as if we were old friends, then turned inquiringly towards Adam, as if she had no idea who he was.

'Adam, this is Gail. Gail, Adam.'

Adam said nothing but took her hand and held it for a moment. She looked at him. 'Sylvie was right.' She giggled. She was drunk already.

'Happy birthday, Gail,' I said drily, and she forced her attention back to me.

The room was full of people holding glasses of wine or cans of beer. There was a raggle-taggle band of musicians clutching their instruments in one corner, but they weren't playing. Music was booming from the stereo instead. I took two glasses from the table and glugged some wine into them for Adam and me, and looked around. Jake was standing near the window, talking to a tall woman wearing a strikingly short leather skirt. He hadn't noticed me come in, or he was pretending that he hadn't.

'Alice.'

I turned. 'Pauline. Nice to see you.' I moved forward and kissed her cheek, but she was unresponsive. I introduced Adam awkwardly.

'I gathered,' she said.

Adam took her by the elbow and said in a clear, carrying voice, 'Pauline, life is too short to lose a friend.'

She looked taken aback but at least she managed to speak. I drifted away from them, towards Jake. I had to get this over with. He had seen me now. He was still talking to the woman in the skirt, but his glance kept turning towards me. I went over. 'Hello, Jake,' I said.

'Hello, Alice.'

'Did you get my letter?'

The woman turned and left us. Jake smiled at me, and said, 'God, that was hard going. It's difficult being single again. Yes, I got your letter. At least you didn't say you hoped we could still be friends.'

At the other end of the room I saw Adam talking to Sylvie and Clive. Pauline was still beside him; and he was still holding her arm. I saw how all the women eyed him, drifted over towards him, and I felt a twinge of jealousy. But then he looked up, our eyes met, and he gave a funny twisted grin.

Jake saw the glance. 'Now I know why you were suddenly so interested in climbing literature,' he said, with a painful smile. I didn't reply. 'I feel so ridiculously stupid. All that happening under my nose and me not knowing. Oh, and congratulations.'

'What?'

'When is it going to be?'

'Oh. In two and a half weeks' time.' He winced. 'Yes, well, why wait . . . ?' I stopped. My voice sounded too bright and cheery. 'Are you all right, Jake?'

Now Adam was talking just to Sylvie. His back was to me, but she was staring up at him with a rapt expression I knew too well.

'It's no longer your concern,' said Jake, in a voice that was trembling slightly. 'Can you tell me something?' I saw that his eyes had filled with tears. It was as if my going had released a new Jake – one who had lost his mellow cheerfulness and his irony; who wept easily.

'What?' I realized that Jake was a bit drunk. He bent closer to me, so I could feel his breath on my cheek.

'If it hadn't been for, you know, him, would you have stayed with me and –?'

'Alice, it's time to go.' Adam put both arms round me from behind, and rested his head on my hair. He was holding me too tightly. I could hardly breathe.

'Adam, this is Jake.'

The two men didn't say anything. Adam let go of me and held out his hand. Jake didn't move at first; then, with a puzzled expression, he put his hand into Adam's. Adam nodded. Man to man. A desire to giggle rose in my throat, which I suppressed.

'Goodbye, Jake,' I said awkwardly. I was about to reach up and kiss him on the cheek, but Adam pulled me away.

'Come on, my love,' he said, leading me from the room. I sketched a half-wave at Pauline and left.

Outside the house, Adam stopped and turned me towards him. 'Satisfied?' he said, and kissed me savagely. I slid my arms under his jacket and shirt and leaned into him. When I pulled away, I saw Jake, still standing at the window and looking out. Our eyes met but he made no gesture.

Thirteen

I tried to make the question seem casual, although I had been shaping it and rephrasing it in my mind for days. We were lying in bed, exhausted, long after midnight, coiled round each other in the dark, when I sensed an opportunity.

'Your friend Klaus,' I said. 'Writing about what happened on Chunga-whatever-it-is. I can never remember the name.'

'Chungawat,' said Adam.

He didn't say anything else. He would need more prompting.

'He said you were pissed off with him for writing the book.'

'Did he now?' Adam said.

'Are you? I don't see why it's a problem. Deborah told me what you did, what a hero you were.'

Adam sighed. 'I wasn't . . .' He paused. 'It wasn't about hero-ism. They shouldn't have been there, most of them. I . . .' He tried again. 'At that height, in those conditions, most people, even fit people who are experienced in other conditions, can't survive on their own if things start to go wrong.'

'Is that your fault, Adam?'

'Greg shouldn't have organized it, I shouldn't have gone along. The rest of them shouldn't have thought there was an easy way of climbing a mountain like that.'

'Deborah said that Greg had worked out a foolproof way of getting them up the mountain.'

'That was the idea. Then there was a storm and Greg and Claude got sick and the plan didn't work out so well.'

'Why?'

His tone turned irritable. He was impatient with me for pressing him, but I wasn't going to stop.

'We weren't a team. Only one of the clients had ever been to the Himalayas before. They couldn't communicate. I mean, for God's sake, the German guy, Tomas, could hardly speak a single word of English.'

'Aren't you just curious to see what Klaus has to say in his book?'

'I know what he has to say.'

'How do you know?'

'I've got a copy.'

'What! Have you read it?' I asked.

'I've looked through it,' he said, almost with contempt.

'I thought the book hadn't been published yet.'

'It hasn't. Klaus sent me one of those rough, early versions – what are they called?'

'Proof copies. Have you got the book here?'

'It's in a bag somewhere.'

I kissed my way down his chest, his stomach and beyond, until I could taste myself on him.

'I want to read it. You don't mind, do you?'

I made a private rule for myself that I would never try to compare Adam with Jake. It seemed a last, feeble way of trying to be fair to Jake. But I couldn't help it sometimes. Jake never just did something, never just went out. He was too considerate and attentive. He asked my permission or informed me or planned it in advance and probably asked me to come with him, or what I was doing. Adam was completely different. Much of the time he was utterly absorbed in me, wanting to touch, taste, penetrate or just look at me. At other times he would make a precise arrangement for where and when we would next meet, then he would throw on a jacket and go.

The next morning he was standing at the door when I remembered. 'Klaus's book,' I said. He frowned. 'You promised,' I said.

He didn't say anything but walked across to the spare room and I heard sounds of rummaging. He emerged with a book with a floppy light blue cover. He tossed it over to where I sat on the sofa. I looked at the cover: *Ridge of Sighs* by Klaus Smith.

'It's only one man's view,' he said. 'So I'll see you at the Pelican at seven.'

And he was gone, rattling down the stairs. I went to the window, as I always did when he went out, and watched him appear and cross the pavement. He halted, turned and looked up. I blew him a kiss and he smiled and turned away. I went back to the sofa. I had, I suppose, some idea of reading for a bit, making some coffee, having a bath, but I didn't move for three hours. At first I flicked ahead, looking for his lovely name and finding it, and looking for photographs, and not finding them, because they wouldn't be in until the final published version. Then I turned to the beginning, to the very first page.

The book was dedicated to the members of the 1997 Chungawat expedition. Beneath the dedication there was a quotation from an old mountaineering book of the thirties: 'May we, who live our lives where the air is thick and minds are clear, pause before we judge men who venture into that wonderland, that looking-glass realm on the roof of the world.'

The phone rang and I listened to the silence for a few seconds before putting it down again. Sometimes I could persuade myself that I recognized the breathing; that it was someone I knew at the other end. Once I said, tentatively, 'Jake?' to see if there was any response, any sharp intake of breath. This time, I didn't really care. I wanted to get on with *Ridge of Sighs*.

The book began more than twenty-five million years ago, when the Himalayan range ('younger than the Brazilian rainforest') was pushed up in folds by the northward drift of the Indian sub-continent. It leaped forward to a catastrophic British expedition up Chungawat just after the First World War. The attempt on the summit was abruptly halted when a British Army major lost his footing and pulled three of his comrades down with him, falling, as Klaus put it drily, around three thousand metres from Nepal into China.

I read quickly through a couple of chapters that described expeditions in the late fifties and sixties in which Chungawat was first climbed and then climbed from various routes and using different climbing methods, which were meant to be purer or harder or more beautiful. This didn't interest me much, except that my attention was caught by a statement that Klaus quoted from 'an anonymous American climber in the sixties': 'A mountain is like a chick. First you just want to fuck her, then you want to fuck her in a few different ways and then you move on. By the early seventies Chungawat was fucked out and nobody was interested any more.'

Apparently Chungawat didn't present enough interesting technical challenges to élite mountaineers but it was beautiful and poems had been written about it, and a classic travel book, and in the early nineties that was what had given Greg McLaughlin his big idea. Klaus described a talk with Greg in a Seattle bar in which Greg had rhapsodized about package tours above eight thousand metres. People would pay thirty thousand dollars and Greg and a couple of other experts would lead them to the peak of one of the highest mountains in the Himalayas with a view into three countries. Greg thought he would be the Thomas Cook of the Himalayas and he had a plan for making it happen. It involved each guide laying a series of lines, fixed on pickets to which the climbers would be attached by carabiners. The lines would lead along a safe route from camp to camp. One guide would be responsible for each line, designated by different colours, and it would be just a matter of making sure that the clients wore the correct equipment and that they were fastened securely to the line. 'The only danger,' he had told Klaus, 'was dying of boredom.' Klaus was an old friend and Greg asked him to come along on the first expedition and help him with some of the logistics in return for a discount. Klaus was unsparing about his own motives. He had had doubts from the first, he despised the idea of turning mountaineering into tourism, yet he accepted because he had never been to the Himalayas before and he wanted to go.

Klaus was also pretty jaundiced about his fellow packagers, who included a Wall Street stockbroker and a Californian cosmetic surgeon. But about one person he wasn't jaundiced. When Adam was first mentioned I felt a lurch:

> The dreamboat of the expedition was Greg's second guide, Adam Tallis, a lanky, good-looking, taciturn Englishman. At thirty years of age, Tallis was already one of the most brilliant climbers of the younger generation. Most important for my own peace of mind, he had extensive experience in the Himalayan and Karakoram mountain ranges. Adam, a long-time friend, is not one for unnecessary talk but he obviously shared my doubts about the whole basis of the expedition. The difference was that if things went wrong, the guides would have to put their lives on the line.

Then my stomach lurched again as Klaus described how Adam had suggested that his ex-girlfriend, Françoise Colet, who was desperate for a Himalayan climb, come along as the doctor. Greg was reluctant, but agreed to take her as a client with a huge discount.

There was too much stuff (for me) about bureaucracy, sponsorship, rivalry with other climbers, the initial trek in Nepal through the foothills and then, like a revelation, the first sight of Chungawat with its notorious Gemini Ridge, leading down from the col just below the summit which divides into two, one side leading to a precipice (down which the English major and his comrades had slipped) and the other leading gently down the slope. I seemed to be living it as I read, experiencing the brightening of the light and the thinning of the air. At first there were elements of lightheartedness, with toasts, prayers to the presiding deity. Klaus described sex in one of the tents, which amused and shocked the Sherpas, but discreetly omitted to mention who had been involved. I wondered if it was Adam who had been in her sleeping bag with her, whoever she was – probably the cosmetic surgeon, Carrie Frank, I thought. I had come to assume that Adam had slept with virtually everybody who had crossed his path, almost as a matter of course. Deborah, for example, the climbing medic in Soho. There had been an expression in her eye that made me think they must have had a fling.

As they moved up the mountain, establishing camps, the book almost stopped being a book and turned into a feverish dream, a hallucination that I shared as I read. The members of the party were blinded by headaches, unable to eat, doubled over with stomach cramps, even dysentery. They debated and bickered. Greg McLaughlin was distracted by administration, divided between his concerns as a guide and his responsibilities as a tour operator. At over eight thousand metres everything was reduced and slowed. There was no actual climbing but even the shallowest slopes became a huge physical effort. Older members of the party slowed everybody up, causing resentment. Through it all, Greg was tormented by his need to get everybody to the top, to show that this form of tourism could work. Klaus described him not only as obsessed but babbling incoherently about the need to hurry, to get to the top in the window of fine weather at the end of May, before June brought storms and disaster. Then, at the camp before the summit, there was a lowering, cloudy day in which Klaus overheard arguments between Greg, Adam and Claude Bresson. The weather held that day and before dawn the party set off up Gemini Ridge along a fixed rope that had been prepared by Greg and two of the Sherpas. It was all done with, as Greg himself put it, a simplicity that might have been designed for kids at kindergarten. Greg's fixed lines were red, Claude's were blue, Adam's were yellow. The clients were told a colour and told to follow it. After they had moved beyond the ridge and were just fifty – vertical – metres below the summit, Klaus, at the back of the group with Claude, saw clouds rolling in ominously from the north. He questioned Claude, who didn't respond. In retrospect, Klaus didn't know whether Claude was stubbornly determined to get to the summit, whether he was already ill, or whether he just hadn't heard. They pressed on and perhaps half an hour later the weather broke and everything went dark.

Much of the rest of the book was delirium as Klaus described the disaster the way he – sick, disoriented, terrified – had experienced it. He couldn't see, he couldn't hear; occasionally figures emerged from the blizzard and disappeared back into it. The climbers had made their way across the col to where Claude, theoretically, had laid the blue line that would lead them towards the summit but by that time nobody could see more than a few feet or hear anything unless it was shouted into their ear. The one figure who emerged with clarity out of the chaos, like a figure in a thunderstorm illuminated by flashes of lightning, was Adam. He appeared out of the storm moving down, disappeared, re-appeared. He was everywhere, keeping up communication, leading the two parties of clients into a place of relative shelter on the col. The immediate priority was to save the lives of Greg and the acutely ill Claude. With Klaus's help they almost carried Claude down the line to the highest camp. Klaus then returned with Adam and they helped Greg down.

By this time Klaus himself was incoherent with fatigue, cold and thirst and collapsed in his tent, unconscious. Adam went back up the mountain to fetch the virtually helpless clients. He took the first group, which included Françoise and four others, to the beginning of the line: they would have to feel their way down to the camp. Adam left them and went back to the second group. But by the time he had brought them back, the fixed line was nowhere to be seen. It had evidently been blown away. It was now beginning to get dark and wind-chill had brought the temperature down to fifty degrees below zero. Adam took his second party back to the col. Then he went down the ridge alone, without a line, in order to fetch his own line and in search of possible help. Greg, Claude and Klaus were unconscious and there was no sign of the first group.

Then Adam went back up the ridge, laid the yellow line and

brought the second group down himself. Some of these needed urgent medical help, but once he had attended to them, he went out once more, alone and in the dark, to search for the missing group. It was hopeless. Late that night, Klaus woke and deliriously assumed that Adam, too, had been lost until he burst into the tent and collapsed.

The first party was found the following day. What had happened was a tragically simple mistake. In the dark and the snow and the noise, with the fixed line unfixed and blown into the abyss, they had blundered down on the wrong side of the Gemini Ridge, which had taken them hopelessly and irrevocably astray on to an exposed ridge that tapered away, leaving steep drops on each side. The bodies of Françoise Colet and an American client, Alexis Hartounian, were never found. They must have gone over the edge, perhaps while struggling back up the ridge or pressing forward to the camp they thought was in front of them. The others huddled together in the dark storm and died slowly. The following morning they were found by the sherpas searching for them. All dead, Klaus wrote, except for one: another American, Pete Papworth, who was just mumbling the single pathetic word, 'Help,' over and over again. Help. Help. Calling, Klaus wrote with the pain of a man who had been asleep through all of it, for help that nobody would bring to him.

I read the final pages in a daze, scarcely able to breathe, and then just lay on the sofa where I must have slept for hours.

When I awoke, there was barely time. I showered and pulled on a dress. I caught a cab down to the Pelican in Holland Park although I would have been quicker walking, except that in my present frame of mind I wouldn't have found my way anywhere. I paid the driver and went inside. Only a couple of tables were occupied. In one corner was Adam, with a man and a woman I didn't recognize. I walked straight up to them. They looked round, startled.

'Excuse me,' I said to the others. 'Adam, could you come outside for a second?'

He looked wary. 'What?'

'Just come. It's very important. I'll only take a second.'

He shrugged and nodded an apology to the others at the table. I took him by the hand and led him out. As soon as we were out of view of his friends I turned to him and took his face in my hands so that I could look him right in the eyes. 'I've read Klaus's book,' I said. His eyes gave a flicker of alarm. 'I love you, Adam. I love you so much.'

I started to cry and I couldn't see, but I felt his arms around me.

Fourteen

'The lady has narrow feet, Mr Tallis.' He held my foot as if it were a piece of clay, and turned it in his thin hands.

'Yeah, well, make sure it's secure around the ankle. She doesn't want blisters, all right?'

I had never been into this kind of shop before, although I had passed them by and peered into their dim, expensive depths. I wasn't trying on shoes, I was being measured and fitted for them. My sock – violet and balding – looked shabby in this company.

'And a high instep.'

'Yeah, I'd noticed that.' Adam took hold of my other foot and examined it. I felt like a horse being shod by a blacksmith.

'What style of walking boot were you thinking of?'

'Well, since I haven't . . .'

'Basic trekking. Quite high, to support her ankle. Light,' said Adam firmly.

'Like the one I made for –?'

'Yes.'

'Made for who?' I asked. They both ignored me. I pulled my feet out of their grip and stood up.

'I need to collect it by next Friday,' said Adam.

'That's our wedding day.'

'That's why I need to collect it by then,' he said, as if it were obvious. 'Then we can go walking at the weekend.'

'Oh,' I said. I'd figured on a two-day honeymoon in bed, with champagne and smoked salmon and hot baths between sex.

Adam looked across at me. 'I'm doing a demonstration climb

in the Lake District that Sunday,' he said briefly. 'You can come
with me.'

'Very wifely,' I said. 'Do I get a say in all of this?'

'Come on. We're in a hurry.'

'Where are we going now?'

'I'll tell you in the car.'

'What car?'

Adam seemed to exist on a barter system. His flat belonged to
a friend. The car that was parked down the road belonged to a
climbing acquaintance. Equipment was stashed away in various
people's attics and other places. I didn't know how he kept track
of it. He picked up odd jobs by word of mouth. Almost always
they were doing him a favour in order to repay him for something
he had done up one mountain or another. Some frostbite he had
prevented, some arduous piece of guiding he had carried out,
some calmness under duress, some kindness in a storm, some
life he happened to have saved.

I was trying now not to think of him as a hero. I didn't want
to be married to a hero. The thought of it frightened me, aroused
me, and put a subtle and erotic distance between us. I knew I
was looking at him differently since yesterday and reading the
book. His body, which I had until twenty-four hours ago thought
of as the body that fucked me, had become the body that endured
when no one else could. His beauty, which had seduced me, now
seemed miraculous. He had staggered through a thin soup of air
in a cracking cold, blasted by wind and pain, and yet he seemed
unblemished by it. Now that I knew, everything about Adam
was charged with his reckless, calm courage. When he looked at
me broodingly or touched me, I couldn't help thinking that I was
the object of desire he had to risk himself on and conquer. And
I wanted to be conquered; I did. I wanted to be assaulted and
won. I liked him to hurt me, and I liked to fight back and then
yield. But what about afterwards, when I was mapped and claimed
as victory? What would happen to me then? Walking through
slushy grey snow to the borrowed car, just six days away from

III

our wedding day, I wondered how I could ever live without Adam's obsession.

'Here we are.'

The car was an ancient black Rover with squashy leather seats and a lovely walnut dashboard. It smelt of cigarettes. Adam opened the door for me, then stepped into the driver's seat as if he owned it. He turned the ignition, then eased into the Saturday-morning traffic.

'Where are we going?'

'Just west of Sheffield, the Peak District.'

'What is this, a magical mystery tour?'

'To see my father.'

The house was grand, and also rather bleak, in its flat situation, exposed to winds from all sides. It was, I suppose, beautiful in an uncompromising way, but today I was looking for comfort, not austerity. Adam parked to one side of the house beside a series of ramshackle outhouses. Large feathery flakes of snow were falling slowly through the air. I expected a dog to run out barking at us, or an old-fashioned retainer to meet us at the door. But no one greeted us, and I had the uneasy impression that no one was there at all.

'Is he expecting us?' I asked.

'No.'

'Does he actually *know* about us, Adam?'

'No, that's why we're here.'

He walked up to the double front door, gave a perfunctory knock, then opened it.

It was freezing inside, and rather dark. The hall was a chilly square of polished floorboards, with a grandfather clock in the corner. Adam took my elbow and led me into a living room full of aged sofas and armchairs. At the end of the room, a large fireplace looked as if it had been many years since it had seen a fire. I pulled my coat round me. Adam took off his scarf and wrapped it round my neck.

'We won't be here long, my sweetheart,' he said.

The kitchen, with its cold quarry tiles and wooden surfaces, was empty as well, although a crumb-scattered plate and knife lay on the kitchen table. The dining room was one of those rooms used only once a year. There were unused candles on the round, polished table and on the stern mahogany sideboard.

'Did you grow up here?' I asked, for I couldn't imagine children ever playing in this house. Adam nodded, and pointed to a black-and-white photograph on the mantelpiece. A man in uniform, a woman in a frock, and, between them, a child, posed outside the house. They all looked very grave and formal. The parents looked much older than I had expected.

'Is that you?' I picked up the photograph and held it to the light to see better. He must have been about nine, with dark hair and scowling brows. His mother's hands were rested on his recalcitrant shoulders. 'You look just the same, Adam, I would have recognized you anywhere. How beautiful your mother was.'

'Yes. She was.'

Upstairs, in all the separate rooms, all the single beds were made, pillows fluffed up. There were ancient dried flower arrangements on each window-sill.

'Which was your room?' I asked Adam.

'This one.'

I looked around, at the white walls, the yellow flocked bedspread, the empty wardrobe, the boring landscape picture, the small, sensible mirror.

'But you're not here at all,' I said. 'There's not a trace of you.' Adam looked impatient. 'When did you leave?'

'Completely, you mean? Fifteen, I suppose, although I was sent away to school when I was six.'

'Where did you go when you were fifteen?'

'Here and there.'

I was beginning to learn that direct questions were not a good method of eliciting information from Adam.

We went into a room that he said had been his mother's. Her

portrait hung on the wall and – a weird touch, this – a pair of silk gloves was folded by the side of the dried flowers.

'Did your father love her very much?' I said to Adam.

He looked at me a bit strangely. 'No, I don't think so. Look, there he is.' I joined him at the window. A very old man was walking up the garden towards the house. There was a frost of snow on his white hair, and his shoulders were touched with snow too. He wore no overcoat. He looked so thin as to be almost transparent, but was quite upright. He carried a stick, but seemed to be using it to swipe at squirrels, which were corkscrewing up the old beech trees.

'How old is your father, Adam?' I asked.

'About eighty. I was an afterthought. My youngest sister was sixteen when I was born.'

Adam's father – Colonel Tallis, as he told me to call him – seemed alarmingly ancient to me. His skin was pale and papery. There were liver spots on both hands. His eyes, startling blue like Adam's, were cloudy. His trousers hung slackly on his skeletal frame. He seemed quite unsurprised to see us.

'This is Alice,' said Adam. 'I am going to marry her next Friday.'

'Good afternoon, Alice,' he said. 'A blonde, eh? So you're going to marry my son.' His look seemed almost spiteful. Then he turned back to Adam. 'Pour me some whisky, then.'

Adam left the room. I wasn't quite sure what to say to the old man and he seemed to have no interest in talking to me.

'I killed three squirrels yesterday,' he announced abruptly, after a silence. 'With traps, you know.'

'Oh.'

'Yes, vermin. But they still come back for more. Like the rabbits. I shot six.'

Adam came into the room with three tumblers full of amber-coloured whisky. He gave one to his father and handed another to me. 'Drink up and then we'll go home,' he said.

I drank. I didn't know what time it was, except that outside it was already getting dark. I didn't know what we were doing here, and I would have said that I wished we hadn't come, except that I had a new and vivid image of Adam as a boy: lonely, dwarfed by two aged parents, losing his mother when he was twelve, living in a large cold house. What kind of life must he have had, growing up alone with this stand-in for a father? The whisky burned my throat and warmed my chest. I had eaten nothing all day, and was obviously not going to get anything here. I realized I hadn't even taken off my coat. Well, there wasn't much point now.

Colonel Tallis also drank his whisky, sitting on the sofa and saying nothing. Suddenly his head tipped back, his mouth parted slightly, and a crackly snore came from him. I took the empty tumbler out of his hand and put it on the table beside him.

'Come here,' said Adam. 'Come with me.'

We went back up the stairs and into a bedroom. Adam's old room. He shut the door and pushed me on to the narrow bed. My head swam. 'You're my home,' he said harshly. 'Do you understand? My only home. Don't move. Don't move an inch.'

When we came downstairs again, the Colonel half woke.

'Going already?' he said. 'Do come again.'

'Do have a second helping of shepherd's pie, Adam.'

'No, thank you.'

'Or salad. Please have some more salad. I've made too much, I know. It's always so hard to get quantities right, isn't it? But that's why the freezer is so useful.'

'No thank you, no more salad.'

My mother was pink and garrulous with nerves. My father, taciturn at the best of times, had said almost nothing. He sat at the head of the table and plodded through the lunch.

'Wine?'

'No wine, thank you.'

'Alice used to love my shepherd's pie when she was little, didn't you, Alice dear?' She was desperate. I smiled at her but couldn't think of anything to say, for, unlike her, I become tongue-tied when nervous.

'Did she?' Unexpectedly, Adam's face lit up. 'What else did she love?'

'Meringues.' My mother's face sagged with the relief of finding a topic of conversation. 'And the crackling on pork. And my blackberry and apple pie. Banana cake. She was always such a slim little thing, you wouldn't believe how much she could eat.'

'Yes, I could.'

Adam put his hand on my knee. I felt myself flushing. My father coughed portentously and opened his mouth to speak. Adam's hand pushed under the hem of my skirt and stroked my upper thigh.

'It seems a bit sudden,' announced my father.

'Yes,' agreed my mother hurriedly. 'We are very pleased, of course we are very pleased, and I am sure that Alice will be very happy, and it's her life anyway, to do what she wants with, but we thought, why rush? If you're sure of each other, why not wait, and then . . .'

Adam's hand moved higher. He put one sure thumb on my crotch. I sat quite still, with my hammering heart and throbbing body.

'We are marrying on Friday,' he said. 'It's sudden because love is sudden.' He smiled rather gently at my mother. 'I know it's hard to get used to.'

'And you don't want us to be there?' she warbled.

'It's not that we don't want you, Mum, but . . .'

'Two witnesses from the street,' he said coolly. 'Two strangers, so it will really be just me and Alice. That's what we want.' He turned his full gaze on me and I felt as if he were undressing me in front of my parents. 'Isn't it?'

'Yes,' I said softly. 'Yes, it is, Mum.'

In my old bedroom, museum of my childhood, he picked up each object as if it was a clue. My swimming certificates. My old teddy bear, with one ear missing now. My stack of old, cracked LPs. My tennis racket, still standing in the corner of the room by the wicker wastepaper basket I had woven at school. My collection of shells. My porcelain lady, present from my grand-mother when I was about six. A jewellery box with pink silk lining, containing just one bead necklace. He put his face into the fold of my old towelling dressing-gown, which still hung on the door. He unrolled a school photograph, 1977, and quickly located my face, smiling uncertainly from the second row. He found the picture of me and my brother, aged fifteen and fourteen, and scrutinized it, frowning, turning from me back to the picture. He touched everything, running his fingers over every surface. He ran his fingers over my face, exploring every flaw and blemish there.

We walked along the river, over the icy mud, our hands touch-ing lightly, electric currents running up my spine, wind in my face. We stopped of one accord and stared at the slow, brown water, full of glinting bubbles and bits of debris and sudden, sucking eddies.

'You're mine now,' he said. 'My own love.'

'Yes,' I said. 'Yes. I'm yours.'

When we got back to the flat, late and sleepy on Sunday night, I felt something under my feet on the mat when I went through the door. It was a brown envelope with no name or address on it. Just 'Flat 3'. Our flat. I opened it and pulled out a single sheet of paper. The message was written in large black felt-tip:

I KNOW WHERE YOU LIVE.

I handed it to Adam. He looked at it and pulled a face.

'Bored with using the phone,' I said.

I'd got used to the silent calls, day and night. This seemed different. 'Somebody came to our door,' I said. 'Pushed it through our door.'

Adam seemed unmoved. 'Estate agents do the same thing, don't they?'

117

'Shouldn't we call the police? It is simply ridiculous just to let this go on and on and do nothing.'

'And tell them what? That somebody knows where we live?'

'It's for you, I suppose.'

Adam looked serious. 'I hope so.'

Fifteen

I took the week off work. 'To prepare for the wedding,' I said
vaguely to Mike, although there was nothing really to prepare.
We were going to be married in the morning, in a town hall that
looked like the presidential palace of a Stalinist dictator. I would
wear the velvet dress Adam had bought me ('and nothing underneath,' he'd instructed me), and we would haul two strangers off
the street to witness the ceremony. In the afternoon we were
driving up to the Lake District. He had somewhere to take me
he said. Then we would come home, and I would go back to
work. Perhaps.

'You deserve time off,' said Mike enthusiastically. 'You've
been working too hard recently.'

I looked at him in surprise. Actually, I had hardly been
working at all.

'Yes,' I lied. 'I need a rest.'

There were a few things I needed to do before Friday. The
first I had been putting off for a long time.

Jake had arranged to be there when I turned up on Tuesday
morning with a rented van to collect the rest of my things. I
didn't particularly want them, but I didn't want to have them in
our old flat either, as if one day I might return to that life, step
back into those clothes.

He made me a cup of coffee, but stayed in the kitchen,
bent ostentatiously over a folder of work, which I'm sure he
hardly looked at. He had shaved that morning, and put on a
blue shirt, which I had bought him. I looked away, tried not to

see his tired, clever, familiar face. How could I have thought he had made those phone calls or sent those anonymous notes? All my Gothic thoughts died down, and I just felt dreary and a bit sad.

I was as businesslike as possible. I stashed clothes into plastic bags, wrapped china in newspaper and put it into the cardboard boxes I had brought along, pulled books off the shelves and then closed the gaps that marked where they had been. I loaded the chair I'd had as a student into the van, my old sleeping bag, some CDs.

'I'll leave my plants, shall I?' I asked Jake.

'If you'd prefer.'

'Yes. And if there's anything I've overlooked . . .'

'I know where you live,' he said.

There was a silence. I swallowed the tepid remains of my coffee, then said, 'Jake, I'm very sorry. There's nothing I can say except sorry.'

He looked at me steadily, then smiled, a thin smile. 'I will be fine, Alice,' he said then. 'I haven't been, but I will be. Will you be fine?' He put his face closer to mine, until I could no longer focus on it. 'Will you?'

'I don't know,' I said, drawing back. 'There's nothing else I can do.'

I had thought of driving to my parents' house and leaving all the stuff I didn't need there, but just as I didn't want things to be waiting for me at Jake's so I didn't want them to be waiting for me anywhere at all. I was beginning again, fresh. I had a giddy sense of burning off my past. I stopped at the first Oxfam shop I saw and gave the astonished assistant everything: books, clothes, china, CDs and even my chair.

I had also arranged to see Clive. He had rung me at work, insistent we get together before I got married. On Wednesday we met for lunch at a dark little tavern in Clerkenwell. We kissed each other awkwardly on both cheeks, like amiable strangers, and then sat at a small table by a fire and ordered artichoke soup with hunks of brown bread, and two glasses of house red.

'How's Gail?' I asked.

'Oh, probably all right. I haven't seen her that much recently, actually.'

'Do you mean it's over?'

He grinned ruefully at me, a flash of the Clive I knew so well and had never stopped feeling uneasy about. 'Yeah, probably. God, you know how hopeless I am with relationships, Alice. I fall in love, then as soon as it gets serious I panic.'

'Poor Gail.'

'I didn't come to talk about that.' He poked his spoon moodily into the thick, greenish soup.

'You wanted to talk to me about Adam, right?'

'Right.' He drank some wine, stirred his soup again, then said, 'Now that I'm here, I don't know how to say it. This isn't about Jake, okay? It's . . . well, I met Adam remember, and, sure, he made every other man in the room look feeble. But are you sure you know what you're doing, Alice?'

'No, but that doesn't matter.'

'What does that mean?'

'Literally, it doesn't matter.' I found that for the first time since meeting Adam I wanted to talk about how I felt. 'Look, Clive, I just fell utterly in love with him. Have you ever been desired so much that –'

'No.'

'It was like an earthquake.'

'You used to make fun of me for saying things like that. You used words like "trust" and "responsibility". You used to say' – he pointed his spoon at me – 'that only *men* said things like "it just happened" *or* "it was like an earthquake".'

'What do you want me to say?'

Clive looked at me with a clinical interest. 'How did you meet?' he asked.

'We saw each other on a street.'

121

'And that was that?'

'Yes.'

'You just saw each other and leaped into bed?'

'Yes.'

'It's just lust, Alice. You can't throw away your whole life for lust.'

'Fuck off, Clive.' He seemed to accept that as a reasonable answer. So I continued, 'He's everything. I'd do anything for him. It's like a spell.'

'And you call yourself a scientist.'

'I *am* a scientist.'

'Why do you look as if you're about to cry?'

I smiled. 'I'm happy.'

'You're not happy,' he said. 'You're unbalanced.'

And I had arranged to meet Lily, although I didn't know why. A note had been left for me at the office, addressed only to 'Alice'. Perhaps she didn't know my full name.

'I need to talk to you about the man you stole from me,' it read, which should have made me throw it away at once. 'It is urgent and must remain secret. Do not tell him.' She had given a phone number.

I thought of the note that had been pushed through our door. The paper was different, the writing was small and neat, like a schoolgirl's. Completely different, but what did that mean? Anyone could disguise their handwriting. I realized that I wanted it to be Lily, and not Jake. I should have shown it at once to Adam, but I didn't. I persuaded myself that he already had too much to worry about. Klaus's book was coming out soon. Already two journalists had rung Adam, wanting to interview him 'about being a hero', and asking questions about Greg and his moral responsibility for the death of the amateur climbers whom he had led up the mountain and left to die. He was contemptuous of the word 'hero', and simply refused to comment on Greg's behaviour. But I often heard him and Klaus talking about it.

Klaus kept going on about the fixed line, and how he didn't want to be judgemental, but how could Greg have been so careless? Adam repeated, over and over, that above eight thousand metres people cannot be held responsible for their acts.

'There, but for the grace of God, go all of us,' he said.

'But you didn't,' I interjected, so that the two men turned to me, benign and patronizing.

'That was my luck,' he replied, very soberly. 'And Greg's bad luck.'

I didn't believe him. And I still thought something had happened up in the mountains that he wasn't disclosing to me. I would watch him at night, sometimes, as he lay asleep, one arm on my thigh and one flung above his head, his mouth slightly open and puffing with each exhaled breath. What dreams sucked him under to where I could not follow?

Anyway, I decided to meet Lily without telling Adam. Maybe I just wanted to see what she was like; maybe I wanted to compare myself to her, or to get a glimpse into Adam's past. I phoned her, and she told me, talking quickly in a low hoarse voice, to meet her at her flat in Shepherd's Bush on Thursday morning. The day before the wedding.

She was beautiful. Of course she was beautiful. She had silvery hair, which looked natural and a bit greasy, and the tall leggy look of a model. Her grey eyes were huge and wide apart in her pale triangle of a face. She wore a faded pair of jeans and, in spite of the inclement weather, a tiny grubby T-shirt that showed her perfect midriff. Her feet were bare and slender.

I gazed at her and wished I hadn't come. We didn't shake hands or anything. She led me down into her basement flat, and when she opened the door I recoiled in horror. The tiny, muggy flat was a tip. Clothes were flung everywhere: bowls were heaped up in the sink or stood in dirty piles on the kitchen table; a stinking cat-litter tray stood in the middle of the floor. There were magazines, or bits of magazines, strewn about. The large bed, which was in the corner of the living room, was a mess of stained sheets and old newspapers. There was a plate with half a piece of toast on the pillow, and a half-empty bottle of whisky nearby. On the wall – and this nearly made me flee – there was a huge black-and-white photograph of Adam, very serious. And as soon as I saw that, I started to notice other signs of Adam. Several photographs, which had obviously been ripped out of books about climbing, were propped up on the mantelpiece, and he was in each of them. A yellowing newspaper article was Blu-tacked to the wall with Adam's picture gazing out of it. By the bed was a picture of Lily and Adam together. He had his arm around her and she was gazing up at him, rapt. I closed my eyes briefly and wished there was somewhere to sit down.

'I haven't cleaned for a bit,' said Lily.

'No.'

We both stayed standing.

'That was our bed,' she said.

'Yes,' I said, looking at it. I wanted to vomit.

'I haven't changed the sheets since he left. I can still smell him.'

'Look,' I said, with an effort, for I felt that I had walked into a terrible dream, and was trapped in it, 'you said you had something urgent to tell me.'

'You stole him from me,' she continued, as if I hadn't spoken. 'He was mine and you came along and stole him from under my nose.'

'No,' I said. 'No. He chose me. We chose each other. I'm sorry, Lily. I didn't know about you, but anyway . . .'

'You just smashed up my life without thinking of me,' she looked around her disastrous flat. 'You didn't care about me.' Her voice sank. 'Now what?' she said, in a kind of listless horror. 'Now what am I supposed to do?'

'Listen, I think I ought to just go,' I said. 'This doesn't help either of us.'

'Look,' she said, and took off her T-shirt. She stood there, pale and slim. Her breasts were small, with large brownish nipples. I couldn't make myself look away. Then she turned around. Livid weals striped her back. 'He did that,' she said triumphantly. 'Now what do you say?'

'I've got to go,' I said, rooted to the spot.

'To show how much he loved me. He branded me his. Has he done that to you? No? But he's done it to me because I belong to him. He can't just throw me off.'

I walked to the door.

'That's not all,' she said.

'We are marrying tomorrow.' I opened the door.

'That's not all that he . . .'

A thought occurred to me. 'Do you know where he lives?'

She looked puzzled. 'What do you mean?'

'Goodbye.'

I shut the door on her and ran back up the steps to the pavement. Even the exhaust fumes smelt clean after Lily's flat.

We had a bath together, and washed each other meticulously. I shampooed his hair and he mine. Warm lather floated on the surface of the water and the air was steamy and fragrant. I shaved his face very carefully. He combed out my hair, holding it with one hand while he teased out little knots so as not to hurt me.

We dried each other. The mirror had fogged over, but he told me I did not need to look at my reflection this morning, except in his eyes. He wouldn't let me put on any makeup. I put my dress on over my naked body and slipped on shoes. He pulled on a pair of jeans and a long-sleeved black T-shirt.

'Ready?' he asked.

'Ready,' I said.

'You're my wife now.'

'Yes.'

'Is this all right? Don't flinch.'

'Yes.'

'And this?'

'No – yes. Yes.'
'Do you love me?'
'Yes.'
'Always?'
'Always.'
'Tell me if you want me to stop.'
'Yes. Do you love me?'
'Yes. Always.'
'God, Adam, I'd die for you.'

Sixteen

'How much further?' I tried to keep my voice steady, but it came out in a raggedy gasp, and the effort of speaking hurt my chest.

'Only about eight miles,' said Adam, turning back towards me. 'If you could manage to walk a bit faster we should get there before it begins to get dark.' He looked down at me dispassionately, then unslung his backpack, in which he was carrying all my stuff as well as his, and took out a flask. 'Have a cup of tea and some chocolate,' he said.

'Thanks. Some honeymoon, *darling*. I wanted a four-poster bed and champagne.' I took the plastic cup of tea in my mittened hands. 'Have we done most of the steep bit?'

'Honey, this is a stroll. We're going up there.'

I twisted my neck back to see where he was pointing. The wind bit into my face; my chin felt raw. 'No,' I said. 'You might be. I'm not.'

'Are you tired?'

'Tired? Oh, no, not at all, I'm fit from all my walks to the underground station. I've got blisters under my new boots. My calves are burning. I've got this stitch in my side that feels like a knife jabbing at me. My nose is freezing cold. My fingers have gone numb. And I'm scared of fucking heights. I'm staying right here.' I sat down in the thin covering of snow and pushed two squares of cold, hard chocolate into my mouth.

'Here?' Adam looked around us, at the lonely moorland rimmed with jagged hills. In the summer, apparently, quite a few walkers came this way – but not on this Saturday in late February, when all the grass was iced into spiky tufts, the few bare trees stooped against the wind, and our breath curled into the grey air.

'All right. I'm not staying here, I'm just making a fuss.'

He sat down beside me and started to laugh. I think it was the first time I had heard him laugh properly. 'I've married a wimp,' he said, as if it were the funniest thing in the world. 'I spend my life climbing mountains, and I've married a woman who can't climb a gentle slope without getting a stitch.'

'Yeah, and I've married a man who drags me into the wilderness and then laughs when I'm in difficulty and feeling embarrassed.' I scowled at him.

Adam stood up and pulled me to my feet. He adjusted my mittens so there wasn't a band of naked wrist between them and the sleeves of my jacket. He took a scarf out of the backpack and wrapped it around my neck. He tied my laces more tightly, so that my boots were not so loose on my feet. 'Now,' he said, 'try and get into a rhythm. Don't hurry yourself. Not that you have been. Just get into a stride and then keep going. Let your breathing come evenly. Don't look ahead where we're going, just one foot in front of the other until it feels like a meditation. Ready?'

'Yes, Captain.'

We walked in single file along the track, which gradually became steeper until we were almost scrambling up it. Adam looked as if he were loitering, yet he drew ahead of me in seconds. I didn't attempt to catch up with him, but tried to follow his instructions. Left, right; left, right. My nose was runny and my eyes were rheumy. My legs ached and felt like lead. I set myself some mental arithmetic. I tried to sing to myself an old song about the chemical elements that I had performed in a show at college. 'There's antimony, arsenic, aluminium, selenium . . .' What came next? I didn't have the breath for it anyway. Occasionally I stumbled over small rocks in the pathway, or snagged myself on thick brambles. It never quite got to feel like a meditation, but I kept going, and soon the stitch dulled to a mild ache and my hands warmed up, and the clean air felt fresh rather than harsh when I breathed in.

At the top of one rise, Adam made me stop and look around.

'It's as if we were all alone in the world,' I said.

'That's the point.'

It was getting dark when we saw the cabin just below.

'Who uses it?' I asked, as we made our way down to it, shapes of huge boulders and stunted trees looming out of the dusk.

'It's a climbers' and hikers' hut. It belongs to the British Alpine Club. Members can stay. I've got the key here.' And he patted the side pocket of his jacket.

It was freezing inside, and without obvious comforts. Adam lit a large gas lamp hanging from one of the beams, and I stared at the narrow wooden ledges round the room that were meant to be beds, at the empty fireplace, the small basin with a single cold tap over it.

'This is it?'

'Yep.'

'Where's the toilet?'

'There.' He pointed back out through the door, to the snowy spaces outside.

'Oh.' I sat on a hard bed. 'Comfy.'

'Wait a minute.'

There were several large boxes of logs and sticks in the corner. He pulled one of these towards the fireplace and started to break the smaller twigs into pieces, arranging them into a neat dome around a few crumpled balls of newspaper. Then he piled some larger logs on top. He struck a match and lit the paper and flames began to lick at the wood. At first the fire was bright but heatless, but soon it was giving out enough warmth to make me consider taking off my jacket and mittens. The cabin was small and well insulated: in half an hour or so it would be warm.

Adam unstrapped the small gas stove from the base of his rucksack, unfolded it, and lit it. He filled a battered copper kettle from the tap and set it on the heat. He shook out the two sleeping bags and unzipped them so that they were like duvets and laid them in front of the fire.

'Come and sit down,' he said. I took off my jacket and joined him by the flames. He pulled a bottle of whisky from the bottom of the backpack, then a long salami and one of those whizzy penknives that are also screwdrivers, bottle-openers and compasses. I watched him as he cut thick slices of salami and laid them on the greased paper. He screwed open the whisky bottle and passed it to me.

'Supper,' he said.

I took a gulp of whisky and then a couple of chunks of salami. It was about seven o'clock and utterly silent. I had never in my life been in silence like this, so thick and complete. Outside the uncurtained window it was inky black, save for the pinpricks of stars. I needed to pee. I stood up and went to the door. When I opened it, the freezing air hit me like a blast. I closed it behind me and walked out into the night. I had a shivery feeling that we were quite, quite alone – and that we would always be alone now. I heard Adam come out of the cabin and close the door behind him. I felt his arms wrap around me from behind, hugging me into his solid warmth.

'You'll get cold again,' he said.

'I don't know if I like this.'

'Come inside, my dear love.'

We drank more whisky and watched the shapes in the flames. Adam threw on more logs. It was quite hot now, and there was a lovely resiny smell in the small room. We didn't talk or touch each other for a long time. When at last he put his hand on my arm, my skin jumped. We got undressed separately, watching each other. We sat cross-legged and naked opposite each other and looked into the other's face. I felt oddly shy, self-conscious. He lifted my hand, with its new band of gold on the third finger, brought it to his mouth and kissed it.

'Do you trust me?' he said.

'Yes.' Or: no no no no.

He handed me the bottle of whisky and I took a swig, feeling it burn as it went down.

'I want to do something to you that no one has ever done before.'

I didn't reply. I felt as if I were in some kind of dream. Some kind of nightmare. We kissed, but very gently. He ran his fingers over my breasts and trailed them down on to my stomach. I tracked his vertebrae down his spine. We held each other very carefully. One side of my body was too hot from the fire, the other chilly. He told me to lie on my back and I did. Maybe I had drunk too much whisky and eaten too little salami. I felt as if I were suspended above an abyss, somewhere in the cold, cold darkness. I closed my eyes but he turned my face towards him and said, 'Look at me.'

Shadows fell across his face; I could only make out parts of his body. It started out so tender, and only gradually became so savage; notch by notch to pain. I remembered Lily and her ridged back. In my mind, I saw Adam up in his high mountains, among all that fear and death. How was it that I was here, in this terrible silence? Why was I letting him do this to me and who had I become that I would let him? I shut my eyes again and this time he didn't tell me to open them. He put his hands around my neck and said, 'Don't move now, don't worry.' Then he began to squeeze. I wanted to tell him to stop but somehow I didn't, couldn't. I lay on the sleeping bags by the fire, in the dark, and he pressed down. I kept my eyes closed and my hands still: my wedding present to him, my trust. The flames danced on my closed lids, and my body writhed under his, as if I had no control over it. I felt the blood roaring round my body; my heart hammering; my head thundering. This was neither pleasure nor pain any longer. I was somewhere else, in some other world where all boundaries had disintegrated. Oh, Christ. He must stop now. He must stop. Darkness rolled in behind the bright lines of pure sensation.

'It's all right, Alice.' He was calling me back. His thumbs eased off my windpipe. He bent forward and kissed my neck. I opened my eyes. I felt sick and tired and sad and defeated. He pulled me upright and held me to him. My nausea ebbed away, but my throat ached badly and I wanted to cry. I wanted to go home. He picked up the whisky bottle, took a swig, then held it to my mouth and tipped it down my throat as if I were a baby. I sank down on the sleeping bags, he covered me over and I lay there for a while gazing into the flames, while he sat there beside me, stroking my hair. I slipped very slowly towards sleep, while Adam fed the dying fire beside me.

At some point in the night I woke, and he was lying by me, full of heat and strength. Someone to depend on. The fire had gone out, though the embers still glowed. My left hand was cold where it had slipped from under the sleeping bag.

Seventeen

'No,' said Adam, and brought his fist heavily down on the table, making the glasses on it jump. Everyone in the pub looked round. Adam didn't seem to notice; he lacked all sense of what my mother would call social decorum. 'I don't want to give an interview to any crappy journalist.'

'Look, Adam,' began Klaus soothingly, 'I know that you –'

'I don't want to talk about what happened up on the mountain. It's past, over, finished. I'm not interested in going over the whole messy fuck-up, not even to help you sell your book.' He turned to me. 'Tell him.'

I shrugged at Klaus. 'He doesn't want to, Klaus.'

Adam took my hand and pressed it against his face and closed his eyes.

'If you gave just one, then –'

'He doesn't want to, Klaus,' I repeated. 'Can't you hear the man?'

'OK, OK.' He put his hands in the air in mock surrender. 'Anyway, I've got a wedding present for you two.' He leaned down and took a bottle of champagne out of a canvas bag at his feet. 'I, um, wish you luck and great happiness. Drink this in bed sometime.'

I kissed his cheek. Adam gave a half-laugh and sat back in his chair.

'All right, you win, one interview.' He stood up and held out his hand for me.

'Are you going already? Daniel said he might turn up later.'

133

'We're going to drink the champagne in bed,' I said. 'It can't wait.'

When I got back from work the next day, the journalist was there. She was sitting opposite Adam, their knees almost touching, and on the table beside her a tape-recorder was running. She had a notebook on her lap, but she wasn't writing anything. Instead, she was gazing intently at Adam, nodding when he spoke.

'Ignore me,' I said, when she made to stand up. 'I'm going to make myself a cup of tea then disappear. Do you want anything to drink?' I took off my coat and gloves.

'Whisky,' said Adam. 'This is Joanna, from the *Participant*. And this is Alice.' He took my wrist and pulled me towards him. 'My wife.'

'Pleased to meet you, Alice,' said Joanna. 'None of the cuttings said you were married.'

Shrewd eyes, behind heavy frames, peered at me.

'None of the cuttings knew,' said Adam.

'Do you climb too?' asked Joanna.

I laughed. 'Not at all, not even stairs when there's a lift available.'

'It must be strange for you, waiting behind,' she went on. 'Worrying about him.'

'I haven't done the waiting yet,' I said vaguely, moving off to put the kettle on. 'And I have my own life,' I added, wondering if that was a lie now.

I thought again about our honeymoon weekend in the Lake District. What had happened between us in that cabin – the violence he had done to me, with my permission – bothered me still. I tried not to think of it too much; it had become a dark zone in my mind. I had put myself into his hands and for a few moments, as I lay beneath him, I had thought he would kill me and I had still not struggled against him. Part of me was aghast at that, and part of me stirred.

As I stood by the kettle, half listening to the interview, I noticed a scrumpled-up sheet of paper with heavy black writing on it. I

134

opened it up, knowing in advance what to expect. 'I WON'T LET YOU REST,' it said. They made my skin crawl, these letters. I didn't know why we hadn't gone to the police long ago. It was as if we had let ourselves become accustomed to them, so that their threats were like stormclouds in our life, which we simply took for granted. I looked up and saw that Adam was watching me, so I gave him a grin, tore the paper up into small shreds and dropped them disdainfully into the bin. He gave me a small nod of approval and turned his attention back to Joanna.

'You were telling me about the last few hours.' Joanna turned back to Adam. 'Did you have any intimations of disaster?'

'If you mean, did I think all those people would die up there, no, of course not.'

'So when did you realize it was all going wrong?'

'When it all went wrong. Can I have that whisky, Alice?'

Joanna looked down at her notebook and tried another tack. 'What about the fixed ropes?' she asked. 'From what I understand, Greg McLaughlin and other expedition leaders fixed the different-coloured ropes that led up the ridge to the summit. But at some point the last bit of rope became untied, which might have made all the difference to the climbers.'

Adam stared at her. I brought him over a large shot of whisky. 'Do you want some, Joanna?' I said. She shook her head and went on waiting for Adam's response. I poured myself a slug and downed it.

'How do you think it happened?'

'How the fuck do I know?' he said eventually. 'It was freezing cold. There was a storm. Everyone was out of it. Nothing functioned any more, nobody. I don't know what happened to the rope, nor does anyone else. Now, you want blame, don't you?' He slurped some whisky back. 'You want to write a nice, neat story saying so-and-so led a group of people to their death. Well, lady, it ain't like that up in the death zone. No one's a hero and no one's a villain. We're all just people stuck up a mountain with our brain cells cascading away.'

135

'The book implies that you were a hero,' said Joanna, quite unperturbed by his outburst. Adam said nothing. 'And,' she went on, carefully, 'it also half implies that the leader of the expedition must bear some responsibility. Greg.'

'Can you get me another, Alice?' Adam held out his glass. When I took it from him I bent down and kissed him. I wondered at what point I should tell Joanna to go.

'I gather that Greg is now in a bad condition. Is that guilt, do you think?'

Once again, Adam said nothing. He closed his eyes briefly, and tipped his head back. He looked very weary.

She tried again. 'Do you think the trip was an unnecessary risk?'

'Obviously. People died.'

'Do you regret the way that the mountains have been commercialized?'

'Yes.'

'Yet you are part of that.'

'Yes.'

'One of the people who died,' Joanna said, 'was very close to you. An ex-girlfriend, I think.'

He nodded.

'Were you badly affected by not being able to save her?'

I took the second whisky over and Adam put his arm around my waist as I leaned towards him.

'Don't go,' he said, as if he was talking about our whole relationship. I sat on the arm of his chair, and rested my hand on his tangled hair. He stared assessingly at Joanna for a moment. 'What the fuck do you think?' he answered at last. He stood up. 'I think that's enough, don't you?'

Joanna didn't move, except to check that the spools of the tape-recorder were still turning.

'Have you got over it?' she asked. I leaned over and turned off her tape-recorder and she looked up at me. Our eyes met and she nodded at me, approvingly, I thought.

136

'*Got over*.' His tone was withering. Then he said, in an altogether different tone, 'Shall I tell you my secret, Joanna?'

'I'd be delighted.'

I'd bet she would.

'I've got Alice,' he said. 'Alice will save me.' And he gave a rather cracked laugh.

Now Joanna did stand up.

'One last question,' she said, as she put on her coat. 'Will you go on climbing?'

'Yes.'

'Why?'

'Because I'm a climber. That's who I am.' His voice was slightly blurred with the whisky. 'I love Alice and I climb mountains.' He leaned against me. 'That is where I find grace.'

'I'm pregnant,' said Pauline. We were walking in St James's Park, arm in arm but awkward together still. It had been her idea to meet, and I had been half unwilling. All my old life seemed far off, almost unreal, as if it had happened to someone different. In that life, I had loved Pauline and depended on her; in this life, I had no room for such an intense friendship. I realized, walking to meet Pauline on that frosty Saturday afternoon in March, that I had put our friendship by for a rainy day. I assumed that I would be able to return to it, but not just yet. We had walked through the park together until it started to get dark, gingerly feeling our way round subjects where once we had been able to say more or less anything to each other. 'How's Jake?' I had asked, and she, wincing slightly, had said he was all right.

'How's your new life?' she'd said, not really wanting to know, and I hadn't really told her.

Now I stopped and took her thin shoulders. 'That is wonderful news,' I said. 'How pregnant?'

'Eight or nine weeks. Enough to feel sick most of the time.'

'I'm very happy for you, Pauline,' I said. 'Thanks for telling me.'

137

'Of course I told you,' she replied formally. 'You're my friend.'

We came to the road. 'I go this way,' I said. 'I'm meeting Adam just up there.'

We kissed each other on both cheeks, relieved, and I turned away, into the unlit street. As I did so a tall young man stepped in front of me and, before I had time to register much except his dead white face and his garish mop of ginger hair, yanked my bag off my shoulder.

'Oi!' I yelled, and lunged at him as he ducked away from me. I got hold of the bag, although there was almost nothing in it of any value, and pulled it from him. He whipped round to face me. There was a spider-web tattoo on his left cheek, and a line round his throat read 'CUT HERE'. I kicked at his shin but missed, so I kicked again. There, that must have hurt.

'Leggo, you cunt,' he snarled at me. The straps of my bag cut into my fingers then slipped from me. 'You stupid fucking cunt.' He lifted his hand and struck me across the face, and I staggered and put a hand up to my cheek. Blood was running down my neck. His mouth was open and I saw that his tongue was fat and purple. He lifted his hand again. Oh, God, he was a madman. I remember thinking that he must be the man who was sending us those notes; our stalker. Then I closed my eyes: better get it over with. No blow came.

I opened them again and saw, as if in a dream, that he had a knife in his hand. It was not pointed towards me, but at Adam. Then I saw Adam slamming his fist into the man's face. He cried out in pain, and dropped the knife. Adam hit him again, a cracking blow into his neck. Then into his stomach. The tattooed man was buckled over; blood was streaming down from his left eye. I saw Adam's face: it was stony, quite without expression. He hit the man again and stepped back to let him fall to the ground, where he lay at my feet, whimpering and holding on to his stomach.

'Stop!' I gasped. A small crowd had gathered. Pauline was there; her mouth was an O of horror.

Adam kicked him in the stomach.

'Adam.' I grabbed hold of his arm and clung on. 'For Chrissakes, stop, will you? That's *enough*.'

Adam looked down at the body writhing on the pavement. 'Alice wants me to stop,' he said. 'So that's why I am stopping. Otherwise I'd murder you for daring to *touch* her.' He picked up my bag from the ground, and then turned to me and took my face in both his hands. 'You're bleeding,' he said. He licked some of the blood away. 'Darling Alice, he made you bleed.'

I saw dimly that people were gathering, talking, asking each other what had happened. Adam held me. 'Does it hurt much? Are you all right? Look at your beautiful face.'

'Yes. Yes, I don't know. I think so. Is he all right? What's he . . . ?'

I looked at the man on the ground. He was moving, but not much. Adam paid no attention. He took a handkerchief out of his pocket, licked it and started to wipe the cut on my cheek. A siren wailed close by us and over Adam's shoulder I could see a police car followed by an ambulance.

'Nice one, mate.' A hefty man in a long overcoat came up and held out his hand to grip Adam's. 'Put it there.' I looked at them, appalled, as they shook hands. This was a nightmare, a farce.

'Alice, are you all right?' It was Pauline.

'I'm all right.'

Policemen were here now. There was a car. It was an official incident, which somehow made it seem manageable. They leaned over the man and pulled him to his feet. He was led away out of my sight.

Adam took off his jacket and draped it over my shoulders. He smoothed back my hair.

'I'm going to get us a cab,' he said. 'The police can wait. Don't move.' He turned to Pauline. 'Look after her,' he said, and sprinted off.

'He could have killed him,' I said to Pauline.

She looked at me oddly. 'He really adores you, doesn't he?' she said.

'But if he had . . .'

'He saved you, Alice.'

The next day the journalist, Joanna, rang up again. She had read about the fight in the evening paper and it was going to make all the difference to her interview, all the difference. She just wanted both of us to comment about it.

'Piss off,' said Adam mildly, and handed me the phone.

'How does it feel,' she asked me, 'to be married to a man like Adam?'

'What kind of man is that?'

'A hero,' she said.

'Great,' I said, but I wasn't exactly sure how it felt.

We lay opposite each other in the half-dark. My cheek stung. My heart was hammering. Would I never get used to him?

'Why are you scared?'

'Please touch me.'

The orange street lamps were shining in through the bedroom window's thin curtains. I could see his face, his beautiful face. I wanted him to hold me so hard and so close that I would disappear into him.

'Tell me first why you are scared.'

'Scared of losing you. There, put your hand there.'

'Turn over, like that. Everything will be fine. I will never leave you and you will never leave me. Don't close your eyes. Look.'

Later, we were hungry, for we hadn't eaten that evening. I slid out of the high bed on to the cold floorboards, and put on Adam's shirt. In the fridge I found some Parma ham, some ancient button mushrooms and a small wedge of hard cheese. I fed Sherpa, who was twisting his small body round my bare legs, and then I made us a giant sandwich with some slightly stale, thin Italian bread. There was a bottle of red wine in our inadequate box of groceries by the door, which I opened. We ate in bed, propped up on pillows and scattering crumbs.

'The thing is,' I said, between bites, 'I'm not used to people behaving like that.'

'Like what?'

'Beating someone up for me.'

'He was hitting you.'

'I thought you were going to kill him.'

He poured me another glass of wine. 'I was angry.'

'You don't say. He had a knife, Adam, didn't you consider that?'

'No.' He frowned. 'Would you prefer me to be the kind of person who asked him politely to stop? Or ran to get the police?'

'No. Yes. I don't know.'

I sighed and settled back against the pillows, drowsy with sex and wine. 'Will you tell me something?'

'Maybe.'

'Did something happen in the mountains . . . ? I mean, are you protecting someone?'

Adam didn't seem startled by my question, or cross about it. He didn't even look round. 'Of course I am,' he said.

'Will you ever tell me about it?'

'Nobody needs to know,' he said.

Eighteen

A few days later I went down to get the post and found another brown envelope. It had no stamp but on it was written: TO MRS ADAM TALLIS.

I opened it immediately, down there in the common passage, feeling the doormat prickle the soles of my feet. The paper was the same, the writing was the same, though a bit smaller because the message was longer:

CONGRATULATIONS ON YOUR WEDDING MRS TALLIS.
WATCH YOUR BACK
P.S. WHY DON'T YOU MAKE YOUR HUSBAND
SOME TEA IN BED?

I took the note up to Adam and put it on the bed by his face. He read it with a sombre expression.

'Our correspondent doesn't know that I've kept my own name,' I said, with an attempt at a light tone.

'Knows I'm in bed, though,' said Adam.

'What does that mean? Tea?'

I went to the kitchen and opened the cupboard. There were only two packets of tea-bags, Kenyan for Adam, poncy Lapsang Souchong for me. I tipped them out on to the counter. They looked normal enough. I noticed that Adam was behind me.

'Why should I make you tea in bed, Adam? Could it be something about the bed? Or the sugar?'

Adam opened the fridge. There were two milk bottles in the door, one half full, one unopened. He took them both out. I looked in the cupboard under the sink and found a large red plastic bowl. I took the bottles from Adam.

'What are you doing?' he asked.

I emptied the first bottle into the bowl.

'Looks like milk to me,' I said. I opened the other bottle and started to pour.

'This is . . . oh, Jesus.'

There were little shadows in the milk and they bobbed to the surface of the bowl. Insects, flies, spiders, lots of them. I very carefully put the bottle down and then emptied the milk down the sink. I had to concentrate very hard in order to stop myself vomiting. First I was frightened, then I was angry. 'Somebody's been in here,' I shouted. 'They've fucking been in this flat.'

'Hmm?' said Adam absently, as if he had been thinking hard about something else.

'Somebody broke in.'

'No, they didn't. It's the milk. They put that bottle on the step after the milk was delivered.'

'What shall we do?' I asked.

'Mrs Tallis,' said Adam thoughtfully. 'It's aimed at you. Shall we call the police?'

'No,' I said aloud. 'Not yet.'

I accosted him as he came out of the front door, briefcase in hand.

'Why are you doing this to me? Why?'

He stepped back from me as if I were a mugger. 'What on earth are –?'

'Don't give me that crap, Jake. I know it's you now. For ages I tried to pretend it was someone else, but I know it was you. Who else knows I'm scared of insects?'

'Alice.' He tried to put a hand on my shoulder but I shook him off. 'Calm down, people will think you're mad.'

'Just tell me why the fuck you put spiders in my milk, dammit. Revenge?'

'Now *I* think you're mad.'

'Come on, tell me. What else have you got up your sleeve? Are you trying to send me slowly off my head?'

He looked at me and that stony look made me feel ill. 'If you ask me,' he said, 'you're already off your head.' And he turned on his heel and walked steadily up the road, away from me.

Adam showed no interest at all, but over the next few days whenever I passed a newsagent I checked to see if they had printed the story. On the next Saturday it was there. I saw it straight away, a little photograph of a mountain in a box on the front page: 'Social Climbing: Mountains and Money. See Section Two.' I quickly pulled the other bit of the paper out to see what Joanna had written. There seemed to be pages of the story, too much to read in the shop. I bought it and took it back home.

Adam had already gone out. I was pleased, for once. I made myself a pot of coffee. I wanted to settle down and give this the time it deserved. The cover of the second section of the *Participant* consisted of a sublime photograph of Chungawat in bright sunshine across a blue sky. Beneath it was a caption as if it was being displayed in an estate agent's window: 'One Himalayan peak for rent, £30,000. No previous experience required.' I was captivated once more by the lonely beauty of the mountain. Had Adam been to the top of that? Well, not quite to the top. I opened the paper and checked. Four pages. There were photographs, Greg, Klaus, Françoise, beautiful in big boots, I noted with a stab of jealousy. There were a couple of the other climbers who had died. Adam, of course, but I was used to seeing pictures of him by now. There was a map, a couple of diagrams. I took a sip of coffee and started to read.

In fact, at first I didn't exactly read it. I just flicked my eyes over the text seeing which names were mentioned and how often. Adam came mainly at the end. I read that to see that there was nothing startlingly new. There wasn't. Reassured, I went back to the beginning and read carefully. Joanna had told the story I already knew from Klaus's book, but from a different perspective. Klaus's version of the Chungawat disaster was complicated by his own feelings of excitement, failure, admiration, disillusion, fear, all mixed together. I respected him because he had owned up to all the confusion of what it had been like to be there in the storm with people dying and to his own inability to behave as he would have liked.

Joanna saw it as a morality tale about the corrupting effects of money and a cult of heroism. On the one hand there were heroic characters who needed money; on the other hand there were rich people who wanted to climb difficult mountains, or, rather, wanted to say that they had climbed difficult mountains, since it was a matter of debate whether in a strict sense they had actually climbed them. None of this was big news to me. The tragic victim in all of this, needless to say, was Greg, whom she had not managed to talk to. After beginning her article with the terrible events on Chungawat, which still made me shiver however melodramatically they were described, Joanna went back to talk about Greg's earlier career. His achievements really were startling. It wasn't just the peaks he had climbed – Everest, K2, McKinley, Annapurna – but the way he had climbed them: in winter, without oxygen, blasting for the summit with a minimum of equipment.

Joanna had obviously been through the press cuttings. In the eighties Greg had been a climbing mystic. A major peak was a privilege to be earned through years of apprenticeship. By the early nineties he had apparently been converted: 'I used to be a mountaineering élitist,' he was quoted as saying. 'Now I'm a democrat. Climbing is a great experience. I want to make it available to everybody.' Everybody, Joanna commented drily, who could stump up $50,000. Greg had met an entrepreneur called Paul Molinson and together they had set up their company, Peak Experiences. For three years they had been taking doctors, lawyers, arbitrageurs, heiresses up to peaks that, until recently, had been beyond all but a select group of advanced climbers.

Joanna focused on one of the Chungawat party who had

died, Alexis Hartounian, a Wall Street broker. A scornful (and anonymous) climber was quoted as saying: 'This man achieved some of the world's great climbs. By no stretch of the imagination was he a climber yet he was telling people that he'd done Everest as if it were a bus stop. Well, he learned the hard way.'

Joanna's account of what had happened on the mountain was simply a distilled version of Klaus's narrative accompanied by a diagram showing the fixed rope up the west side of the ridge. She portrayed a chaotic situation with incompetent climbers, people who were ill, one of them not able to speak a word of English. She quoted anonymous climbing experts, who said that the conditions above eight thousand metres were just too extreme for climbers who couldn't take care of themselves. It wasn't just that they were risking their own lives but those of everybody with them. Klaus had told her that he agreed with some of that, but a couple of the anonymous commentators went further. A peak like Chungawat requires absolute commitment and concentration, especially if the weather turns. They suggested that Greg had been so preoccupied with business complications and the special requirements of his unqualified clients that it had affected his judgement and, worst of all, his performance. 'When you've expended your energy on all the wrong things,' one person said, 'then things go wrong at the wrong time, fixed lines come loose, people go in wrong directions.'

It was a cynical story of corruption and disillusion, and Adam appeared towards the end as the symbol of lost idealism. He was known for having been critical of the expedition, not least of his own participation in it, but when it came down to it, he was the man who had gone up and down the mountain saving people who couldn't save themselves. Joanna had managed to contact a couple of survivors who said that they owed their lives to him. Obviously he appeared all the more attractive for his refusal to blame anybody – indeed, his reluctance to make any comment at all. There was also the pathos of his own girlfriend having been among the fatalities. Adam had said little about this to her but she had found somebody else who described him as going out again and again in search of her before collapsing unconscious in his tent.

When Adam came back, he showed no interest in the article beyond a contemptuous frown at the cover: 'What the fuck does *she* know?' was his only comment. Later, in bed, I read the anonymous criticisms of Greg out to him. 'What do you think of that, my love?' I asked.

He took the paper from my hands and tossed it on to the floor. 'I think it's crap,' he said.

'You mean it's an inaccurate description of what happened?'

'I forgot,' he said, laughing. 'You're a scientist. You're interested in the truth.' He sounded derisive.

It was like being married to Lawrence of Arabia or Captain Scott or the boy on the burning deck or somebody. Almost everybody I knew found a reason to ring me up in the next couple of days for a chat. People who had been disapproving of the indecent haste with which I had got married suddenly got the point. My dad rang up and chatted about nothing in particular, then casually mentioned having seen the article and suggested we come round some time. In the office on Monday morning, everybody suddenly had something urgent they needed to run by me. Mike came in with his coffee and handed me an unimportant piece of paper. 'We're never really tested, are we?' he said, with a musing gleam in his eyes. 'It means that we never really know ourselves because we don't know how we would react in an emergency. It must be wonderful for your . . . er, husband, to have been at the centre of a disaster and to have come through as he did.'

'What do you mean my *er* husband, Mike? He's my husband. I can show you the piece of paper if you like.'

'I didn't mean anything like that, Alice. It just takes some getting used to. How long have you known him?'

'A couple of months, I suppose.'

'Amazing. I must say that when I first heard about it, I thought you'd gone off your rocker. It didn't seem like the Alice Loudon I knew. Now I can see that we were all wrong.'

'*We?*'

'Everybody in the office.'

I was aghast. 'You all thought I'd gone mad?'

'We were all surprised. But now I can see that you were right and we were wrong. It's just like in the article. It's all about the ability to think clearly under pressure. Your husband has it.' Mike had been looking into his coffee cup, out of the window, anywhere but at me. Now he turned and looked at me. 'You've got it too.'

I tried to stop myself giggling at the compliment, if that's what it was. 'Well, thank you, kind sir. Back to business.'

By Tuesday I felt I had talked to everybody in the world who had my phone number in their book, except Jake. Even so I was surprised when Claudia told me there was a Joanna Noble on the phone for me. Yes, it was really me she wanted to talk to and not just as a way of getting to Adam. And, yes, it was important and she wanted to meet face to face. That very day, if possible. She would come to somewhere near my office, right now if I had the time. It would only be for a few minutes. What could I say? I told her to come to Reception and an hour later we were sitting in an almost empty sandwich bar round the corner. She hadn't spoken except to shake my hand.

'Your story has given me a sort of reflected glory,' I said. 'At least I'm the wife of a hero.'

She looked uncomfortable and lit a cigarette. 'He *is* a hero,' she said. 'Between ourselves, I had qualms about some of the piece, dishing out blame the way I did. But what Adam did up there was incredible.'

'Yes,' I said. 'He is, isn't he?' Joanna didn't respond. 'I assumed you would be on to another story by now,' I said.

'Several,' she said.

I saw she had a piece of paper which she was fingering. 'What's that?'

She looked down, almost as if it had arrived in her hands without her knowing and she was startled by it.

'This arrived in the mail this morning.' She handed me the paper. 'Read it,' she said.

It was a very short letter.

Dear Joanna Noble,

What you wrote about Adam Tallis made me sick. I could tell you the truth about him if you were interested. If you are interested, look up in newspapers for 20 October 1989. If you want you can talk to me and I'll tell what he's like. The girl in the story is me.

Yours sincerely,
Michelle Stowe

I looked up at Joanna, puzzled. 'Sounds deranged,' I said.

Joanna nodded. 'I get plenty of letters like that. But I went to the library – I mean the archive of newspapers and cuttings at the office – and found this.' She handed me another piece of paper. 'It's not a very big story. It was on an inside page, but I thought . . . Well, see what you think.'

It was a photocopy of a small news item headed: 'Judge Raps Rape Girl'. A name in the first paragraph was underlined. Adam's:

A young man walked free on the first day of his trial for rape at Winchester Crown Court yesterday when Judge Michael Clark instructed the jury to find him not guilty. 'You leave this courtroom without a stain on your character,' Judge Clark told Adam Tallis, 25. 'I can only regret that you were ever brought here to answer such a flimsy and unsubstantiated charge.'

Mr Tallis had been charged with raping Miss X, a young woman who cannot be named for legal reasons, after what was described as 'a drunken party' in the Gloucester area. After a brief cross-examination of Miss X, which focused on her sexual history and her state of mind during the party, the counsel for the defence, Jeremy McEwan QC, moved for a dismissal, which was immediately accepted by Judge Clark.

Judge Clark said that he regretted 'that Miss X had the benefit of the cloak of anonymity while Mr Tallis's name and reputation were dragged through the mire'. On the court steps, Mr Tallis's solicitor, Richard Vine, said that his client was delighted with the judge's verdict and just wanted to get on with his life.

When I had finished, I picked up my coffee cup with a steady hand and took a sip. 'So?' I said. Joanna said nothing. 'What is this? Are you planning to write something about it?'

'Write what?' said Joanna.

'You've built Adam up,' I said. 'Maybe it's time to knock him down.'

Joanna lit another cigarette. 'I don't think I deserve that,' she said coolly. 'I've said everything I have to say about mountaineering. I have no intention of contacting this woman. But . . .' Now she paused and looked uncertain. 'It was more about you than anything else. I didn't know what was the right thing to do. In the end, I decided it was my responsibility to show you it. Maybe I'm being pompous and interfering. Just forget about it now, if you want.'

I took a deep breath and made myself speak calmly. 'I'm sorry I said that.'

Joanna gave a thin smile and blew out a cloud of smoke. 'Good,' she said. 'I'll go now.'

'Can I keep these?'

'Sure. They're only photocopies.' Her curiosity visibly got the better of her. 'What are you going to do?'

I shook my head. 'Nothing. He was found innocent, wasn't he?'

'Yes.'

'Without a stain on his character, right?'

'Right.'

'So I'm going to do nothing at all.'

Nineteen

Of course, it wasn't quite that simple. I told myself that Adam had been found not guilty. I told myself that I had married him and promised to trust him. This was the first test of that trust. I wasn't going to say anything to him; I wasn't going to honour the slander with a response. I wasn't going to think about it.

Who was I fooling? I thought about it all the time. I thought about this unknown girl, woman, whatever, drunk with a drunk Adam. I thought about Lily, taking off her T-shirt to reveal her pale mermaid's body and her livid back. And I thought about the way Adam was with me: he tied me down, put his hands around my neck, ordered me to follow his instructions. He liked to hurt me. He liked my weakness under his strength. He watched me carefully to track my pain. As I examined it, sex between us, which had seemed like delirious passion, became something else. When I was alone in my office, I would close my eyes and remember different excesses. Remembering gave me a queasy and peculiar kind of pleasure. I didn't know what to do.

The first night after I had seen Joanna, I told him I felt lousy. My period was about to start. I had back cramps.

'It isn't due for another six days,' he said.

'Then I'm early,' I retorted. God, I was married to a man who knew my menstrual patterns better than I did. I tried to joke away my discomfort. 'It just shows how much we need the Drakloop.'

'I'll give you a massage. That'll help.' He was helping someone in Kennington rebuild a wooden floor, and his hands were more callused than ever. 'You're all tense,' he said. 'Relax.'

★　　★　　★

I lasted two days. On Thursday evening he arrived home with a great bag of groceries and announced he was going to cook, for a change. He had bought swordfish, two fresh red chillies, a gnarled hand of ginger, a bunch of coriander, basmati rice in a brown paper bag, a bottle of purplish wine. He lit all the candles and turned out the lights, so that the dismal little kitchen suddenly looked like a witch's cave.

I read the paper and watched him as he washed the coriander carefully, making sure each leaf was free from grit. He laid the chillies on a plate and chopped them finely. When he felt my gaze on him, he put down the knife and came over and kissed me, keeping his hands away from my face. 'I don't want you to get stung by chilli,' he said.

He made a marinade for the fish, rinsed the rice and left it to stand in a pan of water, washed his hands thoroughly, then opened the wine, pouring some into two unmatching glasses.

'It will be about an hour,' he said. He put his hand into his trouser pockets and pulled out two slender leather thongs. 'I've been thinking all day about tying you up.'

'What if I say no?' My voice came out in a blurt. Suddenly my mouth was dry so I found it hard to swallow.

Adam lifted his glass to his mouth and took a small sip. He looked at me consideringly. 'How do you mean, no? What kind of no?'

'I've got to show you something,' I said, and went over to my bag and took out the photocopied letter and article. I handed them to Adam.

He put his wine down on the table and read them through, taking his time. Then he looked up at me. 'Well?'

'I . . . the journalist gave them to me and . . .' I came to a halt.

'What are you asking me, Alice?' I didn't reply. 'Are you asking if I raped her?'

'No, of course not. I mean, look at what the judge said and – oh, shit, we're married, remember? How could you not tell me something like this? It must have been a big thing in your life. I want to know what happened. Of course I do. What the hell do you expect?' To my surprise, I banged the table with my fist so that the glasses jumped.

For a moment he just looked sad, instead of angry as I had expected. 'I expect you to believe in me,' he said in a quiet voice, almost to himself. 'And be on my side.'

'I am. Of course. But . . .'

'But you want to know what happened?'

'Yes.'

'Exactly what happened?'

I took a breath and said firmly, 'Yes, exactly.'

'You asked for it.' He poured himself some more wine and sat back in his chair and looked at me. 'I was at a party at a friend's house in Gloucestershire. It was eight years ago, I guess. I'd recently returned from America, where I'd been climbing in Yosemite with a mate. We were pretty strung out, ready to have a good time. There were lots of people there, but I didn't really know any of them, except the guy who was holding the party. There was plenty of drink flowing. Some drugs. People were dancing, kissing. It was summer, hot outside. There were a few couples in the bushes. This girl came up to me and pulled me up to dance. She was pretty drunk. She tried to undress me on the dance floor. I took her outside. She had her dress off while we were still walking across the lawn. We went behind this big tree; I could hear another pair going at it a few yards away. She kept going on about her boyfriend, and how they'd had this big row, and how she wanted me to fuck her, do things to her that he didn't do. So I did just that. Then she said I had raped her.'

There was a silence.

'Did she want you to?' I asked, in a low voice. 'Or did she ask you not to?'

'Well, now, Alice, that's an interesting question. Tell me, have you ever said no to me?'

'Yes. But . . .'

'And have I ever raped you?'

154

'It's not that simple.'

'Sex is not that simple. What I do to you, do you like it?'

'Yes.' Beads of sweat were standing out on my forehead.

'When I tied you up, you asked me to stop, but did you like it?'

'Yes, but . . . This is ghastly, Adam.'

'You asked for it. When I . . .'

'That's enough. It's still not that simple, Adam. It's about intention. Hers, yours. Did she want you to stop?'

Adam took another sip of his drink, swallowed it slowly. 'Afterwards. She wanted me to have stopped. She wished it hadn't happened, sure. She wanted her boyfriend back. Then, we want to change things we've done.'

'Let's be clear here. There was no point at which you thought she was resisting or unwilling?'

'No.'

We stared at each other.

'Although sometimes' – he went on gazing at me, as if he were testing me – 'it's difficult to tell with women.'

This struck a horribly wrong note. 'Don't talk about *women* like that, as if we were all just generic objects.'

'Well, of course she *was* an object. So was I. I met her when we were both drunk at a party. I don't think I knew her name, nor she mine. That's what we wanted. We both wanted sex. What's wrong with that?'

'I'm not –'

'Has it never happened to you? It has, you've told me so yourself. And isn't that part of the pleasure at the time?'

'Maybe,' I admitted. 'But part of the shame later.'

'Not for me.' He glared across at me, and I could feel his considerable anger. 'I don't believe in worrying about things we can't change.'

I tried to keep my voice steady. I didn't want to cry. 'That night after we got married. In the cabin. I wanted you to, Adam. I wanted you to do anything that you wanted to do. The next morning when I woke up I felt wrong about it. I felt we'd gone too far, gone somewhere we shouldn't have.'

Adam poured me some more wine, and then some for himself. Without me noticing, we'd almost finished the bottle.

'Have you never felt anything like that?' I asked.

He nodded. 'Yes.'

'After sex?'

'Not necessarily. But I know what you mean.' He grimaced at me. 'I recognize the feeling.'

We drank our wine together, and the candles flickered.

'The swordfish will be marinated enough soon,' I said.

'I wouldn't rape someone.'

'No,' I said. But I thought: how would you know?

'Shall I cook the fish now?'

'Not yet.'

I hesitated. It was as if my life was on a hinge. I could push it one way or the other; close off one avenue or another. Trust and go mad. Distrust and go mad. From where I stood, it didn't seem, in the end, to make much difference after all. It was quite dark outside and I could hear the steady drip of rain. The candles were guttering, casting shadows that fluttered on the walls. I stood up and crossed over to where he had dropped the leather thongs. 'Come on, then, Adam.'

He didn't move from his chair. 'What are you saying?' he asked me.

'I'm saying yes.'

But I wasn't saying yes, not quite. The next day at work I rang up Lily, and arranged to see her early that evening, straight after I left the office. I didn't want to go to her seamy little basement flat. I didn't think I could sit on the stained sheets surrounded by old photographs of Adam again. I suggested the coffee bar in John Lewis, on Oxford Street – it was the most neutral, least atmospheric place I could think of.

Lily was there already, drinking cappuccino and eating a large chocolate-chip muffin. She was wearing black woollen trousers, a shaggy mulberry-coloured jersey, ankle boots, and no makeup. Her silver hair was tied back in a loose knot. She looked rather normal and, when she smiled at me, rather sweet. Not so deranged. I smiled back tentatively. I didn't want to like her.

'Trouble?' she said genially, as I sat down opposite.

'Do you want another coffee?' I replied.

'No, thanks. I wouldn't mind another muffin, though – I haven't eaten all day.'

I ordered a cappuccino for me, and another muffin. I stared at her over the rim of my cup and didn't know where to begin. Clearly Lily didn't mind the silence, or my discomfort. She ate hungrily, smearing chocolate over her chin. She was a bit like a little child, I thought.

'We didn't really finish our conversation,' I said lamely.

'What do you want to know?' she asked sharply. 'Mrs Tallis,' she added.

I felt a ripple of alarm.

'I'm not Mrs Tallis. Why do you call me that?'

'Oh, for fuck's sake.'

I let it go. After all, there had been no more phone calls or letters for several days now. Not since I had confronted Jake.

'Was Adam ever really violent with you?'

She gave a yelp of laughter.

'I mean, *really* violent,' I said.

She wiped her mouth. She was enjoying this.

'I mean, were you ever unconsenting?'

'What's that supposed to mean? How do I know? It wasn't like that. You know what he's like.' She smiled at me. 'By the way, what do you think he'd make of you seeing me like this? Of you checking up on his credentials?' Again, she gave her quick, spooky giggle.

'I don't know what he would say.'

'I don't mean what would he say. What would he do?'

I didn't reply.

'I wouldn't like to be in your shoes.' Then, suddenly, she gave a violent shudder and leaned across the table until her face was close to mine. There was a bit of chocolate on one of her perfect white teeth. 'Except I also would, of course.' She closed her eyes, and I had a horrible sensation that I was watching her re-enact in her imagination some fetishistic act with Adam.

'I'm going now,' I said.

'Do you want a word of advice?'

'No,' I said, too quickly.

'Don't try and get in his way, or change him. It won't work. Go with him.'

She got up and left. I paid.

Twenty

I went straight up to Klaus and gave him a hug. He wrapped his arms around me. 'Congratulations,' I said.

'Good party, yes?' He beamed. Then his smile turned ironic. 'So, those people didn't die on the mountain entirely in vain. Some good has come out of it in the form of my book. Let it not be said that I have failed to profit from the misfortunes of other people.'

'That's what other people are there for, I suppose,' I said, and we let each other go.

'Where is your husband, the hero?' Klaus asked, looking around.

'Hiding in the crowd somewhere, fighting off admirers. Is anybody else from the expedition here?'

Klaus looked around. The party for his book was in the library of the Alpinists' Society in South Kensington. It was a cavernous space lined with shelves of leatherbound volumes, of course, but there were also ancient, crusty-looking walking boots in glass cases and ice axes like trophies on the wall and photographs of stiff men in tweeds, and mountains, lots and lots of mountains.

'Greg is somewhere in the room.'

I was astonished. 'Greg? Where is he?'

'Over there, talking to that old man in the corner. Go over and introduce yourself. That's Lord Montrose. He is a man from the great early days of Himalayan climbing when they considered it unnecessary to issue their porters with crampons.'

I pushed my way through the crowd. Deborah was in one corner. There were lots of tall, fantastically healthy women dotted around. I couldn't help imagining to myself which of them Adam had slept with. Stupid. Stupid. Greg was bent over Lord Montrose, shouting in his ear, when I approached them. I stood there for a minute until Greg looked round at me suspiciously. Perhaps he thought I was a reporter. Greg looked like the old idea I would have had of a climber, before I met people like Adam and Klaus. He wasn't tall, like them. He had an unfeasibly large beard, like the man in the Edward Lear limerick who found two larks and a wren in it. His hair was long and unkempt. He must still have been in his thirties but thin lines were engraved on his forehead and around his eyes. Lord Montrose looked at me and then backed away surreally into the crowd, as if I were a magnet repelling him.

'My name's Alice Loudon,' I said to Greg. 'I've just got married to Adam Tallis.'

'Oh,' he said, with a crinkle of acknowledgement. 'Congratulations.'

There was a silence. Greg turned to look at the photograph next to us on the wall. 'Look,' he said. 'On one of the first expeditions up here, a Victorian vicar stepped back to admire the view and pulled four of his colleagues off with him. They landed among their own tents which, unfortunately, were nine thousand feet beneath them.' He moved along to the next photograph. 'K2. Beautiful, isn't it? Just under fifty people have died on it.'

'Where's K *one*?'

Greg laughed.

'It doesn't exist any more. In 1856 a British lieutenant who was working on the great Trigonometric Survey of India climbed a mountain and saw two peaks in the Karakoram range a hundred and thirty miles away. So he jotted them down as K1 and K2. They later discovered that K1 already had a name, Masherbrum. But K2 stuck.'

'You've climbed it,' I said. Greg didn't reply. I knew what I had to say. I blurted it all out in one go. 'Have you talked to

Adam this evening? You have to. He feels very bad about what's appeared in the press about Chungawat. Can I take you over to him now? Then you'll be doing me a favour as well, and rescuing him from all those gorgeous and adoring women.'

Disconcertingly, Greg didn't catch my eye but looked around the room, the way people do at parties if they are half-listening to you and half checking if there is somebody more interesting to talk to. He must have known I wasn't a mountaineer and he can't have had much interest in anything I had to say, so I felt embarrassed.

'He feels bad, does he?' Greg said softly, still not looking at me. 'And why is that?'

Why was I doing this? I took a deep breath. 'Because it's being portrayed in terms that have nothing to do with what it was really like on the mountain, in the storm and everything.'

At this Greg did look round at me, and allowed himself a tired laugh. When he spoke it was with an obvious effort, as if it was still freshly painful for him. 'I think,' he said slowly, 'that the person who leads an expedition has to take responsibility for it.'

'It wasn't a funfair ride,' I said. 'Everybody on the expedition knew that they were going into a very dangerous place. You can't make guarantees about the weather on a mountain like that as if it were just a package holiday.'

The lines in his face crinkled up. It was somehow as if all his time in the Himalayas, in that unprotected sunlight and oxygen-depleted air, had given him the aura of an ancient Buddhist monk. In the midst of that messy, sunburned face, there were the beautiful clear blue eyes of a baby. I felt he had taken the entire burden of what had happened on himself. I liked him enormously.

'Yes, Alice,' he replied. 'That's right.'

The way it came out it sounded less like a form of exoneration than a further example of his misjudgement.

'I wish you'd talk to Adam about all this,' I said desperately.

'Why should I talk to him, Alice? What would he tell me?'

I thought for a moment, trying to get it clear in my mind. 'He would tell you,' I said finally, 'that it's a different world up there about eight thousand metres and it is wrong to moralize about what happened.'

'The problem,' Greg said, almost in bafflement, 'is that I don't agree with that. I know that . . .' He stopped for a moment. 'I know that Adam feels it's something different up there, different from everything else. But I think you *can* moralize about behaviour at the top of mountains like anywhere else. The only problem is getting it right.'

'What do you mean?'

He sighed and looked around to see if anybody was eavesdropping on our conversation. Fortunately they weren't. He took a sip of his drink, then another sip. I was drinking white wine, he was drinking whisky.

'Do I have to punish myself all over again? Maybe it was irresponsible of me to take relatively inexperienced climbers up Chungawat. I thought I was properly prepared.' He looked hard at me, with a new steeliness in his gaze. 'Maybe I still do. I got sick on the mountain, really sick, and I had to be half dragged down to base camp. It was a very bad storm, one of the worst I've ever seen in May. But I thought I had created a system of fixed lines and support, using the porters and the professional guides, that was foolproof.' We looked at each other and then I saw his face relax until he just looked very, very sad. 'But – you will say, or people will say – five people died. And then it seems . . . well, inappropriate to start making protests about whether this rope gave way or that fastening or that pole and whether my mind was on other things.' He gave a little shrug.

'I'm sorry,' I said. 'I don't know about that sort of technical stuff.'

'No,' Greg said. 'People don't.'

'But I know about emotions, the aftermath. It was terrible for everybody else too. I've read Klaus's book. He feels bad that he was so powerless up there. And Adam. He's still tortured because he failed to save his girlfriend, Françoise.'

'Ex-girlfriend,' said Greg distantly. He didn't seem consoled. Suddenly a young woman came up to us.

'Hello,' she said brightly. 'I'm Kate from Klaus's publishers.'

There was a pause while Greg and I looked at each other, conspirators suddenly.

'My name is Alice,' I said.

'I'm Greg.'

The woman's face lit up in recognition.

'Oh, you were . . .'

Then she stopped in confusion and went red.

'It was terribly embarrassing,' I said. 'There was this black hole of a pause. Obviously Greg couldn't break in and finish her sentence identifying himself as the one who was to blame for the whole disaster and I didn't think it was for me to step in and help her out. So she just went redder and redder and then drifted away. It was . . . oh, that's cold.'

Adam had pulled the duvet off me.

'What did you talk to Greg about?'

As he spoke he began to arrange my limbs and turn me around as if I were a mannequin.

'Careful. I felt I had to meet somebody who was so important in your life. And I wanted to tell him how badly you felt about all the coverage.' I tried to twist myself around to look Adam in the face. 'Do you mind?'

I felt his hands on the back of my head, then he seized my hair tightly and pushed my face really hard into the mattress. I couldn't help crying out.

'Yeah, I do mind. It's nothing to do with you. What do you know about it?' I had tears in my eyes. I tried to twist around but Adam was holding me down on the bed with an elbow and a knee and running his fingers over my body at the same time. 'Your body is so inexhaustibly lovely,' he said tenderly, his lips

163

brushing against my ear. 'I am completely in love with every bit of it and I am in love with you.'

'Yes,' I groaned.

'But,' and now his tone hardened but it was still little more than a whisper, 'I don't want you interfering in things that have nothing to do with you because it makes me very angry. Do you understand?'

'No,' I said. 'I don't really understand at all. I don't agree.'

'Alice, Alice,' he said reproachfully, running his fingers from my hair down my spine, 'we're not interested in each other's worlds, each other's past life. All that matters is us here, in this bed.'

Suddenly, I flinched. 'Ow, that hurts,' I cried.

'Wait,' he said. 'Wait, all you have to do is relax.'

'No, no, I can't,' I said, twisting around, but he pushed me back down so that I could hardly breathe.

'Relax and trust me,' he said, 'trust me.'

Suddenly there was this jolt of pain right through my body, like a flash of light that I could see as well as feel and it ran through me and through me and wouldn't stop and I heard a scream that seemed to come from somewhere else and it was me.

My GP, Caroline Vaughan, is only about four or five years older than I am and when I see her, usually just about a prescription or a vaccination, I always feel we are the sort of people who would be friends if we had met under other circumstances. Which made it a bit awkward on this occasion. I'd rung and pleaded with her to give me an emergency appointment on my way to work. Yes, it was essential. No, I couldn't wait until tomorrow. The internal examination was agonizing and I lay on the table biting my knuckles to stop myself crying out. Caroline had been chatting with me and then she fell silent. After a while she took off her gloves and I felt her warm fingers on the top of my back. She told me I could get dressed and I heard the sound of her washing her hands. When I came back out from behind the screen she was sitting at her desk writing notes. She looked up. 'Can you sit down?'

'Just about.'

'I'm surprised.' Her expression was serious, almost sombre. 'You won't be surprised to learn that you have an acute anal fissure.'

I tried to look at Caroline with a composed expression as if this were just flu. 'So what happens?'

'It will probably heal by itself but you should eat plenty of fruit and fibre over the next week or so to avoid damaging it any more. I'm going to prescribe a mild laxative as well.'

'Is that it?'

'What do you mean?'

'It hurts so much.'

Caroline thought for a moment and then wrote something more on her prescription. 'This is for an anaesthetic gel which should be a help. Come and see me next week. If it hasn't healed then we'll need to consider anal dilatation.'

'What's that?'

'Don't worry. It's a simple procedure but it has to be done under general anaesthetic.'

'God.'

'Don't worry.'

'Right.'

She put her pen down and handed me the prescriptions. 'Alice, I'm not going to give you some moral lecture. But, for God's sake, treat your body with respect.'

I nodded. I couldn't think of what to say.

'You've got bruises on your inner thigh area,' she continued. 'On your buttocks, on your back and even on the left side of your neck.'

'You'll have noticed I'm wearing a high-collared shirt.'

'Is there anything you want to talk about with me?'

'It looks worse than it is, Caroline. I've just got married. We got carried away.'

'I suppose I should offer my congratulations,' said Caroline, but she didn't smile when she said it.

I stood up to go, wincing. 'Thanks,' I said.

'Alice.'

'Yes.'

'Violent sex –'

'It's not like that . . .'

'As I was saying, violent sex can be a spiral that's difficult to get out of. Like being battered.'

'No. You're wrong.' I felt hot all over, furious and humiliated. 'Sex is often about pain as well, isn't it? And power and submission and stuff like that.'

'Of course. But not about anal fissures.'

'No.'

'Be careful, OK?'

'Yes.'

Twenty-one

She was easy to track down. There was the letter that I had stared at until my eyes ached. I knew her name; her address was on the headed notepaper in curlicued lettering. I simply rang directory inquiries from work one morning and got her telephone number. I spent a few minutes staring at the digits I had written down on the back of a used envelope, and wondering if I was actually going to call her. Who should I pretend to be? What if someone else answered? I went down the corridor to the drink dispenser, fetched myself a polystyrene mug of orange tea, and settled down in my office with the door firmly pulled shut. I pushed a soft cushion under me, but still felt sore.

The phone rang for a quite a long time. She must be out; probably at work. Part of me was relieved.

'Hello.'

She was there, after all. I cleared my throat. 'Hello, is that Michelle Stowe?'

'Yes, it is.'

Her voice was high and quite thin, with a West Country burr to it. 'My name is Sylvie Bushnell. I'm a colleague of Joanna Noble's at the *Participant*.'

'Yes?' The voice was cautious now, tentative.

'She passed your note on to me, and I wondered if I could talk to you about it.'

'I dunno,' she said. 'I shouldn't have written it. I was angry.'

'We wanted to get your side of the story, that's all.'

There was a silence.

'Michelle?' I said. 'You would only need to tell me what you felt able to.'

'I dunno.'

'I could come and see you.'

'I don't want you publishing anything in the paper, not unless I agree to it.'

'There's no question of that,' I said, accurately enough.

She was reluctant, but I pressed and she agreed and I said I would come to see her the following morning. She lived only five minutes from the station. It was all so easy.

I didn't read on the train. I sat still, wincing with the jolting of the carriage, and stared out of the window as the houses of London petered out, and countryside took over. It was a dank grey day. The previous evening Adam had rubbed me all over with massage oil. He'd been very gentle round the bruising, stroking the swollen purple abrasions tenderly as if they were glorious battle scars. He had bathed me and wrapped me in two towels, and laid his hand on my forehead. He had been so solicitous, so proud of me for my suffering.

The train went through a long tunnel and I saw my face in the window: thin, swollen lips, shadows under my eyes, hair awry. I pulled a brush and an elastic band out of my bag and tied my hair back severely. I remembered I hadn't even brought a notebook or a pen. I'd get them when I arrived at the station.

Michelle Stowe answered the door with a baby clutched to her breast. It was feeding. Its eyes were screwed shut in its wrinkled, reddened face. Its mouth was working voraciously. As I stepped in through the front door, it lost its grip for a second and I saw it make a blind instinctual movement, mouth gaping, tiny fists uncurling and scrabbling at air. Then it found the nipple once more and settled back to its rhythmic suckling.

'I'll just finish feeding him,' she said.

She took me through to a small room filled with a brown sofa. A bar fire glowed. I sat on the sofa and waited. I could hear her cooing softly, the baby whimpering. There was a sweet smell of talcum powder. There were photographs of the baby on the mantelpiece, sometimes with Michelle, sometimes with a thin, bald-headed man.

Michelle came in, without the baby now, and sat down at the other end of the sofa.

'Do you want tea or anything?'

'No, thanks.'

She looked younger than me. She had dark curly hair, and full pale lips in a round, watchful face. Everything about her seemed soft: the glossy curls in her hair, her small white hands, her milky breasts, her plump post-natal tummy. She looked both voluptuous and comfortable, wrapped in a shabby cream cardigan, feet in red slippers, a trace of milk on her black T-shirt. For the first time in my life I felt the tug of maternal instinct. I took the spiral-bound notebook out of my bag and put it on my lap. I picked up the pen.

'Why did you write to Joanna?'

'Somebody showed me the magazine,' she said. 'I don't know what they thought. I'd been raped by somebody famous.'

'Do you mind telling me about it?'

'Why not?' she said.

I kept my eyes on the notepad, and occasionally made a scrappy little doodle that might look like shorthand. Michelle spoke with the weary familiarity of somebody telling an anecdote they'd told many times before. At the time of the incident – she used that odd word, maybe because of the police and court proceedings – she had been eighteen years old, and was at a party in the country just outside of Gloucester. It was being thrown by a friend of her boyfriend ('Tony was my boyfriend then,' she explained). On the way to the party, she'd argued with Tony, and he'd left her there and driven off with two mates to the nearby pub. She was cross and embarrassed and she'd got drunk, she said, on cider and cheap red wine and an empty stomach. By the time she met Adam, the room was spinning. She was standing in a corner, talking to a friend, when he and another man came in.

'He was good-looking. You've seen his picture probably.' I nodded. 'There they were, these two men, and I remember saying to Josie, "You have the blond one and I'll go for the dish."'

So far, this was Adam's story too. I drew a droopy flower in the corner of the pad.

'What happened then?' I asked. But Michelle didn't really need asking. She wanted to tell her story. She wanted to talk to a stranger and be believed at last. She thought I was on her side, the journalist-therapist.

'I went up and asked him to dance. We danced for a bit and then started kissing. My boyfriend still hadn't come back. I thought that I'd show him.' She looked up at me to see if I was shocked by the admission, by the sort of statement that must have been brought out under cross-examination. 'So I did start it all off. I kissed him and put my hands under his shirt. We went outside together. There were other people outside already, kissing and stuff. He pulled me towards the bushes. He's strong. Well, he climbs mountains, doesn't he? When we were still on the lawn, with all these people watching, he unfastened my dress a bit at the back.' She gave a sharp little intake of breath, like a half-sob. 'It sounds stupid, I'm not naïve or anything, but I didn't want –' She stopped, then sighed. 'I just wanted a laugh,' she said lamely. She put up both hands and pushed back her dark hair. She looked too young to have been eighteen eight years ago.

'What happened, Michelle?' I asked.

'We moved away from the others, behind a tree. We were kissing, and it was still all right.' Her voice was very low now, and I had to lean forward to catch what she was saying. 'Then he put his hand between my legs, and I let him at first. Then I said I didn't want that. That I wanted to go back inside. It felt all wrong, suddenly. I thought my boyfriend would come back. He was so tall and strong, and if I opened my eyes I could see his eyes staring right at me, and if I closed them then I felt horribly sick and the whole world lurched. I was pretty drunk.'

While Michelle described the scene to me, I tried to concentrate

170

on the words, and not make any picture out of them. When I looked up at her to nod encouragingly or make some affirming grunt, I tried not to see her face properly but to let it become an unfocused blur, a pale expanse of skin. She told me that she had tried to pull away. Adam had pulled her dress off her, thrown it behind them into the darkness of bushes, and kissed her again. This time it hurt a bit, she said, and his hand between her legs hurt, too. She started to get frightened. She tried to get free of his arms, but he held her more firmly. She tried to scream, but he put his hand over her mouth so no sound came out. She remembered trying to say 'please' but it was muffled by his fingers. 'I thought if he could hear me begging him, he would stop,' she said; she was near to tears now. I drew a big square on my notepad, and a smaller one inside it. I wrote the word inside the smaller square: 'please'.

'Part of me still didn't believe this was happening. I still thought he would stop in the end. Rape doesn't happen like this, I thought. It's a man in a mask jumping out of a dark alleyway, you know the kind of thing. He pushed me down on the ground. It was all prickly. There was a stinging nettle under my calf. He still had a hand over my mouth. Once he took it away to kiss me, but it didn't feel like a kiss any longer, just another kind of gag. Then he jammed it back. I kept thinking I would be sick. He put his other hand between my legs and tried to make me want him. He really worked hard at that.' Michelle looked through me. 'I couldn't help feeling some pleasure, and that made it worst of all, do you see?' I nodded again. 'To want to be raped: that makes it not rape, doesn't it? *Doesn't it?*'

'I don't know.'

'Then he did it to me. You don't know how strong he is. He seemed to enjoy hurting me as he did it. I just lay there, all limp, just waiting for it to finish. When he'd done, he kissed me again as if it had all been something we'd agreed to do. I couldn't speak, I couldn't do anything. He went and found my dress, and my knickers. I was crying and he just looked at me as if he found me

171

interesting. Then he said to me, "It's just sex," or "It's only sex," or something like that, and he just went off. I got dressed and I went back inside. I saw Josie with her blond man and she winked at me. He was dancing with another girl. He didn't look up.'

Michelle looked numb, almost unmoved. She'd been through this too often. I asked, in a neutral voice, when she had gone to the police. She told me that she had waited a week.

'Why so long?'

'I felt guilty. I'd been drunk, I'd led him on, I'd gone behind my boyfriend's back.'

'What made you decide to report it then?'

'My boyfriend heard about it. We had a row and he walked out on me. I was confused, I went to the police.'

Suddenly she looked round. She got up and left the room. I took a few deep breaths to calm myself before she returned, carrying her baby. She sat down again, with him bundled into the crook of her arm. Every so often she put her little finger into his mouth, and he sucked it contemplatively.

'The police were quite sympathetic. There were still some bruises. And he . . . he did things to me, there was a doctor's report. But the trial was awful.'

'What happened?'

'I gave evidence and then I realized that it was me on trial. The lawyer asked me about my past – I mean my sexual past. How many people I'd slept with. Then he took me through what had happened at the party. How I'd had a row with my boyfriend, what I'd been wearing, how much I'd drunk, how I'd kissed him first, led him on. He – Adam – just sat there in the dock and looked all serious and sad. The judge stopped the trial. I wanted the ground to swallow me up – everything was dirty suddenly. Everything in my life. I have never hated anyone so much as I hated him.' There was a silence. 'You believe me?' she said.

'You've been very honest,' I said. She wanted something more from me. Her face seemed plumply girlish and she gazed at me with an urgent look of appeal. I felt so sorry for her, and for me too. She picked up the baby and pushed her face into the squashy concertina of his neck. I stood up. 'And you were brave,' I forced myself to say.

She lifted her head and stared at me. 'Will you do something about this?'

'There are legal problems.' The last thing I wanted was to build up her hopes.

'Yes,' she said, in a fatalistic tone. Her expectations seemed low. 'What would you have done, Sylvie? Tell me.'

I forced myself to look into her eyes. It was as if I was staring down the wrong end of a telescope. A fresh sense of my double betrayal flooded me. 'I don't know what I would have done,' I said. Then a thought occurred to me. 'Do you ever get up to London?'

She frowned in puzzlement. 'With this?' she asked. 'Why would I want to?'

She seemed quite genuine; and anyway the phone calls and notes seemed to have stopped.

The baby started crying and she lifted him so his head was butting up under her chin. He lay against her chest, arms akimbo, like a little climber pressed against the rockface. I smiled at her. 'You've got a gorgeous little boy,' I said. 'You've done well.'

Her face broke into an answering smile. 'I have, haven't I?'

Twenty-two

'You did *what*?'

Until then I had always thought that the expression about jaws dropping was a metaphor or a poetic exaggeration but there was no doubt about it: Joanna Noble's jaw dropped.

On the train back, already shocked and distressed, I had suffered a virtual panic attack as it occurred to me for the first time what I had actually done. I imagined Michelle ringing the *Participant* and asking to speak to Sylvie Bushnell in order to complain or add something to her story, and discovering there was no one of that name, and then talking to Joanna instead. The trail to me was hardly long and winding. What would Michelle feel about what had been done to her? A further, and not entirely irrelevant, question was what would happen to me. Even if I hadn't exactly broken the law, I imagined myself explaining to Adam what I had done.

I settled the matter, to the extent that it was possible, immediately. I phoned Joanna Noble from a call-box on the way home and was at her flat over in Tufnell Park at breakfast-time the next day.

I looked at Joanna. 'Your ash needs tapping,' I said.

'What?' she asked, still stupefied.

I found a saucer on the table and dangled it under the teetering cylinder of ash at the end of the cigarette in her right hand. I tapped the cigarette myself and the ash snowed down on to the saucer. I braced myself to amplify the stark sentence of confession I had just spoken. I had to be as clear as I could possibly be.

'I feel very ashamed, Joanna. Let me tell you exactly what I

174

did and then you can tell me what you think of me. I rang up Michelle Stowe and I pretended to be a colleague of yours working on the newspaper. I went and talked to her and she told me about what happened between her and Adam. I couldn't stop myself from wanting to find out and I couldn't think of any other way of doing it. But it was wrong. I feel terrible.'

Joanna stubbed out her cigarette and lit another. She ran her fingers through her hair. She was still in her dressing-gown. 'What the *fuck* did you think you were doing?'

'Investigating.'

'She thought she was talking to a reporter. She thought she was making a brave declaration on behalf of rape victims and instead she was satisfying your nosiness about what your *hubby*' – this last uttered with bitter contempt – 'got up to with his little cock before you were married.'

'I'm not trying to defend myself.'

Joanna took a deep drag on her cigarette. 'You gave her a false name?'

'I told her my name was Sylvie Bushnell.'

'*Sylvie Bushnell?* Where did you get *that* from? You . . .' But then it was all too much for her. Joanna started giggling, then laughed uncontrollably. She put her head down on the table and banged her forehead lightly twice. She took another drag and started coughing and laughing at the same time. Finally she controlled herself. 'You've certainly got a taste for the jugular. You should be doing my job. I need some coffee. You want some?'

I nodded and she boiled some water and spooned the ground beans into a cafetière as we talked.

'So what did she tell you?'

I gave a summary of what Michelle had said.

'Hmm,' said Joanna. She didn't seem especially disconcerted. She poured two mugs of coffee and sat back down opposite me at her kitchen table. 'So what do you feel after your escapade?'

I took a sip of coffee. 'I'm still trying to sort it out in my mind. Rocked. That's one of the things I feel.'

Joanna looked sceptical. 'Really?'

'Of course.'

She lit another cigarette. 'Is it any different from what you read in the paper? Based on what you told me, I would still acquit Adam. I'm amazed it ever came to court.'

'I don't care about the legal technicalities, Joanna. All I care is what happened. What *may* have happened.'

'Oh, for God's sake, Alice, we're grown-ups.' She topped up her coffee. 'Look, I don't think of myself as an especially promiscuous person. Well, nobody does, do they? But I've had sex with men to make them go away, or because they went on and on about it. I've had sex with people while drunk who I wouldn't have had sex with sober. I've done it not really wanting to, and I've regretted it the next morning, or ten minutes later. Once or twice I've humiliated myself so that I felt sick with it. Haven't you?'

'On occasion.'

'All I'm saying is that most of us have gone out into that grey area and played around with what we really want to do. I mean, it's difficult, but all I'm saying is that it's not like the man who climbs through your window with a mask and a knife.'

'I'm sorry, Joanna, I'm not comfortable with that.'

'You're not supposed to be comfortable with it. That's the point. Look, I don't know about you and Adam. How did you meet?'

'Well, let's just say it wasn't exactly having tea with the vicar and all very Jane Austen.'

'Quite. When I met Adam he was rude to me, prickly, difficult. I suspect his attitude to me was a combination of being uninterested, suspicious and contemptuous and I felt turned on by him. The man is sexy, right?' There was a silence I made no attempt to fill.

'Well, he is, isn't he?'

'He's my husband,' I said primly.

'For Christ's sake, Alice, don't play Pollyanna with me. The

176

man is an epic in himself. He single-handedly saved the lives of almost everybody in that expedition. Klaus was telling me about his life. He walked out of Eton when he was sixteen and made his way to the Alps. He bummed around there for a couple of years before finding his way out to the Himalayas where he spent years trekking and climbing. How dare you find this man before me?'

'I know all this, Joanna. It's a shock finding this other side to him.'

'What other side?'

'That he can be violent, dangerous.'

'Has he been violent to *you*?'

'Well . . . you know.' I gave a shrug.

'Oh, you mean in *nice* ways.'

'I don't know if *nice* is the right word.'

'Mm,' said Joanna approvingly, almost carnivorously. 'You have got a problem, Alice.'

'Have I?'

'You've fallen in love with a hero, an extraordinary man who's not like anybody I've ever heard of. He's strange and unpredictable and I think that sometimes you wish he was like a solicitor coming home at six thirty for dinner and a cuddle and the missionary position once a week. What was your last relationship?'

'I left somebody for Adam.'

'What was he like?'

'He was nice. But not like that solicitor you're talking about. He was good fun, considerate, we were friends, shared the same interests, we had a good time together. Sex was good.'

Joanna leaned across the table and looked at me closely. 'Miss him?'

'It's all so different with Adam. We don't "do things together", the way I used to with other boyfriends. We're never just casually, easily, together, the way I was with Jake. It's all so . . . so intense, so tiring in a way. And sex – well, sure it's great, but it's also disturbing. Troubling. I don't know the rules any more.'

'Do you miss Jake?' Joanna asked again.

It was a question I had never asked myself. I had virtually never had time to ask myself.

'Not for a single second,' I heard myself say.

Twenty-three

It was the middle of March, nearly the beginning of British Summer Time again. There were crocuses and daffodils in all the parks, brighter faces on the street; the sun rose higher each day. Joanna Noble was right. I would never know what happened in the past. Everyone has their secrets and their betrayals. No one's life is untouched by shame. Best keep dark things in the dark, where they can heal and fade. Best put away the torments of jealousy and paranoid curiosity.

I knew that Adam and I could not spend the rest of our lives together by shutting out the world and exploring each other's bodies in strange, darkened rooms. We had to let the world in a bit. All the friends we had ignored, relatives we had abandoned, duties we had put aside, movies we hadn't seen, papers we had failed to read. We had to act a bit more like normal people. So I went out and bought some new clothes. I went to the super-market and bought ordinary kinds of food: eggs, cheese, flour, things like that. I made arrangements, as I had in my previous life.

'I'm going to a film with Pauline tomorrow,' I said to Adam, when he came in.

He raised his eyebrows. 'Why?'

'I need to see some friends. And I thought we could invite people round for a meal here on Saturday.'

He looked at me inquiringly.

'I thought I'd ask Sylvie and Clive,' I persevered. 'And what about having Klaus here, or Daniel, and maybe Deborah? Or whoever you want.'

'Sylvie and Clive and Klaus and Daniel and Deborah? Here?'

'Is that strange?'

He took my hand and fiddled with the wedding ring. 'Why are you doing this?'

'Doing what?'

'You know.'

'It can't all be . . .' I struggled for a word. 'Intensity. We need ordinary life.'

'Why?'

'Don't you ever want just to sit in front of the TV? Or go to bed early with a book?' The memory of my last weekend with Jake suddenly came flooding in on me: all that unremarkable domestic happiness that I had so euphorically thrown off. 'Or fly a kite or go ten-pin bowling?'

'Bowling? What the fuck is this?'

'You know what I mean.'

He was silent. I put my arms around him and hugged him, but he felt resistant. 'Adam, you're my dearest love. I'm in this for life. But marriage is about ordinary things, chores, boring duties, work, squabbles, sorting out squabbles. Everything. Not just, well, burning desire.'

'Why?' Adam said simply. It wasn't a question. It was a statement. 'Who says?'

I stopped hugging him and went and sat on the armchair. I didn't know if I felt angry or forlorn, if I should shout or weep.

'I want to have children one day, Adam, or maybe I do. I want to get a house sometime and be middle-aged and ordinary. I want to be with you when I'm old.'

He crossed the room and knelt at my feet and put his face in my lap. I stroked his tangled hair, smelt the sweat of his day on him. 'You'll always be with me,' he said, his voice muffled.

Pauline's pregnancy was beginning to show, and her face, normally so pale and severe, looked plump and rosy. Her dark hair, which she usually tied back, fell on to her shoulders. She looked young and pretty and happy. We were shy with each other, courteous and making an effort. I tried to remember what we used to talk about when we saw each other back in the pre-Adam days: everything and nothing, I suppose; casual bits of gossip, hushed confidences, intimate inanities which were like verbal acts of affection. We used to giggle. Be silent. Argue and make up. This evening, however, we had to work hard to keep our conversation from flagging, and whenever there was a pause one of us would rush to fill it.

After the film we went to a pub. She had tomato juice and I had gin. When I pulled a note out of my wallet to pay for the drinks, the photograph that Adam had taken of me the day he had asked me to marry him fell out too.

'That's a strange picture,' she said, picking it up. 'You look as if you've seen a ghost.'

I stuffed it back between the credit cards and the driving licence. I didn't want anyone else peering at it – it was for my eyes only.

We discussed the bad film rather tamely, until suddenly I couldn't bear it any longer. 'How's Jake?' I asked, as I always did.

'All right,' she said blankly.

'No, I *really* mean how is he. I want to know.'

Pauline looked at me shrewdly. I didn't look away, or smile meaninglessly, and when she spoke it felt like a kind of victory for something. 'The plan was that you two were going to get married, have children. Then it all changed. He told me that everything was going well and that it came out of the blue. Is that true?'

I nodded. 'Pretty much.'

'He's shaken. He was so wrong about you.' I didn't speak. 'He was, wasn't he? Did you love him?'

I thought back to the distant days of me and Jake. I could hardly remember what his face looked like any more. 'Of course

181

I did. And there was you, and the Crew, Clive and Sylvie and the rest, like a big family. I think I thought the same as Jake. I felt I was betraying all of you. I still think that. It's as if I've become an outsider.'

'That's what it's all about, isn't it?'

'What?'

'Being an outsider. Choosing the heroic loner and giving everything up for him. Great fantasy.' Her voice was flat and faintly contemptuous.

'That's not what I want.'

'Has anyone told you that you look completely different from three months ago?'

'No, they haven't.'

'Well, you do.'

'How?'

Pauline looked at me reflectively with an almost hard expression. Was she hitting back at me?

'You look thinner,' she said. 'Tired. You're not as tidy as you used to be. You always wore neat clothes and your hair was well cut and everything about you seemed ordered and composed. Now' – she stared at me, and I was uncomfortably aware of the bruise on my neck – 'you look a bit, well, wasted. Ill.'

'I'm not composed,' I said, truculently. 'I don't think I ever was. But you, on the other hand, look wonderful.'

Pauline smiled a smile of contained satisfaction. 'It's the pregnancy,' she purred. 'You should try it sometime.'

When I got back from the film Adam was not in. At about midnight, I gave up waiting for him and climbed into bed. I stayed awake until one, reading, listening for his feet pounding up the stairs. Then I slept fitfully, waking every so often to look at the luminous hands on the alarm clock. He didn't come home until three. I heard him throw off his clothes and shower himself. I wasn't going to ask him where he'd been. He climbed into bed and spooned himself behind me, warm and clean, smelling of soap. He put his hands on my breasts and kissed my neck. Why do people shower at three in the morning?

'Where've you been?' I said.

'Letting air into our relationship, of course.'

I cancelled the meal. I bought all the food and the drink, but then I couldn't go through with it after all. I came in with the shopping that Saturday morning; Adam was in the kitchen drinking a beer. He jumped up and helped me unpack everything. He took my coat off and rubbed my fingers, which were cramped from carrying the bags back from the supermarket. He made me sit down while he put the ready-roasted chicken and the different cheeses in the small fridge. He made a pot of tea for me and eased my shoes off, rubbed my feet. He put his arms around me as if he worshipped me and kissed my hair, and said, ever so softly, 'Did you go out of London the week before last, Alice?'

'No, why?' I was too startled to think clearly. My heart was banging uncomfortably, and I was sure he must be able to feel it through my cotton shirt.

'Not at all?' He kissed the side of my jaw.

'I worked all of last week, you know that.'

He had found something out. My brain worked furiously.

'Of course I do.' His hands slid down and cupped my buttocks. He held me very tightly, kissed me again.

'I went to a meeting in Maida Vale one day, but that's all.'

'What day would that be?'

'I can't think.' Maybe he'd phoned the office that day, maybe that's what had happened. But why ask me now? 'Wednesday, I think it was. Yes.'

'Wednesday. That's a coincidence.'

'What do you mean?'

'Your skin feels all silky today.' He kissed my eyelids, then started very slowly to undo the buttons on my shirt. I stood quite still as he took the shirt off. What had he found out? He undid my bra and took that off as well.

183

'Careful, Adam, the curtains are open. Someone could see us.'

'That doesn't matter. Take off my shirt. That's it. Now my belt. Take my belt out of my jeans.'

I did.

'Now feel in my pocket. Go on, Alice. No, not that pocket, the other one.'

'There's nothing there.'

'Yes, there is. It's only small, though.'

My fingers felt a stiff piece of paper. I drew it out.

'There you are, Alice. A train ticket.'

'Yes.'

'For last Wednesday.'

'Yes. So?' Where had he found that? I must have left it in my coat or bag or something.

'The day you were out of the office in – where did you say?'

'Maida Vale.'

'Yes, Maida Vale.' He started to undo my jeans. 'Though the train ticket is for Gloucester.'

'What is this about, Adam?'

'You tell me.'

'What has a train ticket got to do with anything?'

'There. Step out of your jeans. It was in your coat pocket.'

'What were you doing going through my coat pocket?'

'What were you doing, Alice, going to Gloucester?'

'Don't be stupid, Adam, I never went to Gloucester.' It never occurred to me to tell him the truth. At least I still had a trace of self-preservation left.

'Take your knickers off.'

'No. Stop this.'

'Why Gloucester, I wonder?'

'I never went there, Adam. Mike went there a few days ago – maybe it was Wednesday – to visit some warehouse space. Maybe it's his ticket. But why does it matter?'

'Why was it in your pocket, then?'

'Fuck knows. Look, if you don't believe me, ring him up and ask him. Go on. I'll dictate the number to you.'

I glared at him defiantly. I knew Mike was away for the weekend anyway.

'We'll forget about Mike and Gloucester, then, shall we?'

'I'd already forgotten it,' I said.

He pushed me to the floor and knelt over me. He looked as if he were about to cry and I held my arms out to him. When he struck me with his belt, the buckle biting into my flesh, it didn't even hurt very much. Nor the second time. Was this the spiral my GP had warned me of?

'I love you so very much, Alice,' he groaned, afterwards. 'You've no idea how very much I love you. Don't ever let me down. I wouldn't be able to bear it.'

I put off the meal, saying to everyone I called that I had flu. It was true that I felt so exhausted it was like being ill. We ate the chicken I had bought in bed and went to sleep early, locked in each other's arms.

Twenty-four

A temporary hero and celebrity, Adam began to get communications from the world outside, relayed from the newspapers and publishers to which they'd been sent. People wrote to him as they might have written to Dr Livingstone or Lawrence of Arabia, complicated theories and grievances outlined over a dozen pages in minuscule handwriting and unusual colours of ink. There were adoring letters from young girls that made me smile, and become a little worried. There was a letter from the widow of Tomas Benn – who had died on the mountain – but it was in German, and Adam didn't bother to translate it for me. 'She wants to see me,' he said, wearily, tossing the letter on to the pile.

'What does she want?' I asked.

'To talk,' he said curtly. 'To hear that her husband was a hero.'

'Are you going to see her?'

He shook his head. 'I can't help her. Tommy Benn was a rich man out of his class, that's all.'

Then there were people who wanted to go on expeditions. And there were people with projects, ideas, obsessions, fantasies and a great deal of hot air. Adam ignored most of them. Once or twice he was lured out for a drink and I would join him in some bar in central London being talked at by a magazine editor or a bright-eyed researcher.

One day there was another unpromising approach, a foreign accent on a bad line early on a rainy Tuesday morning. I picked up the phone and was discouraging. I handed the receiver across the bed to Adam who was downright rude. But the caller persisted and Adam agreed to meet him.

'So?' I asked Adam, when he slouched in late one evening and took a beer from the fridge.

'I don't know,' he said, banging the bottle open in his macho way on the edge of the table. He looked puzzled, almost stunned.

'What was it about?'

'A man in a suit who works for a German TV company. Knows a bit about climbing. He says they want to do a documentary about a climb. They'd like me to lead it. Any time I want, anywhere in the world, with whoever I want, the more challenging the better and they'll organize finance.'

'That sounds amazing. Isn't that perfect?'

'There must be a catch. There must be something wrong with the plan, but I haven't worked out what it is yet.'

'What about Daniel? I thought you were going with him next year.'

'Fuck Daniel. That was just for the money. I just can't believe it's for real.'

Apparently it *was* for real. There were more drinks, then meetings. One evening, late at night when we were a bit drunk, Adam told me what he would like to do. He would like to go up Everest and not even attempt to get to the top: just clear the mountain of all the shit, bits of tent and frayed line, empty oxygen bottles, litter, even some of the dead bodies that were still up there, crammed into their last useless shelters. I thought it was beautiful and I coaxed him into scrawling the idea on a piece of paper, which I then typed into a presentable form. The TV company said yes to everything. It would make a great film. It had mountains and ecology.

It was wonderful. *I* felt wonderful. Adam had been like a boiling pot, spluttering and splattering on the stove, and it was as if he had suddenly been turned down to a more manageable simmer. Adam's life was climbing and me, and for a couple of months it had been almost entirely me, and I had begun to wonder if I would get worn out, literally worn out, by the intensity of his attention. I loved Adam, I adored Adam, I lusted after Adam,

187

but it was a relief now sometimes to lie in bed, sipping wine while he talked of the number of people he should take, when he should go, and I contributed nothing. I just nodded and enjoyed his enthusiasm. It was nice, just nice but nothing transcendent, and that was good too but I was careful not to say that to Adam.

For my part, I was also, gradually, becoming calmer about Adam's past. The whole Michelle thing was now part of the landscape, the sort of thing we all get involved with when we're young in one way or another. And Michelle had her baby and her husband now. She didn't need my help. His previous girlfriends, the long-term ones, didn't really mean much more to me than, say, the mountains he had summitted. If, when I was talking to Klaus or Deborah or Daniel or another of his older climbing friends, a mention of one of them came up I wouldn't pay particular attention. But obviously you are interested in everything to do with the person you are in love with and to say nothing at all would have been an affectation. So I picked up information about them here and there and began to form a picture of them in my mind, to consider them in chronological order.

One evening we were back at Deborah's Soho flat, but as guests this time. Daniel was going to be there. I had suggested that Daniel could go along on the Everest expedition. Adam was generally about as likely to take my advice on the subject of mountaineering as he was that of the doorknob of our bedroom, but on this occasion he looked reflective rather than dismissive. For most of the evening, he and Daniel were deep in conversation leaving Deborah and me to talk by ourselves.

It was a simple meal, just ravioli bought from across the street, salad from round the corner, and bottles of Italian red wine poured into dangerously large glasses. After we had finished the meal, Deborah took one of the bottles from the table and we went and sat on the floor in front of the open fire. She topped up my glass yet again. I didn't feel exactly drunk, but I felt that my edges had gone fuzzy and as if there was a soft mattress between me and the floor. Deborah stretched out.

'I sometimes feel there are ghosts in this flat,' she said, with a smile.

'You mean, people who used to live here?' I said.

She laughed. 'No, I mean you and Adam. This was where it all started.'

I supposed that the colour of my cheeks would be camouflaged by the fire and the wine. 'I hope we tidied up properly,' was all I could manage.

She lit a cigarette and reached across to the table for an ashtray. She lay back down on the floor. 'You're good for Adam,' she said.

'Am I? I sometimes worry that I'm not enough of a part of his world.'

'That's what I mean.'

I looked across at the table. Adam and Daniel were drawing diagrams and even talking about spreadsheets. Deborah winked at me. 'It's going to be the most glamorous trash collection in history.' She laughed.

I looked across. They wouldn't be listening to what we were saying.

'But his last er . . . girlfriend, Lily, she wasn't involved with climbing, was she? Did you meet her?'

'A few times. But she was nothing. That was just a transitional thing. She was all right, but she was a pain, whining after Adam all the time. When he woke up and saw what she was like he dumped her.'

'What was Françoise like?'

'Ambitious. Rich. A pretty good technical climber.'

'Beautiful, as well.'

'Beautiful?' said Deborah ironically. 'Only if you like long-legged, thin, sun-tanned women with long fine black hair. Unfortunately most men do.'

'It was a terrible thing for Adam.'

'Worse for Françoise. Anyway,' she pulled a face, 'it was finished, wasn't it? She was a climbing groupie. She liked the guys.' She dropped her voice a little. 'It may have taken Adam a little time to discover that, but he's a grown-up man. He knows what happens when you sleep with climbing doctors.'

And then I knew.

'So you and . . .' and I nodded over at Adam.

Deborah leaned over and put her hand on mine. 'Alice, it was nothing, for either of us. I just didn't want to have a secret between us.'

'Of course,' I said. I didn't mind. That much. 'Then before Françoise there was the girl called Lisa,' I said, prompting her.

'You want to do this?' asked Deborah, with amused suspicion. 'Adam dumped Lisa when he fell for Françoise.'

'Was she American?'

'No. British. Welsh, Scottish, one of those things. Part-time climber, I think. They were A Couple,' she pronounced the words as if they were inherently comic, 'for years. But, Alice, you mustn't get all of this wrong. They were A Couple,' she made invisible quotation marks in the air with her fingers, 'but they never lived together. Adam's never been committed to anybody the way he has been to you. It's just a different thing.'

I continued to press. 'There was always someone in the background. Although he had other affairs that didn't mean anything – as you say – there was always a permanent relationship. When one finished another started.'

Deborah lit another cigarette and frowned with thought. 'Maybe. I can't remember who he was connected with, as it were, before Lisa. Maybe I never met her. There was a girl a few years before that when I first knew him. What was she called? Penny. She married another old friend of mine, a climber called Bruce Maddern. They live in Sydney. I haven't seen them in a decade.' She looked round at me then snatched another glance across at Adam. 'Jesus, what are we doing? You don't want to bother about all of this. The only point of it is that Adam stayed committed to people he wasn't really in love with.' She smiled. 'You can rely on him. He won't let you down. And you mustn't let him down. I've climbed with the guy. He doesn't tolerate you failing to do what you've committed to do.'

'That sounds alarming,' I said cheerfully.

'How about climbing, Alice? Any ambitions? Hey, Adam, are you going to take Alice along next year?'

Adam turned to me amiably. 'Maybe you should ask her.'

'Me?' I said alarmed. 'I get blisters. I get tired and bad-tempered. I'm unfit. And what I really like is being warm and wrapped up. My idea of happiness is a hot bath and a silk shirt.'

'That's why you should climb,' said Daniel, coming over with two mugs of coffee and then sitting with us on the floor. 'You know, Alice, I was on Annapurna a few years ago. There had been some fuck-up with the supplies. There are always fuck-ups of some kind or another. Usually it's something like finding yourself at twenty thousand feet with two left mitts, but this time someone, instead of packing five pairs of socks, had ordered fifty. What it meant was that every time I got into the tent I could get an entirely fresh clean pair of socks and put it on and luxuriate in that. You've never been on the mountain so you can't imagine what it was like to put my wet feet into those warm dry socks. But just picture every warm bath you've ever had mixed into one.'

'Trees,' I said.

'What?' said Daniel.

'Why don't you climb trees? Why does it have to be mountains?'

Daniel smiled broadly. 'I think that I will leave that question for the famous buccaneering mountaineer Adam Tallis to deal with.'

Adam thought for a moment. 'You can't pose for photographs on top of a tree,' he said finally. 'That's why most people climb mountains. To pose for photographs on the top.'

'But not you, my darling,' I said, and then was embarrassed by my own serious tone.

191

There was a silence as we all lay and looked in the fire. I sipped my coffee. Then, on an impulse, I leaned over, took Deborah's cigarette, dragged on it and then returned it to her.

'I could so easily start again,' I said. 'Especially on an evening like this, lying on the floor in front of the fire, a little drunk with friends after a lovely dinner.' I looked across at Adam who was looking at me, the light from the fire shimmering on his face. 'The real reason isn't any of that. I think I might have wanted to do something like that before I met Adam. That's the funny thing. It's Adam who's made me understand what a wonderful thing it is to climb a mountain and at the same time he's made me not want to do it. If I were going to do it, I'd want to be looking out for other people. I wouldn't want them to have to be looking out for me all the time.' I looked around. 'If we were climbing together, you'd all be dragging me up. Deborah would probably fall down a crevasse, Daniel would have to give me his gloves. I'd be all right. You are the ones who would pay for it.'

'You looked beautiful this evening.'

'Thanks,' I said sleepily.

'And what you said about trees was funny.'

'Thanks.'

'It almost made me forgive you for quizzing Debbie about my past.'

'Ah.'

'You know what I want? I want it to be as if our lives began at the moment we first saw each other. Do you think that's possible?'

'Yes,' I said. Meaning, no.

Twenty-five

The history I had learned at school, but mostly forgotten now, fell into convenient categories: the Middle Ages, the Reformation, the Renaissance, the Tudors and Stuarts. For me, Adam's earlier life now fell into similar categories: stripes of separated time, like coloured sand in a bottle. There was the Lily Age, the Françoise Age, the Lisa Age, the Penny Age. I never talked to Adam about his past now: it was a forbidden subject. But I thought about it. I picked up little details about the women he had loved, and slotted them into the larger picture. As I did so, I realized that there was a gap in the chronology – an empty space where a woman should have been but wasn't. It might just have been a year or so without a committed relationship, but that didn't seem to fit into what I had come to see as the pattern of Adam's life.

It was as if I was watching a beloved figure walking across the landscape towards me, always getting closer, when it was suddenly swallowed up in mist. I calculated that it was about eight years ago, this hiatus. I didn't want to interrogate anybody about it, but the sense of needing to fill in the gap grew stronger. I asked Adam if he had any photos of himself when he was younger, but apparently he had none. I tried to find out, from casual questions, what he was doing at that time, as if I would eventually be able to join the insignificant dots to reveal a significant answer. But while I discovered names of peaks and perilous routes, I never found a woman to fill in the space between Lisa and Penny. But I was the world expert on Adam. I needed to be sure.

One weekend in late March, we returned to his old family

house. Adam needed to fetch some of his equipment, which he kept stashed away in one of the large outhouses, so he had hired a van. 'I don't have to return it until Sunday. Maybe we could find a hotel for Saturday night.'

'With room service,' I said. It never occurred to me to suggest we should stay with his father. 'And an *en suite* bathroom, please.'

We set off early. It was a glorious early-spring morning, icily clear. There was new blossom on some of the trees, mist rolling off the fields we passed by on our way northwards. Everything felt newly hopeful. We stopped at a motorway service station for breakfast. Adam drank coffee and didn't eat his Danish pastry while I had a large bacon sandwich – stringy pink rashers between slices of greasy white bread – and a mug of hot chocolate.

'I like women with an appetite,' he said. So I finished off his pastry too.

We arrived at about eleven and, like a fairy story, everything was as it had been on our last visit. There was no one to greet us, and no sign of Adam's father. We went into the dark hall, where the grandfather clock stood guard, and took off our coats. We went into the chilly living room, where a single empty tumbler stood on a side table. Adam called out for his father, but there was no reply. 'We might as well start,' he said. 'It shouldn't take long.'

We put our coats back on and went out by the back door. There were several old outhouses of varying sizes behind the house for, as Adam explained, there had been a working farm attached to the estate. They were mostly derelict but a couple had been patched up, new slates put on the roof and weeds cleared from their doorways. I peered in through the windows as we passed. In one, there was broken furniture, boxes of empty wine bottles, old storage heaters and, shoved into the corner, a netless table-tennis table. Wooden tennis racquets were stacked on a broad shelf, a couple of cricket bats. There were numerous tins of paint ranged on the shelf above them, their sides dripping with different colours. Another shed was used for tools. I made out a lawn-mower, a couple of rakes, a rusty scythe, spades, forks, hoes, great bags of compost and cement mix, toothy saws.

'What are those?' I asked, pointing to several gleaming silver contraptions hanging from large hooks screwed into the wall.

'Squirrel traps.'

There was one building I wanted to go into, for through the broken glass I had seen a grand china teapot without its spout poking out of a large box, and hanging from a hook, a ripped, useless kite. It looked like the place where all the worn-out family effects were kept, the ones that no one wanted, but no one could quite throw away. There were trunks on the floor and stacked containers. It all looked so well ordered and so sad. I wondered if all the things that had belonged to Adam's mother had been put here, long ago, and never been touched since. I asked Adam, but he pulled me away from the window. 'Leave it alone, Alice. It's just stuff he should have got rid of years ago.'

'Don't you ever look through it?'

'What for? Here, this is where my stuff is kept.'

I had never imagined there would be so much of it. It almost filled the long, low room. Everything was neatly packed and stored; lots of the boxes and bags had labels on them, with Adam's bold script slanting across. There were ropes, of different thickness and colours, in steep coils. An ice axe hung from the beams. There were a couple of backpacks, empty and fastened down against the dust. One slim nylon bag was a tent, the other, shorter, was a Gore-Tex sleeping bag. A box of crampons stood by a box of long thin nails. A box full of assorted clips, screws, clamps. Bandages in Cellophane wraps stood on a thin shelf, and on a broader one a Calor gas stove, a few canisters of gas, pewter mugs and several water bottles. Two well-used pairs of climbing boots lay to one side.

'What's in this?' I asked, poking a squashy nylon sack with my toe.

'Gloves, socks, thermal underwear, that kind of thing.'

'You don't travel light.'

'As light as I can,' he replied, looking around. 'I don't carry this stuff for fun.'

'What are we here for?'

'This, for a start.' He pulled out a largish bag. 'This is a Portaledge. It's like a tent you can bolt on to a sheer cliff side. Once I spent four days in it, in a raging storm.'

'Sounds terrifying,' I shivered.

'Cosy.'

'Why do you want it now?'

'It's not for me. It's for Stanley.'

He rifled through a Tupperware box packed with tubes of ointment, picking out a couple and stuffing them into his jacket pocket. He took one of the ice axes off the beam and laid it beside the tent. Then, hunkering down on his haunches, he started pulling out little cartons and boxes and examining their labels. He looked entirely focused on his task.

'I'm going for a wander,' I said eventually. He didn't look up.

Outside, it was warm enough to take off my coat. I walked over to the vegetable garden, where a few decayed bolted cabbages swayed, and weeds climbed the frames meant for runner beans. Someone had left the hose tap running slightly, and there was a great puddle of mud in the centre of the garden. It was all rather depressing. I turned it off, then looked around to see if Adam's father was anywhere in sight, and marched firmly towards the ramshackle building where I'd glimpsed the china teapot and the kite. I wanted to look through the boxes, pick up the objects that Adam had had as a child, find photographs of him and of his mother.

There was a large key in the lock that turned easily. The door opened inwards. I shut it quietly behind me. Someone had been in here quite recently, for the thick dust only lay over some of the boxes and trunks, whereas others were fairly clean. In one corner I saw the skeleton of a bird. There was a thick, stale smell in the room.

I had been right, though: it was where old family things were stored. The teapot was part of a china tea-set. There were faint brownish rings round some of the cups still, tidemarks from long-ago drinks. There was a packing case piled high with paired wellington boots. Some of them were small. They must have belonged to Adam when he was a boy. The largest black trunk had the gilt initials V. T. on its lid. What had his mother's name been? I couldn't remember if he'd ever told me. I opened it furtively. I told myself I was doing nothing wrong, just poking around, but I didn't think Adam would see it like that. The trunk was full of clothes, smelling strongly of musty age and pungent mothballs. I fingered a spotted navy-blue frock, a crocheted shawl, a lavender-coloured cardigan with pearl buttons. Graceful but sensible clothes. I shut the lid, and opened a battered white suitcase beside it. It was full of baby clothes: Adam's. Jerseys with boats and balloons knitted into the pattern, striped dungarees, woollen hats, an all-in-one-suit with a pixie hood, tiny leggings. I almost cooed. There was a christening gown in there too, yellowing with age, now. The chest of drawers to one side, which was missing several knobs and was badly scratched down one side, was full of little booklets which, on closer inspection, turned out to be things like school magazines and school reports. The two girls' and Adam's, from Eton. I opened one at random from 1976. He would have been twelve. It was the year his mother died. Maths: 'If Adam applied his considerable ability to learning rather than disrupting,' ran the neat italic script in blue ink, 'then he would do well. As it is . . .' I shut up the booklet. This wasn't just snooping; it felt more like spying.

I wandered over to the other corner of the room. I wanted to find photographs. Instead, in a small case with a strap wrapped round it twice to keep it shut, I found letters. At first I thought they were letters from Adam's mother, I don't know why. Maybe because I was looking for traces of her, and something about the handwriting made me sure they were from a woman. But when I picked up the top bundle and leafed through it, I realized at once that they were from lots of different people, and were written in lots of different kinds of handwriting. I glanced at the top one, scrawled in blue Biro, and gasped.

'Darling darling Adam,' it began. It was from Lily. Some vestigial scruple stopped me reading it. I put down the bundle, but then picked it up again. I didn't read through the letters, although I couldn't help noticing certain memorable phrases, which I knew I would be unable to forget. I just looked to see who they were from. It was, I told myself, as if I were an archaeologist, digging through the layers of Adam's history, through all his familiar periods.

First there were letters – short and scrappy – from Lily. Then, in black ink and with the familiar looped and cursive elegance of French script, letters from Françoise. These were usually long. They weren't passionate, like Lily's, but their raw intimacy made me wince. Her English was exceptionally vivid, charming even in its occasional slips. Under Françoise were a couple of miscellaneous letters. One from a rapturous Bobby and the other from a woman who signed herself 'T', and then a succession of postcards from Lisa. Lisa liked exclamation marks and underscorings.

And then, below Lisa – or before Lisa – came a series of letters from a woman I had never heard of. I squinted at the signature: Adele. I sat back on my heels and listened. Everything was quite quiet. All that I could hear was the rattle of wind in the loose slates above me. Adam must still be sorting through his stuff. I counted through Adele's letters; there were thirteen, mostly rather short. Under her letters were six from Penny. I had found the woman between Lisa and Penny, Penny and Lisa. Adele. Starting with the bottom one, presumably the first that she wrote to him, I began to read them.

The first seven or eight letters were short and to the point: she was making arrangements where to meet Adam, naming a place, a time, urging caution. Adele was married: so that was why Adam had remained silent. He was keeping their secret even now. The next letters were longer and more tormented. Adele clearly felt guilty about her husband, whom she called her 'trusting Tom', and a host of others, parents, sister, friends. She kept begging Adam to make things easy for her. The final letter was her goodbye. She wrote that she could no longer continue to betray Tom. She told Adam that she loved him and he would never know how much he had meant to her. She said that he was the most wonderful lover she had ever had. But she couldn't leave Tom. He needed her, and Adam clearly didn't. Had she been asking him for something?

I laid the thirteen letters on my lap. So Adele had left Adam for her marriage. Maybe he had never got over her, and that was why he didn't talk about her. He may have felt humiliated by her. I pushed my hair back behind my ears with hands that were slightly sweaty with nerves, and listened again. Was that a door I heard shutting? I gathered up the letters and put them on top of the ones from Penny.

Just before placing the rest on top, covering up that layer of the past with more recent pasts, I noticed that Adele had written her final letter, unlike all the others, on formal family paper, with a letterhead, as if she were emphasizing her bonded state. Tom Funston and Adele Blanchard. I felt a stirring of memory, like a prickle down my spine. Blanchard: the name was dimly familiar.

'Alice?'

I shut the case and pushed it, unstrapped, back into position.

'Alice, where are you?'

I scrambled to my feet. There was dust all over the knees of my trousers, and my coat was filthy.

'Alice.'

He was near by, calling me, getting closer. I walked as quietly as I could towards the shut door, smoothing my hair as I did so. It would be better if he didn't find me here. There was a broken armchair piled high with yellow damask curtains in the corner of the room, to the left of the door. I pulled the chair out slightly and crouched down behind it, waiting for the footsteps to go past. This was ridiculous. If Adam found me in the middle of the room I could just say that I was looking around. If he found me hiding behind a chair, there was nothing at all I could say. It wouldn't just be embarrassing; it would be violent. I knew my husband. I was about to stand up when the door was pushed open and I heard him step into the room.

'Alice?'

I held my breath. Maybe he would be able to see me through the heap of curtains.

'Alice, are you there?'

The door shut again. I counted to ten and stood up. I went back to the case of letters, opened it and retrieved Adele's final letter, adding theft to my list of marital crimes. Then I shut the case and this time I strapped it up. I didn't know where to put the letter. Obviously not in any of my pockets. I tried stuffing it into my bra but I was wearing a tight-fitting ribbed top, and the wodge of paper showed. What about my knickers? In the end I took off one shoe and hid it in there.

I took a deep breath and went to the door. It was locked. Adam must have locked it when he went out again, as a matter of course. I gave a hard push, but it was solid against me. I looked around in panic for some kind of implement. I took the old kite off the wall and slid the central arm out of the ripped material. I poked this through the lock, though I am not sure what I hoped to achieve. I heard the key clunk to the ground outside the door.

The lower pane in the window was broken. If I removed the jagged remains of the glass, I would be able to squeeze through. Perhaps. I started to pull shards from the pane. Then I chucked my coat through the hole. I pulled a trunk under the window and, standing on it, swung one leg through. The window was too high: I couldn't touch the ground on the other side. Painfully, I manoeuvred myself through the hole until my toes touched a firm surface. I felt a spike of glass I had failed to remove pierce my jeans and puncture my thigh. I hunched my body and pushed through, head emerging into bright daylight. If anyone caught me now, what would I say? Second leg out. There. I bent down and picked up my coat. My left hand was bleeding. There was dirt and cobwebs and dust all over me.

'Alice?'

I heard his voice in the distance. I took a deep breath. 'Adam.' It sounded steady enough. 'Where are you, Adam? I've been looking for you everywhere.' I slapped dirt off me, licked my forefinger and rubbed it over bits of my face.

'Wherever did you get to, Alice?' He came round the corner, looking so eager and handsome.

'Where did *you* get to, more like?'

'You've cut your hand.'

'It's nothing serious. I ought to wash it, though.'

In the cloakroom – an old-fashioned affair, where the guns were kept, as well as the tweed caps and the green wellies – I rinsed my hands and splashed water all over my face.

His father was sitting in an armchair in the living room, as if he had been there all along and we had simply failed to notice it. He had a fresh glass of whisky by his side. I went over and shook his hand, feeling the thin bones under the loose skin.

'So you've got yourself a wife, Adam,' he said. 'Are you staying to lunch?'

'No,' said Adam. 'Alice and I are going to a hotel now.' He helped me into the coat that I still had bundled under my arm. I smiled up at him.

Twenty-six

One evening, about fifteen people came round to the flat to play poker. They sat on the floor, on cushions, and drank large quantities of beer and whisky, and smoked until all the saucers were overflowing with fag ends. By two in the morning, I was about three pounds down, and Adam was twenty-eight pounds up.

'How come you're so good?' I asked, after everyone had left except Stanley, who was crashed out on our bed, dreadlocks spread over the pillow and pockets quite emptied of cash.

'Years of practice.' He rinsed a glass and put it on the draining board.

'Sometimes it seems so strange to think about all those years when we weren't together,' I said. I picked up a stray tumbler, and drained it. 'That when I was with Jake, you were with Lily. And you were with Françoise, Lisa and . . .' I stopped. 'Who was before Lisa?'

He looked at me coolly, not fooled at all. 'Penny.'

'Oh.' I tried to sound nonchalant. 'Was there no one between Lisa and Penny?'

'No one special.' He did his shrug.

'Talking of which, there's a man in our bed.' I stood up and yawned. 'Sofa do you?'

'Anywhere will do me if you're there too.'

There's a large difference between not revealing something, and positively concealing it. I rang her from work, between two wrangling meetings about the delay on the Drakloop. This, I promised myself, would be the last time, the very last time, that I would poke around in Adam's past. Just this one thing, and then I would lay it all to rest.

I shut my door, swivelled round in my chair so that I was facing my window, with its view of a wall, and dialled the number at the head of the letter. The line was dead. I tried again, just in case. Nothing. I asked the exchange to test the line, and they told me it was no longer in use. So I asked if they could give me the number of Blanchard, A., in West Yorkshire. They had no Blanchards at all there. What about Funston, T.? Nothing under that name either. Sorry, caller, they said blandly. I almost howled in frustration.

What do you do when you want to track someone down? I read through the letter again, hunting for clues, which I already knew weren't there. It was a good letter: straightforward and heartfelt. Tom, she wrote, was her husband and Adam's friend. Their affair was never free of his presence. One day he was bound to discover, and she wasn't prepared to hurt him that much. Nor could she live with the guilt that she was feeling at the moment. She told Adam that she adored him, but that she couldn't see him again. She told him that she was going to stay with her sister for a few days, and he was not to try to change her mind, or to get in touch with her. She was resolute. The affair would remain their secret: he must tell no one, not even his closest friends; not even the women who came after her. She said that she would never forget him but that she hoped one day he would forgive her. She wished him luck.

It was a grown-up kind of letter. I laid it down on my desk and rubbed my eyes. Perhaps I should just let it go now. Adele had implored Adam never to tell anyone, not even future lovers. Adam was simply honouring her request. That fitted his character. He would keep a promise. There was something scarily literal about Adam.

I picked up the letter again and stared at it, letting the words blur. Why did I feel a faint tug of memory at her name? Blanchard.

Where had I heard it before? Maybe from one of Adam's climbing cronies. She and her husband were clearly climbers. I fretted for a few minutes longer, then went into my next meeting with the marketing department.

Adele wouldn't go away. Once you start being jealous, anything feeds that state. You can prove suspicions, but you can never disprove them. I told myself that after I knew about Adele I would be free from the grip of my sexual curiosity. I rang up Joanna Noble and asked if I could use her professional expertise.

'What now, Alice? More wifely paranoia?' She sounded weary of me.

'Nothing like that.' I gave a brisk laugh. 'This is quite unrelated. It's just – I need to track someone down. And I think she was mentioned in the papers recently. I know that you have access to newspaper files.'

'Yes,' she said cautiously. 'Unrelated, you say?'

'Yes. Completely.'

There was a tapping sound at the end of the line, as if she were bouncing a pencil against her desk. 'If you come first thing in the morning,' she said at last, 'nine, say, we can pull up any mentions of the name on the computer, and do a printout of anything relevant.'

'I owe you one.'

'Yes,' she said. There was a pause. 'All fine on the Adam front?' It sounded as if she were talking about the Somme.

'Yup,' I said cheerily. 'All quiet.'

'See you tomorrow, then.'

I got there before nine, and Joanna hadn't arrived. I waited in the reception area, and I saw her before she saw me. She looked tired and preoccupied, but when she noticed me sitting there she said, 'Right, let's go then. The library is in the basement. I've only got about ten minutes.'

The library consisted of rows and rows of sliding shelves filled with brown files, categorized according to subject, and then alphabetically. Diana, Diets, Disasters/natural, that kind of thing. Joanna led me past all of these, to a largish computer. She pulled over a second chair, gestured for me to fill it, and then sat down in front of the screen. 'Tell me the name, then, Alice.'

'Blanchard,' I said. 'Adele Blanchard. B-L- . . .' But she had already typed it in.

The computer beeped into life; numbers filled the top right-hand corner and on the clock icon a hand ticked round. We waited in silence.

'Adele, you say?'

'Yes.'

'There is no Adele Blanchard coming up, Alice. Sorry.'

'That doesn't matter,' I said. 'It was just a long shot. I'm really grateful to you.' I stood up.

'Hang on, there's another Blanchard coming up, though. I thought the name was familiar.'

I looked over Joanna's shoulder. 'Tara Blanchard.'

'Yes, this is just a paragraph or two about a young woman who was fished out of a canal in East London a couple of weeks back.'

That was why the name sounded so familiar. I felt a stab of disappointment. Joanna pressed a key to call up any further items: there was only one, which was more or less identical.

'Do you want a printout?' she asked, with a touch of irony. 'Adele might be her middle name.'

'Sure.'

While the printer was stuttering out the single sheet about Tara Blanchard, I asked Joanna if she had heard anything from Michelle. 'No, thank God. Here you are.'

She handed me the printout. I folded the paper in half, then half again. I should really just chuck it in the bin, I thought. I didn't, though. I pushed it into my pocket, and caught a taxi to work.

I didn't look at the cutting until lunch-time, when I bought a cheese and tomato sandwich and an apple from a café up the road and took them back up to my office. I read the few lines again: the body of twenty-eight-year-old Tara Blanchard, a receptionist, had been found in a canal in East London on 2 March by a group of teenagers.

Adele's letter had mentioned a sister. I hauled the residential telephone directory off the shelf and flicked through it, not expecting to find anything. But there it was: Blanchard, T. M., of 23B Bench Road, London EC2. I picked up the phone, then changed my mind. I rang through to Claudia, said I was going out, and could she take my calls. I wouldn't be long.

Twenty-three Bench Road was a thin, beige, pebble-dashed terrace house, squashed between others, and exuding a general air of neglect. There was a dead plant in one window, and a pink cloth instead of curtains at another. I rang the B bell, and waited. It was one thirty and if anyone had lived here with Tara they were probably out. I was about to press the other bells to see if I could unearth a neighbour or two when I heard footsteps and saw, through the thickly ribbed glass, a shape coming towards me. The door opened on a chain, and a woman stared through the crack. I had clearly woken her up: she was clutching a dressing-gown to her, and her eyes were puffy. 'Yes?'

'I'm really sorry to bother you,' I began, 'but I'm a friend of Tara's, and since I was just passing . . .'

The door closed, I heard the chain being slid back, and then it opened wide. 'Come in, then,' she said. She was a small, plump woman, young, with a mop of gingery hair and tiny ears. She looked at me expectantly.

'I'm Sylvie,' I said.

'Maggie.'

I followed her up the stairs and into her kitchen.

'Do you want a cup of tea?'

'Not if it's a bad time.'

'I'm awake now, aren't I?' she said, quite amiably. 'I'm a nurse, on nights at the moment.'

She filled the kettle, then sat down opposite me at the grubby kitchen table. 'You were a friend of Tara's?'

'That's right,' I said confidently. 'I never came here.'

'She didn't bring people back.'

'I really knew her from childhood actually,' I said. Maggie busied herself with the tea. 'I read about her death in the papers and I wanted to know what happened.'

'It was awful,' said Maggie, standing up to drop two tea-bags into a teapot and pour on the boiling water. 'Sugar?'

'No. Do the police know how it happened?'

'A mugging. Her purse was missing when they found her. I always told her she shouldn't walk along the canal when it was dark. But she always did. It cuts half the distance from the station.'

'Awful,' I said. I thought of the dark canal and shuddered. 'I was mostly a friend of Adele actually.'

'Her sister?' A wave of exhilaration rushed through me: so Tara was Adele's sister, after all. Maggie plonked down my cup of tea. 'Poor thing. Poor parents too. Imagine what they must feel. They came here to collect her stuff a week or so ago. I didn't know what to say to them. They were so very brave, but there can't be anything worse than losing a child, can there?'

'No. Did they leave their address or phone number? I'd love to get in touch with them to tell them how sorry I am.' I'd become too good at deceit.

'I've got it somewhere. I don't think I wrote it in my book, though. I didn't think I'd need it. But it's probably in a pile. Hang on.' She started rummaging through a stack of papers by the toaster – bills in black and red, junk mail, postcards, take-away menus – and finally found it scrawled on the telephone directory. I copied it down on a scrap of used envelope, then put it in my wallet.

'When you speak to them,' she said, 'tell them I've thrown away all the odd stuff they left, like they said I should, apart from the clothes, which I gave to Oxfam.'

'Didn't they take all her things, then?'

'They took almost everything; all the personal things, of course, jewellery, books, photos. You know. But they left some bits. Amazing how much rubbish one has, isn't it? I said I'd deal with it.'

'Can I look at it?' She stared at me in surprise. 'Just in case there's a memento,' I added feebly.

'It's in the dustbin, unless the binmen have taken it.'

'Can I have a quick look?'

Maggie seemed dubious. 'If you want to go through orange peel and cat-food tins and tea-bags, then I guess it's your look-out. The bins are just outside the front door – you probably saw them on your way in. Mine is the one with 23B painted on it in white.'

'I'll have a look on my way out, then. And thanks a lot.'

'There's nothing there. It's all bits of old rubbish.'

I must have looked crazy, a woman in a smart grey trouser suit rooting through a bin. What did I think I was doing, trying to find out about Tara, who was nothing to me except a shabby means of finding her parents? Whom I'd already found, and who were also nothing to me, except as a way of finding the woman who might be Adele. Who should mean nothing to me. She was just a lost fragment of someone else's past.

Chicken bones, empty tuna and cat-food tins, a few lettuce leaves, an old newspaper or two. I was going to reek when I got back to work. A broken bowl, a light-bulb. I'd better do this methodically. I started pulling things out of the bin and piling them on to the bin lid. A couple walked past and I tried to look as if this was quite normal behaviour. Tubes of lipstick and eyeliner pencils: this had probably belonged to Tara. A sponge, a torn bathcap, several glossy magazines. I put them on the pavement, beside the overflowing pile on the bin lid, and then peered back into the nearly empty bin. A face stared back at me. A familiar face.

Very slowly, as in a nightmare, I pushed my hand down and picked up the scrap of newspaper. Tea-leaves were stuck to it.

'The hero returns,' read the headline. By the bin, crammed in a corner, I found a plastic shopping bag. I unfolded it and put the newspaper inside. I scrabbled around in the bottom of the bin and came up with several more scraps of newspaper. They were dirty and sodden, but I could make out Adam's name, Adam's face. I found other sodden papers and envelopes and transferred them all to the shopping bag, cursing the smell and the damp.

A tiny old woman, with two enormous dogs on a double lead, came past and looked at me with distaste. I grimaced. I was even talking to myself now. A madwoman, going through dustbins, scaring herself to death.

Twenty-seven

My hands were oily and stained. I couldn't go back to the office, not like this, and I wanted to go home and scrub everything about this experience off my body, out of my hair, out of my brain. I couldn't take this bag of sodden paper back to the flat. I had to find a place to sit down where I could straighten out my thoughts. I had fabricated so much, concealed so much from Adam, that it was now impossible for me to go spontaneously to him. Always I had to think what it was that I had previously told him, what my story had to be in order to fit in with previous lies. That was the advantage of telling the truth. You didn't have to concentrate all the time. True things fitted together automatically. The thought of this gap I had created between myself and Adam suddenly made the grey day seem even greyer and less bearable.

I walked aimlessly through residential streets looking for a café or anywhere I could rest and think, plan what to do. I saw nothing but an occasional corner shop but eventually I came to a small patch of grass next to a school with a drinking fountain and a climbing frame. Some young mothers were there with babies in prams and raucous toddlers teetering on the apparatus. I went over to the fountain, drank from it then rinsed my foul hands in the dribble of water and dried them on the inside of my jacket.

One bench was free and I sat on it. It must have been Tara who had made the phone calls and left the messages and tampered with the milk, all out of some sick infatuation with Adam that was a hangover from his relationship with her sister. I might once have thought that such behaviour was inconceivable, out of all proportion to the emotion, but now I had become something of an expert in obsession. I tried to calm myself down. For a time I hardly dared to look into the bag.

When I was at school, one of my boyfriends had had a cousin who was in a punk band which became famous for a year or two. Every so often I would notice a mention of his name, or even a picture of him in a magazine and sometimes I would tear it out to show to a couple of my friends. What could be more natural than that Tara should be interested in newspaper articles about Adam? That she should tear them out? After all, almost everybody I knew in any capacity had been fascinated by the Adam they read about in the press. Tara had actually known him. I lifted my fingers to my nose. There was still a sweet, rancid reek to them. I considered the image of myself secretly rummaging in the dustbin belonging to the dead sister of an ex-girlfriend of my husband's. I thought of how I had deceived Adam over and over again. Was this any different from my earlier betrayal of Jake?

The thought came to me that the right thing would be to stuff this bag into the nearest bin and go home to Adam, tell him everything I had done and had discovered, admit everything and ask for his understanding. If I was too cowardly to own up to what I had done, then at least I could draw a line under it and allow us to get on with our lives. I dared myself. I actually stood up, looked around for a bin and saw one. But I couldn't get rid of it.

On the way home I went into a stationer's and bought some cardboard folders. As soon as I was out of the shop I unwrapped them and wrote on one: 'Drakloop. Conf: Apr 1995, notes.' That sounded boring enough to repel anybody's interest. I gingerly extracted Tara's sad little clippings from the shopping bag, trying to avoid spilling grease on my clothes. I put them in the file and tossed away the bag. Then I got paranoid and wrote some more meaningless words on three of the other files. When I got them home I had them casually in my hand. They looked just like work stuff.

★　　★　　★

'You look tense,' said Adam. He had come up behind me and touched my shoulders. 'There's a stiff muscle just there.' He began to knead the area in a way that made me groan with pleasure. 'What is there to make you tense?'

What was there to make me tense? A thought occurred to me. 'I don't know, Adam. It may be those calls and messages, they were getting me down.' I turned and took him in my arms. 'But I'm actually feeling better now. They've stopped.'

'They have, haven't they?' Adam frowned.

'Yes. There's been nothing for more than a week.'

'You're right. Were you really worried about them?'

'They were escalating. But I wonder why they stopped like that.'

'It all comes from getting your name in the papers.'

I kissed him. 'Adam, I've a suggestion.'

'What?'

'A year of boredom. Not completely, of course. But below eight thousand metres or whatever it is. I want everything involving me to be completely dull.'

Then I gave a scream. I couldn't help it, because Adam had picked me up in a sort of fireman's lift. He carried me across the flat and then tossed me on to the bed. He looked down at me, grinning. 'I'll see what I can do,' he said. 'And as for you,' he picked up Sherpa and kissed him on the nose, 'this is not going to be a suitable sight for a cat of tender years.' He set him gently down outside the bedroom and closed the door.

'What about me?' I said. 'Should I leave as well?'

He shook his head.

The next morning we left at the same time and went on the tube together. Adam was taking the train out of town. He wouldn't be back until eight. I had a frantic day of meetings at work, which occupied my entire attention. When I emerged, blinking, out of Drakon into the shock of unfiltered air I felt as if there was a swarm of bees inside my head. On the way home I bought a bottle of wine and a prepared meal that needed nothing more than heating up and prising out of a foil container.

When I arrived back home the outside door was unlocked but there was nothing unusual about that. A music teacher lived on the first floor and she unlocked the front door on the days when she had lessons. But when I reached the front door of our flat everything was wrong and I let the shopping fall. The flimsy door had been forced open. There was something taped to it. It was the familiar brown envelope. My mouth was dry, my fingers trembling, as I pulled it away and roughly tore it open. There was a message in crude black capital letters:

HARD DAY, ADAM? TAKE A BATH

I pushed the door gently inwards and listened. There was no sound.

'Adam?' I said feebly, pointlessly. There was no reply. I wondered if I should just go away, call the police, wait for Adam, anything but go in. I waited and listened some more and evidently nobody was there. Out of some curious, automatic sense of neatness I picked up the shopping from the floor and walked into the flat. I put the bag on the kitchen table. I almost tried to pretend to myself for a moment that I didn't know what I had to do. The bathroom. I had to go and look in the bathroom. The person had now gone further and had come and played some joke, left something, just to show that they could get in if they wanted. That they could make us see what they wanted us to see.

I looked around. Nothing had been disturbed. So, inevitably, numbly, I went to the bathroom. I paused outside. Could it be a trap? I pushed at the door. Nothing. I pushed it open and jumped back. Still nothing. I went in. It was probably stupid, nothing at all, and then I looked in the bath. At first, I thought that somebody must have taken a fur hat and splashed it in deep crimson paint for a joke and tossed it into the bath. But I leaned forward and saw it was Sherpa, our cat. He had been difficult to

213

recognize because he hadn't only been slit open right down his torso but it was almost as if an attempt had been made to turn the little thing inside out. He was a horrid disgusting bundle of blood, but still I bent down and touched the top of his stained head, to say goodbye.

When Adam found me I had been lying in the bed, fully dressed, my head under the pillow, for an hour, two hours, I had lost count. I saw his face, puzzled. 'Bathroom,' I said. 'The note's on the floor.'

I heard him go and come back. His face was icy but when he lay beside me and held me I saw there were tears in his eyes. 'I'm so sorry, my darling Alice,' he said.

'Yes,' I sobbed. 'I mean, don't be.'

He shook his head. 'No, I mean . . . I . . .' His voice faltered and he hugged me. 'I didn't listen to you, I was . . . Police. Can I just dial 999?'

I shrugged, tears running down my face at an angle. I couldn't speak. I dimly heard quite a long conversation on the phone, Adam insistent. By the time two police officers arrived, an hour and a half later, I had sorted myself out. They were large, or they made the flat look small, and they stepped inside awkwardly as if they were concerned they might knock something over. Adam led them into the bathroom. One of them swore. Then they came back out, both were shaking their heads.

'Bloody hell,' said one of them. 'Bastards.'

'Do you think there was more than one of them?'

'Kids,' the other one said. 'Out of their heads.'

So it hadn't been Tara, after all. I didn't understand anything any more. I had been so very sure it had been her. I looked up at Adam.

'Look,' he said, giving them the last note. 'We've been getting these over the last couple of weeks. And phone calls as well.'

The officers looked at it without much interest.

'Are you going to be taking fingerprints?' I asked.

They exchanged glances.

'We'll take a statement,' one of them said, extracting a small notebook from his bulky jacket. I told him that I had found our cat cut up in our bath. That our door had been forced open. That we had received anonymous phone calls and notes, which we hadn't bothered to report or keep, but then they seemed to have stopped. He wrote it down laboriously. Half-way his pen ran out and I gave him one from my pocket.

'It's kids,' he said, when I had finished.

On the way out, the two of them looked critically at the door.

'You want something more solid,' one of them said reflectively. 'My three-year-old could kick this open.' And they were gone.

Two days later Adam received a letter from the police. 'Dear Mr Tallis' was handwritten at the top but the text was a blurry photocopy. It continued: 'You have reported a crime. No arrest has been made, but we will keep the case on file. If you have any further information, please contact the duty officer at Wingate Road Police Station. If you require assistance from a Victim Support Group, contact the duty officer at Wingate Road Police Station. Yours sincerely.' The signature was a squiggle. A photo-copied squiggle.

Twenty-eight

Lying gets easier. This is partly a matter of practice. I became an actress secure in her role as Sylvie Bushnell, the journalist or the concerned friend. I had discovered also that other people generally assume that what you are saying to them is true, especially if you are not trying to sell them insurance or an industrial-sized vacuum cleaner.

So, three days after rummaging through the bin of a murdered woman I had never met, I was sitting in a house in a village in the middle of middle England drinking tea made for me by her mother. It had been so easy to phone up, to say that I had known Tara, that I was in the area, that I wanted to pay my respects. Tara's mother had been eager, almost effusive.

'This is very kind of you, Mrs Blanchard,' I said.

'Jean,' the woman said.

Jean Blanchard was a woman in her late fifties, about the age of my own mother, dressed in slacks and a cardigan. Her medium-length hair was streaked with grey, there were deep wrinkles in her face that looked as if they had been chiselled in hard wood and I wondered what her nights were like. She held out a plate of biscuits to me. I took a small thin one and nibbled the end of it, trying to stow into a dark corner of my mind the thought that I was stealing it from her.

'How did you know Tara?'

I took a deep breath. But I had it all planned out. 'I didn't know her that well,' I said. 'I met her through a group of mutual friends in London.'

Jean Blanchard nodded. 'We worried about her, when she

went down to London. She was the first of the family to move away from the area. I knew that she was grown-up, though, and able to take care of herself. How did she seem?'

'London is a big place.'

'That's exactly what I felt,' Mrs Blanchard said. 'I've never been able to bear it. Christopher and I went to see her and, to be frank, we didn't enjoy being there, with the noise and the traffic and the people. We didn't much care for the flat she was renting. We had plans to help her find somewhere, but then this . . .' She faltered.

'What did Adele think?' I asked.

Mrs Blanchard looked puzzled. 'I'm sorry? I don't understand.'

I had gone wrong somewhere. I felt a lurch, almost of vertigo, as if I had been near a cliff edge and had stumbled. I tried desperately to think of what I might have misunderstood. Had I somehow got the wrong family? Could Adele and Tara be the same person? No, I'd mentioned her to the woman in the flat. Say something noncommittal.

'Tara used to talk about Adele.'

Mrs Blanchard nodded, unable to speak. I waited, not daring to say anything further. She took a handkerchief from her pocket and wiped her eyes then blew her nose. 'Of course, that was why she moved to London. She never got over Adele . . . And then Tom's death.'

I leaned over and put one hand on Mrs Blanchard's. 'I'm so sorry,' I said. 'It must have been so terrible for you. One thing after another.' I needed more information. 'When did it happen?'

'Tom?'

'Adele.'

Mrs Blanchard gave a sad smile. 'I suppose it's a long time ago to other people. January nineteen ninety. I used to count the days.'

'I never knew Adele,' I said, which was almost the first true sentence I had uttered in Mrs Blanchard's presence. 'But I think

I know, *used* to know,' I corrected myself prudently, 'some of her friends. Climbers. Deborah, Daniel, Adam . . . whatever he's called.'

'Tallis?'

'I think so,' I said. 'It's a long time.'

'Yes, Tom used to climb with him. But we knew him when he was a boy. We were friends of his parents, long ago.'

'Really?'

'He's become rather famous. He saved some people's lives on a mountain and he's been written about in the newspapers.'

'Really? I didn't see that.'

'He'll be able to tell you about it himself. He's coming here this afternoon for tea.'

I was almost scientifically interested in the way that I was able to continue leaning forward with a concerned expression on my face, even as it seemed that the polished wooden floor was moving towards me and would strike me in the face. I had seconds to think of something. Or should I just relax and let myself go, allow disaster to take its course? A vestigial part of my mind, somewhere deep inside, survived, was still fighting for survival.

'That would have been lovely,' I heard myself say. 'Unfortunately I've got to get back. I'm afraid I've really got to go. Thank you so much for the tea.'

'But you've only just arrived,' Mrs Blanchard protested anxiously. 'Before you go I must show you something. I've been going through Tara's things and I thought you might be interested to see her photograph album.'

I looked at her sad face. 'Of course, Jean, I would love to,' I said. I looked at my watch quickly. It was twenty-five to three. The trains arrived in Corrick on the hour and it had taken me ten minutes to walk from the station, so Adam couldn't be coming on the last train. Could he be driving? It seemed unlikely. 'Do you know when the train goes back to Birmingham?' I asked Mrs Blanchard, who was returning with the photograph album clutched under her arm.

218

'Yes, it goes at four minutes past . . .' She looked at her watch. 'Four minutes past three would be the next one.'

'So I've got plenty of time,' I said to her, with a forced smile.

'More tea?'

'No, thank you,' I said. 'But I would love to see the photographs. If you can bear it.'

'Of course, my dear.'

She pulled her chair closer to mine. All the time she spoke I was making calculations in my head. If I left by a quarter to three I would be able to get to the station before Adam arrived – and, of course, maybe he wouldn't arrive at four, but if he did then I would be safely on the other platform and could find somewhere to conceal myself. Mrs Blanchard would mention that somebody who knew him had just been there but I couldn't remember anything I had done to give away my real identity. As far as Adam was concerned I would just be one of those dozens, hundreds of girls in his past.

If I'd got it wrong? What would happen if Adam arrived while I was still there? I made dismal half-formed attempts to plan something I might say, but I dismissed everything as disastrous. I needed all my concentration just to stay upright, to remain capable of speech. I had known nothing of Tara Blanchard except that her body had been found in an East London canal. Now I saw her as a cherub-cheeked toddler in the sandpit at her nursery school. In pigtails and blazer. In swimsuits and party dresses. Adele was often there as well. She had looked dumpy and cross as a small child but then became long-legged and beautiful. Adam was consistent, I had to admit. But it was going too slowly. I looked at my watch repeatedly. At eighteen minutes to three we seemed to be about half-way through the book. Then Mrs Blanchard paused for a story I couldn't make myself listen to. I pretended to be so interested that I had to turn the page to see what was coming up. A quarter to. We were still not at the end. Thirteen minutes.

'There's Adam,' said Mrs Blanchard.

I forced myself to look. He was much the same as the Adam I knew. The hair was longer. He was unshaven. In a smiling group with Adele, Tara, Tom, a couple of others I didn't know. I looked for a hint of complicity between him and Adele but saw none. 'No,' I said. 'I must have mixed him up with someone else.'

It might even stop Mrs Blanchard from mentioning me to Adam. But I mustn't make too much of it. Ten to. With a sudden desperate relief I saw Mrs Blanchard reach a blank page of the album. The book wasn't full. I had to be firm. I took her hand. 'Jean, that was . . .' I stopped, as if the emotions were too great to be expressed. 'And now I must go.'

'Let me drive you,' she said.

'No,' I said, trying to stop my voice rising into a howl. 'After this, all this, I would like to walk on my own.'

She stepped forward and took me in her arms. 'Come again, Sylvie,' she said.

I nodded and within seconds was walking down the path. But it had taken longer than I thought. It was six minutes to. I considered going in the other direction, but that seemed even worse. As soon as I had turned out of the driveway into the road I broke into a run. My body was not ready for this. After a hundred yards my breath was coming in gasps, there were sharp pains in my chest. I turned another corner and saw the station ahead, too far ahead. I made myself run but as I reached the car park, full of commuter vehicles, I saw a train pulling in. I couldn't risk entering a station and running into Adam. I looked around desperately. There seemed to be no cover. All I saw was a phone-box. In desperation I ran inside and took the phone from the hook. With care I turned my back to the station but I was directly beside the entrance. I looked at my watch. One minute past. I heard the sound of the train pulling out. Mine would be here in another minute or two. I waited. What if Adam came out of the station and wanted to make a phone call?

I was probably making a fool of myself. I became sure that

Adam hadn't been on the train. The temptation to turn around became almost irresistible. I heard the footsteps of several people emerging from the station and then descending to the gravel of the park. One set of footsteps stopped behind me. I could see the fragmentary reflection in the glass in front of me of somebody standing outside the box waiting for me to finish. I couldn't make it out properly. There was a rap at the door. I remembered myself and spoke a few random sentences into the phone. I turned very slightly. There he was, looking a little smarter than usual. He had put on a jacket. I couldn't see if he was wearing a tie. He had passed the phone-box and was down in the car park. He stopped an old woman and said something to her. She looked around and pointed up the street. He set off.

I heard another train arrive. Mine. I remembered with horror that my train was on the other side. I would have to cross a bridge. Don't look round, Adam, don't look round. I replaced the receiver, ran out of the phone-box and actually collided with the woman. She gave a shout of annoyance. She started to say something but I was gone. Had Adam looked round? The automatic doors of the train were closing as I reached the platform. I pushed my arm between their snapping jaws. I assumed that some central electronic intelligence would take note of this and re-open them. Or would the train leave regardless? I had visions of being dragged under the wheels and found horribly mangled at the next station. That would give Adam something to puzzle about.

The doors opened. I felt it was more than I deserved. I sat at one end of the carriage, far from anybody else, and started to cry. Then I looked at my arm. The rubber of the door had left a neat black impression, like a memorial armband. It made me laugh. I couldn't help it.

Twenty-nine

I was alone. I realized at last how alone I was now, and with that realization came fear.

Of course, Adam hadn't been there when I returned from the Blanchards although I supposed he might return soon. I hurriedly pulled on an old T-shirt and crept into bed like a guilty thing. I lay in the dark. I hadn't eaten anything all day and every so often my tummy rumbled, but I didn't want to get up and go into the kitchen. I didn't want Adam to come home and find me exploring the fridge or eating at the kitchen table or any ordinary domestic situation. What could I say to him? All I had were questions, but they were questions that I couldn't ask him. With each fresh deception I had pinned myself into a corner and I couldn't see how I could escape from it. But he had deceived me too. I shuddered when I remembered hiding in that phone-box while he walked by me. What a ghastly farce it all was. Our whole marriage was built on desire and deception.

When he came in, whistling softly, I lay quite still and pretended to be asleep. I heard him open the fridge door, take something out, close it again. I heard a beer can being opened, then drunk. Now he was taking off his clothes, dropping them on the floor at the foot of the bed. The duvet was pulled back as he slid in beside me, and I felt cold air. His warm hands slid round me from behind. I sighed as if in deepest sleep and moved away from him slightly. He moved after me and wrapped his body along the contours of mine. I kept my breathing deep and steady. It wasn't long before Adam was asleep, his breath hot against my neck. Then I tried to think.

What did I know? I knew that Adam had had a secret affair with a woman to whom, it was now clear, something had happened. I knew that that woman had a sister who had collected newspaper cuttings about Adam and had been fished out of a canal a few weeks ago. I knew, of course, that another of his lovers, Françoise with the long black hair, had died up on the mountains, and that Adam had been unable to rescue her. I thought about these three women while he slept beside me. Five in the bed.

Adam was a person who, all his life, had been surrounded by violence and loss. But then, after all, he lived in a world where men and women knew that they might die before their time and where risk was part of the point. I wriggled carefully out of his grasp and turned in the bed to watch him. In the light that shone from the street lamps outside I could just make out his face, serene in sleep, full lips puffing gently with each breath. I felt a sharp pang of pity for him. No wonder he was sometimes gloomy and strange and his love came out as violence.

I woke again as it was getting light and slipped out of our bed. The boards creaked but Adam didn't wake. One arm was flung out above his head. He looked so trusting, lying there naked and dreaming, but I found that I couldn't lie there beside him any longer. I pulled out the first clothes that came to hand – black trousers, boots, a high-necked orange sweater that was wearing through at the elbows – and dressed in the bathroom. I didn't bother to clean my teeth or wash. I could do all that later. I just had to get out of here, be alone with my thoughts, not be there when he awoke and wanted to pull me down to him. I let myself out of the flat, wincing at the bang of the door as I pulled it shut.

I didn't know where I was going. I walked briskly, jacketless and cold, and breathed the air deep into my lungs. I felt calmer now that it was daytime: I was going to be all right, somehow. At a café near Shepherd's Bush I stopped for a coffee, bitter and black. The smell of grease and bacon made me feel faintly queasy. It was nearly seven o'clock and already the roads were clogged with traffic. I set off again, remembering Adam's instructions to me when we were in the Lake District. Get into a rhythm, one step at a time, breathe properly, don't look too far ahead. I wasn't thinking at all, just walking. Newsagents were open and so were some food shops. After a bit, I realized where my feet were taking me but I didn't stop, although I went more and more slowly. Well, maybe it wasn't such a bad idea after all. I needed to talk to somebody and there were precious few people left.

I got there at ten past eight, knocked firmly on the door and felt suddenly and horribly nervous. But it was too late to run away. There was the sound of footsteps, then there he was and there was I.

'Alice.'

He didn't sound shocked to see me but he didn't sound too happy either. Nor did he ask me in.

'Hello, Jake.'

We stared at each other. The last time we had met, I'd accused him of putting spiders in my milk bottle. He was still in his dressing-gown, but it was a dressing-gown I didn't recognize, a post-Alice one.

'Just passing?' he said, with a glimmer of his old irony.

'Can I come in? Only for a minute.'

He pulled the door wider and stepped back.

'It's all changed here,' I said, looking around me.

'What did you expect?'

There was a new sofa and curtains, and large new cushions on the floor near the fireplace. A couple of pictures I'd not seen before hung on the walls (green now, not off-white). There were none of the old photographs of him and me.

I hadn't thought about it properly, or at all. But I now knew that I had somehow assumed that I would step into my old, rejected home and find it waiting for me, although I had made it cruelly clear that I would never return. If I was honest with myself, I had probably also assumed that Jake would be waiting for me, whatever I'd done to him. That he would wrap an arm round me and sit me down and make me tea and toast and listen to me pouring out my married woes.

'It's no good,' I said at last.

'Would you like a cup of coffee, now that you're here?'

'No. Yes, all right.'

I followed him into the kitchen: new kettle, new toaster, new matching mugs hanging on new hooks, lots of fresh plants on the window-sill. Flowers on the table. I sat down on a chair.

'Have you come to collect the last of your things?' he asked.

I saw now that it was useless to have come here. I'd had some quaint idea, last night, that even though I had lost everyone else, I somehow wouldn't have lost Jake. I persevered for a few more ghastly sentences.

'I'm a bit out of my depth,' I said.

Jake raised his eyebrows at me and handed me my coffee. It was too hot to drink, so I put it in front of me and twisted it round on the table, spilling some. 'Everything's got a bit strange.'

'Strange?' he said.

'Can I use the lavatory?'

I stumbled into the tiny room and stared at myself in the mirror. My hair was greasy and my cheeks were pasty and thin, and there were great shadows under my eyes. I hadn't washed last night or this morning, so mascara and grime smudged my face. My orange jumper was inside out, though I didn't bother to change it. What was the point?

I washed my face, at least, and as I was flushing the lavatory I heard a scraping noise in the room above. The bedroom. Someone else was here.

'Sorry,' I said, as I came out, 'it was a mistake.'

'What's wrong, Alice?' he asked, with a hint of real concern. But not as if he still loved me – more as if I were a stray cat who was suffering on his doorstep.

'I'm just being a bit melodramatic.' A thought struck me. 'Can I use your phone, though?'

'You know where it is,' he said.

I phoned directory inquiries and asked for the police station in Corrick. I wrote the number down on the palm of my hand with a felt-tip that was lying on the floor. I started to dial, then I remembered the phone calls that Adam and I had been receiving. I had to be careful. I replaced the receiver.

'I've got to go,' I said.

'When did you last have something to eat?' Jake asked.

'I'm not hungry.'

'Shall I call you a taxi?'

'I can walk.'

'Where to?'

'What? I don't know.'

Upstairs, someone was having a bath. I stood up. 'Sorry, Jake. You know, sorry.'

He smiled. 'That's okay now,' he said.

Thirty

I bought a phonecard in a newsagent's, the most expensive in the shop, and then found a phone-box.

'Police station,' said a metallic female voice.

I had prepared an opening sentence. 'Can I talk to whoever is in charge of the Adele Blanchard file?' I said, authoritatively.

'What department?'

'God, I don't know.' I hesitated. 'Criminal?'

There was a pause at the other end of the line. Exasperation? Bemusement? Then I heard a dim sound of talking. Obviously she had her hand over the receiver. Then she was back with me. 'Let me see if I can connect you to somebody.'

There was a beeping as she transferred me.

'How may I help you?' said another voice, male this time.

'I am a friend of Adele Blanchard,' I said confidently. 'I've been away for several years in Africa, and I just wanted to know what progress has been made on her case.'

'Could you give me your name please?'

'My name is Pauline,' I said. 'Pauline Wilkes.'

'I'm afraid we can't give out information over the phone.'

'Have you heard of her?'

'I'm sorry, madam, do you have anything to report?'

'I . . . no, sorry, goodbye.'

I put the phone down and dialled directory inquiries. I found the number of the Corrick public library.

As I arrived in Corrick for the second time, I felt a slight unease. What if I met Mrs Blanchard? Then I dismissed the thought from my mind. What did it matter? I would lie, as usual. I hadn't been to a public library since I was a child. I think of them as old-fashioned municipal buildings, like town halls, dark, with heavy iron radiators and tramps hiding out from the rain. The Corrick public library was bright and new, and next to a supermarket. There seemed to be as many CDs and videos as books, and I was worried that I would have to fiddle around with a mouse or a microfiche. But when I asked at the front desk about the local paper, I was directed to shelves where eighty years of the *Corrick and Whitham Advertiser* was stored in huge bound volumes. I hauled out 1990 and dropped it heavily on to a table.

I checked the four front pages for the month of January. There was a dispute about a bypass, a lorry crash, a factory closure and something to do with the council and waste-disposal but nothing about Adele Blanchard, so I went back to the beginning of the month and skimmed the inside news pages for the whole of January. Still nothing. I didn't know what to do and I didn't have much time. I hadn't been inclined to go by train again and had borrowed the car belonging to my assistant, Claudia. If I left at nine, drove straight there and back, then I could be back in time for a two o'clock meeting with Mike and the pretence of a proper day's work.

I hadn't reckoned on the search through the papers taking such a long time. What was I to do? Perhaps Adele had lived somewhere else, except that her mother had talked of Tara as the first to move away from the area. I read through the first February issue. Still nothing. I looked at my watch. Almost half past eleven. I would read the February papers and then I would leave, even if I found nothing.

Such as it was, it was in the issue of the last Friday of the month, the twenty-third. It was a small story at the bottom of page four:

LOCAL WOMAN 'MISSING'
Concern is growing over the fate of a young Corrick woman. Adele Funston, 23, has been reported missing. Her husband,

Thomas Funston, who had been working abroad, told the *Advertiser* that Adele had planned to go on a hiking holiday while he was away in an undetermined location: 'It was when I didn't hear anything that I started to get anxious.' He joined with his father-in-law, Christopher Blanchard, also of Corrick, in expressing a hope that Mrs Funston was just on an extended holiday. Detective Superintendent Horner told the *Advertiser* that he was 'not unduly worried. If Mrs Funston is safe, I would like to appeal to her to come forward,' he told us. Mrs Funston was best known locally as a teacher at St Eadmund's primary school in Whitham.

Missing. I looked round. Nobody was nearby. As quietly as I could, I tore the item out of the paper. Malicious damage, I thought to myself grimly.

Thirty-one

Joanna Noble lit a cigarette. 'Before we start, do you mind if I say something that might sound harsh?'

'Before we start? You make it sound as if you're a doctor or lawyer.'

'Well, what am I? That's part of my point. Hang on, wait a second.' She filled our glasses from the bottle of white wine I'd bought at the bar.

'Cheers,' I said ironically.

She took a gulp of wine, and jabbed in my direction with her cigarette. 'Look, Alice, I've interviewed loads of people and sometimes I hated them and a few times I've thought we might become friends but we never did, for whatever reason. Now it looks as if I'm becoming friendly with the *wife* of somebody I interviewed, except . . .'

'Except what?'

She took a drag of her cigarette. 'I don't know what you're up to. If you want to meet me, is it because I'm such a nice supportive reassuring person and you can't think of anybody better to pour out your troubles to? Or is it that you think I have some kind of professional expertise that you can draw on? What are we doing here? I suppose I'm wondering whether the sort of thing I expect you're going to say to me wouldn't be better being said to a friend or a relative or –'

'Or a psychiatrist?' I interrupted angrily, and then stopped myself. It wasn't fair to blame her for being suspicious. I was suspicious of myself. 'You're not a friend, I know, but this is something I couldn't talk to a friend about, or a relative. And you are right to distrust me. I'm turning to you because you know things other people don't know.'

'Is that our bond?' Joanna asked, almost with a sneer, but then smiled more sympathetically. 'Never mind. I'm also pleased, in a way, that you wanted to talk to me. So what is it?'

I took a deep breath, then told her in a low voice of what I had done over the previous days and weeks: of the details I had exchanged with Adam about our sexual history, about the letters from the unknown Adele I had found, about the death of her sister, of going to see their mother. At this Joanna raised her eyebrows but said nothing. It felt utterly strange to me to put all this into words and I found myself listening to myself as I talked, as if I were hearing a story told by a woman I didn't know. It made me realize the hermetic existence I had been leading, going over and over this in my head with nobody to confide in. I tried to tell it like a story, chronologically and clearly. When I had finished, I showed Joanna the cutting about Adele's disappearance. She read it with a frown of concentration, then handed it back to me.

'Well?' I said. 'Am I mad?'

She lit another cigarette. 'Look,' she said in an uncomfortable tone, 'if it's all gone wrong, why don't you just leave the guy?'

'Adele left Adam. I've got the letter in which she broke with him. It's dated the fourteenth of January 1990.'

Joanna looked genuinely startled and made a visible effort to gather her thoughts and speak.

'Let me just spell this out,' she said finally, 'so that we can acknowledge what is being talked about. You are saying that when this Adele broke up with Adam – your husband – he killed her and managed to dispose of the body so brilliantly that it was never found.'

'Somebody disposed of her body.'

'Or she killed herself. Or she just left home and never called.'

'People don't just disappear like that.'

'Oh, don't they? Do you know how many people are currently listed as missing in Britain?'

'Of course I don't.'

'It's as many people as live in Bristol or Stockport or some medium-sized town or other. There's a whole secret ghostly town in Britain, which consists of the disappeared and lost. People do just leave.'

'Her last letter to Adam wasn't desperate. It was all about staying with her husband, about committing herself to her life.'

Joanna filled our glasses again. 'Do you happen to have any evidence of any kind about Adam? How do you know he wasn't on a climbing expedition?'

'It was the winter. Anyway, her letter was sent to him at a London address.'

'For God's sake, it's not just a matter of having no evidence at all. Do you really think he's capable of coolly killing a woman and just carrying on with his life?'

I thought for a moment. 'I don't think that there's anything Adam couldn't do if he wanted to do it.'

Joanna smiled. 'I can't make you out. For the first time today, you really sounded like you loved him.'

'Of course. That's not the point. But what do you think, Joanna? About what I've told you.'

'What do you mean, what do I think? What are you asking for? I feel responsible for this in a way. It was me who told you about the rape case and sent you off into this lunacy. I feel that I've put you under this pressure so that you want to prove something, anything, just so that you can really know. Look . . .' She gestured helplessly. 'People don't do things like that.'

'That's not true,' I said. I was feeling unexpectedly calm. 'You of all people know that. But what should I do?'

'Even if this were true, which it isn't, there is no evidence and no way of finding any. You're stuck with what you know now, which is nothing. So that means that you've got two choices. The first is to leave Adam.'

'I couldn't. I don't dare to do it. You don't know him. If you were me, you'd just know that that was impossible.'

'If you're going to stay with him, you can't spend the rest of your life living like a double agent. You'll poison everything. If you're going to make a go of it, then you owe it to both of you to tell him about everything. Explain your fears to him.'

I laughed. It wasn't funny at all but I couldn't help it.

'You want to put some ice on it.'

'Which bit, Bill? All the bits hurt.'

He laughed. 'But think what a favour you've done to your cardiovascular system.'

Bill Levenson may have looked like a retired lifeguard but in fact he was the senior executive from Pittsburgh in charge of our division. He had arrived at the beginning of the week and had been conducting meetings and making assessments. I had expected to be summoned for a grilling in the boardroom but instead he had invited me to meet him at his health club to play a game called racquetball. I told him I'd never heard of it.

'Have you played squash?'

'No.'

'Have you played *tennis*?'

'At school.'

'Same thing.'

I turned up with some rather fetching checked shorts and met him outside what looked like a normal squash court. He handed me an eye-guard and a racquet that looked like a snowshoe. Racquetball turned out not to be at all the same thing as tennis. I had a few distant memories of tennis at school: a bit of pretty scampering up and down the baseline, some delicate swings of the racquet, lots of giggling and flirting with the male coach. Racquetball consisted of desperate sweaty lunges and sprints, which quickly reduced me to a tubercular wheeze while muscles started to flutter and spasm in strange recesses of my thighs and upper arms. It was good for a few minutes to devote myself to

233

an activity that drove all my worries from my mind. If only my body had been able to tolerate the burden.

After twenty minutes of the scheduled half-hour I fell to my knees, mouthed, 'Enough,' and Bill led me from the court. At least I was in no condition to observe the response of the other lithe, tanned members of Bill's club. He led me to the door of the women's changing room. When I rejoined him in the bar, I was at least looking better, but walking had become something I had to concentrate on, as if I had only just learned.

'I ordered a bottle of water for us both,' Bill said, standing to receive me. 'You need rehydrating.'

What I needed was a double gin and tonic and a lie-down, but I cravenly accepted the water. Bill removed his wristwatch and laid it on the table between us. 'I read your report and we're going to deal with it in precisely five minutes.'

I opened my mouth to protest but for once I couldn't think of anything to say.

'It was bullshit. As you know. The Drakloop is going into a black hole fast and we're paying for it. From your, shall I say detached?, tone in the report, I would infer that you are aware of that.'

All I could have said honestly in reply was that the tone of my report was detached because for the last few months my mind had been on other things. So I said nothing.

Bill continued, 'The new design hasn't yet worked. I don't believe it's going to work. And *you* don't believe it's going to work. What I ought to do is shut the division down. If there's anything else I should do instead, tell me now.'

I buried my head in my hands and for a second I considered just leaving it there until Bill had gone away. Or maybe I should leave myself. The other bit of my life was now a disaster as well. Then I thought, Oh, fuck it. I raised my head and looked at the slightly surprised face of Bill. Perhaps he thought I had gone to sleep. 'Well,' I said, giving myself time to think, 'the impregnated copper was a waste of time. The benefits weren't significant and they haven't managed to make it anyway. The emphasis on ease of fitting was a mistake as well. That makes it less reliable as a contraceptive.' I took a sip of water. 'The problem isn't with the design of the Drak III. The problem is with the design of the cervixes that they are attached to.'

'So?' said Bill. 'What do we do?'

I shrugged. 'Dump the Drak IV. Give the Drak III a few tweaks and call it the Drak IV. Then spend money on advertisements in women's magazines. But not with soft-focus pictures of couples watching the sunset on a beach. Give detailed information about the women IUDs are suitable for and those they aren't. Above all, give them advice on getting them fitted. Competent fitting would achieve a greater improvement than the Drak IV would have managed, even if it had worked.' A thought struck me. 'And you could get Giovanna to organize a programme of retraining GPs for fitting it. There you are. I'm done.'

Bill gave a grunt and picked up his watch. 'The five minutes is up anyway,' he said, fastening it back on to his wrist. Then he lifted a small leather case from the ground, placed it on the table and snapped it open. I assumed he was going to produce my redundancy papers but instead he had a glossy magazine in his hand. It was called *Guy* and was evidently for men. 'Look at this,' he said. 'I know something about you.' My heart sank but I carried on smiling. I knew what was coming. 'Jesus,' he said, 'your husband is incredible.' He opened the magazine. I saw a flash of mountain peaks, faces in goggles – some familiar ones: Klaus, the elegant snap of Françoise that seemed to be the only one anybody could get hold of, a gorgeous one of Adam caught off-guard talking to Greg.

'Yes, he's incredible,' I said.

'I used to do some hiking when I was in high school and I do some skiing but those climbers – that is something. That's what we'd all like to be able to do.'

'Lots of them died, you know,' I said.

'I don't mean that. I mean what your husband did. You know,

235

Alice, I'd give up everything, my career, everything, to be able to know that about myself, to have proved myself in that way. It's an amazing article. They've interviewed everybody, and he did it. Adam was the man. Look, I don't know how you're fixed but I'm flying out on Sunday. Maybe we can all get together.'

'That would be good,' I said warily.

'It would be my privilege,' Bill said.

'Can I borrow this?' I said, pointing at the magazine.

'Sure,' said Bill. 'It'll be a treat for you.'

Thirty-two

I had obviously woken him up, even though it was past eleven o'clock: he was puffy and squint-eyed with sleep, and was wearing grubby pyjamas, wrongly buttoned up. His hair stood out from his head, making him look even hairier than I had remembered him.

'Greg?'

'Yes?' He stared at me from the doorway, showing no sign of recognition.

'It's Alice. I'm sorry to disturb you.'

'Alice?'

'Alice, as in Alice-and-Adam Alice. We met at the book launch.'

'I remember.' There was a pause. 'You'd better come in. As you can see, I wasn't really expecting visitors this morning.' And he smiled suddenly; baby-blue eyes very sweet in his crumpled, unwashed face.

I had been expecting Greg to live in a mess, but it was a neat little house, everything in its proper place, every surface wiped and clear. And there were pictures of mountains everywhere – great snowy peaks in black-and-white or colour on every white wall. It felt a bit strange, standing in this over-tidied house, to be surrounded by such epic vistas.

He didn't ask me to sit down, but I did anyway. I had crossed London to see him, although I didn't know why. Perhaps I had just remembered liking him when we had met briefly, and clung on to that. I cleared my throat and he looked suddenly amused. 'Tell you what, Alice,' he said. 'You feel uncomfortable because you've just turned up on my doorstep uninvited, and you don't

237

know how to begin. And I feel uncomfortable too, because I'm not dressed when any respectable person would be, and I've a cracking hangover. So why don't we go into the kitchen? I'll show you where the eggs are and you can scramble some and make a pot of coffee while I put some clothes on. Then you can tell me why you're here. This isn't just a social call, I take it?'

I stood dumb.

'And you don't look as if you've eaten in weeks.'

'Not very well,' I confessed.

'Eggs, then?'

'Eggs would be great.'

I whisked four eggs in a saucepan and set them over a low heat, stirring all the while. Scrambled eggs should be cooked very slowly, and served soft rather than like rubber. Even I know that. I made the coffee – far too strong, but we could probably both do with a jolt of caffeine – and toasted four slices of stale bread. When Greg came back into the kitchen breakfast was on the table. I found that I was ravenous, and the salty, creamy eggs and buttery toast soothed and steadied me. The world ceased swimming in front of my eyes. I took gulps of bitter coffee between mouthfuls. Opposite me Greg ate with methodical pleasure, distributing the eggs evenly over the toast and pushing neat squares on to his fork. It felt strangely companionable. We did not speak.

When he had cleared his plate, he laid down his knife and fork and pushed his plate away from him. He looked at me expectantly. I took a deep breath, smiled at him, and to my consternation felt tears hot on my cheeks. Greg pushed a box of tissues at me and waited. 'You must think I'm mad,' I said, and blew my nose. 'I thought perhaps you could help me understand.'

'Understand what?'

'Adam, I suppose.'

'I see.'

He stood up abruptly. 'Let's go for a walk.'

'I haven't got my coat. I left it in the office.'

'I'll lend you a jacket.'

Outside, we set off at a lick along the busy road that led down to Shoreditch and, beyond that, the Thames. Suddenly Greg led us down some steps and we were on a canal towpath. The traffic was left behind and it was as quiet as the countryside. It seemed reassuring, but then I thought of Tara. Was it in this canal that her body had been found floating? I didn't know. Greg walked as fast as Adam, with the same effortless stride. He stopped and looked at me. 'Why ask me, of all people?'

'It happened so fast,' I said. 'Me and Adam, I mean. I thought the past didn't matter, that nothing mattered. But it doesn't work like that.' I stopped again. I couldn't tell Greg all my fears. He was the man whose life Adam had saved. He was Adam's friend, sort of. I looked at the water. Motionless. Canals don't flow like rivers. I wanted to talk about Adele, or Françoise, or Tara. Instead, I said, 'Do you mind the way everyone thinks he's the hero and you're the villain?'

'Villain?' he said. 'I thought I was just the coward, the weakling, the Elisha Cook Junior role.'

'Who?'

'He was an actor who played cowards and weaklings.'

'Sorry, I didn't mean . . .'

'I don't mind people thinking he was a hero, because he was. His courage, fortitude, coolness, all that, was extraordinary that day.' He glanced sideways at me. 'Is that what you want to hear? As for the rest of it, I'm not sure I want to talk over with you how I feel about my failure. Wife of the hero and all that.'

'It's not like that, Greg.'

'It is, I think. Which is why you found me in my pyjamas this morning, nursing a hangover. But I don't understand it, and that is what torments me. What does Adam say about it?'

I took a deep breath. 'I think what Adam believes is that there were people in the expedition who didn't belong on Chungawat.'

Greg gave a laugh that dissolved into a racking cough. 'He can say that again,' he said, when he was recovered. 'Carrie Frank, the skin doctor, she was a fit hiker but she'd never climbed before. She didn't know how to put her crampons on. And I remember screaming a warning to Tommy Benn when he had attached himself wrongly to the belay. He was about to fall off the mountain. He didn't respond and I remembered he didn't understand any English at all. Not a single word. God, what was he doing with us? I had to slide down and reattach his 'biner. But I thought I'd handled that, that I'd created a foolproof system. It failed and the lives of five people under my protection were lost.' I put a hand on his arm but he went on, 'When it came to it, Adam was the hero and I wasn't. You don't understand things about your life. Join the club.'

'But I'm scared.'

'Join the club, Alice,' he repeated, with a half-laugh.

Suddenly and incongruously, there was a small garden on the other side of the canal, with ranks of red and purple tulips.

'Was it something in particular that's scared you?' he asked eventually.

'It's all of his past, I guess. It's all so shadowy.'

'And so full of women,' Greg added.

'Yes.'

'Difficult for you.'

We sat on a bench together.

'Does he talk about Françoise?'

'No.'

'I was having an affair with her, you know.' He didn't look at me as he said it, and I had the impression that he had never said it before. For me, it was like a blow, sharply unexpected.

'An affair with Françoise? No. No, I didn't know. God, Greg, did Adam know?'

Greg didn't answer at once. Then he said, 'It began on the expedition. She was very funny. Very beautiful.'

'So they say.'

'It was over between her and Adam. She told him when we

240

all arrived in Nepal that it was ended. She was sick of all his infidelities.'

'*She* finished it?'

'Didn't Adam tell you?'

'No,' I said slowly. 'He didn't say anything about it.'

'He doesn't take kindly to rejection.'

'Let me get this straight,' I said. 'Françoise ended her long-standing relationship with Adam, and a few days later you and she started having an affair?'

'Yes. And then, if you want me to spell it out for you, a few weeks after that she died up in the mountains because I fucked up with the fixed lines, and Adam saved me, his friend who had usurped him.'

I tried to think of something to say that could be plausibly comforting and gave up.

'I must be getting back.'

'Listen, Greg, did Adam know about you and Françoise?'

'We didn't tell him at the time. We thought it might be a distraction. It wasn't as if he was being celibate himself. And afterwards . . .' He let the sentence die away.

'He's never mentioned it?'

'No. Are you going to discuss it with him?'

'No.'

Not that, not anything else either. We were long past the point of telling.

'Don't stay silent on my account. It doesn't matter any more.'

We walked back and I took off his jacket and handed it to him. 'I'll catch a bus along here,' I said. 'Thanks, Greg.'

'I've not done anything.'

Impulsively, I put my arms around his neck and kissed him on the mouth, feeling the prickle of his beard.

'Take care of yourself,' I said.

'Adam's a lucky man.'

'I thought that *I* was supposed to be the lucky one.'

Thirty-three

It had sometimes felt to me as if when I was with Adam I was dazzled so that I couldn't really see him, let alone analyse or make judgements about him. There was sex, sleep, fragmentary conversation, food and occasional attempts at arrangements, and even those took place in an atmosphere of emergency, as if we were doing what we could before the boat went down, before the fire consumed the house with us inside it. I had just given in helplessly, grateful at first to be free from thought, from chat, from responsibility. The only way of assessing him in any rational way was in the mediated form of what people said about him. This more distant Adam could be a relief, and useful too, like a photograph of the sun at which you could stare directly as a way of learning about that thing above, out of direct vision, burning down on you.

When I got back from seeing Greg, Adam was sitting watching TV. He was smoking and drinking whisky. 'Where have you been?' he asked.

'Work,' I said.

'I rang. They said you were out of the office.'

'A meeting,' I said vaguely.

The important thing about lying is not to offer unnecessary information that can catch you out. Adam looked round at me, but didn't reply. There was something wrong about the movement, as if it was just a bit too slow or too fast. He might have been a bit drunk. He was moving between channels, watching a programme for a few minutes, changing to another, watching for a few minutes, changing again.

I remembered the magazine I had borrowed from Bill Levenson.

'Did you see this?' I said, holding it up. 'More stuff about you in it.'

He looked round briefly but didn't speak. I knew the story of the Chungawat disaster intimately but I wanted to read about it in the light of what I had learned about Adam and Françoise and Greg to see if it was different, so I sat at the kitchen table and leafed impatiently through the ads for running shoes, cologne, fitness machines, Italian suits, pages and pages of male stuff. Then I came to it, a long prominent article called 'The Death Zone: Dreams and Disaster at 28,000 feet'.

The article was longer and much more detailed than Joanna's. The author, Anthony Kaplan, had talked to every surviving member of the expedition, including, I saw with a pang, Adam himself. Why did he never tell me these things? It must have been one of those long phone conversations or one of those bar-room meetings that had occupied so much of his time during the previous month or two.

'I didn't know you'd talked to this journalist,' I said, in what I hoped was a light-hearted tone.

'What's his name?' asked Adam, who was refilling his glass.

'Anthony Kaplan.'

Adam took one sip and then another. He flinched slightly. 'The guy was a jerk,' he said.

I felt cheated. It was common enough to know the trivial, mundane details about the life of a friend or colleague, but nothing of their passionate inner life. With Adam that was all I knew. His imagination, his fantasy life, his dreams, but only accidental fragments of what he actually did during his days. So I was hungry for anything about Adam, about his capacity to carry other people's equipment when they were slowed to a crawl by altitude sickness. Everybody talked about his carefulness, his prudence, his clear-headedness.

There was one new detail concerning Adam. Another expedition member, an interior designer called Laura Tipler, had told Kaplan that she had shared a tent for a few days with Adam on the way up to base camp. That was what Greg must have been referring to when he'd said Adam hadn't been celibate after Françoise. Then, without any ado, Adam had moved out. To husband his resources, no doubt. I didn't mind very much. It was all very adult and consensual, with no hard feelings on either side. Tipler told Kaplan that Adam's mind was evidently elsewhere, on the arrangements for the move up the mountain, the assessment of various risks and the ability of the different expedition members to manage them, but his body had been enough for her. The bitch. She described the episode almost casually to Kaplan, as if it were an optional extra selected from the brochure. But had he slept with absolutely every woman he had ever met? I wondered what he would have thought if I had led a sex life like that.

'Twenty questions,' I said. 'Who's Laura Tipler?'

Adam thought for a moment then laughed harshly. 'A bloody liability is what she was.'

'You shared a tent with her. She says.'

'What are you saying, Alice? What do you want me to say?'

'Nothing. It's just that I keep learning things about you from magazines.'

'You won't learn anything about me from that crap.' He looked cross. 'Why do you bother with it? Why are you poking around?'

'I'm not poking around,' I said warily. 'I'm interested in your life.'

Adam took another drink. 'I don't want you to be interested in my life. I want you to be interested in *me*.'

I looked sharply round. Did he know anything? But his attention was back on the television, moving from channel to channel, flick, flick, flick.

I carried on reading. I had hoped, or feared, that there would be some more detail about Adam's break-up with Françoise and about the tensions there may have been between them on the mountain. But Kaplan only mentioned briefly that they had been a couple and apart from that she barely featured in the article at all until near the end when she had disappeared. The thought had been running in my mind that the two women who had rejected Adam had died. Could it be that he hadn't made as much effort to rescue Françoise's group as he had with the others? But it was speedily contradicted by Kaplan's evocation of what it had been like on the mountain in the storm. Both Greg and Claude Bresson had been out of action. The remarkable thing was not that five of the party died but that anybody at all had survived and that was almost entirely down to the efforts of Adam, going out again and again into the storm. But it nagged away at me and I wondered if that accounted for the composure with which he had recalled that nightmare.

Adam hadn't said very much, as usual, but at one point Kaplan had asked him if he was driven by the great romantic tradition of British explorers like Captain Scott: 'Scott died,' was Adam's response. 'And his men with him. My hero is Amundsen. He approached the South Pole as if he were a lawyer drawing up a legal document. It's easy to gloriously kill the people in your charge. The difficult thing is to make sure the knots are tied properly and bring the people back.'

Kaplan went from that quotation to the problem of the knots that hadn't stayed tied. As he pointed out, the cruel paradox of the disaster was that, through Greg McLaughlin's own innovation, there had been no way of dodging responsibility in the aftermath of the expedition. Claude Bresson had been in charge of the red line, Adam had been in charge of the yellow line and Greg had given himself the ultimate responsibility of securing his blue line, the line that would take the expedition up the Gemini Ridge to the col just below the summit.

It was so horribly simple, but just to make it simpler still, a detailed diagram showed the disposition of the blue line on the

245

west ridge and where it had gone astray at the apex so that one group of climbers had missed the line and blundered down the east ridge to their deaths. Poor Greg. I wondered if he had heard of this latest eruption of publicity.

'Poor Greg,' I said aloud.

'Eh?'

'I said, "Poor Greg." Back in the spotlight again.'

'Vultures,' said Adam bitterly.

There was virtually nothing in Kaplan's article that differed even in emphasis from what I had read in Joanna's article and, from a more personal perspective, in Klaus's book. I read through the article a second time looking for anything at all that was different. All I could find was a trivial correction. In Klaus's book, the climber found barely alive the following morning, mumbling, 'Help,' had been Pete Papworth. Kaplan had collated the accounts of everybody involved and had established, for what it was worth, that Papworth had died overnight and it was the German, Tomas Benn, who had been found dying. Big deal. Apart from that, the accounts agreed completely.

I went over and sat on the arm of Adam's chair, ruffled his hair. He passed his drink to me and I took a sip, passed it back.

'Do you dwell on it, Adam?'

'What?'

'Chungawat. Do you go over and over it in your mind? Think how it might have worked out differently, how the dead people might have been saved or that you might have died?'

'No, I don't.'

'I do.'

Adam leaned forward and snapped off the television. The room was suddenly very quiet and I could hear noises from the street, a plane going over. 'What the fuck for?'

'The woman you loved died on the mountain. It haunts me.'

Adam's eyes narrowed. He put his glass down. He raised himself up and took my face in his hands. They were big, very

246

strong. I felt he could snap my head off, if he wanted to. He was looking hard into my eyes. Was he trying to see in?

'You're the woman I love,' he said, without taking his eyes off me. 'You're the woman I trust.'

Thirty-four

'It's Bill Levenson for you.' Claudia held out the phone with a sympathetic look on her face, as if she were handing me over to a hangman.

I took the phone from her with a grimace. 'Hello, Alice here.'

'Okay, Alice.' He sounded jovial for a man who was about to downsize me. 'You're on.'

'What?' I raised my eyebrows to Claudia who was hovering by the door, waiting to see my face collapse.

'You're on,' he repeated. 'Do it. Drakloop mark IV, she's your baby.'

'But . . .'

'You haven't had second thoughts, have you, Alice?'

'Not at all.'

I hadn't had any thoughts at all. Drakloop had been the last thing on my mind in the previous couple of days. Even now, I could barely summon up the energy to sound interested.

'Then you can do whatever you have to do. Make a list of your requirements and your schedule and e-mail them to me. I've banged heads together, and they're ready. Now, I've given you the ball, Alice. Run with it.'

'Fine,' I said. If he wanted me to sound excited or grateful, he was going to be disappointed. 'What's happening to Mike and Giovanna and the others?'

'Leave the fun stuff to me.'

'Ah.'

'Well done, Alice. I'm sure you are going to make a great success of Drakloop IV.'

I left work later than usual, so that I didn't have to meet Mike. Later, I told myself, I would take him out and we would get drunk together and curse the senior management and their grubby machinations, as if we were both quite untainted by their ways. But not now. I had other things to worry about, and I could only care about Mike in a provisional sort of way. That side of my life was in abeyance. I brushed my hair and tied it in a knot at the back of my head, then I picked up my overflowing in-tray and dumped all of its contents in the bin.

Klaus was waiting by the revolving doors, eating a doughnut and reading yesterday's paper, which he folded away when he saw me.

'Alice!' He kissed me on both cheeks, then looked at me searchingly. 'You're looking a bit tired. Are you all right?'

'What are you doing here?'

To his credit, he looked slightly embarrassed. 'Adam asked me if I would see you home. He was worried about you.'

'There's nothing wrong with me. It's a waste of your time.'

He tucked my arm through his. 'It's a pleasure. I wasn't doing anything anyway. You can give me a cup of tea at your flat.'

I hesitated, showing my obvious reluctance.

'I promised Adam,' said Klaus, and started to tow me towards the underground station.

'I want to walk.'

'Walk? From here?'

This was getting irritating. 'There's nothing wrong with me, and I'm walking home. Coming?'

'Adam always says that you're stubborn.'

'It's spring. Look at the sky. We can walk through the West End and Hyde Park. Or you can fuck off and I can go alone.'

'You win, as always.'

'So what's Adam doing that he couldn't come himself to accompany me?' I asked, after we had crossed the road, the very place I had first set eyes on Adam, and he on me.

'I think he was going to meet up with some cameraman or other who might climb on the expedition.'

'Have you seen the piece on Chungawat in *Guy* magazine?'

'I talked to Kaplan on the phone. He sounded like a pro.'

'He doesn't say anything much new.'

'That's what he told me.'

'Except for one thing. You said the man who survived overnight and was found dying and calling out for help was Pete Papworth, and Kaplan says it was actually Tomas Benn.'

'The German guy?' Klaus was frowning, as if trying to remember, then he smiled. 'Kaplan must have got it right. I wasn't exactly *compos mentis* at the time.'

'And you didn't mention Laura Tipler sharing Adam's tent.'

He looked at me strangely, without breaking his stride. 'It seemed like a violation of privacy.'

'What was she like?'

Klaus's expression became faintly disapproving, as if I were breaking some kind of unspoken rule. Then he said, 'It was before he met you, Alice.'

'I know. So I'm not allowed to know anything about her?' He didn't reply. 'Or about Françoise? Or any of them?' I stopped myself. 'Sorry. I didn't mean to go on about it like this.'

'Debbie said you were dwelling on things a bit.'

'Did she? She had a fling with him once, too.' My voice sounded unnaturally high-pitched. I was beginning to alarm myself.

'God, Alice.'

'Maybe we shouldn't walk. Maybe I'll get a taxi home. I feel a bit tired.'

Without a word, Klaus stepped out into the road and hailed a passing black cab. He handed me in, then stepped in after me in spite of my protestations.

'Sorry,' I said again.

We sat in uncomfortable silence for a while, as the cab edged its way through the evening traffic.

'You have no reason to be jealous,' he said at last.

'I'm not jealous. I'm sick and tired of secrets and mysteries, and finding out about Adam from articles I read in papers, or from little things people let slip when they're not thinking. It's like being ambushed all the time. I never know which direction the surprise is going to come from.'

'From what I hear,' said Klaus, 'the surprises aren't exactly springing out at you. It's more like you are rooting around trying to find them.' He laid a warm, callused hand over mine. 'Trust him,' he said. 'Stop tormenting yourself.'

I laughed, and then the laugh turned into a hiccuping sob. 'Sorry,' I said again. 'I'm not usually like this.'

'Perhaps you should get some help,' said Klaus.

I was aghast. 'You think I'm going mad? Is that what you think?'

'No, Alice, just that it might help to talk to an outsider about all of this. Look. Adam's a buddy, but I know what a stubborn bastard he can be. If you're having problems, get help to sort them out.'

'Maybe you're right.' I sat back in the taxi and closed my stinging eyes. I felt bone-tired and horribly dreary. 'Maybe I've been a fool.'

'We're all fools sometimes,' he said. He looked relieved at my sudden acquiescence.

When the taxi stopped, I didn't ask him in for the cup of tea he had promised himself, and I don't think he minded at all. He hugged me at the front door and strode rapidly down the road, coat flapping. I trudged up the stairs, dispirited and somewhat ashamed of myself. I went to the bathroom, stared into the mirror and didn't like what I saw there. Then I gazed around the flat, which was as I had left it that morning. There were dishes that had been in the sink for several days, drawers left open, jars of honey and jam with their lids off, bread going stale on the cutting board, a couple of filled bin-bags stacked by the door, crumbs and dirt on the linoleum floor. In the living room, there were old mugs everywhere, newspapers and magazines on the floor together with emptied bottles of whisky and wine. A bunch of daffodils were shrivelled and brown in a jam jar. The carpet looked as if it had not been vacuumed for weeks. Come to think of it, we hadn't changed the sheets or done the laundry for weeks either.

'Shit,' I said in disgust. 'I look like shit and this place looks like shit. Right.'

I rolled up my sleeves and started in the kitchen. I was going to get my life under control. With every surface I cleaned, I felt better. I washed the dishes, threw away all the stale or rotting food, all the candle stubs, all the junk mail, and I scrubbed the floor with hot soapy water. I gathered all the bottles and the old papers and threw them away, not even stopping to read last week's news. I threw away Sherpa's bowl, trying not to remember the last sight I had had of him. I stripped the bed and put the sheets in the corner of the room, ready to go to the laundry. I put shoes into pairs, books into neat piles. I cleaned the tidemark from the bath and the limescale from the shower. I added the towels to the laundry pile.

Then I made myself a cup of tea and started on the cardboard boxes under our high bed, where Adam and I had got into the habit of tossing anything we weren't actually going to deal with but didn't want to throw away just yet. For a second, I considered simply putting them outside by the dustbins without even going through them. But then I saw a scrap of paper with Pauline's work number scribbled on it. I mustn't throw that away. I started to plough through the old bills, the new bills, the postcards, the scientific journals I hadn't yet read, the photostats of Drakloop material, the scraps of paper with messages I had left for Adam, or Adam had left for me. 'Back at midnight; don't go to sleep,' I read, and tears pricked my eyelids again. Empty envelopes.

Unopened envelopes addressed to the owner of the flat. I took them over to the writing desk in the corner of the bedroom and began to sort them into three piles. One to discard, one to deal with at once, and one to put back in the box. One of the piles slipped over and several of the papers fell down behind the desk. I tried to reach down after them but the gap was too narrow. I was tempted to leave them there but, no, I was going to clear up everything in the flat. Even the invisible bits. So, with an immense effort, I pulled the desk out from the wall. I retrieved the papers and, of course, there was the other stuff that gets stuck behind desks: a shrivelled apple-core, a paper clip, a pen top, an old scrap of envelope. I looked at the envelope to see if it could just be thrown away. It was addressed to Adam. Then I turned it round and all at once I felt I had been punched so hard in the stomach that I could only breathe with difficulty.

'Had a bad day?' I read. It was Adam's scrawl, in thick black ink. Then, again, on the next line down, 'Had a hard day, Adam?' Then: 'Hard day, Adam? Take a bath.' Finally, underneath was written in familiar capital letters: HARD DAY.

The words were written repeatedly like an infant's writing exercise: HARD DAY HARD DAY HARD DAY HARD DAY HARD DAY

Then: ADAM ADAM ADAM ADAM ADAM ADAM ADAM

And then, finally: HARD DAY ADAM? TAKE A BATH.

I mustn't be mad. I mustn't be obsessive. I tried and tried to think of the sensible, reassuring explanation. Adam might have been doodling, thinking about the note, writing its words over and over. But that wasn't what was on the paper. This wasn't doodling. It was Adam imitating the handwriting of the previous notes – of Tara's notes – until he got it right, so that the link between Tara and the harassment would be broken. Now I knew. I knew about Sherpa and I knew about everything. I knew what I had known for a long time. The one truth I couldn't stand.

I picked up the envelope. My hands were steady. I hid it in my knicker drawer, with the letter from Adele, and then went

253

back to the bedside and put everything I had taken out and sorted back into the boxes. I pushed the boxes back under the bed, and even rubbed away the depressions they had made on the carpet.

I heard the footsteps coming up the stairs and went, unhurriedly, into the kitchen. He came in and stood over me. I kissed him on the lips and put my arms tightly around him. 'I've spring-cleaned,' I said, and my voice sounded perfectly ordinary.

He kissed me back and looked into my eyes and I didn't flinch or turn away.

Thirty-five

Adam knew. Or he knew something. Because he was always around, always had his eye on me. A detached observer might have thought it the same as the beginning of our relationship when neither of us could physically bear to be apart from the other. Now it was more like a very conscientious doctor who couldn't let an unstable patient out of his sight for a moment because of the suspicion that she might do herself harm.

It wouldn't be accurate to say that Adam followed me everywhere I went. He didn't accompany me to work every single day, nor was he there to meet me every day. He wasn't phoning me there all the time. But it happened enough so that I knew that any more of my private investigations would be risky. He was around, and I was sure that there were times when he was near and I didn't notice. Once or twice, walking along the street, I would look round feeling that I was being watched or that I had glimpsed someone, but I never saw him. But he could still have been there. It didn't matter anyway. I had the feeling that I knew everything I needed to know. It was all there in my head. I just had to think about it all. I had to get the events straight.

Greg was going to fly out to the States for a few months and, on the Saturday before he left, a couple of friends arranged a party to give him a send-off. It rained almost the whole day and Adam and I didn't get out of bed until almost noon. Then Adam suddenly got dressed, briskly, and said he had to go out for a couple of hours. He left me with a cup of tea and a hard kiss on the mouth. I lay in bed and I made myself think about it all – clearly, point by point, as if Adam was a problem I had to solve.

255

All the elements were there, I just needed to get them in the right order. I lay under the duvet, hearing the rain pattering on the roof, the sound of cars accelerating through puddles, and I thought about everything until my head hurt.

In my mind I was going over and over the events on Chungawat, the storm, the altitude sickness of Greg and Claude Bresson, the extraordinary achievement of Adam in directing the climbers down the Gemini Ridge, the failure of the guiding line and the consequent disastrous wrong turning of the five climbers: Françoise Colet, Pete Papworth, Caroline Frank, Alexis Hartounian and Tomas Benn. Françoise Colet, who had just broken off with Adam, and who had been conducting an affair with Greg.

Adele Blanchard had broken off with Adam. How would the Adam I knew respond to being left? He would have wanted her to die and she disappeared. Françoise Colet broke off with Adam. He would have wanted her to die and she died on the mountain. That didn't mean he killed her. If you wanted someone to die and they died, did that mean you bore some responsibility, even if you hadn't caused it? I went over and over it. What if he didn't try hard enough to rescue her? But, then, as everybody else said, he had already done more than anybody else could have done in the same circumstances. What if he put her group last on the list of priorities while he saved the lives of other people? Did that make him just a bit responsible for her death and the deaths of the other members of the expedition? But somebody had had to assess priorities. Klaus, for example, couldn't be blamed for the deaths because he hadn't been in a condition even to rescue himself, let alone decide the order in which other people were rescued. It was all stupid. Adam couldn't have known about the storm anyway.

Yet there was something, like a little itch that is so tiny you can't even locate it exactly, you can't decide whether it is on the surface of the skin or somewhere underneath but it won't let you relax. Maybe there was some technical mountaineering detail, but none of the experts had mentioned anything like that. The only relevant technical detail was that Greg's fixed line had come loose at the crucial point, but that had affected all the descending groups equally. It was just a matter of chance that it was Françoise's group who took the wrong route down. Something wouldn't leave me alone. Why couldn't I stop thinking about it?

I gave up. I had a long shower, put on some jeans and one of Adam's shirts, and made myself a piece of toast. I didn't have time to eat it because the doorbell rang. I wasn't expecting anybody and I certainly didn't want to see anybody, so at first I didn't answer. But it rang again – longer this time – and I ran down the stairs.

A middle-aged woman was standing outside under a large black umbrella. She was quite stout, with short, greying hair, wrinkles around her eyes, and running down from her nose to the corners of her mouth. I thought at once that she looked unhappy. I had never seen her before.

'Yes?' I said.

'Adam Tallis?' she said. She had a thick accent.

'I'm sorry, he's not here at the moment.'

She looked puzzled.

'Not here,' I repeated, slowly, watching her stricken expression and the slump of her shoulders. 'Can I help you?'

She shook her head, then laid her hand on her mackintoshed chest. 'Ingrid Benn,' she said. 'I am the wife of Tomas Benn.' I had to strain to understand her, and talking seemed to require an immense effort. 'Sorry, my English not . . .' She made a helpless gesture. 'I want to speak with Adam Tallis.'

I opened the door wide, then. 'Come in,' I said. 'Please come in.' I took the umbrella from her and closed it, shaking off the drops of water. She stepped inside and I shut the door firmly behind her.

I remembered now that several weeks ago she had written to Adam and to Greg, asking if she could come and see them to talk about her husband's death. She sat at the kitchen table, in her smart, sensible suit, with her neat brogues, holding a cup of

257

tea but not drinking it, and gazed at me helplessly, as if I might be able to provide some kind of answer, although like Tomas she spoke almost no English, and I knew no German at all.

'I'm so sorry,' I said. 'About your husband. I really am sorry.'

She nodded at me and started to cry. Tears streamed down her cheeks and she didn't wipe them away but sat patiently, a waterfall of sorrow. There was something rather impressive about her mute, unresisting grief. She put no obstacles in its way but let it flow over her. I handed her a tissue and she held it in her hand as if she didn't know its function. 'Why?' she said eventually. 'Why? Tommy say . . .' She searched for the word then gave up.

'I'm sorry,' I said, very slowly. 'Adam is not here.'

It didn't seem to matter all that much. She took out a cigarette and I fetched a saucer for her and she smoked and cried and talked in fragments of English but also in German. I just sat and looked into her large sad brown eyes, shrugging, nodding. Then gradually she subsided and we sat for a few moments in silence. Had she been to see Greg yet? The image of them together was not appealing. The article on the disaster in *Guy* magazine was open on the table and Ingrid caught sight of it and pulled it across. She looked at the group photograph of the expedition and she touched the face of her dead husband. She looked at me with the hint of a smile. 'Tomas,' she said, almost inaudibly.

She turned the page and looked at the drawing of the mountain, which showed the arrangement of fixed lines. She started jabbing at it. 'Tommy say *fine*, he say. No problem.'

Then she switched to German again and I was lost, until I heard a familiar word, repeated several times. 'Yes,' I said. 'Help.' Ingrid looked puzzled. I sighed. 'Help,' I said slowly. 'Tomas's last word. Help.'

'No, no,' she said insistently. '*Gelb.*'

'Help.'

'No, no. *Gelb.*' She pointed at the magazine. '*Rot.* Here. *Blau.* Here. *Und gelb.*'

I looked blank. '*Rot* is, er, red, yes? And *blau* is . . .'

'Blue.'

'And *gelb* . . .'

She looked around the flat, pointed to a cushion on the sofa.

'Yellow,' I said.

'Yes, yellow.'

I couldn't help laughing at the mix-up and Ingrid smiled sadly as well. And then it was as if a dial had been turned in my head; the last number in a combination lock ratcheting into place. The doors swung open. Yellow. *Gelb*. Yes. He wouldn't have called out in English as he lay dying, would he? Of course not. Not the man who had hampered the expedition by not knowing a word of English. His last word had been a colour. Why? What had he been trying to say? Outside, the rain fell steadily. Then I smiled again. How could I have been so stupid?

'Please?' She was staring at me.

'Mrs Benn,' I said. 'Ingrid. I am so sorry.'

'Yes.'

'I think you should go now.'

'Go?'

'Yes.'

'But . . .'

'Adam cannot help.'

'But . . .'

'Go home to your children,' I said. I had no idea if she had any, but she looked like a mother to me, a bit like my own mother in fact.

She stood up obediently and gathered her mackintosh.

'I'm so sorry,' I said again, thrust her umbrella into her hand, and she left.

Greg was drunk when we arrived. He hugged me a little too boisterously and then hugged Adam as well. It was the same old crowd: Daniel, Deborah, Klaus, other climbers. It struck me that they were like soldiers home on leave, meeting each other at selected refuges because they knew that civilians would never really understand what they had gone through. It was an in-between place and an in-between time, just to be got through until they returned to the real life of extremity and danger. I wondered, not for the first time, what they thought of me. Was I just a folly to them, like one of those mad flings soldiers had on weekend leave in the Second World War?

The atmosphere was fairly jovial. If Adam looked a little distracted, then maybe that was just my over-sensitivity and he was soon caught up in the conversation. But there was no doubt about Greg: he looked dreadful. He drifted from group to group, but didn't say very much. He constantly refilled his glass. After a bit I found myself alone with him.

'I don't feel I really belong,' I said uneasily.

'Nor do I,' said Greg. 'Look. It's stopped raining. Let me show you Phil and Marjorie's garden.'

The party was at the house of an old climbing friend who had given it up after college and gone into the City. While his friends were still vagrants, drifting around the world, raising money here and there, snuffling out sponsorship, Phil had this large beautiful house just off Ladbroke Grove. We walked outside. The grass was damp and I felt my feet getting cold and wet but it was good to be outside. We walked to the low wall at the far end of the garden and looked over at the house on the other side. I turned back. I could see Adam through the window on the first floor in a group of people. Once or twice he glanced at us. Greg and I raised our glasses to him. He raised his own glass back at us.

'I like this,' I said. 'I like it when I know that this evening is lighter than yesterday evening and tomorrow evening will be lighter than today.'

'If Adam weren't standing there looking, I'd feel like kissing you, Alice,' Greg said. 'I mean, I feel like kissing you, but if Adam weren't looking then I *would* kiss you.'

'Then I'm glad he's standing there, Greg,' I said. 'Look.' I fluttered my hand in front of his face displaying my wedding ring. 'Trust, eternal fidelity, that sort of thing.'

'Sorry, I know that.' Greg looked morose again. 'You know the *Titanic*?'

'I've heard of it,' I said, with a thin smile, aware that I was stuck with a very drunk Greg.

'Do you know . . . ?' Then he stopped. 'Do you know that no officer who survived the *Titanic* ever rose to command a ship?'

'No, I didn't know that.'

'Bad luck, you see. Bad on the CV. As for the captain, he was lucky that he went down with it. Which is what captains are supposed to do. You know why I'm going to the States?'

'A climb?'

'No, Alice,' he said, too vigorously. 'No. I'm going to wind up the company. That's it. *Finito*. A line drawn in the sand. I shall be searching for a different line of work. At least Captain Ahab went down with the whale. People under my care died and it was my fault and I'm finished.'

'Greg,' I said, 'you're not. I mean it wasn't.'

'What do you mean?' he asked.

I looked around. Adam was still up there. Mad as it might be, drunk as he was now, I had to tell Greg before he went away. Whatever else I did or didn't do, I owed this to him. I'd probably never have the chance again. Perhaps I thought, too, that with Greg I would have an ally, that I wouldn't be so alone if I told him. I had the crazy hope that he would snap out of his drunken, maudlin state and come to my rescue.

'Did you read Klaus's book?' I asked.

'No,' he said, raising his glass of vodka.

'Don't,' I said, stopping him. 'Don't drink any more. I want you to concentrate on what I'm saying. You must know that when the missing party on Chungawat were brought down to the camp, one of them was just about alive. Do you remember which one?'

Greg's face had an expression of stony gloom. 'I wasn't exactly conscious at the time. It was Peter Papworth, wasn't it? Calling for help, the poor bastard. The help that I failed to give him.'

'No,' I said. 'That was Klaus's mistake. It wasn't Papworth. It was Tomas Benn.'

'Oh, well,' said Greg. 'We were none of us at our best. Down the hatch.'

'And what was Benn's principal characteristic?'

'He was a crap climber.'

'No, you told me yourself. He didn't speak a word of English.'

'So?'

'Help. Help. Help. That's what they heard him say as he was dying, slipping into a coma. A funny time to start speaking English.'

Greg shrugged. 'Perhaps he said it in German.'

'The German for help is *hilfe*. That doesn't sound very similar.'

'Perhaps it was somebody else.'

'It wasn't somebody else. The magazine article quotes three different people who reported his final words. Two Americans and an Australian.'

'So why did they report hearing that?'

'They reported it because that's what they expected him to say. But I don't think it's what he said.'

'What do you think he said?'

I looked around. Adam was still safely inside. I waved at him cheerily.

'I think he said "*gelb*".'

'"*Gelb*"? What the fuck is that?'

'It's German for yellow.'

'*Yellow?* Why the fuck would he gave gone on about yellow while he was dying? Was he hallucinating?'

'No. I think he was pondering on the problem that had killed him.'

'What do you mean?'

'The colour of the line that the party had followed down Gemini Ridge. Down the wrong side of Gemini Ridge. A yellow line.'

Greg started to speak, then stopped. I watched him think slowly about what I'd said.

'But the line down Gemini Ridge was blue. My line. They went down the wrong side of the ridge because the line came out. Because I hadn't secured it.'

'I don't think so,' I said. 'I think the top two pegs of your line came out because they were pulled out. And I think that Françoise, Peter, Carrie, Tomas and the other one – what was he called?'

'Alexis,' muttered Greg.

'They went down the wrong ridge because a line led them there. A yellow line.'

Greg looked baffled, in pain.

'How could a yellow line get there?'

'Because it was put there to lead them in the wrong direction.'

'But who by?'

I turned and looked up at the window once more. Adam glanced down at us then looked back at the woman he was talking to.

'It could have been a mistake,' said Greg.

'It couldn't have been a mistake,' I said slowly.

There was a long, long silence. Several times Greg caught my eye, then looked away. Suddenly he sat down, on the wet soil, against a bush, which sprang back and flicked water over both of us. He was shaking in spasms and sobbing hopelessly.

'Greg,' I hissed urgently, 'pull yourself together.'

He was crying and crying. 'I can't. I can't.'

I bent down and grabbed him firmly, shook him. 'Greg, Greg.' I made him get up. His face was red, tear-stained. 'You've got to help me, Greg. I've got nobody. I'm alone.'

'I can't. I can't. The fucking fucker. I can't. Where's my drink?'

'You dropped it.'

'I need a drink.'

'No.'

'I need a drink.'

Greg staggered back down the garden and into the house. I

263

waited for a moment, breathing heavily, calming myself. I was hyperventilating. It took a few minutes. Now I must go back inside and be normal. At the moment I stepped into the basement kitchen I heard a terrible crash and then shouting from upstairs, breaking glass. I ran up the stone steps. In the front room there was a mêlée, a scrum on the floor. Furniture had been knocked over, a curtain had been pulled down. There were shouts and screams. At first I couldn't even make out who was involved, and then I saw Greg being pulled off somebody. It was Adam, clutching his face. I ran forward to him.

'You fucking fucker,' Greg was shouting. 'You fucking fucker.' He ran out of the room like a madman. The front door slammed. He was gone.

There were expressions of incredulity around the room. I looked at Adam. He had a bad scratch down one cheek. His eye was already swelling. He was looking at me. 'Oh, Adam,' I said, and ran forward.

'What was that all about?' somebody asked. It was Deborah. 'Alice, you were talking to him. What got into him?'

I looked around the room at Adam's friends, colleagues, comrades, all expectant, baffled, enraged by the sudden attack. I shrugged. 'He was drunk,' I said. 'He must have cracked. It all finally got to him.' I turned back to Adam. 'Let me clean that up for you, my love.'

Thirty-six

It was a swimming-pool like the ones I'd gone to as a child –
dank cubicles with green tiles, a straight up-and-down pool with
old plasters and small hairballs drifting near the bottom, signs
telling you not to run, not to dive, not to smoke and not to pet,
tired buntings hanging beneath the unsteady strip-lighting. In
the communal changing room, women came in all shapes and
sizes. It was like a drawing from a children's book illustrating
human difference: dimpled bottoms and veined, pendulous
breasts; gaunt ribcages and bony shoulders. I looked at myself
in the tarnished mirror before pulling on my costume, and was
again alarmed by how unhealthy I looked. Why hadn't I noticed
before? Then I tugged on my swimming cap and my goggles,
tight enough to make my eyeballs bulge. I marched into the pool
area. Fifty lengths: that's what I was going to do.

I hadn't been swimming for months. My legs, corkscrewing
with the breast-stroke or flailing with the crawl, felt heavy. My
chest hurt. Water found its way under my goggles and stung my
eyes. A man on his back, arms like rotating saws, hit me in my
belly and shouted at me. I counted as I swam, staring through
my goggles at the turquoise water. This was so boring; up and
down, up and down. I remembered now why I had given up
before. But after about twenty lengths, I started to find a rhythm
that became almost calming, and, instead of puffing and counting,
I started thinking. Not frantically any more, but slowly and calmly.
I knew that I was in grave danger and I knew that no one was
going to help me. Greg had been my last chance of that. I was
on my own now. The muscles in my arms ached as I swam.

It seemed absurd, and yet I was almost relieved. I was on my own and I felt that, for the first time in months, I was myself again. After all that passion, rage and terror, all that vertiginous loss of control, I was clear-headed, as if I'd emerged from a feverish dream. I was Alice Loudon. I had been lost and now I was found. Forty-two, forty-three, forty-four. I made a plan as I forged up and down the pool, avoiding all the men doing the crawl. The knots in my shoulders eased.

In the changing room I towelled myself briskly, put on my clothes without getting them wet on the puddly floor, and then put on makeup in front of the mirror. There was a woman next to me, also applying eyeliner and mascara. We grinned at each other, two women arming themselves for the outside world. I blow-dried my hair, then tied it back so that no locks were escaping on to my face. Soon I was going to cut it off, a new-look Alice. Adam loved my hair: sometimes he would bury his face in it as if he were drowning. It seemed such a long time ago, that rapturous, obliterating darkness. I would get myself cropped at the hairdresser's so that I wouldn't have to carry all that voluptuous weight around.

I didn't go back to work at once. I went to an Italian restaurant down the road from the pool and ordered a glass of red wine, a bottle of fizzy water and a seafood salad with garlic bread. I pulled out the writing paper I had bought that morning, and a pen. At the head of the paper I wrote, in thick capital letters, TO WHOM IT MAY CONCERN, and underlined it twice. My wine was put in front of me and I sipped it cautiously. I had to keep a clear head now. 'If I am found dead,' I wrote, 'or if I disappear and cannot be traced, then I will have been murdered by my husband, Adam Tallis.'

The seafood salad and garlic bread arrived, and the waiter ground black pepper liberally over it with an oversized peppermill. I speared a rubbery ring of squid and popped it into my mouth, chewed vigorously, washed it down with water.

I wrote down everything I knew, in neat script and in as cogent a style as I could muster. I explained the death of Adele, and that her last letter to Adam, written just before she disappeared, was in my knicker drawer, under all of my underwear. I told them about Adele's sister Tara, who had been harassing Adam, and had been fished out of a canal in East London. I even described the murder of Sherpa. Strangely, it was the cat rather than the women who made me realize my own peril most clearly. I remembered him, slashed open in the bath. For a minute I felt my gut clench. I crunched on crusty bread and drank a bit more wine to steady my nerves. Then I went through my analysis of exactly what had happened on the mountain with Françoise. I described Françoise's rejection of Adam, Greg's apparently foolproof system of ropes, the German man's dying words. I drew a diagram as neatly as I could, reproducing it from the magazine article with satisfying arrows and dotted lines. I gave them Greg's address and said they should confirm the accuracy of what I had written with him.

On a separate piece of paper I wrote out a very basic will. I left all my money to my parents. I left my jewellery to Pauline's baby if it was a girl, and to Pauline if it was a boy. I left Jake my two pictures and my brother my few books. That would do. I didn't have much to leave anyway. I thought about my beneficiaries, but in a detached sort of way. When I remembered my life with Jake, I felt no stirrings of regret. It just seemed so very long ago, a different world and a different me. I didn't want the old world back, not even now. I didn't know what I wanted. I couldn't look ahead like that, into the future, perhaps because I didn't dare. I was locked into the disastrous present, and it was one step in front of the other now, edging my way through danger. I didn't want to die.

I folded the documents, sealed them in an envelope and put it into my bag. I finished my lunch, eating methodically, swilling back the last of the red wine. I ordered a slice of lemon tart for pudding, which was satisfyingly creamy and astringent, and a double espresso. After I had paid the bill I fished out my new mobile and called Claudia. I told her that I had been held up and

267

wouldn't be in the office for another hour. If Adam called, she should tell him I was at a lunch meeting. I left the restaurant and hailed a cab.

Sylvie was in a meeting with a client, and her assistant told me that she was terribly busy for the rest of the afternoon.

'If you could tell her it's Alice to see her on a matter of urgency, and that I'll only need a few minutes of her time.'

I waited in the lobby, reading last year's copies of women's magazines, learning how to lose weight and have multiple orgasms and cook carrot cake. After about twenty minutes a woman with red eyes came out of Sylvie's office and I went in.

'Alice.' She hugged me and held me away from her. 'You look fabulously skinny. Sorry you had to wait. I've been holed up since lunch with a hysterical divorcée.'

'I'll not keep you long,' I said. 'I know you're very busy. I wanted to ask you a favour. It's quite a simple one.'

'Sure, ask away. How's that gorgeous husband of yours?'

'That's why I'm here,' I said, and sat down opposite her, her large and chaotic desk between us.

'Is something wrong with him?'

'In a way.'

'You don't want a divorce, do you?'

She looked curious in a rapacious sort of way.

'It's just a favour. I want you to keep something safe for me.' I fished the sealed envelope out of the bag and pushed it across the desk. 'Now, I know that this will sound ridiculously melodramatic, but if I am found dead or if I disappear I want you to give this to the police.'

I felt embarrassed. There was an absolute silence. Sylvie's mouth was open; she had a vacuous expression on her face. 'Darling Alice, is this a joke?'

'No. Is there a problem?'

The phone on her desk rang, but she didn't pick it up and we both waited until it stopped.

'No,' she said absently. 'I suppose not.'

268

'Good.' I stood up and picked up my bag. 'Give my love to the Crew. Say that I miss them. That I've always missed them, although I didn't know it at first.'

Sylvie stayed sitting in her chair, staring at me. When I reached the door, she leaped up and rushed after me. She put her hand on my shoulder.

'Alice, what's wrong?'

'Sorry, Sylvie.' I kissed her on the cheek. 'Some other time, perhaps. Take care of yourself. And thanks for being my friend. It helps.'

'Alice,' she said again, helplessly. But I was gone.

I was back at work by four. I spent an hour briefing the marketing department, and half an hour with accounts, arguing over my future budget. In the end, they backed down because I obviously wasn't going to. I swept through the paperwork on my desk, and left earlier than usual. Adam was waiting for me, as I had known he would be. He wasn't reading a paper, or gazing around him or looking at his watch; he was standing quite still, as if to attention, with his patient gaze fixed on the revolving doors. He'd probably been like that for an hour.

When he saw me he didn't smile, but he took my bag from me and then put his arms round me and stared into my face. 'You smell of chlorine.'

'I went swimming.'

'And perfume.'

'You gave it to me.'

'You look beautiful today, my love. So fresh and beautiful. I can't believe you're my wife.'

He kissed me, hard and long, and I kissed him back and pressed against him. My body felt as if it was made of some inert heavy matter that would never again shudder with desire. I shut my eyes because I couldn't bear to see his eyes staring into mine so intensely, never looking away from me. What could he see? What did he know?

'I'm going to take you out for a meal tonight,' he said. 'But before that we're going home so I can fuck you.'

'You've got it all worked out,' I said, acquiescent and smiling in the closed circle of his arms.

'I have. Right down to the last detail, my Alice.'

Thirty-seven

I hadn't protested when he took my foil card and popped the small yellow pills, one by one, down the lavatory. If anyone had told me, six months ago, that I would be allowing my lover – my *husband* – to flush away my contraceptives without my consent, I would have laughed in their face. He had shaken out the last pill and then taken me by the hand and led me, without a word, to the bedroom and made love to me very gently, making me look into his eyes. And I hadn't protested. But all the time my mind was making furious calculations. Probably he didn't know that the effect of the Pill lasts for a bit, and by that time I would be past this month's window of opportunity. I wouldn't, I guessed, get pregnant for the next couple of weeks at least. I had time. Yet I felt, nevertheless, as if he were planting a child in me and all I was doing was lying back and receiving it, and not protesting. It made me realize how unimaginative I had always been about battered wives or the partners of alcoholics. Disaster creeps up, a tidal wave on the tourist beach. By the time you can see it, you are powerless or unable to resist it and it rolls you up and away. I suppose I had been unimaginative about a lot of things, though. I had spent most of my life untouched by tragedy, and not properly thinking about the way that other people lived and suffered.

When I looked back over the past few months, I felt freshly ashamed of how very easily I had sloughed off an old and loved life: my family, friends, my interests, my sense of the world. Jake had accused me of burning bridges, which made my behaviour sound reckless and fine. But I had abandoned *people* as well. Now

I needed to get my affairs in order, or at least make a gesture of reconciliation towards those I might have hurt. I wrote a letter to my parents, saying that I knew I hadn't been in contact much but they should always remember that I loved them very much. I sent a postcard to my brother, whom I had lasted visited a year ago, in which I tried to be jaunty and affectionate. I rang Pauline, and left a message on the answering-machine asking after the pregnancy and saying that I would like to see her very soon and that I had been missing her. I posted a belated birthday card to Clive. And, taking a deep breath, I rang up Mike. He sounded subdued rather than bitter, and not displeased to hear from me. He was going on holiday with his wife and young son the next day, to a house in Brittany, his first holiday in months. I was saying goodbye to everyone, but they wouldn't know it.

I had wrecked my old world decisively, and now I was trying to figure out a way of bringing my new world crashing down too, so that I could escape from it. There were still times – fewer as each day passed – when it felt impossible to believe that I was actually living this. I was married to a murderer, a beautiful, blue-eyed murderer. If he ever found out that I knew, he would kill me too, I had no doubt about that. If I tried to leave, he would also kill me. He would find me and kill me.

That evening I had arranged to go to a lecture examining new figures on the link between fertility treatments and ovarian cancer, partly because it was distantly connected to my work, partly because it was given by an acquaintance of mine, but mainly because it would be a way of spending time away from Adam. He would be waiting outside for me and, of course, I couldn't stop him coming with me if he insisted. But we would be together in my world for once, a world of reassuring scientific inquiry, empiricism, and of temporary safety. I wouldn't have to look at him, or talk to him, or be held down by him, moaning in pretended passion.

Adam wasn't waiting outside. The relief I felt was so intense it was like exhilaration. I was immediately lighter-footed, clearer-headed. Everything looked different without him standing there, watching for me as I came through the doors, staring at me with that persistent, brooding gaze that I could no longer decipher. Was it hate or love, passion or murderous intent? With Adam the two had always been too closely linked, and again I remembered – with a shudder of pure revulsion now, mixed with a tingling shame – the violence of our honeymoon night in the Lake District. I felt trapped in a long, grey morning-after.

I walked to the lecture hall, which took about a quarter of an hour, and as I rounded the corner towards the building I saw him standing there, holding a bunch of yellow roses. Women looked longingly at him as they passed by, but he seemed not to notice. His eyes were for me only. He was waiting for me, although expecting me to come from another direction. I stopped and backed into the nearest doorway as a wave of nausea came over me. I would never get away from him: he was one step ahead of me, always waiting for me, always touching me and clasping me to him, never letting me go. He was too much for me. I waited until the panic subsided and then, careful not to be seen by him, I turned round and ran back down the road until I was round the corner. Then I hailed a cab.

'Where to, love?'

Where to? Where could I go to? I couldn't run away from him because then he would know I knew. I shrugged in dispirited defeat and asked the driver to take me home. Prison. I knew that I couldn't continue like this. The horror that had swamped me when I had seen Adam had felt utterly physical. How much longer could I pretend to love him, pretend to be in bliss when he stroked me, pretend that I didn't feel very scared? My body was in revolt. But I didn't know what else to do.

As I came through the door, the phone was ringing.

'Hello.'

'Alice?' It was Sylvie, and she sounded flustered. 'I didn't think you'd be there.'

'So why ring?'

'Actually I was wanting to speak to Adam. This is a bit awkward.'

I suddenly felt cold and clammy, as if I were about to throw up. 'Adam?' I said. 'Why were you wanting to speak to Adam, Sylvie?'

There was a silence at the other end of the phone.

'Sylvie?'

'Yes. Look, I wasn't going to tell you, I mean, he was going to speak to you, but since this has happened, well.' I heard her take a drag on her cigarette. Then she said, 'The fact is, and I know you'll think this is a betrayal but one day you'll realize it was an act of friendship, I looked at the letter. And then I showed it to Adam. I mean, he turned up at my house out of the blue, and I didn't know what to do, but I showed it to him because I think you're having a breakdown or something, Alice. What you wrote, it's crazy, completely crazy, you're deluded. You must see that, of course you must. So I didn't know what to do, and I showed it to Adam. Hello, Alice, are you still there?'

'To Adam.' I didn't recognize my own voice, it was so flat and expressionless. I was thinking hard: there was no time left any more. Time had gone.

'Yes, he was wonderful, absolutely wonderful. He was hurt, of course, God, he was hurt. He was crying when he read the letter and kept saying your name over and over again. But he doesn't blame you, you must understand that, Alice. And he's worried you might, you know, do something stupid. That was the last thing he said to me. He said that he was worried that in the state you are you might, you know, harm yourself.'

'Do you have any idea of what you've done?'

'Now, look, Alice . . .'

I put the phone down on her pleading voice and stood for a few seconds, paralysed. The room seemed very cold and quiet. I could hear every little sound in it, the creak of a floorboard when I shifted my weight, a murmur in the water pipes, the tiny sigh of wind outside. That was it. When I was found dead, Adam had already expressed the fear that I might harm myself. I raced across to the bedroom and pulled open the drawer where I had hidden Adele's letter and Adam's forged note to himself. They were gone. I ran for the front door and then I heard his footsteps, distant still at the bottom of the long flight of stairs.

There was no way out. Our flat was at the top of the stairs. I looked around, knowing there were no other exits, that there was nowhere to hide. I considered ringing the police, but I wouldn't even have time to dial. I ran to the bathroom and turned the shower full on, so that it was splashing noisily on to the tiled floor. Then, tweaking shut the shower curtains and leaving the bathroom door very slightly open, I raced back into the living room, picked up my keys and ducked into the poky kitchen, where I stood behind its open door, barely out of sight. The copy of *Guy* magazine was there within reach on the worktop. I picked it up. That was something at least.

He came in, and pulled the flat door shut behind him. My heart pounded in my chest, thundering away so that I couldn't believe he couldn't hear it too. I suddenly remembered that he was carrying a bunch of flowers. He would come into the kitchen first to put them in water. Oh, God, please please please. My breath came in raggedy gasps, hurting my chest. I gave a little ratchety sob. I couldn't stop it.

But then, like a miracle, fear ebbed away and what was left was a kind of curiosity, as if I were a spectator at my own disaster. Drowning people are supposed to see their lives flash past them as they die. Now, in those few seconds as I waited, my mind reeled through the images of my time with Adam; such a brief time, really, although it had obliterated everything else that had gone before. I watched as if I were my own observer: our first glance, across a crowded street; our first sexual encounter, so feverish it seemed almost comic now; our wedding day, when I was so happy I wanted to die. Then I saw Adam with his hand upraised; Adam holding a buckled belt; Adam with his hands around my neck. The images all led to now: this moment ahead,

275

when I would see Adam killing me. But I wasn't scared any longer. I almost felt peaceful. It had been such a long time since I had felt peaceful.

I heard him walk across the room. Past the kitchen. Towards the bathroom, and the gushing shower. I took the new Chubb lock between my thumb and forefinger, ready for use, and tensed my body to run.

'Alice,' he called. 'Alice.'

Now. I sprinted out of the kitchen, into the hall, and wrenched open the front door.

'Alice!'

He was there, striding towards me, yellow flowers crushed against his chest. I saw his face, his gorgeous murderer's face.

I pulled shut the door and thrust the heavy key into the lock and twisted it frantically. Come on, please, come on. It turned in the lock, and I pulled it free and ran blindly towards the stairs. As I did so I heard him hammering on the door. He was strong, oh, God, he was strong enough to break it. He'd done it easily enough before, when he'd broken into our own flat to kill Sherpa.

I kept on running down the stairs, taking them two at a time. At one point, my knees buckled under me and I twisted my ankle. But he wasn't coming. The hammering grew fainter. The new lock was holding. If I came through this I would gain a bitter kind of satisfaction from the fact that he had trapped himself when he had broken the door to murder our cat.

Now I was on the pavement. I sprinted up the road towards the high street and only when I was at the top did I turn my head quickly to see if I could see him. Was that him, that figure running towards me in the distance? I hurtled across the main road, between cars, dodging a bicycle. I saw the rider's angry face as he swerved to avoid me. I had a sharp pain in my side but I didn't slow down. If he caught up with me I would yell and howl, but people would just think I was a madwoman. Nobody ever interferes in domestic quarrels anyway. I thought I heard someone shout my name, but maybe it was just my screaming imagination.

I knew where I was headed. It was near here. Only a few more yards. If I could only make it in time. I saw the blue light, a numbered van parked outside. I summoned up my last energy and sprang in through the doors, coming to an abrupt, undignified stop at the front desk, where a policeman's bored face was staring up at me.

'Yes?' he said, picking up his pen, and I started to laugh.

Thirty-eight

I sat in a corridor and waited and watched. I saw everything as if I were looking through the wrong end of a telescope. People in and out of uniform bustled up and down, phones rang. I'm not sure whether I had an over-dramatic sense of what I'd find in a central London police station, whether I had expected to see pimps and prostitutes and lowlifes being hustled through and booked, whether I'd expected that I myself would be led into an interview room with a false mirror where I'd be alternately grilled by a nice and a nasty cop. But I hadn't expected to sit aimlessly on a moulded plastic chair getting in the way in a corridor, as if I had shown up in a casualty department with an injury that was insufficiently serious to merit speedy treatment.

In normal circumstances I would have been intrigued by these glimpses of other people's dramas but now I was quite lost to such things. I was wondering what Adam was thinking and doing outside. I had to make a plan. It was almost certain that whoever talked to me would consider that I was mad and usher me back out into the frightening world behind the Plexiglass at the front desk and all that was waiting for me there. I had an uncomfortable feeling that accusing my husband of seven murders was seven times as unconvincing as accusing him of just one, which in itself would have been implausible enough.

What I wanted more than anything else in the world was for a paternal, or maternal, figure to tell me that they believed me, that they would deal with it from here on in and that my troubles were over. There was no chance of that happening. I had to take control. I remembered once when I was a teenager coming back

278

drunk from a party and forcing myself to do an imitation of the way a sober person behaved. But I took such immense pains to walk around the sofa and the chairs so that I wouldn't stumble over them, I was so extremely sober, that my mother instantly asked me what I'd been up to. I probably reeked of Babycham as well. I needed to do better than that today. I needed to convince them. After all, I had convinced Greg, for all the good that had done me. It wasn't essential to convince them entirely. It was just a matter of keeping them intrigued enough so that they might think there was something to investigate. I mustn't go back out there – into the world where Adam was waiting for me.

For the first time in years, I badly wanted my mother and father; not as they were now, though, ageing and uncertain, fixed in their disapproval and determinedly blind to the bitterness and terror of the world. No, I wanted them as they had seemed to me as a little girl, before I had learned to distrust them: tall, solid figures telling me what was right and what was wrong, protecting me from hurt, guiding me. I remembered my mother sewing buttons back on to shirts, sitting in the bulky armchair under the window, and how she had seemed so entirely competent and reassuring to me. My father carving the joint on a Sunday afternoon, very particular as he shaved off thin pink slices of beef. I could see myself sitting between them, growing in their shelter. How had that sensible little girl, with braces and ankle socks, turned into me, here in this police station, scared for my life? I wanted to be that little girl again, and rescuable.

The female police officer who had brought me through came back with a middle-aged man in a shirt with rolled-up sleeves. She looked like a schoolgirl returning with an exasperated senior teacher. I guessed that she had gone around the office looking for somebody who wasn't on the phone or deep in filling out forms and this man had agreed to come into the corridor for a second, preferably to make me go away. He looked down at me. I wondered if I should stand up. He looked a bit like my father, and that resemblance made my eyes fill with tears. I blinked them back, fiercely. I must seem calm.

'Miss . . . ?'

'Loudon,' I said. 'Alice Loudon.'

'I understand you have some information you want to report,' he said.

'Yes,' I said.

'Well?'

I looked around. 'Are we going to talk out here?'

The man frowned. 'I'm sorry, love, but we're pressed for space at the moment. If you could bear with us.'

'All right,' I said. I clenched my fists in my lap so he wouldn't see them trembling, cleared my throat and tried to keep my voice steady. 'A woman called Tara Blanchard was found murdered in a canal a few weeks ago. Have you heard about it?' The detective shook his head. People kept pushing past but I continued, 'I know who killed her.'

The detective held up a hand to stop me. 'Hang on, my dear. The best thing is if I go off and find the station that's dealing with the case and then I'll give them a ring and you can pop over and have a chat with them. All right?'

'No, it isn't. I came here because I was in danger. The person who killed Tara Blanchard is my husband.'

I expected some reaction to this statement, if only a laugh of disbelief, but there was nothing.

'Your husband?' said the detective, catching the eye of the WPC. 'And why do you think that?'

'I think that Tara Blanchard was blackmailing, or at least harassing, my husband so he killed her.'

'Harassing him?'

'We were getting phone calls constantly, late at night, early in the morning. And there were threatening notes.'

He looked blank. Was he going to have to start trying to make sense of what I was saying? The prospect can't have been appealing. I looked around. I couldn't continue in this setting.

What I was going to say might seem more convincing if it were conducted in a more formal style.

'I'm sorry, Mr . . . I don't know your name.'

'Byrne. Detective Inspector Byrne.'

'Well, can't we talk somewhere a bit more private? It feels strange talking in a corridor.'

He gave a weary sigh to show his impatience. 'There are no rooms free,' he said. 'You can come through and sit by my desk, if that's any better.'

I nodded and Byrne led me through. On the way he got me a coffee. I accepted it though I didn't feel like it. Anything that would make us seem as if we had a trusting relationship.

'Now, where were we, can you remember?' he asked, as he sat down by his desk with me on the other side.

'We were getting these threatening notes.'

'From the murdered woman?'

'Yes, Tara Blanchard.'

'Did she sign them?'

'No, but after her death I went to her flat and found newspaper articles about my husband among her rubbish.'

Byrne looked surprised, not to say alarmed. 'You searched her rubbish?'

'Yes.'

'What were these newspaper articles?'

'My husband – his name is Adam Tallis – is a well-known mountaineer. He was involved in a terrible disaster on a Himalayan mountain last year in which five people died. He's a sort of hero. Anyway, there was the problem that we received another of those notes after Tara Blanchard had died. Not only that. The note was connected to a break-in at our flat. Our cat was killed.'

'Did you report the break-in?'

'Yes. Two officers from this police station came round.'

'Well, that's something,' Byrne said wearily, and then, as if it were almost too much effort to be worth pointing out, 'but if this happened after this woman apparently died . . .'

'Exactly,' I said. 'It was impossible. But a few days ago I was clearing out the flat and under a desk I found a scrunched-up envelope. On the paper Adam had clearly been practising writing the note that was left that last time.'

'So?'

'So Adam had been trying to break any possible connection between the notes and this woman.'

'Can I see this note?'

I had been dreading this moment. 'Adam found out about what I suspect him of. When I got back to the flat today, the paper was gone.'

'How did he find out?'

'I wrote everything down and put it in an envelope and gave it to a friend of mine, in case anything should happen to me. But she read it. And she gave it to Adam.'

Byrne gave a half-smile then quickly suppressed it. 'Maybe she had your best interests at heart,' he said. 'Maybe she wanted to help.'

'I'm sure she wanted to help. But she didn't help. She put me in danger.'

'The problem is, er, Mrs . . .'

'Alice Loudon.'

'The problem is that murder is a very serious offence.' He was talking to me as if he were instructing a primary-school child about road safety. 'And because it's such a serious offence, we need evidence, not just suspicion. People quite often feel suspicious about people they know. They suspect them of crimes when they've had arguments. The best thing is to sort out those differences of opinion.'

I could feel him slipping away from me. I had to continue.

'You haven't let me finish. The reason Tara was harassing Adam was that, I believe, she suspected that he had killed her sister, Adele.'

'Killed her *sister*?'

Byrne raised a disbelieving eyebrow. Worse and worse. I

pressed my hands against the desk, to stop the sense that the ground was tilting beneath me; tried not to think of Adam waiting outside the police station for me. He would be standing there, quite still, blue eyes fixed on the door, which I would come out of. I knew what he looked like when he was waiting for something that he wanted: patient, absolutely focused.

'Adele Blanchard was married and lived in Corrick. It's a village in the Midlands, fairly near Birmingham. She and her husband were trekkers, climbers, and were part of a group of friends that included Adam. She had an affair with Adam and broke it off in January nineteen ninety. A couple of weeks later she disappeared.'

'And you think your husband killed her?'

'He wasn't my husband then. We only met this year.'

'Is there any reason for thinking he killed this other woman?'

'Adele Blanchard rejected Adam and she died. He had one other long-term girlfriend. She was a doctor and a mountaineer called Françoise Colet.'

'And where is she?' asked Byrne, with a slightly sarcastic expression.

'She died on the mountain in Nepal last year.'

'And I suppose your husband killed her as well.'

'Yes.'

'Oh, for God's sake.'

'Just wait, let me take you through it properly.' Now he thought I was insane.

'Mrs, er, I'm very busy. I've got . . .' He pointed vaguely at the piles of paper on his desk.

'Look, I know this is difficult,' I said, trying to suppress a feeling of panic that was rising in me, like a flood about to engulf me entirely. My voice came out in a gasp. 'I really appreciate you listening to me. If you could just give me a few more minutes and I can take you through it. After that, if you want me to, I'll just go away and forget about the whole thing.'

There was a visible expression of relief on his face. That was evidently the most hopeful news he had heard since I had arrived.

'All right,' he said. 'But briefly.'

'I promise,' I said, but of course I wasn't brief. I had the magazine with me and with all the questions and repetitions and explanations the account lasted almost an hour. I took him through the details of the expedition, the arrangements involving the coloured lines, the non-English-speaking Tomas Benn, the chaos of the storm, the repeated descents and ascents made by Adam while Greg and Claude were disabled. I talked and talked, gabbling against my death sentence. As long as he was listening, I would be alive. As I told him the final details, fading away into unwilling silence, a slow smile spread across Byrne's face. I had his attention at last. 'So,' I said at the end, 'the only possible explanation is that Adam deliberately arranged for the group with Françoise in it to go down the wrong side of the Gemini Ridge.'

Byrne gave a broad grin. '*Gelb?*' he said. 'That's German for yellow, you say?'

'That's right,' I said.

'It's good,' he said. 'I've got to give you credit. It's good.'

'So you believe me.'

He shrugged. 'I don't know about that. It's possible. But, then, maybe they misheard him. Or maybe he really did shout, "Help."'

'But I've explained why that's impossible.'

'It doesn't matter. It's a matter for the authorities in Nepal or wherever that mountain was.'

'But that's not my point. I've established a psychological pattern. Can't you see that, on the basis of what I've told you, it's worth investigating the other two murders?'

Byrne had a hunted, cornered look by this time and there was now a long silence as he considered what I'd said and how to answer me. I clung to the desk as if I were about to fall.

'No,' he said finally. I started to protest but he continued, 'Miss Loudon, you must agree that I've done you the politeness of listening to what you had to say. The only thing I can recommend to you is that if you wish to take these matters further you should talk to the police forces concerned. But unless you have anything concrete to offer them, I don't believe there's anything they can do.'

'It doesn't matter,' I said. My voice sounded flat, drained of all expression. And, indeed, it didn't matter any more. There was nothing left to do.

'What do you mean?'

'Adam knows about it all now. This was my only chance. You're right, of course. I've got no evidence. I just know. I just know Adam.' I was going to stand up, say goodbye, leave, but on an impulse I leaned across the desk and took Byrne's hand. He looked startled. 'What's your first name?'

'Bob,' he said uneasily.

'If, in the next few weeks, you hear that I've killed myself or fallen under a train or drowned, there'll be lots of evidence that I've behaved madly over the last few weeks so it will be easy to conclude that I killed myself while the balance of my mind was disturbed or that I was having a breakdown and was an accident waiting to happen. But it won't be true. I want to stay alive. All right?'

He delicately removed my hand from his. 'You'll be all right,' he said. 'Talk it over with your husband. You can sort it out.'

'But . . .'

Then we were interrupted. A uniformed officer beckoned Byrne away and they talked in low voices, occasionally looking across at me. Byrne nodded at the man, who went back the way he had come. He sat down at his desk once more and looked at me with an expression of great solemnity.

'Your husband is at the front desk.'

'Of course,' I said bitterly.

'No,' said Byrne gently. 'It's not like that. He's here with a doctor. He wants to help you.'

'A doctor?'

'I understand that you have been under pressure lately. You've been acting irrationally. I gather there's some suggestion of pretending to be a journalist, that sort of thing. Can we bring them through?'

'I don't care,' I said. I had lost. What was the point of fighting it? Byrne picked up the phone.

The doctor was Deborah. The two of them looked almost glorious as they walked across the seedy office, tall and tanned, among the pale, sallow detectives and secretaries. Deborah gave a tentative smile as she caught my eye. I didn't smile back.

'Alice,' she said. 'We're here to help you. It'll be all right.' She nodded at Adam then addressed Byrne. 'Are you the officer of record?'

He looked puzzled. 'I'm the one to talk to,' he said warily.

Deborah spoke in a calm, soothing voice as if Byrne, too, were one of her patients. 'I'm a general practitioner and under section four of the Mental Health Act of nineteen eighty-three I am making an emergency application to take charge of Alice Loudon. After discussion with her husband, Mr Tallis here, I am convinced that she urgently needs hospital admission and assessment for her own safety.'

'Are you sectioning me?' I asked.

Deborah looked down, almost shiftily, at a notebook she held in her hand. 'It's not really that. You mustn't think of it like that. We only want what's best.'

I looked at Adam. He had a soft, almost loving expression. 'My darling Alice,' was all he said.

Byrne looked uncomfortable. 'It's all a bit far-fetched but . . .' he said.

'It's a medical call,' said Deborah firmly. 'In any case, that's for the psychiatric assessment. Meanwhile, I ask for Alice Loudon to be released into the care of her husband.'

Adam put out his hand and touched my cheek, so tenderly. 'Sweetest love,' he said. I looked up at him. His blue eyes shone down at me, like the sky. His long hair looked windswept. His mouth was slightly apart, as if he were about to speak or to kiss me. I put my hand up and touched the necklace he had given me, long ago in the first days of our love. It was as if there was nobody in the room except me and him, everything else was just blur and noise. Maybe I had been wrong about it all. Suddenly the temptation seemed irresistible just to give myself up to these people and be cared for, people who really loved me.

'I'm sorry,' I heard myself say, in a feeble voice.

Adam bent down and took me in his arms. I smelt his sweat, felt the roughness of his cheek against mine.

'Love's a funny business,' I said. 'How can you kill someone you love?'

'Alice, my darling,' he said, soft against my ear, hand on my hair, 'didn't I promise that I would always look after you? For ever and ever.'

He held me close and it felt wonderful. For ever and ever. That was the way I had thought it was going to be. Maybe it could still be like that. Maybe we could turn the clock back, pretend he had never killed people and I had never known. I felt tears running down my face. A promise to look after me for ever and ever. A moment and a promise. Where had I heard those words? There was something in my mind, blurred and indistinct, and then it took shape and I saw it. I stepped back, out of Adam's arms, and I looked clearly at Adam's face.

'I know,' I said.

I looked round. Byrne, Deborah and Adam were looking puzzled. Did they think now that I had really and finally gone over the edge? I didn't mind. I was in control again, my mind clear. It wasn't me that was mad.

'I know where Adam put her. I know where Adam buried Adele Blanchard.'

'What do you mean?' asked Byrne.

I looked at Adam and he looked back steadily, unwavering. Then I fumbled in my coat and found my purse. I opened it and pulled out a season ticket, receipts, some foreign currency, and there it was: me, photographed by Adam at the moment he asked me to marry him. I handed the photograph to Byrne, who took it and looked at it with a puzzled expression.

'Careful with that,' I said. 'It's the only copy. Adele's buried there.'

I looked round at Adam. He didn't look away, even then, but I knew he was thinking. This was his genius, making calculations in a crisis. What was he planning inside that beautiful head?

Byrne turned away from me and showed the photograph to Adam. 'What's this?' he said. 'Where is it?'

Adam gave a baffled, sympathetic smile. 'I don't know exactly,' he said. 'It was just on a walk somewhere.' He turned his gaze back to me.

At that moment I knew that I was right.

'No,' I said. 'It wasn't just a walk somewhere. Adam took me there to this special spot. He had been let down before, he told me. But now in that special place he wanted to ask me to marry him. A moment and a promise. We vowed to be faithful to each other over the dead body of Adele Blanchard.'

'Adele Blanchard?' said Adam. 'Who's she?' He looked at me very closely. I could feel his eyes on mine trying to assess what I knew. 'This is crazy. I don't remember where we were on that walk. And you. You don't remember either, do you, darling? You slept all the way up in the car. You don't know where it is.'

I looked at the photograph with a sudden lurch of horror. He was right. I didn't. I looked at the grass, so green, tantalizingly graspable and so far away. Adele, where are you? Where is your betrayed, broken, lost body? And then I had it. Here I am. Here I am.

'St Eadmund's,' I said.

'What?' said Byrne and Adam, at the same time.

'St Eadmund's with an A. Adele Blanchard taught at St Eadmund's primary school near Corrick, and the church of St Eadmund's is there as well. Take me to the church of St Eadmund's and I'll take you to this spot.'

Byrne looked from me to Adam and then back again. He didn't

know what to do but he was wavering. I took a step closer to Adam so that our faces were almost touching. I looked into his clear, blue eyes. There wasn't the smallest flicker of disquiet. He was magnificent. Perhaps for the first moment I had a clear sense of this man on a mountain, saving a life or taking it away. I raised my right hand and touched his cheek as he had touched mine. He flinched very slightly. I had to say something to him. Whatever happened, I would never have another chance.

'I understand that you killed Adele and Françoise because, in some terrible way, you loved them. And I suppose that Tara was threatening you. Had her sister told her something? Did she know? Or suspect? But what about the others? Pete. Carrie. Tomas. Alexis. When you went back up the mountain, did you actually push Françoise over the edge? Did somebody see you? Was it just *convenient*?' I waited. There was no response. 'You'll never say, will you? You won't give lesser mortals the satisfaction.'

'This is ridiculous,' Adam said. 'Alice needs help. I can legally take custody of her.'

'You've got to take note of this,' I said to Byrne. 'I've reported the existence of a murdered body. I've identified the location. You are obliged to investigate.'

Byrne looked between us. Then his face relaxed into a sardonic smile. He sighed. 'All right,' he said. Then he looked over at Adam. 'Don't worry, sir. We'll take good care of your wife.'

'Goodbye,' I said to Adam. 'Goodbye, Adam.'

He smiled at me, a smile of such sweetness that he looked like a little boy, full of terrifying hope. But he didn't say anything, just looked at me as I walked away, and I didn't look back.

Thirty-nine

WPC Mayer looked about sixteen. She had bobbed brown hair and a round, slightly spotty face. I sat in the back of the car – a plain blue one, not the police car I'd been expecting – and looked at the back of her plump neck above her crisp white collar. It looked stiff to me, disapproving, and her listless handshake and brief, shallow glance had seemed indifferent.

She made no effort to talk to me, except to tell me at the start of the journey to fasten my seat-belt, please, and I was grateful for that. I leaned against the cool plastic and stared at the London traffic outside, seeing almost nothing. It was a bright morning, and the light gave me a headache, but when I closed my eyes it was no better, for then images chased across the lids. Particularly Adam's face, my last sight of him. My whole body felt sore and hollow. It was as if I could feel all the different bits of me: my heart, my guts, my lungs, my aching kidneys, the blood coursing round me, my ringing head.

Every so often, WPC Mayer's radio would crackle into life and she would speak into the car, a strange formulaic kind of language about rendezvous and times of arrival. Outside this car was ordinary real life – people going about their daily business, irritated, bored, contented, indifferent, excited, tired. Thinking about their work, or what to cook for supper, or what their daughter had said at breakfast that morning, or thinking of the boy they fancied, or how their hair needed cutting or how their back ached. It was hard to imagine I had ever been there, in that life. Dimly, as in a dream half forgotten, I remembered evenings in the Vine with the Crew. What had we talked about, night after night, as if time didn't matter, as if we had all the time in the world? Had I been happy then? I didn't know any more. I could barely recall Jake's face now, or not Jake's face when I was living with him, not his lover's face, not the way he had looked at me when we lay in bed together. Adam's face got in the way, his gazing eyes. How he had pushed his way between me and the world, blotting out my view so that all I could see was him.

I had been Alice-with-Jake, then Alice-with-Adam. Now I was just Alice. Alice alone. No one to tell me how I looked or ask me how I felt. No one to make plans with or test thoughts against or be protected by or lose myself in. If I survived this, I would be alone. I looked down at my hands, lying inert on my lap. I listened to my breathing, steady and quiet. Maybe I wouldn't survive. Before Adam, I had never been too scared of death, mainly because death had always seemed far off, happening to some comfy white-haired old woman whom I couldn't connect with myself. Who would miss me, I wondered. Well, my parents would miss me, of course. My friends? In a way – but for them I had already gone missing when I walked out on Jake and the old life. They would shake their heads over me as over a curiosity. 'Poor thing,' they would say. Adam would miss me, though; yes, Adam would miss me. He would weep for me, genuine tears of grief. He would always remember me and he would always mourn me. How strange that was. I almost smiled.

I took the photograph out of my pocket again and stared at it. There I was, so happy at the miracle of my new life that I looked like a madwoman. There was a hawthorn bush behind me, and grass and sky, but that was all. What if I couldn't remember? I tried to recall the route from the church but as I did so a sense of utter blankness came over me. I couldn't even visualize the church itself. I tried to stop myself thinking about it, as if by doing so I might drive away the last shreds of memory. I looked at the photograph again and I heard my own voice: 'For ever,' I had said. For ever. What had Adam said back? I couldn't think about that, but I remembered that he had cried. I had felt his tears on my cheek. For a moment, I nearly cried myself, sitting in that chilly police car, on my way to find out if I was going to win or be defeated by him, live or be destroyed by him. Adam was my enemy now but he had loved me, whatever that meant. I had loved him, too. For one disastrous moment, I wanted to tell WPC Mayer to turn round and go home; it was all a terrible mistake, a mad aberration.

I shook myself and looked out of the window again, away from the photograph. We were off the motorway now, and driving through a little grey village. I remembered nothing of this journey. Oh, God, maybe nothing would come back to me at all. WPC Mayer's neck was unyielding. I closed my eyes once more. I felt so frightened that I was almost calm with it, sickly calm; frozen calm. My spine felt thin and brittle when I shifted in the seat; my fingers were cold and stiff.

'Here we are.'

The car drew up at St Eadmund's church, a stocky grey building. A notice outside announced proudly that the foundations of the church were more than a thousand years old. With a surge of relief, I remembered it. But this was where the test began. WPC Mayer got out of the car and opened the door for me. I got out and then saw that three people were waiting for us. Another woman, a bit older than Mayer, wearing slacks and a thick sheepskin jacket, and two men in yellow jackets, like the jackets that construction workers often wear. They were carrying spades. My knees felt wobbly, but I tried to walk briskly, as if I knew exactly where I wanted to go.

They hardly looked at me as we approached. The two men were talking to each other. They glanced up at me then resumed their conversation. The woman stepped forward and introduced herself as Detective Constable Paget, took Mayer by the elbow and steered her away from me.

'We should be finished with this in a couple of hours,' I heard her say. So no one believed me at all. I looked down at my feet. I was wearing inappropriate ankle boots with heels, hopeless for walking over moorland and through muddy fields. I knew which direction we were going to set off in. I was just going to continue walking up the road, past the church. That much was easy. It was what happened next that was the problem. I caught the two men staring over at me, but when I stared back at them their glances fell away, as if they were embarrassed by me. The madwoman. I pushed my hair behind my ears and did up the top button of my jacket.

The two women returned, looking purposeful.

'Right, Mrs Tallis,' said the detective, nodding at me. 'If you'd like to show us the way, then.'

My throat felt as if there was some obstruction in it. I started to walk along the lane. One foot in front of another, clip clop along the silent lane. Childhood surged back on me in a rhyme: 'Left, left, had a good home and I left. Right, right, it serves you jolly well right.' WDC Paget walked beside me and the other three fell behind a little way. I couldn't make out what they were saying to each other, but every so often I could hear one of them laugh. My legs felt heavy, like lead. The road stretched out in front of me, on and on, featureless. Was this my last walk?

'How far is it from here?' asked WDC Paget.

I had no idea. But round a bend, the road forked and I saw a war monument with a chipped stone eagle on the top.

'This is it,' I said, trying not to sound relieved. 'This is where we came.'

WDC Paget must have heard the surprise in my voice for she cast me a quizzical glance.

'Right, here,' I said, for although I had not remembered the monument, now that we were here it came clearly back to me.

I led them along the narrow lane, which was more like a track. My legs felt lighter now. My body was showing me the way to go. Somewhere along here there would be a path. I looked anxiously from left to right and kept stopping to peer into the undergrowth, in case it had become overgrown by weeds since I was last here. I could sense the growing impatience of the group.

Once, I saw W P C Mayer exchange a look with one of the diggers – a thin young man with a long, lumpy neck – and shrug.

'It's somewhere near here,' I said.

A few minutes later I said, 'We must have gone past it.' We stood in the middle of the lane while I dithered, and then W D C Paget said, quite kindly, 'I think there's a turning up ahead. Shall we just go and look at that?'

It was the path. I almost hugged her in gratitude then set off, at a shambling trot, with the police coming after me. Bushes snagged at us, brambles whipped at our legs, but I didn't mind. This was where we had come. This time I didn't hesitate, but turned off the path into the trees, for I had seen a silver birch that I recognized, white and straight among the beech trees. We scrambled up a slope. When Adam and I had come here, he had held my hand and helped me through the slippery fallen leaves. We came upon a crowd of daffodils and I heard W P C Mayer exclaim in pleasure, as if we were out on a country walk.

We reached the top of the slope, the trees cleared and we were out in what was almost moorland. As if he were beside me I heard Adam's voice reaching me from the past: 'A patch of grass that's off a path that's off a track that's off a road.'

Now, suddenly, I didn't know where to go. There had been a hawthorn bush, but I couldn't see it from where I stood. I took a few uncertain steps, then stopped and gazed around me hopelessly. W D C Paget came up beside me and said nothing, just waited. I took the photograph out of my pocket. 'This is what we are looking for.'

'A bush.' Her voice was expressionless but her glance was not. There were bushes all around us.

I shut my eyes and tried to think myself back. And then I remembered. 'Look with my eyes,' he had said. And we had gazed down on the church beneath us, and the fields. 'Look with my eyes.'

It was as if I was truly looking with his eyes, following in his footsteps. I stumbled, almost ran, along the patch of moorland,

and there, in the break in the trees, I could see down to where we had come from. There was St Eadmund's, with the two cars parked beside it. There was the table of green fields. And here was the hawthorn bush. I stood in front of it, as I had stood then. I stood on the spongy earth and prayed that the body of a young woman was lying underneath me.

'Here,' I said to WDC Paget. 'Here. Dig here.'

She beckoned over the men with their spades and repeated what I had said: 'Dig here.'

I stepped away from where I was standing and they started to dig. The ground was stony and it was obviously hard work. Soon I could see beads of sweat standing out on their foreheads. I tried to breathe evenly. With each strike of the spade, I waited for something to appear. Nothing. They dug until there was a sizeable hole. Nothing. Eventually they stopped and looked at WDC Paget, who looked at me.

'It's there,' I said. 'I know it's there. Wait.'

Again, I closed my eyes and tried to remember. I took out the photograph and stared at the bush.

'Tell me exactly where to stand,' I said to WDC Paget, thrust the photo into her hand and positioned myself by the bush.

She looked at me wearily then shrugged. I stood just as I had stood for Adam, and stared at her as if she were about to take my photograph herself. She stared back through narrowed eyes.

'Forward a bit,' she said.

I stepped forward.

'That's it.'

'Dig here,' I said to the men.

Again they started to shift the earth. We waited in silence, the dull thump of the spade, the laboured breathing of the working men. Nothing. There was nothing, just coarse reddish earth and little stones.

Again they stopped and looked at me. 'Please,' I said, and my voice came out hoarse. 'Please dig a bit more.' I turned to WDC Paget and put my hand on her sleeve. 'Please,' I said.

295

She frowned in deep thought before speaking. 'We could spend a week up here digging. We've dug where you said and we've found nothing. It's time to call a halt.'

'Please,' I said. My voice was cracked. 'Please.' I was begging for my life.

WDC Paget gave a deep sigh. 'All right,' she said. She looked at her watch. 'Twenty minutes and that's that.'

She made a gesture and the men moved across with an array of sarcastic grunts and expressions. I moved away and sat down. I looked into the valley. Grasses were rippling in the wind like the sea.

Suddenly, behind me, I heard a murmur. I ran across. The men had stopped digging and were on their knees by the hole, clearing earth with their hands. I crouched down beside them. The earth was suddenly darker here and I saw a hand, just its bones, protrude, as if it were beckoning us.

'It's her!' I cried. 'It's Adele! Do you see? Oh, do you see?' and I started scrabbling away myself, tearing at the soil, though I could hardly see myself. I wanted to hold the bones, cradle them, put my hands around the head, which was beginning to appear, a ghastly grinning skull, poke my fingers through the empty eyes.

'Don't touch,' said WDC Paget, and hauled me back.

'But I must!' I howled. 'It's her. I was right. It's her.' It was going to be me, I wanted to say. If we hadn't found her it would have been me.

'It's evidence, Mrs Tallis,' she said sternly.

'It's Adele,' I said again. 'It's Adele, and Adam murdered her.'

'We have no idea who it is,' she said. 'Tests will have to be carried out, identifications.'

I looked down at the arm, hand, head poking out from the soil. All the tension went out of me and I felt utterly weary, utterly sad.

'Poor thing,' I said. 'Poor woman. Oh dear. Oh, dear God, oh, Christ.'

WDC Paget handed me a large tissue, and I realized I was crying.

'There's something round the neck, Detective,' said the thin digger.

I put my hand to my own neck.

He held up a blackened wire. 'It's a necklace, I think.'

'Yes,' I said. 'Yes, he gave it to her.'

They all turned and looked at me, and this time they were looking at me attentively.

'Here.' I took off my necklace, silver and gleaming, and laid it by its blackened counterpart. 'Adam gave me this, it was a token of his love for me, his undying love.' I fingered the silver spiral. 'This will be on hers too.'

'She's right,' said WDC Paget. The other spiral was black and clotted with earth, but it was unmistakable. There was a long silence. They all looked at me and I looked at the hole where her body lay.

'What did you say her name was?' asked WDC Paget at last.

'Adele Blanchard.' I gulped. 'She was Adam's lover. And I think . . .' I started to cry again, but this time I wasn't crying for me, but for her and for Tara and for Françoise. 'I think she was a very nice woman. A lovely young woman. Oh, sorry, I'm so, so sorry.' I put my face into my muddy hands, blindfolding myself, and tears seeped through my fingers.

WPC Mayer put her arm around my shoulder. 'We'll take you home.'

But where was my home now?

Detective Inspector Byrne and one of his female officers insisted on accompanying me to the flat, although I told them Adam wouldn't be there and I was only going to pick up my clothes and leave. They said that they had to check the flat anyway, although they had already tried to ring there. They had to try to find Mr Tallis.

I didn't know where I was going to go, although I didn't tell them that. Later there would be statements to make, forms to sign in triplicate, solicitors to see. Later, I would have to face up to my past and confront my future, try to climb out of the ghastly wreckage of my life. Not now, though. Now I was just inching along numbly, trying to put words in the right order until I was left on my own somewhere, to sleep. I was so tired I thought I could go to sleep standing up.

Detective Inspector Byrne steered me up the stairs to the flat. The door hung uselessly on its hinges, where Adam had broken it down. My knees buckled, but Byrne held my elbow and we walked in, followed by his officer.

'I can't,' I said, stopping abruptly in the hall. 'I can't. I can't go in here. I can't. I can't. I just can't.'

'You don't have to,' he said. He turned to the woman. 'Pick up some clean clothes for her, will you?'

'My bag,' I said. 'I only need my bag, really. My money's in there. I don't want anything else.'

'And her bag.'

'It's in the living room,' I said. I thought I was going to throw up.

'Have you got family you can go to?' he asked me, as we waited.

'I don't know,' I said feebly.

'Can I have a word with you, sir?' It was the woman officer, with a grave face. Something had happened.

'What . . . ?'

'Sir.'

I knew then. It was knowledge that went through me like a ripple of pure sensation.

Before they could stop me I had run through into the living room. My beautiful Adam was there, turning ever so slowly on the rope. I saw that he had used a length of climbing rope. Yellow climbing rope. A chair lay on its side. His feet were bare. I touched the mutilated foot very gently, then I kissed it, as I had done that first time. He was quite cold. He was wearing his old jeans and a faded T-shirt. I looked up at his puffy, ruined face.

'You would have killed me,' I said, staring up at him.

'Miss Loudon,' said Byrne at my side.

'He would have killed me,' I said to him, without taking my gaze away from Adam, my dearest love. 'He would have done.'

'Miss Loudon, come away now. It's over.'

Adam had left a note. It wasn't a confession, really, nor a self-explanation. It was a love letter. 'My Alice,' he had written, 'To see you was to adore you. You were my best and my last love. I am sorry it had to end. For ever would have been too short a time.'

Forty

In the middle of the evening a few weeks later, after the clamour, after the funeral, there was a knock at the door. I went down and there was Deborah, looking unusually smart in a skirt and dark jacket, tired-looking after a day at the hospital. We gazed at each other, unsmiling. 'I should have got in touch earlier,' she said at last.

I stepped aside and she walked past me up the stairs. 'I've brought two things for you,' she said. 'This.' She removed a bottle of Scotch from a plastic bag. 'And this.' She unfolded a page from a newspaper and handed it to me. It was an obituary of Adam. It was by Klaus, for a newspaper that I didn't normally get. 'I thought you might like to see it.'

'Come through,' I said.

I took the whisky, a couple of glasses and the newspaper cutting and went into the living room. I poured us each a drink. Like a good North American, Deborah went back into the kitchen in search of ice. I looked at the cutting.

Above the article itself, across four columns, was a picture of Adam I hadn't seen before, sunburned, no hat, on a mountain somewhere, smiling at the camera. How rarely had I seen him smile or look carefree. In my mind he was always grave, intense. Behind him was a range of mountains like sea waves in a Japanese etching, caught at the moment of still perfection. That was what I had always found difficult to grasp. When you saw the photographs from high up, it was so clear and beautiful. But what they'd all told me – Deborah, Greg, Klaus, Adam, of course – was that the real experience of being up there was everything that couldn't be captured in the photograph: the unbelievable cold, the struggle to breathe, the wind that threatened to pick you up and blow you away, the noise, the slowness and heaviness of the brain and body and, above all, the sense of hostility, the feeling that this was a non-human world you were ascending briefly in the hope that you could survive the assault of the elements and your own physiological and psychological degeneration. I stared at Adam's face and wondered who he was smiling at. In the kitchen I heard the chink of ice.

Klaus's text made me wince at first, as I glanced through it. He was partly writing a personal memorial to his friend and also trying to fulfil the professional obligation of the obituarist. Then I read it through word by word:

> The mountaineer, Adam Tallis, who died recently by his own hand, achieved fame through his heroic actions during the disastrous storm last year on the Himalayan mountain of Chungawat. It was a fame he had not looked for, and he was uncomfortable in the spotlight – but he was as graceful and charismatic as ever.
>
> Adam was the product of a military family, which he rebelled against (his father participated in the first day of the Normandy landings in 1944). He was born in 1964 and educated at Eton but was unhappy at school and indeed was never willing to submit himself to any form of authority or institution that he considered undeserving. He left school for good when he was sixteen and literally set off alone across Europe, travelling overland.

Klaus then gave a précis of the account in his book of Adam's early mountaineering career and of the events on Chungawat. He had taken note of the correction in *Guy* magazine. It was now Tomas Benn who was poignantly calling for help before he sank into a coma. This led to the climax of Klaus's article:

> In asking for help, too late, Benn was speaking for a form of

humanity that Adam Tallis embodied. There have, especially in recent years, been those who have claimed that normal morality ceases to operate as we approach the summits of the highest mountains. This brutal approach may have been encouraged by the new trend in commercial expeditions in which the leader's obligation is to the client who has paid him and the client depends on the expert guides to keep him or her alive. Adam himself had strongly voiced reservations about these 'yak trails' by which unqualified but prosperous adventurers were ushered up climbs which had previously been the province of teams of élite climbers.

Yet, and here I speak as a man whose life was saved by Adam Tallis, in the middle of that terrible storm he lived up to the greatest traditions of Alpine and Himalayan fellowship. It seemed that the pressures of the market place had taken over even in that rarefied world above 8,000 metres. But somebody had forgotten to tell the mountain god of Chungawat. It was Adam Tallis who showed that, *in extremis*, there are deeper passions, more basic values.

On his return from Chungawat, Adam was far from idle. Always a man of strong impulses, he met and married a beautiful and spirited woman, Alice Loudon,

Deborah was back in the room. She sat down beside me and sipped at her whisky, studying my face as I read on:

a scientist with no background in mountaineering at all. The couple were passionately in love, and Adam's friends thought he had found the stable centre of his life that this troubled rover had always been searching for. It was, perhaps, significant that his planned expedition to Everest next year was not to summit but to clean the mountain, perhaps his own form of reparation to deities that had been defied and insulted for too long.

Yet it was not to be. Who can speak of an individual's inner torments? Who knows what drives the men and women who seek their fulfilment at the top of the world? It may be that the events on Chungawat had taken more out of him than even his friends realized. To us, he had seemed happier and steadier than at any time in his life, yet in his final weeks he became edgy, prickly, uncommunicative. I cannot help feeling that we were not there for him in the way that he had been there for us. Perhaps when the strongest men break they break terribly and irreversibly. I have lost a friend. Alice has lost a husband. The world has lost a rare kind of heroism.

I laid the paper down beside me, photograph turned away so I wouldn't see his face, and blew my nose on a tissue. Then I gulped some of my drink, which burned my aching throat as it went down. I wondered if I would ever feel normal again. Deborah laid her hand tentatively on my shoulder and I smiled slightly at her. 'It's all right,' I said.

'Does it bother you?' she asked. 'Don't you want everybody to know?' The question seemed to come from a long way off.

'Not everybody,' I said at last. 'There are a couple of people I've got to go and see, people I lied to and tricked. They deserve to know the truth. It's probably for my benefit as much as for theirs. For the rest, it doesn't matter now. It really doesn't matter.'

Deborah leaned forward and clinked her glass against mine. 'Dear Alice,' she said, in a strained and formal voice. 'I'm saying that in that way because I'm quoting from the letter I kept trying to write to you and then throwing away. Dear Alice, if I hadn't been saved from myself, I would have been responsible for kidnapping you and God knows what else. I'm so, so sorry. Can I buy you dinner?'

I nodded at her, answering the unasked question as well as the asked one. 'I'd better change,' I said. 'To compete with you. I've had a sweaty day at work.'

'Oh, I've heard. Congratulations.'

A quarter of an hour later we were walking along the road arm in arm. It was a warm evening and I felt I could really believe that there would be a summer at last, with heat and long evenings and fresh dawns. Still we didn't talk. I felt that there were no words left in me, no thoughts. We walked smoothly, in rhythm. Deborah led me into a new Italian restaurant she had read about, ordered pasta and salad and a bottle of expensive red wine. To assuage her guilt, she said. The waiters were dark and handsome and very attentive to us. When Deborah took a cigarette from its packet two of them sprang forward with lighters. Then Deborah looked me in the eye. 'What are the police doing?' she asked.

'I spent a day last week with detectives from different forces. I told them roughly the same story I told just before you and Adam arrived.' Deborah winced. 'But this time they were paying attention and asking questions. They were pretty cheerful about it. "No further suspects are currently being sought" was the expression, I think. Detective Inspector Byrne, the one you met, was being very nice to me. I think he felt a bit guilty.'

A waiter bustled forward with an ice-bucket. There was a soft pop of a cork held inside a napkin. 'With the compliments of the gentlemen.'

We looked round. Two young men in suits were raising their glasses to us, grinning.

'What kind of place is this?' said Deborah loudly. 'Who are those assholes? I should go and pour this over their heads. God, I'm sorry, Alice. This is the last thing you need.'

'No,' I said. 'It's not important.' I poured the smoking champagne into our glasses and waited for the froth to subside. 'Nothing like that is important now, Deborah. Stupid men buzzing around like gnats, stupid battles, little rages, it's not worth it. Life's too short. Don't you see?' I clinked my glass against hers. 'To friendship,' I said.

And she said, 'To coming through.'

Deborah walked me home afterwards. I didn't ask her up and we kissed goodbye at the door. I climbed upstairs, to the flat I was going to move out of next week. This weekend I would have to pack my few possessions and decide what to do with Adam's. They still lay all round the rooms: his faded jeans; his T-shirts, and rough jerseys that smelt of him so that if I closed my eyes I could believe he was still there in the room, watching me; his leather jacket that seemed to hold the shape of him still; his backpack stuffed with climbing gear; the photographs he had taken of me with his Polaroid. Only his precious scuffed climbing boots were gone: Klaus – dear Klaus with his face swollen by weeping – had laid them on his coffin. Boots instead of flowers. So he didn't leave very much at all. He had always travelled light.

I had thought, immediately afterwards, that I wouldn't be able to stay in this flat for an hour, for a single minute. Actually, I had found it perversely hard to leave. But on Monday I would close the brand new door, double lock it, and hand the keys to the agent. I would take my bags and bits and get a taxi to my new home, a comfortable one-bedroom apartment very near work, with a small patio, a washing-machine, a microwave, central heating and thick carpets. Pauline had once said to me, after she was through the worst of her stunned unhappiness, that if you behave as if you are all right, then one day you will be. You have to go through the motions of surviving in order to survive. Water finds its way into the ditches you have dug for it. So I would buy a car. Maybe I would get a cat. I would start learning French again and buying clothes. I would arrive at work early each morning and I knew I could do my new job well. I would see all my old friends. A kind of life could flow into these prepared spaces; not a bad life, really. People looking at me would never guess that these things meant little; that I felt as deep and empty and sad as the sky.

I could never slide back into my old self. My self before him. Most people would never know. Jake, happy with his new girlfriend, wouldn't know. He would look back on the end of our affair and remember the pain and the mess and embarrassment, but it would be a dim memory and would lose all power to hurt

305

him, if it hadn't already. Pauline, heavily pregnant, wouldn't know either. She had asked me, very shyly, if I would consider being her child's godmother and I had kissed her on both cheeks and said that I didn't believe in God but, yes, I would be very proud. Clive, ricocheting from attachment to attachment, would think of me as the woman who had known true romantic love; he would ask me for advice every time he wanted to go out with a woman or wanted to leave her. And I could never tell my family, or his, or Klaus and the community of climbers, or anyone at work.

To all of them, I was the tragic widow of the hero who had died too young, by his own hand. They spoke to me and probably of me with a hushed kind of respect and sorrow. Sylvie knew, of course, but I couldn't speak to her about it. Poor Sylvie, who had thought she was acting for the best. She had come to the funeral and afterwards, in a frantic whisper, had begged my forgiveness. I said that I forgave – what else could I say? – and then turned and continued speaking to someone else.

I was tired, but I was not sleepy. I made myself a cup of tea which I drank out of one of Adam's pewter mugs, a mug that had hung from his backpack when we went to the Lake District for our honeymoon, that dark and starry night. I sat on the sofa in my dressing-gown, legs tucked under me, and thought about him. I thought about the first time I had set eyes on him, across the road and gazing at me, hooking me with his stare, reeling me in. I thought about the last time, in the police station, when he had smiled at me so sweetly, letting me go. He must have known it was the end. We had never said goodbye. It had begun in rapture and finished in terror and now in such loneliness.

A few days ago, Clive had met me for lunch and, after all the exclamations of distress and support, had asked, 'How will anyone ever measure up to him, Alice?'

Nobody ever would. Adam had murdered seven people. He would have murdered me even while he wept over my body. Every time I remembered the way he used to look at me, with such intensely focused love, or saw in my mind's eye his dead body swinging slowly on the yellow rope, I also remembered that he was a rapist and a killer. My Adam.

But, after everything, I still remembered his lovely face and how he had held me in his arms and stared into my eyes and said my name, so tenderly, and I didn't want to forget that someone had loved me so much, so very much. It's you I want, he had said, only you. Nobody would ever love me like that again.

I stood up and opened the window. A group of young men walked past on the street below, lit by the lamp, laughing drunkenly. One of them looked up and, seeing me there at the window, blew me a kiss and I waved at him and smiled and turned away. Oh, it has been such a sad story, my love, my heart.